"I'M NOT GOOD ENOUGH FOR YOU," CALUM SAID FIERCELY

Gillian heard the torment in his voice. She reached out and cupped her palm against his cheek. Hesitantly, she lifted her other hand to his mane of fire-gold hair. He went still.

"Not true," she whispered. "'Tis not true."

Calum pulled her into a desperate embrace. His lips moved on hers in a wild kiss of possession that ignited an answering blaze within her. Gillian moved against his body, wanting to feel him, the burning heat of his skin. She closed her eyes and yielded to the tide of desire that rose in her.

CELEBRATE
101 Days of Romance with
HarperMonogram

FREE BOOK OFFER!

Books by Terri Lynn Wilhelm

Fool of Hearts
Shadow Prince

Available from HarperPaperbacks

Fool of Hearts

 TERRI LYNN WILHELM

HarperPaperbacks
A Division of HarperCollinsPublishers

This is a work of fiction. The characters, incidents, and dialogues are products of the author's imagination and are not to be construed as real. Any resemblance to actual events or persons, living or dead, is entirely coincidental.

HarperPaperbacks   *A Division of* HarperCollins*Publishers*
10 East 53rd Street, New York, N.Y. 10022

Cover illustration by Doreen Minuto

First printing: June 1995

Printed in the United States of America

HarperPaperbacks, HarperMonogram, and colophon are trademarks of HarperCollins*Publishers*

❖ 10 9 8 7 6 5 4 3 2 1

Fool of Hearts

1

Yorkshire, England, 1783

       "O-o-oh, good King George, he knows the way—"

Splash!

"—to keep all Englishmen *lo*y-al."

Splash! Splash!

Gillian Ellicott awoke from her dream of a rippling, golden field of ripe oats, ready for the scythe, to the bellowed lyrics of a ribald ditty.

Her father was in the fountain again.

Heaving a weary sigh, she fumbled sleepily with the steel and flint and managed to light the candle on her bedside table. She slid off the side of the high tester bed and dragged on her brocade dressing gown.

Life had been so much simpler before her father had returned from his latest adventures in the Orient, she thought irritably—and instantly felt contrite. He was her father, she reminded herself, no matter how seldom he'd chosen to acknowledge that fact.

She flung open the door of her bedchamber and hurried down the stygian corridor. The flame of her candle cast a net of golden illumination that caught and released plush Savonnerie carpets, dark oak flooring, and classical alabaster statues in their shadowed niches.

Zerrin, her lady's maid, met her at the staircase. "Lady sister, your father—he again dances in the fountain," she said quietly, her Turkish accent as exotic as her garb. In the many years since her arrival at Treymoor, she'd refused to exchange her modest, comfortable style of dressing for the more restrictive English clothing. Now, as they hastened down the staircase, an opaque veil fluttered against the lower half of her face.

They were met halfway down by Pym, the butler. Tall, in his middle years, he was attired in his dressing gown and an extravagant tasseled nightcap. "I'm sorry to disturb you, Lady Gillian, but it seems Lord Molyneux—"

"Yes, I heard the . . . singing."

She saw Mrs. Withecombe waiting at the foot of the stairs. The slim, regal housekeeper wore night-clothes too, and her brown-gray hair hung down her back in a neat plait. George Jenkins, the footman, trotted up to stand behind her, his hands busy tying the sash of his dressing gown.

Gillian managed a smile for them all, aware that their concern was for her. "My father—"

Odgers, the wiry valet of whom her father so

seldom made use, dashed into the hall and nearly skidded by them, his slippers sliding on the polished floor. "Lord Molyneux—"

"—Is enjoying another balmy summer's evening." Her smile kept tightly in place with a regimental will, Gillian nodded to them and kept going, sailing through the great entry hall and out the front doors.

The summer air was soft and warm, and she drew in a deep, wistful breath as she led them quickly down the steps, away from the house. Gravel crunched under their feet as they crossed the circular drive to the marble fountain. There, clad in a soaked night-shirt, his three-cornered hat set at a ridiculous angle on his head, the Earl of Molyneux cavorted with an Italian marble Pan and two dryads.

"And a derry-o, derry-o, *high*-o-o-o!" The earl caught sight of his daughter and grinned widely. "Oh, there you are. I'm leaving for Istanbul in two days."

He's foxed, she thought, exasperated. This was the third night in a row. Until this visit, she'd seldom seen her father in his cups. Of course, in her twenty years, she'd seldom seen her father in any condition. "Yes, I know you're leaving." If she didn't get him into the house and out of those wet clothes, he might catch a fever.

He frowned. "There was something I meant to tell you, child. Something important, I'm sure." His eyebrows drew down even farther in concentration. "Now it quite escapes me."

"I'm certain you will think of it as soon as you're in nice dry clothes," she coaxed, holding out her hands to him. "Please, Papa, climb out of the fountain pool. Let us go inside."

Pym and Odgers both stepped forward, ready to remove the earl from the dark water.

Suddenly the earl brightened. "Ah, now I remember!" He clumsily dodged the grasps of the butler and the valet as he waded determinedly toward his daughter. "I wanted to tell you—"

At that instant, his feet went out from under him, and the earl toppled, plunging backward into the water. An explosion of spray surged up and out, drenching his rescuers in tepid, fishy-smelling water.

"S'truth!" Odgers swore.

Gillian scraped her sodden nightcap off her forehead. "Really, Papa," she began, a stinging scold poised on her lips—until she noticed that her father was not moving, that he made no attempt to lift his face from the water. Stark terror seized her. "Papa! Dear Lord!" She lunged forward, trying to reach him, but he was too far from her.

Quickly, the men dragged him from the pool, up onto the wide marble coping, where he weakly coughed up water. When Pym brought his hand away from the back of the earl's head, his palm and fingers were stained dark with blood.

Gillian's horrified gaze met the butler's; then he bent to examine the wound.

"Don't bother," the earl said, his voice surprisingly free of the usual effects of inebriation, yet terrifyingly feeble. "I'm feeling . . . decidedly queer. Just listen."

Fear for her father clutched at Gillian. "Odgers, go for the doctor," she ordered.

"No," her father countermanded. "Stay."

"But, Papa—"

The butler slipped off his dressing gown and tucked it around the injured man.

"Please . . . you will need him," the earl told her. "Allow me to do at least this for you. I know I've neglected you, child. Was never home."

Sharp anguish clenched in her chest. How could she tell him he was little more than a stranger to her? After years of disappointment, how could she express the yearning for a father's love and recognition that had burned in her as a child and that had finally flickered to faint hope as a woman? Sadly, the answer was she could not. She'd invented excuses for his negligence until even she failed to believe them.

"You wrote," she pointed out, her throat tight with emotion.

With a visible effort, he reached out and touched a straggling lock of her hair. "Few times. Know I shipped home furniture, silk"— his eyes moved to the partially veiled maid —"Zerrin."

Moisture filled Zerrin's sloe eyes. She took his hand and pressed her forehead to the back of it.

The earl softly brushed his fingertips along one of her slanting, black eyebrows. He murmured something in a foreign tongue.

Zerrin answered him in the same language. Gillian understood enough Turkish to recognize the word "promise."

Then he turned his gaze back to his daughter. "I left you with the servants because I . . . knew they were loyal," he continued, in a voice little more than a whisper. "You were so vulnerable. And I'd seen power of guardianship abused too often. Knew Pym and Withecombe . . . would take care of you. All that's . . . changed now."

"Your trust in Pym and Mrs. Withecombe and Odgers has been well placed, Papa," she reassured him desperately. He was failing, and she was certain he knew it. Their time together had been so short. It all seemed wrong, horribly unfair. But then, when had fairness ever counted for much with the world? "Aunt Augusta helped, of course," she added in a choked voice.

His lips curved faintly. "You've grown to be . . . quite the lady of the manor. It is time you marry. These . . . past years . . . *you* have provided for *me*. I . . . have not been . . . an adequate father, but . . . you've been . . . most excellent daughter. Now . . . I see you've . . . never really needed . . . my help. Gillian? Child, where are you?"

In the icy light cast by the full moon, she saw his eyes were turned directly toward her. Alarmed at his inability to see, she moved closer to him and with trembling fingers smoothed back a thin wisp of hair from his forehead. Warm tears coursed down her cheeks. "I'm here, Papa." In that moment life seemed so fragile, so easily broken. If only they'd had a chance. . . . She clutched his hand a little tighter, as if her grip could keep his spirit anchored in his body.

"My dear . . . in the past . . . you have asked . . . who . . . will inherit Treymoor. . . ."

"Yes." Gillian's heart began to pound. He must know he was dying, to speak of the estate. It had never seemed to mean much to him beyond a place to keep his daughter and a source of revenue to finance his adventures. He had regularly drawn on the income she and her people had worked so hard to provide, and in turn he allowed her a free hand with Treymoor, though he had never given legal assent to such unheard-of freedom.

She knew the estate was entailed to her father's closest male relative, but she wasn't certain of that man's identity. The earl had no uncles, no brothers, or nephews. Many of his family had died in past wars, and others had left for the opportunities to be found in the colonies. She knew of two men who might have a claim. One was a gambling ne'er-do-well, the other a malicious adventurer. Bile rose in her throat at the thought of either of them possessing Treymoor.

This estate was more than just her sanctuary. Here lived the people she loved, her *true* family: the servants of the manor and the tenants of the land. For their sakes, as well as for her own, Treymoor must go to a responsible master.

"Who shall have Treymoor?" she asked, fearing the answer but needing to know if either of those blackguards would inherit her home.

Her father drew a rattling breath.

She leaned closer and touched his cheek. "Papa?"

A soft sigh escaped his mouth.

Gillian stared at him as a cold, aching knot grew in her chest. "Papa?"

Her father made no answer. Pym reached over and gently closed his eyes.

The Earl of Molyneux was dead.

*　　*　　*

As they walked slowly back to the house, the three men carrying the earl between them, a bleak numbness settled over Gillian. It was hard to accept that her father was no longer alive. While he'd never shown her much attention, she had known he was usually within a letter's distance. She had believed in her heart that, should a dire enough emergency ever have arisen, he would have come at her summons. Now even that small comfort was gone. Soon, another man, a man with a black soul, would claim Treymoor.

What would become of her home? Of her people? Of her?

The numbness melted away as she considered the certain ruin of Treymoor. She had seen with her own eyes what could happen when an estate fell into uncaring hands: the starving tenants and destitute, unemployed servants. . . .

Such was the future of her home and the people who lived there. But what good did it do to think on it? What could *she* do about it? She frowned as she pondered their situation.

They mounted the steps and crossed the portico. Mrs. Withecombe stepped forward to open the front door.

"Take him to the icehouse," Gillian said abruptly.

The man stopped and turned awkwardly to face her, clearly confused.

"The icehouse?" Pym asked.

"Yes," she said with more firmness than she felt. "Bear with me. I will soon explain."

The earl was settled on a trestle horse in the frigid icehouse and draped with a length of canvas.

"A prayer, please," she said softly, and they all bowed their heads.

She squeezed her eyes closed. *Oh, Papa, I'm not certain I can succeed at this, but I must try. I hope you will understand.*

After they had each spoken a prayer for the soul of the late Earl of Molyneux, the survivors left the earth-covered shed by the stream. They hastened through the stately gardens behind the imposing, moonlit mansion, up the stairs, and through dark hallways to the library, where Gillian closed and locked the door.

She waved the others to chairs. "Sit, sit. I have a plan."

One by one, she regarded the five people she trusted most in the world. Elegant, capable James Pym and shorter, adventuresome Thomas Odgers had been both father and uncle to her, George Jenkins an older brother. Elizabeth Withecombe, who would have made a fine ship's captain if she'd been born a man, had stepped in to take over when Lady Molyneux had died in a carriage accident, leaving behind five-year-old Gillian. The housekeeper's correct, no-nonsense demeanor concealed a warm and loving heart. And Zerrin, petite, exotic, dark-eyed Zerrin, who, though slightly younger than Gillian, had a maturity that exceeded her years—Zerrin had been both teacher and confidante, a sister both younger and older.

What would happen to these generous, good people—her family—when the new master of Treymoor took over? She had only to recall what had happened to neighboring Frampton Park to know all too chillingly well.

She cleared her throat, not relishing the undertaking she was about to propose. "This will involve a certain amount of risk," she said, knowing her words for a vast understatement.

"Is this all part of placing your father in the icehouse?" Odgers inquired dryly.

"Yes."

"There is a particular disrespect implied in storing one's parent among cakes of butter and pipkins of cream," Mrs. Withecombe observed primly.

"It is necessary, I believe," Gillian said. "You see, if no one knows my father has died, no one can take Treymoor from us."

Five pairs of eyes widened in shock. "What!" Suddenly, they were all talking at once, exclaiming over her outrageous intent to conceal the earl's death.

"Listen to me," she insisted. "Please hear me out!"

Slowly, they quieted.

"Who shall inherit this estate?" she asked. No one answered. "Remember when Lord Quirval died? Two years ago, Frampton Park was the picture of prosperity. What happened when his heir—a third cousin twice removed—inherited?"

She allowed them to recall the heartbreaking details of the way Frampton Park had been gambled away by Quirval's heir and then stripped by the new owner, a man who never left London. The manor that had once seen the gaiety of balls and the excitement of hunting parties now stood empty, crumbling into disrepair. The few remaining tenants eked out a miserable existence.

"Surely my lord Molyneux would not have left us to the mercy of one so evil," Zerrin protested.

But Gillian saw concern in the expressions of the others, who were more familiar with the system common among the nobility. "Treymoor is entailed, Zerrin," she explained, though she knew everyone was already aware of that fact. Hoping to aid her purpose, she persisted. "This estate and the title of Earl of Molyneux will go to my father's nearest male relative."

"Who is Laurence Ellicott," Pym informed the maid. "Dull but reliable."

"Not so reliable," Gillian said. "He was killed in a duel."

Pym frowned. "Francis Chilcott, then. A man of the cloth. A bit inexperienced, perhaps."

"Yes, Francis *was* a man of the cloth—before the bishop defrocked him. But inexperienced? He died of a heart seizure in the arms of his lovers."

Odgers's eyes widened. "Lovers?"

Gillian nodded.

"But that only leaves Philip Rundle," Pym protested, as if he could argue with fate.

"Killed in the war with the American colonies. At Yorktown," Odgers announced.

"Who has kept you informed of all this?" Mrs. Withecombe asked Gillian. "The circumstances of Mr. Chilcott's demise are certainly not fit for a young lady's ears."

Gillian smiled. "Aunt Augusta."

Mrs. Withecombe rolled her eyes but made no reply.

"Well, if Mr. Ellicott is dead, and so are Mr.

Chilcott and Mr. Rundle, who will inherit?" Pym inquired. "Who is left?"

"Precisely the problem," Gillian pointed out. "I do not know—not of a certainty. The connections are so remote it is difficult to say. Even Aunt Augusta isn't sure, but then you know how she feels about Papa's family." She wrinkled her nose. "I believe I have deduced the two most likely candidates."

"These two, they are better than those who have died?" Zerrin asked hopefully.

"No." Gillian knew she must make them see the danger of their predicament. "They're worse. Much worse."

She let them absorb this dire truth for a moment.

"You have the house in London," Pym stated, as if trying to reassure himself that she, at least, would be provided for.

"It seems Papa sold the house three years ago. He told me yesterday." She had wanted to cry. "I probably could not have afforded to keep it anyway. On to the second point of my plan."

"And what might that be?" Odgers asked gloomily.

"I directly find a nice, manageable husband. When I bear him a son, I will 'receive' a letter from Istanbul, or some other foreign place, notifying me of my father's death."

Pym raised a bushy eyebrow. "Pray, allow me to understand this correctly. We conceal your father's death until you wed and bear a son."

"Correct."

"Then a letter will arrive informing you that your father is dead."

"Yes."

"But your son will already have inherited Treymoor."

Gillian nodded, relieved that her scheme was so clearly understood.

"Insane!" Pym declared.

"It will never work!" Odgers announced.

"Where would you ever find a *manageable* male to wed?" Mrs. Withecombe wanted to know.

Frustrated, Gillian turned to Zerrin and Jenkins. "What about you?" she demanded. "Haven't you anything to add?"

"No," Jenkins said.

Above the white veil, Zerrin's eyes twinkled. "I come from a land where intrigue scents the air we breathe and flavors the food we eat. But have a care, lady sister, that *you* do not become the victim of your designs. Tell us of these two men who may claim the title and the home that belonged to my lord Molyneux."

"Nicholas Vallance likely has first claim, though, as I said, I cannot be certain. He gambled away his inheritance and was said to have stabbed a man in a fight. He fled to France, barely ahead of his creditors."

She saw the others exchange worried glances and continued.

"The second rascal is even worse, a distant cousin to my father; I believe at one time they served together in the East. He is Robert MacFuaran, Marquess of Iolar."

"That's a Scottish name," Odgers exclaimed in a strangled voice.

"It is," Gillian agreed darkly. "Aunt Augusta told me the man cast out his wife for being faithless and repudiated the son she bore as the offspring of her lover. The marquess left Scotland and never returned. He stripped and sold what was left of his holdings—all except the seat of his marquessate." She paused for effect. "But he suffered for his callousness. It seems the son he repudiated engineered the utter destruction of the remaining estate, out of revenge."

"Scotchmen," Jenkins muttered.

Gillian smiled slightly. "Well, at least we won't have to worry about *him*. Since he was disinherited by the marquess, he could not possibly have any claim to Treymoor."

Mrs. Withecombe drew a deep breath and released it in a single huff. "I suppose I could go live with my daughter and her husband. Then they wouldn't have to worry about paying my savings back."

"Your daughter has nine children. Where would you even sleep?" Gillian asked.

"I've put some money by, over the years," Pym said slowly. "I had in mind to buy a little inn. You could come with me, Mrs. Withecombe."

Gillian knew a courtship of sorts had been going on for years between Pym and Mrs. Withecombe. When they did indeed retire from service, she had no doubt they would spend their remaining time together. But she also knew that neither their savings nor their spirits were ready for such retirement. Nor were Odgers or Jenkins ready. They would all end in poverty. And where would Zerrin go?

Treymoor was their home, as it was hers. So she did not scruple to use guilt as a tool in her effort to save their way of life.

"So you plan to abandon me?" she challenged. "You too, Zerrin? Am I left to my own devices? I suppose I must place myself at the mercy of the next Earl of Molyneux, *even* if he is a Scotsman. Perhaps"— she hung her head —"if I am fortunate, he might deign to take me as his mistress."

The heated objections that resulted from her statement gladdened her heart.

"Then we will keep my father's death a secret, and I shall look for a husband," she concluded, eager to take the only action she could think of that might keep them from becoming discards on the playing table of inheritance laws.

"But what if you fail to have a son?" Pym asked, pointing out the most obvious flaw in her plan.

She frowned. Well, yes, there appeared to be a few conspicuous obstacles in her proposed path, but, given time, she had no doubt she could find a way around them. Hadn't she always? She had made her schemes work since she was fifteen and had shouldered the responsibility for running Treymoor, after the death of the old steward. By hook and by crook, she had succeeded in concealing from society the fact that she was a woman alone, a minor, all the while managing to keep everyone on Treymoor sheltered, fed, clothed, and these days even paid. No, Gillian vowed, she would not be defeated now.

"I make no claims of my strategy's perfection," she said. "But is it not preferable to merely waiting for a stranger to strip Treymoor bare or gamble it away? Can anyone here conceive a better scheme?"

Everyone looked at one another, then reluctantly shook their heads.

"You've always been a stubborn miss," Odgers said, the glint of pride dancing in his eyes.

Gillian fixed them all with a fierce gaze. "Are you or are you not with me?"

Hesitantly, one by one, her audience nodded.

"We cannot succeed if any of us lack resolve." Her voice softened. "I need you."

She saw their conviction flicker, then strengthen. They straightened in their chairs, and the uncertainty revealed in their faces metamorphosed into determination.

"Our little lionheart," Pym said quietly. "We will see this through."

The others agreed.

"If we are careful," Gillian said as they left the library to return to their rooms, "we should have no trouble."

Calum MacFuaran, new Marquess of Iolar, reined in his sweating roan to a walk. He and his two kinsmen—sons of his mother's cousins—had been riding hard for days, on their way to some damned English farm called Treymoor.

But for the ridiculous letter stuffed in the pocket of his riding coat, the three Highlanders would now have been on their way to Iolar Glen. For Calum it would have been his first time there in twenty years. Instead, not trusting to the questionable efficiency of the postal service, he had perforce thundered out of Scotland toward Treymoor.

The letter had been written by the Earl of Molyneux, who was a distant relation to Robert

MacFuaran, the late marquess, according to other correspondence that had been left in the solicitor's keeping. It was a simple document, too simple by far. It only specified the Marquess of Iolar as guardian of the earl's illustrious "sweet child," Gillian Ellicott. Though the earl might have intended this to mean Robert MacFuaran, the title was now Calum's—along with the responsibilities.

But this was one responsibility Calum would not—absolutely *refused* to—accept.

Calum seethed with impatience. Leather creaked, and the hooves of four horses thudded on the hard-packed earth. In the field next to the road, a lark trilled.

"D'ye think we'll arrive in time, Calum?" Ian Gunn asked, giving the reins of the docile packhorse that followed him an encouraging twitch. "Did the letter no say the earl was leavin' tomorrow?" At twenty-three, the youngest of the three cousins, Ian was also the quickest with a smile.

"Aye," Calum agreed darkly. "That it does."

"We're all but there, Ian," Hugh Drummond said patiently. "Remember the directions we got from the farmer's woman."

Ian's white teeth flashed in his full blond beard. "I remember she was only too happy to see the backs of us. She dinna like us, I think."

"We frightened her," Hugh stated, not taking his gaze from the vista of cultivated fields that surrounded the road they traveled. During his forty-three years, Hugh had seen much change in Scotland, little of it good. Yet he retained an even-tempered nature and a fairness of judgment that never ceased to be valued by those around him.

Ian laughed. "Och, aye, we frightened her, all right, terrible wild beasties that we are. Ye'd have thought we planned to take her liver."

Observing his younger kinsman's exuberance, a grudging smile tugged at Calum's lips. "The poor woman was used to English gentlemen, Ian, and likely had never seen such handsome, manly fellows as ourselves before."

Hugh chuckled. "She must have been fair blinded by our rare beauty." The three of them laughed.

They rode a little farther before Ian asked, "What kind of father leaves his bairn to the care of a stranger?"

"No a verra good one," Hugh answered flatly.

Calum's mouth curved down. It seemed to him that Molyneux's lack of specificity smacked of a suspicious eagerness to find a keeper for his offspring. "Or one who's certain he'll have no luck with those who know her."

Hugh looked over his shoulder and raised a bushy brown eyebrow. "Ye think she's a brat, Calum?"

"A spoiled, snot-nosed, Sassenach brat," he confirmed. "But it doesna matter a bit, for I'll no be takin' responsibility for her." He had ample problems already. "And once I've informed Molyneux of his mistake, we'll be on our way." To beautiful Iolar Glen. Joyful anticipation surged through Calum, expanding in his chest.

"C'mon, lads," he called out, spurring his horse to a faster gait. "Let's complete this wee errand and be on our way."

*   *   *

The farmer's woman had been right, and it was not long before the three riders turned into Treymoor's well-tended approach. Calum wondered if the fields of oats and barley he'd watched rippling in the summer breeze all belonged to Molyneux.

Their horses cantered down the drive toward a small palace built of grayish limestone. In the center of the front, a colonnade of towering columns was topped by a triangular pediment to form a gracious portico. Rows of tall windows sparkled in the sunlight.

"It looks as though the earl has done well for himself," Ian muttered.

"Aye. *Verra* well." It was, perhaps, a bit more grand than Dunncrannog Castle, where Calum had spent his first seven years, and decidedly more modern than that medieval citadel. But for all its manicured loveliness, he thought Treymoor could not compare with the raw, dramatic beauty of Dunncrannog rising up from the tarn on its narrow island like a crenelated cathedral.

Someone had observed their arrival, for a man came around from the side of the house and offered to take the horses. He regarded the Scots with marked wariness.

The riders removed their saddlebags from their mounts, slinging the heavy leather pouches over their shoulders. Then they ascended the wide curve of steps. As Ian banged the brass knocker, Calum wondered impatiently why someone had been sent to take their horses but no one had thought to greet them at the door.

A tall, impeccably groomed man answered Ian's knock, wearing a butler's aloof expression. In

Edinburgh or Yorkshire, Calum reflected, the look was the same.

The man's glance covered all three of them and came back to rest on Calum, who stood directly in front of him. "Yes?" The tone was as impersonally disinterested as the look.

"I'm here to see Lord Molyneux," Calum announced shortly, faintly annoyed. "Tell him the Marquess of Iolar has arrived," he added, hoping to hurry the servant along. The sooner this matter was concluded the better.

"Lord Molyneux is not at home, sir. He has departed."

Tension built to a small whirlwind in Calum's chest. "Departed to where?"

"Istanbul, sir."

The whirlwind grew in pressure, moving faster, growing larger. He fought the urge to tighten his hands into fists. He wanted to smash something. He needed the distraction of violence. But the only target that could possibly satisfy was Lord bloody Molyneux.

And now he was saddled with the man's daughter.

Calum's first impulse was to turn around, retrieve his horse, and ride back to Scotland. After all, he had important matters of his own to attend. Certainly more important than playing nursemaid to an Englishman's brat. He owed Molyneux nothing. He'd never even met the man. To the devil with him!

But what of the bairn? an insidious voice from the back of his mind whispered. Perhaps—just perhaps—there was an acceptable reason behind her father's actions. Should a child suffer for its father's error? Dark memory twisted around Calum's conscience.

Instead of instructing the butler to have the horses brought round, as he would have preferred, he said, "Molyneux advised me that he dinna plan to leave until tomorrow."

Was it his imagination, or did the man's face whiten slightly? Under Calum's scrutiny, the butler's expression did not change.

"His departure was unexpected," the servant said. "An emergency, I believe."

Unexpected. An emergency. So Molyneux hadn't planned an early departure after all. The man was careless, or maybe even a wee bit daft, but perhaps he'd *expected* Calum to come for her. Perhaps it had always been his intention to personally see his daughter tucked safely in her guardian's care before leaving.

Now Molyneux was gone and Calum was left here, in possession of a document appointing him guardian.

Calum set his teeth. What was his alternative? To abandon the little one to the mercies of her father's servants? As much as he resented the thought of shouldering yet another legacy of Robert MacFuaran, he knew he would not walk away from this charge. No man of honor could.

He regarded the stitching on a corner of the saddlebag that rested against his chest as he considered the matter for a moment. The man had trusted his sweet child to Calum's keeping. . . .

Och, how much trouble could a bairn and her nursie be? Calum would simply take them back to Scotland with him.

The decision made, he felt better, ready to get on with the matter at hand. He looked down at the butler from an advantage of several inches. "Well, man, let us in. I've come for the earl's daughter."

Alarm flashed across the man's features but was gone almost instantly. His eyes narrowed in suspicion. "I'm afraid I was not told to expect you, sir."

Days in the saddle had left Calum sore and tired. He disliked the sweat and grime that filmed his body and clothing, and his last meal was many hours in the past. The news of the earl's early departure had come as a blow. He was in no mood to tolerate a butler's arrogance.

"I've been appointed guardian," he said softly. "Now let us in."

"Guardian?" It was almost a croak.

"Aye."

"Lord Molyneux said nothing of a guardian."

"The earl consults ye regularly, does he?" Calum kept his voice mild.

After a second's hesitation, the butler stepped back and gave them entrance. "I'm sure there must be some mistake," he objected.

Calum ignored him, looking around at the three-story entry hall. The soaring walls were pale blue, while the gleaming floor was of white blue-veined marble. Grecian columns, also of white-and-blue marble, supported the magnificent horseshoe staircase that rose before him on either side of the hall, curving up to the second-floor landing. On the first floor, across the hall from him, paneled white double doors were flanked by two pedestals, each supporting an alabaster bust of a male in Roman attire.

"Take me to the bairn," he ordered.

The butler looked confused. "Bairn?"

"The earl's daughter," Calum elaborated impatiently. No, if the butler was any example, he most definitely was not going to leave her with the servants of this household.

The man nodded, led the way down the hall on the left, and opened a door into a drawing room.

A glance told Calum there was no one inside. He made no move to enter. "Perhaps ye dinna understand me, man," he said, steel in his voice. "I told ye take me to the bairn."

The butler flushed. "It is customary—"

In a short, sharp gesture, Calum sliced the air with his open hand, effectively cutting off the servant's objection. "Now," he ordered with soft menace.

"Very well, my lord." His posture stiff with offended dignity, the butler led them back through the entry hall and into a corridor, where he opened another door.

The room was lined floor to ceiling with precious leather-bound books. Four lofty windows drenched the room with late morning sunlight.

"The Marquess of Iolar and—er, company, my lady," the servant announced to a young woman seated at a walnut library table. An open ledger lay before her, and in her right hand she held a quill poised over a sheet of foolscap.

Hair as black as polished ebony had been caught up into a simple, unfashionable knot high at the back of her head. In her oval face, slanting eyebrows formed inky slashes, which contrasted sharply against the pearl fairness of her skin. Large oblique eyes the soft gray of a Scottish mist widened in surprise as Calum and his cousins stepped into the room. Her face went paler.

Ian all but shut the door in the butler's face.

Immediately the door thrust open again, and the two men glared at each other.

Calum noted the butler had said "my lady." Who was this woman? The document he'd received had mentioned no other females.

"I'd been given to believe Lord Molyneux is a widower," he said bluntly. "Are ye his sister?" She was far too young to be the earl's mother. A member of his dead wife's family, perhaps?

Slowly she stood. "No," she said slowly, "I am not his sister." Her fingers gripped the edge of the table so tightly her knuckles turned white. "I'm Gillian Ellicott, Lord Molyneux's daughter."

2

It took every ounce of Gillian's self-control to keep her knees from buckling. The Marquess of Iolar! How had he discovered her father's death so soon? The earl had only died last night. There had not even been time—or opportunity—to remove him from the icehouse.

The story told by the sheep trader, and later by her aunt, of the cruel marquess must be true. He looked every inch a savage—and there were many more inches to him than one's average marquess. All wide shoulders and long muscular limbs, he towered over the six-feet-tall Pym. Saddlebags, smelling strongly of horse, hung over one shoulder. As she watched, he unslung them and thumped the burden on the floor. His companions followed suit.

"Molyneux's daughter?" he asked. "Have ye a younger sister?"

"No," she said, struggling to conceal her alarm behind a pleasant manner. "I am his only child."

The marquess turned his head, looking around the library. A jaw muscle jumped. Cautiously, she took the opportunity to study him.

He held in one hand a three-cornered hat and was attired in a dusty riding coat of somber brown, a rust-colored waistcoat, and snug leather breeches. His rumpled neckcloth and scuffed boots added the finishing touches to a valet's worst nightmare. Pulled back into a long queue, his hair was the bright red-gold of a newly minted farthing, a color shades lighter than his bushy beard. Above a short straight nose and high broad cheekbones, his widely spaced eyes were what gave Gillian the strongest impression of the danger this man presented. They were a startling light green.

She had seen that color before. It was the green of sun-dazzled sea. But she knew that, while sunshine might twinkle on the surface, turning it to gleaming apple jade, the water beneath remained untouched, unlit . . . fathomless.

Now, gazing into the eyes before her, she sensed their bright color masked a fathomless depth of their own, a darkly haunted soul.

"My lady," Pym said a little too loudly, as though to claim her attention, "the marquess came to see Lord Molyneux. I told him, of course, that your father left for Istanbul yesterday. But he claims—"

"Get out," the marquess commanded the butler over his shoulder, never taking his gaze from Gillian. "This is none of your affair."

But she'd already caught the significance of Pym's

words. Perhaps, she thought a little wildly, these barbarians knew nothing of her father's death after all! Hope and relief surged through her.

"Tea would be nice, Pym," Gillian said quickly, grateful for his warning and wishing she had a reason for him to stay that would not arouse suspicion in this irritable peer and his equally unfriendly looking companions. "And please send Zerrin."

"Very good, m'lady." The door closed quietly behind him.

"Zerrin?" the Scot demanded, his r's rolling off his tongue.

"My lady's maid."

"And just where is your chaperone?" he inquired with a mildness that didn't fool her.

"Why, er . . ."—she groped for an answer—"Aunt Augusta?" She and her aunt had played this game before. Augusta often stayed here with her, just as often expressing her indignation over her brother-in-law's lack of propriety. But then the gaiety of London life always drew the older woman back to her home in Grosvenor Square. "She's—uh, she's in London," Gillian said. And it was the truth, she told herself piously. Aunt Augusta *was* in London— enjoying routs and balls, gossip and shopping. Taking full advantage of her widowhood.

Iolar scowled. "London? Yer chaperone is in London? And ye are here alone?"

"Er . . . yes . . . at the moment." What on earth was she stammering about? She was no schoolgirl caught in the midst of a prank. This man was the enemy, and the welfare of her people and the inheritance of her children-to-be were at stake! If only she knew what Pym had been trying to tell her before the wretched marquess had interrupted him.

She held her breath and cast her bread upon the waters. "Lord Molyneux left, you see."

He made a sound of disapproval. "So I've been told. It seems yer father's early departure left more than one person at a disadvantage."

She breathed a small inward sigh of relief.

"Ye've sent for yer auntie, have ye not?"

"Certainly!" Gillian lied indignantly. "Until then, the rector and his wife are staying at Treymoor." Another lie, but one that could easily be rectified.

Just then, she noticed they were still standing and hastened to correct her omission. "Gentlemen, please be seated." She almost cringed at the thought of what their travel-soiled clothing would do to the brocade upholstery. Instead, she forced her lips to curve up, hoping the smile didn't appear as insincere as it felt.

He made no move to sit. Neither did the other two men. "Thank ye, no. We've been in the saddle since before dawn. Ye look as if ye were no expectin' us," he continued, his deep voice possessing a smoky quality that, despite the circumstances, she found appealing.

The door opened and Jenkins entered with a coal scuttle. "Beggin' your pardon, m'lady," he said with a meaningful glance, "but it seems to be growing a mite chilled."

Actually, it was a warm summer's day, but she was grateful for his presence in this lion's den. She smiled. "Thank you, Jenkins, you're quite right."

He crossed the room and set about making a fire.

The marquess raised an eyebrow but made no comment. Instead, he said, "As yer man meant to tell ye, I'm here as yer guardian. But yer father wrote of a child, which I expected ye to be." His mouth tightened fractionally as his gaze traveled the length of her. "I can well see ye are no bairn."

Gillian bridled at his bold survey.

"I have business in Scotland and dinna wish to tarry here," he continued, either unaware or unconcerned with the offense he had offered. "So I'll ask ye to ready yerself to leave with us as soon as yer auntie arrives."

"*What*?" Panic and outrage exploded within her. She looked briefly over at Jenkins, to find he'd straightened from his kneeling position on the hearth and was standing, open-mouthed, his eyes large with consternation. Quickly she recovered herself, though her heart continued to race.

"My father said nothing of appointing a legal guardian for me. I mean," she added hastily, "he said nothing of appointing *you* my legal guardian." It would not do for this barbarian to know she'd never had a legal guardian in all the time her father had been absent. And she had managed quite well, thank you very much. She eyed the tall Scotsman nervously. She required this . . . this person as urgently as she required a cardamom purgative.

"Aye, well, yer father seems to have taken much for granted," he commented dryly, hefting the full saddlebags back to his shoulder. "I'll thank—"

The door opened and Pym swept in with a large silver tray bearing the accoutrements for tea, accompanied by Zerrin, her veil fluttering below downcast eyes.

"This is a verra busy room," the marquess drawled.

Gillian flushed. "You will stay to tea, will you not, Lord Iolar?" She hoped he understood her implied dismissal for anything beyond tea.

His lips curved in faint amusement. "I'll thank ye to have yer man show us our rooms now and bring up the rest of our things from the packhorse. We'll need hot bathwater, but a cold tray will do nicely. We've ridden from Edinburgh, and the inns we stopped at along the way were no all that scrupulous in their hospitality."

Gillian fumed at his high-handed manner. "Sir, you are a stranger to me, and I have only your word that my father ever had communication with you of any kind."

He regarded her a moment with those light-green eyes, then gave a curt single nod. "Fair enough." He reached into his coat and withdrew an envelope, which he offered to her.

Reluctantly, she took it. A stone dropped in her stomach as she recognized her father's handwriting. Filled with dread, she unfolded a sheet of the thick parchment he had always favored for his letters home, insisting it was more likely to survive the distance it must travel to her. Gillian swallowed hard against the unexpected tears that recollection summoned.

No solicitor had had a hand in the writing of this document, which was short and to the point. The Marquess of Iolar was therein appointed her legal guardian, with all rights thereto.

Why? Why would her father, who had been absent so many years, think to appoint a legal guardian now, when she was quite capable of running her own life? And such a guardian he had chosen! What had possessed him to send her this . . . this *Scotsman*? Well, she would not have it. Too much was at stake. A nice, manageable sort of man was what she needed—she glanced up through her lashes at the unsmiling marquess—and quite soon. But first she must get rid of this odious intruder and his silent minions.

Primly, she refolded the letter but did not extend it to him. "There is a mistake, Lord Iolar. This is not my father's handwriting." Silently she asked forgiveness for her laxity with the Ninth Commandment.

A slow, wicked smile stole across his face. White teeth gleamed in auburn beard. "Aye, there *is* a mistake, lassie, but it is no mine. There was other correspondence from the earl among my late father's and uncle's papers. A comparison yielded that this document"—he deftly plucked the paper from her fingers and tucked it back into his pocket—"is quite authentic."

Color rushed up to heat Gillian's cheeks. Her first urge was to fling the heavy silver sugar bowl at the lout's handsome head.

"Now. Where are our rooms?"

Something he'd said struck her suddenly, with sickening impact. "You said—did you say your *late father's* papers? Are you not Robert MacFuaran?" For the first time, she realized the marked difference in this man's age and what Robert MacFuaran's would have been as her father's contemporary. Which meant . . .

She longed to wet lips suddenly gone dry. "Do you, perchance, have a half brother?"

The humor vanished from his eyes. They grew as cold as the North Sea. "I have no brother."

Gillian felt the blood drain from her face. Oh, God! To have the father as her guardian would have been terrible enough. But to be held in the legal grasp of the malicious bastard son? Her gaze fell to the heavy gold-and-ruby signet he wore on the hand hanging calmly at his side. She barely managed to suppress a shudder. This man had managed to plunder MacFuaran's sole remaining estate while that peer yet lived, which meant he was clever, vindictive, and utterly ruthless.

Out of the corner of her eye she could see the wooden expressions of Pym and Jenkins and knew they had caught the significance of their situation. She slid her gaze over to the other side of the room. The two men who accompanied the marquess looked angry.

"Pym," Lord Iolar said in a quiet voice. There was a soft, deadly quality to it that reminded Gillian of the sound of a rapier sliding from its sheath. "We shall have our rooms now. And our hot water. And our tray."

Pym looked to Gillian, but she could sense he had felt the warning too. Still, it was to her that he turned for instructions, bless his loyal soul.

"Give the gentlemen rooms in the east wing," she instructed him. Those chambers were the farthest from hers, isolated from the rest of the household. "See to their comfort." She would play the part of the gracious hostess—for now.

Pym inclined his head. "Very good, m'lady." To the marquess he intoned, "If you would be good enough to follow me, m'lord?" He moved to the library door and stopped, waiting for Treymoor's unwanted guests.

The marquess met her gaze, his expression revealing nothing. Then he gracefully inclined his head. "Lady Gillian." He turned and led his fellows out the door.

Calum and his cousins followed the butler without a word, mounting the magnificent staircase to the second floor. The servant took them to a deserted wing of the manor, where the only sound was the heavy, hollow thunder of their boots on wood floors, punctuated by the occasional silence the scattered Turkish carpets provided.

As Calum dumped his saddlebags on the floor of the room to which he was shown, Pym informed him that hot water would soon be available in the bathhouse and silently closed the door.

Calum looked around. The walls were covered with silk upon which a richly colored mural of exotic birds, flowers, and trees had been painted. Oriental carpets covered most of the floor. A massive tester bed, draped in heavy crimson damask, faced a fireplace that stood empty. The mantel was in the form of two Doric columns on either side supporting a shelf carved with various Greek goddesses bearing urns and bowls of fruit. Calum recognized quality when he saw it. All the furniture in the chamber, from the carved walnut wardrobe to the mahogany washstand, was finely crafted from excellent materials. But then, everything about Treymoor seemed to be first rate.

Restlessly, he paced to the window, where he stood looking out over the gardens without really seeing them.

Damn Molyneux's soul to eternal fire! Had he no relatives to lay this responsibility on? Had Robert MacFuaran been the man's only friend?

"Sweet child" indeed! That lying female was long from the cradle, and she was as sweet as a viper. Little Lady Gillian had been only too ready to believe the worst of him. Absently, Calum stroked a thumb over the signet he wore, feeling the sharp roughness of the family crest engraved in the cabochon ruby. Aye, he'd seen the color drain from her face when she'd realized who he was. That reaction was too familiar for him to miss its meaning. The Sassenach wench had somewhere heard the contemptible tales of bastardy and revenge that seemed to fly so eagerly from one vicious wagging tongue to the next. And like so many others, she'd embraced base rumors as truth before ever setting eyes on him. As he watched a gardener pull weeds from a rose bed, Calum's lips curved in a bitter smile.

A knock sounded at his door. "Come," he called.

Ian and Hugh entered.

"And what do ye think, cousin?" Ian asked, propping his hip against the writing desk.

Calum cast an uninterested glance around the room. "The accommodations are fair."

"I spoke of Lady Gillian," Ian said. " 'Tis certain she's no a bairn."

Calum's mouth tightened. "Nor has she been for some time now."

Hugh folded his arms over his chest and observed,

"Everything would have been simpler if she'd been a bairn, instead of a bonny lass."

"Beauty is as beauty does," Ian retorted angrily. "Ye saw her face when she discovered who Calum is. She had already judged him a black-hearted bastard."

Hugh shrugged. "Who knows how the tale came to her? Perhaps from friends she trusted, who heard from someone they had no reason to doubt."

"Or perhaps she and hers just prefer to believe the worst of others."

Hugh raised an eyebrow. "And ye've never done this?"

Ian fell silent, color tingeing his cheeks above his beard.

" 'Tis unimportant," Calum stated flatly. "What concerns me now is the delay."

"She's a wee bit old no to be married and with a wean in her arms," Hugh observed. "Still, she is a woman, and ye well know a woman needs the care of a man." He gazed out the window. "But if ye cannot tolerate the delay, why not leave Lady Gillian here and be done? She will be well enough chaperoned by her rector and his wife until her auntie arrives."

Calum folded his arms and leaned his back against the wall. " 'Tis a thought that appeals, but I canna do that." Honor. He recalled how she had denied recognizing the signature on the document as her father's. Had she truly not identified it or had she been lying? Calum set his jaw. He could not abide liars.

And there was something else. Something more.

Calum frowned slightly. She'd been nervous. Of course, that could have been the result of his un-expected arrival. Still, he did find it puzzling that she had not known who had been appointed her guardian. Or even that she had one.

"I wish to meet this rector and his wife," he said. And he would also keep a vigilant eye on Lady Gillian.

There was a light knock at the white-paneled door, and Ian crossed the room to turn the porcelain doorknob. Calum recognized the footman who had come into the library to build the unnecessary fire.

"The bath is ready, m'lord . . . gentlemen," the servant announced, his eyes flicking over the journey-stained Scotsmen. "Please follow me."

They left the manor and strode through the gardens to a small building that looked like a Greek temple with a domed roof.

They walked into a white-walled room with tall cases of shelves. Several stools were scattered about.

"If m'lord and the gentlemen will disrobe and proceed through there, your baths await." The foot-man passed under the archway he had indicated.

The three Scotsmen looked at one another.

"I was expectin' a tub and hot water," Ian said.

Calum scowled. "I'll no be takin' off my clothes until I know what this stiff-rumped servant pro-poses." He stepped through the archway into a long, narrow, windowless room. The high domed ceiling was glass, allowing in the sunlight. The interior walls were covered with brilliant jewel-toned faience tiles. On a long stone step-up shelf five large marble pedestal basins lined the wall under five pairs of brass faucets.

Calum had never seen anything like it. Where was the tub? Surely they were not expected to fit into the basins. He stepped closer to inspect one and felt heat emanating from the tiled wall behind it.

"Are we to splash water on ourselves from these faucets, then?" he inquired. Sweet Jesus, if he'd only wanted to throw a few handfuls of water on himself he could have taken a sponge bath in his room from the ewer on the washstand.

"No, m'lord. You will sit on this stool and I will pour buckets of hot water over you, scrub you with this loofah"—he held up something that looked like a tubular straw sponge—"soap you up—normally we use oil, but in this case I think you'll agree soap is called for—and pour warm water over you."

Calum felt heat rise up his neck to flood his face. "Where is the tub? All I asked for was a simple bath. A *real* bath. Not this . . . this"—he waved his arm to include the entire room—"foolishness!"

"This," the footman replied stiffly, "is a Turkish bath."

"I dinna care if it's a *Spanish* bath, I'll no have ye soapin' me up!"

"As you wish, m'lord. I will leave the soap in your care. Now, if you'll be so good as to return to the changing room and remove your clothes. Of course I will be happy to assist you—"

"Thank ye verra much, but I can manage."

"As you say, m'lord."

Back in the changing area, Calum explained the process to his cousins, his jaw tight with annoyance and an offended sense of propriety. He jerked off his coat, tossed it across a shelf, and then unfastened each button of his waistcoat with a sharp precision born of tightly reined temper.

He had been at Treymoor little more than an hour, and at every turn it seemed he was having to make adjustments to his plans.

"Think of it as a new experience, lad," Hugh suggested, as if he sensed what was going through Calum's mind. "How many men do ye know who can practice a foreign mode of bathing?"

Calum made a noise in his throat in answer as he wrapped a large towel about his naked hips. He cast a baleful look at his older relative, who surprised him with a rare smile.

"We might become the envy of Edinburgh," Hugh continued as the three of them walked slowly to the basins. They took their places on the stools Jenkins had set out, one to a basin. The footman pointedly instructed them that it was customary *here* to bathe in the nude. The towels were dropped to the stone floor.

The water from the brass bucket the footman held over Calum's head was hot. It splashed over him, slicking his unbound hair to his neck, shoulders, and back, soaking his beard, cascading down his bare, saddle-weary body. Jenkins poured bucket after steaming bucket, until Calum's skin was the bright pink of a boiled shrimp.

Under the heat and the sensuous caress of the liquid, Calum finally began to relax. He sighed, content for once to simply sit.

His contentment evaporated at the first abrasive stroke of the loofah across his back. But even that wasn't unpleasant, as he had fully expected it would be.

"How came ye to have a Turkish bath?" he asked as the footman scrubbed.

"My master was—*is*—interested in all things Oriental," Jenkins answered. "He sent Zerrin to us from Turkey, and she conceived of the plan to build this bathhouse."

"Zerrin?" Calum's skin tingled under the scratchy loofah.

"Lady Gillian's maid."

"Ah."

The footman seemed willing to talk. "At first we were all suspicious of this ritual. It seemed . . . unhealthful."

"Aye."

Jenkins completed the scrubbing and rinsed Calum off with only slightly cooler water, then handed him a bar of finely milled soap. Calum lathered it over his wet skin. The sharp, spicy scent of sandalwood filled his nostrils.

"Now we all quite like the Turkish bath." Jenkins moved to the basin next to Hugh. He refilled his container with steaming water from brass faucets and commenced the elder cousin's ablution.

"We?" Calum squeezed his eyes shut against the sting of the soap as he washed his hair.

"The staff and the tenants. Twice a week Lady Gillian opens the bathhouse to us. Men go one night and women the other."

Jenkins came back to pour more hot water over Calum, sluicing off the soap. A dousing with lukewarm water followed. The footman then handed him a fresh towel the size of a sheet. "Wrap yourself in this, m'lord, and go into that room for a little lie-down."

The scrubbing and hot water had left Calum—who was more used to cold-water baths—feeling enervated. As the footman turned his attention to Hugh and Ian, Calum wound the towel around his body and walked through the ogee arch Jenkins had indicated.

Here were cushioned benches long enough to recline on. Vivid tapestries covered the walls. Like the bathing area, light from the glass dome provided illumination. On small Oriental tables set about the room, trays of sliced cold meats, breads, and fruit had been laid out, along with pitchers of ale and a pot of tea.

Calum helped himself to food and drink and then, still waiting for his cousins' baths to be completed, stretched out on one of the benches.

If there was anything in Scotland resembling this bathhouse, he'd not heard of it. He studied the richly colored wool tapestry closest to him. Perhaps some day he could build such a luxury at Castle Dunncrannog. Gradually, his eyelids grew heavier as fatigue caught up with him.

He dreamed of returning to green Iolar Glen, snuggled deep in the Highlands. As he approached the castle, guardian of that mountain valley, a woman walked out to stand at the battlement. Calum shouted up to her to open the castle gate so that he might enter. She refused.

Dark thunderheads rolled across the sky, blotting out the sun, and a storm began to rise. The wind whipped her ebony hair about her head. Lightning illuminated her fair, oval face. Filled with a gut-wrenching yearning to be home, he called to her again to open the gate.

And again, Gillian Ellicott denied him entry.

*   *   *

As soon as the library door closed behind the Scotsmen, Gillian had collapsed into her chair. She sat there for a moment, stunned, swamped by anxiety.

Jenkins hurried over to her. "M'lady, what's to do? The earl— he's still in the icehouse!"

The door flew open, and Mrs. Withecombe and Odgers rushed into the room. Odgers shut and locked the door.

When Gillian had explained what had transpired, Mrs. Withecombe asked, "Are they staying, then?"

Gillian sighed heavily. "It appears so."

The housekeeper frowned. Absently she jingled the ring of keys that perpetually hung at her waist, a ring almost identical to the one Gillian usually wore. "This is most unexpected."

"Lord Iolar has requested a bath," Gillian said, latching onto the most mundane bit of news. First things first.

"He and his companions looked in need of one," Odgers said, wrinkling his nose. "What kind of gentleman presents himself to a lady in such a state?"

Gillian recalled quite clearly the pungent aroma of sweating horse and man mixed with the smell of leather. "I imagine they've been riding for days," she said.

"I will see to his lordship's bath, m'lady," Jenkins promised. He paused, then brightened. "The bathhouse has no windows. If we moved the earl, they couldn't see us."

"But everyone else in the parish could." Gillian stood and began to pace as she considered their predicament. They dared not move the earl from the icehouse in broad daylight. The plan had been for a transfer to the family crypt to take place where, if she could persuade him, the rector would hold a simple service. That still seemed the best course. "We can't take the chance."

Abruptly she sat down again. She pulled a sheet of paper from a drawer and hastily scratched out a note to the little rector and his wife. She explained that unexpected company had arrived at Treymoor, and at the moment Aunt Augusta was in London. Gillian invited them to stay at the manor as her guests while she awaited the arrival of her aunt. She folded and sealed the note, then handed it to Pym. "Please have this delivered at once to Reverend Appleyard."

He went to the bell cord and tugged.

Gillian scribbled another quick message, this one addressed to Augusta. After it was sealed, she handed the folded foolscap to Odgers. "Take this to Aunt Augusta and tell her about Papa yourself. I don't need to tell you how important it is that she makes all haste. Lord Iolar must believe she was coming back tomorrow. I will stall him with the usual story of her coach breaking down."

Odgers nodded. "Very good, m'lady. I'll have the Lady Augusta here fast as you can blink an eye."

"Yes, quite," she said, smiling at his exaggeration. "Do be careful, Odgers." She pressed his hand, suddenly reluctant to part with him. He'd been with her all her life and was dear to her. "Take two men with you."

He leaned forward to give her an affectionate

peck on the forehead. "Don't you worry about me, little Gillyflower. You take care o' yourself."

"I will." She hated the thought of her dear friend traveling the roads to London. Dangers abounded.

There was a light tapping at the door. Odgers unlocked it and took the opportunity to slip out as eight-year-old Sammy Blenkin came in.

"Deliver this note to Reverend Appleyard, lad," Pym instructed the little page. "You must be quick about it."

"There's a nice bit of ginger cake for the lucky boy who's quick as a blink," Mrs. Withecombe added. She consulted the clock on the mantel. "Let's see who can deliver his packet to the good rector and be back to the kitchen in, say . . . oh, half of an hour?"

Sammy's blue eyes widened with excitement. "Right you are, ma'am!" With a decided lack of decorum, he raced out of the library.

Gillian pushed her chair back from the desk and stood. She moved to the window and looked out on the garden. Her interest fixed on the bathhouse.

"Well," she said, never taking her gaze from the temple-like building, "as it seems we are stuck with the marquess, the next step is to remove Papa from the icehouse without being discovered."

3

After Mr. Appleyard and his wife arrived at Treymoor and were settled in their room, Gillian asked to see the rector.

When he entered the drawing room, she swept forward with a greeting on her lips, genuinely pleased to see him.

Gillian realized that, by the standards of many, spectacled Francis Appleyard looked to be of little consequence. At thirty years of age, he was short and slim, and his unremarkable brown hair was already thinning. The dark colors he usually wore were not flattering to him, causing his face to appear somewhat jaundiced. He was a patient, soft-spoken man, but Gillian knew that when the occasion called for it he could be quite firm. Most important of all, Mr. Appleyard truly cared about people. Together with his wife, who was equally mild-mannered and generous of heart, he saw to the spiritual needs of those in the nearby village of Poppleton and the surrounding countryside.

"Thank you so much for coming, Mr. Appleyard," she said warmly, offering her hand. "Do you and Mrs. Appleyard find your room comfortable?"

"Yes, quite. As always. You know, Lady Gillian, if you had a proper chaperone, unanticipated guests would not pose such a problem for you." He had chided her gently in this way many times throughout the past three years, ever since she'd appointed him to the living of Saint Agnes.

She motioned him to the settee and poured two cups of tea from a service Pym had left with her minutes earlier. "As you never fail to remind me." Smiling, she passed him his cup.

He sighed. "It is a shame your father left for Istanbul so unexpectedly. I did wish to discuss that very matter with him."

Gillian cleared her throat. "Unexpectedly. Yes. Well, that was what I wanted to speak with you about." She paused, marshaling her words. Dear Lord, this was not going to be easy!

"Yes?" He smiled and patted her hand encouragingly. "Do not be afraid to share your troubles with me."

She had a feeling he would soon regret those words. She did not like putting him in a difficult situation, but his cooperation was essential to her plan. And, she reminded herself, he had much to lose if authority over Treymoor was transferred, either to the devil Scotsman or to that wastrel Nicholas Vallance, should he return from his refuge in France and assuming he was still alive. If only she knew who was to inherit! She took a gulp of tea.

"My father didn't leave for Istanbul," she said.

Mr. Appleyard tilted his head, directing his good ear toward her. "I fear I did not hear you. Please speak up."

"My father didn't leave for Istanbul," she repeated more loudly.

He frowned in confusion. "Didn't leave . . . ?"

Gillian set her cup and saucer on the satinwood occasional table next to her and turned her full gaze on the rector. "He's dead, Mr. Appleyard."

He drew back so abruptly his spectacles bounced to the tip of his nose. "Dead?"

She nodded. "He was dancing in the fountain— he was foxed, you see—and he fell. Cracked his head, I believe. He—he"—she took two deep breaths and tried again—"he died a few minutes later."

"Oh, my gracious!" The rector took a large swallow of tea and set his cup back in its saucer with a clatter of china. "Oh, my gracious!"

He blinked several times as he stared out the window. Gillian hoped he was thinking of his good wife and their two children, of how change in authority at Treymoor might affect his flock.

"Lady Gillian," he said, turning sympathetic brown eyes on her, "I am so sorry for your loss. Though I only met Lord Molyneux for the first time briefly last week, I—well, he must have been a most devoted father to have such a conscientious daughter. But why did you not notify me immediately? And I've heard nothing from Mr. Fichett."

No, she thought with a sharp twinge of guilt, he wouldn't have heard from the village physician.

"Mr. Fichett is unaware of the situation," she said. "No one knows yet, except certain of my household staff. And now you, of course."

"But why?" His eyebrows drew down as he deposited his cup and saucer on the tea table. "This is not customary. Not customary at all."

She sighed. "I do not know who stands to inherit the title of Earl of Molyneux and—more importantly—Treymoor. Not exactly. I believe one of two infamous rogues stands to gain: either Nicholas Vallance or the Marquess of Iolar. I assure you, neither will leave Treymoor intact. Vallance has already gone through his own fortune and fled to France to escape his creditors. He is a violent man, a gambler. The other possibility is the illegitimate son of the late Marchioness of Iolar."

The little rector's face had grown pale with apprehension as she'd disclosed the possible heirs. "But this is terrible!" he exclaimed. "I've heard nothing of this Vallance person, but I *have* heard of Iolar's—er, offspring. Or rather, his wife's. Of course, it is true that what I heard was perhaps gossip, which may be nothing more than exaggerated untruth," he added quickly, obviously trying to be fair.

Gillian hoped the rector could not see any signs of the desperation she was feeling. She tried to school her features into a solemn expression. "Where there is smoke, I perceive there must be fire."

"Good gracious," he repeated mournfully.

She pounced on his uncertainty. "Either man is a

threat to the well-being of everyone in the parish. Do you remember how the tenants and servants of Frampton Park fared at the hands of Lord Quirval's heir?"

He closed his eyes. "Yes. Yes, I remember. That fiend. I remember also how Mr. Johnston and his family fared," he said, speaking of the rector of that parish. "And his wife, poor soul." His mouth tightened.

Gillian recalled that story with sorrow. "She had only just been delivered of a child. Her great distress over the condition of affairs—"

"And the lack of money for coal."

Gillian looked at him in surprise. "I sent them coal. And food and blankets."

"Which they shared with the less fortunate of their flock. Then the babe came earlier than expected."

Mrs. Johnston and her newborn had died two days later. Her seven surviving children and her bereaved husband were turned out of the rectory shortly after. The heir had sold the estate with no thought to the people who lived there and the new owner, who lived in London, had decided to raise only sheep.

Gillian shuddered. Such a fate would not befall her people. It would not!

Trying to sound as confident as possible, she went on. "I have a plan, Mr. Appleyard, that will save us all from the fate suffered by those at Frampton Park."

He straightened. "Indeed?"

She nodded. "It is, of necessity, somewhat unorthodox, but only a bold plan will see us through.

And"—she snatched up his cup and filled it—"your part in the stratagem is of utmost importance." She turned her full charm into the smile she gave him as she passed the refill.

"My part?" He frowned into his cup, then lifted his gaze to meet hers. "What sort of part?"

"Iolar does not know Papa is . . . has . . . passed to his eternal reward. We hid him, you see."

"Hid Iolar?"

"No, Papa."

Horror dawned in Mr. Appleyard's face. "You *hid* the bod—er, your father? Dear Savior, help us. Where?"

Trying to calm her agitated nerves, Gillian took a convulsive sip of tea. What if Mr. Appleyard would not help them? Her eyes narrowed. He *would* do his part, on that she was determined. "In the icehouse. But the important thing is that I will meet you in the Ellicott family crypt at twelve of the clock this night for my father's funeral. He will be interred there, but no marking shall be made. Secrecy, of course, is vital. No one must know."

"But how will you keep such an occurrence as a peer's death a secret? There are reports to fill out—"

"They will not be filled out. Not yet."

"The—the parish registry—"

"I must ask you not to make your entry at this time. I . . . I know that is asking—"

"You are asking me to break the law!"

She pressed her lips together and shook her head. "No, I am not. I wish only that you help me bend it a little."

Quickly, Gillian explained her plan, hoping she

sounded more calm and decisive than she felt. All the while, she was only too aware that, as he listened, his eyes grew increasingly wider—which made her increasingly nervous.

"So you see," she concluded, "I ask only that you delay some of your official duties. As for my part in the scheme, I shall begin seeking a husband immediately." She searched his face for his reaction.

Mr. Appleyard remained silent for a moment. He stared at a shield-back chair across the room, but Gillian doubted he even saw it, so inward did his thoughts seem to turn.

"Lady Gillian," he finally said, his voice low and solemn, "do you realize the risk you take? The consequences to be faced if the authorities apprehend this . . . masquerade?"

She clutched the teacup and saucer in her lap and nodded slowly. Then she lifted her gaze and met his squarely. "I do."

"Do you doubt that the weight of the King's justice will fall fully on you if what you do is discovered?"

She swallowed, but her gaze did not waver. "No. I comprehend my risk, Mr. Appleyard, and since last night I have given it considerable thought." In truth, she had done little else. There had been no sleep for her last night as the few memories she had of her father spun round and round in her head and anxiety for the future of her people and of Treymoor bore down on her. "I see no other way."

Mr. Appleyard sighed heavily. "It is unfortunate that your father did not give more thought to your future. Had he but appointed a legal guardian for you, had you sent to London for a spring season as the daughter of an earl should have been . . . why, you would be wed by now and perhaps already the mother of a fine son. You would not be reduced to this desperate hunt for a husband."

Gillian stared down into the tepid brown liquid in the bottom of her cup. She had wanted a spring in London. What extravagance to have time to do nothing but indulge in entertainment! But time was not the only thing she'd wanted in London. There her chances would have been better for finding a husband, a special man of her own with whom to share her life. Someone upon whose shoulder she could occasionally lay her head when the world proved to be a more difficult place than usual. Someone who would love her as she loved him. . . .

I will not think of that. Gillian lifted the cup and took a bitter swallow. The hard fact remained: She was twenty years old and unmarried. Compared to the other women of Saint Agnes parish, she was an old maid. How she hated that term!

Something the rector had said intruded on her thoughts. *Had he but appointed a legal guardian for you.*

"Guardian," she muttered under her breath as she recalled the purpose of her talk with Mr. Appleyard. She cleared her throat. "Uh, yes. There is one small detail I may have forgotten to mention."

"Detail?"

"I did advise you that the Marquess of Iolar has arrived unannounced." She absently raised her hand to stroke the perfectly matched Persian pearls about her throat. The feel of the smooth skin-warmed spheres soothed her as always. The necklace with its exquisite ruby pendant was the only real gift her father had ever given her, a present to commemorate the sixteenth anniversary of her natal day. Rarely did she take it off.

Mr. Appleyard frowned in puzzlement. "Certainly you advised me. His presence is the reason Mrs. Appleyard and I are staying at Treymoor."

"Yes." She stood, unable to remain still a moment longer. Her skirts whispered as she paced a few steps. She turned abruptly to face the rector. "He presented me with a document that appoints him my legal guardian."

"*What?*"

"Regrettably, I believe the document is authentic. I cannot understand why my father—"

"Lord Iolar is notorious. Even *I* have heard what is said about him." Color darkened Mr. Appleyard's face to an alarming shade of purple. " 'Pon my word, that man is no fit guardian for a young gentlewoman. For *any* woman. Surely your father—"

"Will you help me, Mr. Appleyard?" she asked quietly.

He huffed a deep sigh but met her gaze squarely. "Yes. Yes, Lady Gillian, I will help you."

Before she could voice her thanks, the door of the drawing room opened and Lord Iolar entered. He regarded them evenly for a moment, his expression neutral, and she hoped he had not overheard any of her conversation.

Iolar looked a different man than the one she'd seen this morning. Oh, he was still tall and imposing. The fact that he was now clean and looked to be refreshed certainly attributed to the difference. But it was the lack of his beard that was most notable. Its absence revealed a strong angular jaw, a firm chin. The man, Gillian grudgingly admitted to herself, was strikingly handsome.

His white lawn stock was conservative, and he wore a well-cut frock coat of sapphire blue, a cream-colored embroidered waistcoat, and buff breeches. Silver buckles gleamed on his shoes.

As Iolar stood there, watching her from across the drawing room, Gillian shifted uneasily. The change was only in his appearance. It touched no deeper.

Mr. Appleyard stood politely. Gillian set her cup down, forcing a smile for her unwanted guest.

"I bid you welcome, my lord."

Iolar's lips curved slightly. "I trust I dinna interrupt anything important?"

"Why, no. No, of course not." To her annoyance, she felt her face grow warm. "Please." She gestured for him to be seated. "Will your companions be joining us this eve?"

"Nay. They've chosen to take their meals in Hugh's room."

She was relieved to hear that she would not be subjected to the company of two more of the interlopers. Immediately on the heels of her relief came concern that they had entirely too much freedom and might wander where she least wanted them to go. She fervently hoped someone was keeping an eye on them. She needed to speak with Pym, to make certain.

She went to the liquor cabinet. "What would you prefer to drink while we wait?" she asked the marquess.

"Whisky."

Facing the liquor cabinet, with her back to him, she surreptitiously nudged the full decanter of good Drumossie whisky to the rear row, hidden from sight. "Oh, dear," she said, feigning surprise, "there seems to be none here." She turned a bright smile on him. "Fear not, I am certain we have some in reserve. I will just be a moment." She started toward the door.

The marquess reached over and tugged the bell chord, effectively stealing her excuse to leave the room. She wanted to shriek in frustration, furious with his presumption. How could her father have been so careless as to saddle her with such an arrogant man as guardian?

One corner of Iolar's sensual mouth quirked up. "Dinna trouble yerself, Lady Gillian. Ye have an army of servants; surely one of them knows where the whisky is kept."

She lifted her chin, favoring him with a frosty look. "I assure you, Lord Iolar, you need not have pulled the bell. I am quite capable of running this household without assistance from guests." With that she turned, determined to get out of the room to caution Pym or Mrs. Withecombe privately about Iolar's henchmen.

To her astonishment, before she could move two brisk steps, Jenkins appeared. To her further surprise, he wore the powdered wig and pale-blue-and-white satin livery usually reserved for the infrequent balls and dinners her aunt insisted upon holding at Treymoor.

"Yes, m'lady?" he asked smoothly.

Since the terminal for the manor's bells was

located in the servants' hall, it would have taken a footman, moving at a quite respectable pace, several minutes to arrive in the drawing room. Yet instantly here was Jenkins, not a hair of his wig out of place, his breathing unhurried, not at all as if he'd just charged from one side of the enormous house to the other. Which meant only one thing: He had been waiting, listening on the other side of the door.

She shot a quick glance at the marquess, hoping he had not arrived at the same conclusion. To her discomfiture, she found him already looking at her.

He lifted an eyebrow. "A miracle of efficiency."

Gillian flushed hotly. "To be sure," she said, wishing she could pull Jenkins aside and give him her message for Pym or Mrs. Withecombe. To do so, however, might raise Iolar's suspicions, and that was the last thing she wanted. "Jenkins, we need whisky for Lord Iolar. There is none in the cabinet."

The servant frowned. "None, m'lady?" She tried to give him what she hoped was a meaningful look. He leaned closer to her, his frown melting into concerned scrutiny.

She continued with her look, focusing on the footman, willing him to understand her message. "If you would bring the whisky, Jenkins. And please convey to Pym that Lord Iolar's companions are taking their meals in their rooms *and are to be accorded every consideration.*"

His face abruptly took on the lack of expression of a well-trained servant, which told Gillian he had received her message. "Very good, m'lady." The picture of dignity, he turned and silently withdrew from the room.

Mrs. Appleyard arrived moments later, and they all went into the dining room, where another liveried footman waited.

Gillian smiled to herself when she saw the elegant table that had been set. Neither Pym nor Mrs. Withecombe, it appeared, was about to let the Marquess of Iolar think anything was amiss or wanting at Treymoor.

The heavy silver candelabra had been fitted with new beeswax candles, as had the wall sconces in the green room, the smaller of Treymoor's two dining halls. The enormous red dining room had been designed for occasions of state and had not been used in Gillian's lifetime. Here in this more intimate chamber, candlelight glowed upon the emerald-and-gold-painted walls and matching draperies at the windows. Reflections of the tiny flames twinkled on silver, china, and Irish crystal. Mellow light performed a shadow dance across the ornate plasterwork of the twenty-foot-high ceiling.

The first course was taken in near silence, the most noticeable sound in the room the intermittent clinking of soupspoons against the sides of the bowls. By the time the salmon trout was served, the lack of conversation apparently had become too much for Mrs. Appleyard.

"Well," she said with forced cheer, her voice echoing against marble and plaster. "Have you visited the English countryside before, Lord Iolar?"

He turned his head to regard the lady solemnly. "Nay, madam. I have traveled, but not around England."

Seeing an easy opportunity to learn something

about her guardian, Gillian said, "Pray be kind enough to tell us of the sights you have seen, Lord Iolar. We lead a tame and quiet life here."

Mr. Appleyard choked on his wine. Immediately, Gillian reached over and patted his back. When he had recovered his composure, she spared him one last, slightly more energetic thump—a pointed warning to be more discreet. He shot her an apologetic look.

The marquess took a helping of vegetable pudding. "In the American colonies I saw great forests and half-naked savages, though in truth the savages I met were mannerly and possessed of great dignity. The colonists are a vigorous hard-working people."

"You speak as if you think well of them, my lord," Mr. Appleyard said. "Yet they defied their king and broke with their mother country."

Iolar looked over at the rector, the movement of his head causing the gleaming red-gold hair of his queue to slip across his back. "Aye, that they did, and so they're colonists no more. They are Americans."

Gillian observed how the muted light traced the strong planes of his face. According to the letter this man had shown her, he was her guardian. The document she had read appeared to be authentic, right down to the paper her father had favored. And it was not as if she could simply walk into the office of her father's solicitor to ask for confirmation of Iolar's appointment. But she could send to Edinburgh to verify the identity of the true Marquess of Iolar.

He glanced at her. Over the candlelit table, their gazes caught and held. Her breath stopped in her throat. Time paused as her world contracted into green eyes, eyes that seemed capable of seeing the secrets that hid in her mind. . . .

Then he looked away. Feeling vaguely stunned, she drew a shaky breath. Foolishness, she told herself sternly. The overactive imaginings of a swooning twit. The man was dangerous. She would need to exercise more caution if she hoped to succeed with her plan.

"Is it not, Lady Gillian?" Mrs. Appleyard asked.

With a start, Gillian realized that she'd missed what had been said. "I . . . I am afraid I did not hear." She managed a smile for Mrs. Appleyard.

"Lord Iolar tells us he has been to the West Indies. That is quite exciting, is it not?"

"Oh. Quite. Yes. Quite exciting." Precisely what this world needs, Gillian thought dryly. Another adventurer. Well, he would not get his hands on Treymoor, to strip it for his cursed expeditions. Unless he already stood to inherit. Unless she could not find a husband, produce a son. . . .

It was all so unjust. She had *wanted* a husband, children. All the local ladies her age were long since wed, and many already had babes. She had not dared to take either the time or the risk of discovery that a proper courtship would have involved. Oh, why hadn't her father come home long enough—

She nearly dropped her fork. Her father! Dear Lord in Heaven, had anyone thought to remove her father's things from his room? Just before the accident, he and Odgers had been packing. Had they finished? Where were the trunks? If the Scots discovered that all her father's possessions—all his *neatly packed* possessions—remained here, they would surely guess something was amiss.

The conversation grew more and more stilted, with Iolar revealing no new facts about himself. While Gillian presented a pleasant face, inwardly she writhed with impatience, desperate to see an end to this gathering.

When finally the marquess bade them all good night, she thought everyone must be relieved. She thanked the Appleyards again for their generosity in accepting her invitation to stay at Treymoor on such short notice and then, wishing them pleasant dreams, hastened to her own chamber.

Zerrin was waiting for her. "You were successful? Mr. Appleyard, he will perform the service for my lord Molyneux this night?"

Gillian nodded. "He agreed. He will meet us in the crypt at the twelfth hour."

Zerrin's dark eyes smiled above her veil. "It is good."

"Oh, Zerrin, I surely hope so. So many people depend on—"

The Turkish woman made a small disapproving sound as she set about undressing Gillian. "Think not of that, my lady sister, for you have the heart of a lioness and your people love you."

"Uh, lioness. Quite." She'd never thought of herself as a lioness.

She stepped out of her skirts. "There is one thing I must do before we go to the crypt."

Zerrin glanced at the clock on the polished marble mantel. "One and one-half hours remain before Pym and Jenkins remove my lord Molyneux from the icehouse." She helped Gillian into a quilted petticoat and a bodice of midnight blue. Briskly, she laced up the front of the bodice. She fussed with her mistress's hair before fitting over it a mobcap adorned with a band of dark blue ribbon.

"Enough," Gillian said impatiently. "I must go."

"Where? What must you do that cannot wait until the morrow?"

At the door of her chamber she turned back to Zerrin. "I'm only going to Papa's room. I wish to see if there is anything that will reveal the name of the rightful heir. Perhaps . . . perhaps there is a third man, one unknown to us. Perhaps the lawful heir to Treymoor is a kind soul who poses no threat." She laughed softly at her own desperation, but the sound held no mirth. "I fear there is little chance of that, but I must know, Zerrin. I must know."

She went to her dressing table and withdrew from an enameled box a small watch. She fastened its silver chain around her neck and checked to see if the time it kept was accurate. "I will meet you here in one hour."

"One hour," Zerrin agreed.

Gillian hastened down the hall, the flame of her single candle flickering. A glow touched the corrugated surfaces of old gilded frames, shadowed canvases, and smooth-limbed statues. The smell of melting wax drifted to her, and here and there she caught the sweet scent of dried rose petals as she passed a bowl of potpourri.

She quietly descended the stairs, into the better-illuminated area of the entrance hall, where moonlight poured through large windows. After passing down the length of another corridor, she arrived at the door of her father's apartments.

She hesitated. On the fingers of one hand, she could count the number of times she'd entered his rooms. It seemed to her that on his rare visits he had always been in the process of leaving.

Drawing a deep fortifying breath, Gillian turned the brass doorknob, entered her father's antechamber, and closed the door behind her. Here, too, moonlight spilled through windows. The silence that filled these apartments weighed down on her as she made her way through the room to the enormous bedchamber.

There she found what she had dreaded. Carefully folded articles of a man's clothing covered the counterpane of the stately canopied bed. Open half-filled trunks formed a neat line, apparently ranked according to content. She crossed the chamber and opened one door of the wardrobe. More clothing, not yet folded and stowed. All damning evidence.

She swallowed hard as her gaze moved about the room, taking in a set of silver-backed hairbrushes, a razor, a nightcap. These things, his personal possessions, were all she had left of her father. These, her pearl necklace, and the few letters he had written her. The house was filled with treasures he had sent from far-off lands, but she found no sentimental value in a carpet or a bolt of silk that he might never have touched or even seen.

Suddenly it seemed too much. She must rid her father's apartments of his belongings and, in an hour, attend his shamefully secret funeral. His limestone sarcophagus would not even bear his name yet. Gillian swallowed against the tightness that gathered in her throat and leaned back against the wall. Her elbow struck an acanthus leaf carved into the wood paneling. A second later, she was leaning forward, clutching her tingling, tortured arm against her body, suppressing a groan of misery. Tears of regret and frustration gathered in her eyes.

No! She would not give in to tears. There was no time for such weakening indulgence. Too much rode on her ability to think swiftly. Too many people depended on her. Slowly she straightened. Her elbow throbbed, but the pain had eased. She looked around the room. Now where was she going to hide everything? There was no time to call for help. She leaned against the wall again—

—And fell backward, into a dark and musty space.

Gillian scrabbled for balance, barely saving her head from a sharp acquaintance with the stone wall, encumbered as she was with ells of petticoat and underskirt. Her hands came away smudged with black mildew and her sleeves were coated with fluttering cobwebs. Revolted, she skipped quickly back into the bedchamber. She regarded the dark hole for a moment, then reluctantly picked up her candlestick and stepped closer to investigate.

A section of the wall's paneling was, in fact, a door. When it was closed, it was undetectable. Gillian poked her head back into the room, holding her candle aloft. This was no small storage space or cache. It appeared to be part of a passageway, which continued as far as her candle's light shone. Where did it lead? she wondered. Judging from the thick cobweb draperies, only spiders had used this corridor in a long time.

She backed into the bedchamber, set her candle-stick on the washstand, and began throwing every-thing lying on the counterpane into the open trunks. The brushes, the razor, and the nightcap followed, along with everything else she thought a man might take on a long sojourn far from home. Then she closed the trunks and applied herself to dragging them into the tunnel.

By the time she had finished, she was panting and weary, and she feared the floorboards were scarred beyond repair. She pulled a carpet from the other side of the chamber over the gouges. It was an odd place for a carpet, true, but for now it would have to suffice. She closed the door into the passage.

"Merciful heavens!" she whispered as she glanced at her watch. There was just enough time to make it back to her room to rendezvous with Zerrin for the funeral.

As her hand touched the doorknob, she heard the outer door close. She froze in place, hardly daring to breathe. Who was out there? Perhaps Zerrin, come to remind her of the hour?

The knob turned. Wide-eyed, Gillian stared at it, even though she knew the door was locked. Her heart pounded as she waited, certain her maid would call to her, if the person at the door was indeed Zerrin.

No call sounded. Again the knob turned.

There was a small clicking sound, and vibration in the lock under her fingers, as if someone was hav-ing difficulty with the key. Zerrin did not have a key to this room. No one but Gillian possessed the key. Who—?

Wildly, she cast about the room for a place to hide. The secret passage! But there was no time to see if the door would open again. She must confront whoever was trying to get in.

She caught a glimpse of herself in a mirror. Her face and hands were smeared, and some hair was sticking out of her crooked mobcap.

Hastily she wiped her hands and face on the only thing she could think of, a bedsheet. She straightened her cap, stuffed her errant hair back into place, and whirled around to face the intruder, her heart beating like the hooves of a runaway horse.

The door swung open.

"Who—who dares to enter my father's room?" she demanded, hoping the intruder could not detect the quaver in her voice.

The light of another candle entered the doorway, revealing the imposing figure of the Marquess of Iolar. He scowled as he strode into the chamber.

"What are ye doin' here?" he demanded in a low voice. "Ye should be all tucked up in yer bed."

"As you should be," she retorted, incensed by his invasion. The man's presumption knew no bounds! "Just what are *you* doing, wandering through this house? My father's house, in which you are a guest?"

The marquess moved closer. She longed to step back but refused to give ground before him. He stood too near, his height and broad shoulders making her only too aware of how vulnerable she was before his strength. She stiffened her back and met his eyes. But they were unreadable.

"Aye, yer father's house, lassie, but let us settle one matter now. I am no a guest here. I'm yer legally

appointed guardian." One corner of his mouth
pulled up. "Until Lord Molyneux returns, *I* am master of Treymoor."

Gillian wanted to shout her denial of him, but
what purpose would that serve? She knew the document she had read to be of her father's making. To
oppose the marquess might prompt him to take the
matter up with the authorities, a situation she
devoutly wished to avoid.

"Now," he said quietly, "I'll ask ye once more:
What are ye doin' here?"

"This is my father's room," she pointed out,
struggling with her anger.

"Aye, I am aware of that. I am also aware of the
hour."

The hour! Gillian suppressed an urge to look at
her watch. Zerrin would be waiting for her, Pym and
Jenkins would be in the icehouse, Mr. Appleyard
would be fretting in the Ellicott crypt. And here she
was, trapped by this large Scottish barbarian.

"I . . . I miss my father. I . . . uh, feel closer to him
when I'm surrounded by his things." A lie. She
could stay in this room day and night and feel no
closer to her father. She had tried that long ago.

The marquess's hard expression softened, and for
the first time she realized he was younger than she'd
first thought. "Poor lassie. Are ye pinin' for him then?"

"I—" Did she truly miss her father? Or did she
simply regret that there was not much she could
miss, having been allowed such brief glimpses into
his life? Gillian dropped her gaze to the floor.
Foolish to think on that now.

Then she noticed Iolar's bare feet. Surprised, she

drew her eyes up, taking in his nankeen breeches
and full-sleeved white cambric shirt. Like her, he
had changed out of the clothes he had worn for dinner into something more practical.

She scowled. "Your feet are bare."

He smiled, revealing even white teeth. Amusement
danced in his eyes. "Aye, well, I could no verra well
go sneakin' around this great mountain of a house
with my boots on, now, could I?"

Gillian stiffened. "Sneaking? What need of sneaking has the *master* of Treymoor, when all he surveys
is his to command?"

He raised a warning eyebrow at her sarcasm but
answered her question. " 'Twas merely that I knew
ye to be anxious over my arrival. I thought to satisfy
my curiosity without awakenin' anyone."

"You picked the lock of this door!"

He nodded, staring down at his feet. "Aye, that I
did. Easily, too. 'Tis no a verra good lock." He gave
her a slantwise look. "Before I go to bed I intend to
check the locks on the outside doors."

She glared at him.

"I think it would be a good thing were I to keep
the keys." He held out his hand, palm up.

Gillian wanted to strike him. "You may be the
master of Treymoor, Lord Iolar, but *I* am the mistress. It is necessary for me to have the keys."
Especially if she was going to slip in and out of the
house at night undetected. "My duties require
them." She had no intention of telling him the scope
of her responsibilities. If she said nothing to the contrary, he would believe her duties to be strictly
domestic. The less he knew the better.

His hand remained out. "The keys, Mistress Gillian."

Defiantly, she clenched her fingers over the bunch of keys that hung at her waist but made no move to hand them over.

"I'll no ask again." Somehow, the mild way he spoke the words, rather than the words themselves, conveyed the stronger warning.

With bad grace she smacked the jangling bundle into his palm.

"Now, pray, will you tell me what you are doing in my father's room?" The room she had to escape if her father was to be buried this night. The longer he remained in the icehouse, the greater the danger of discovery.

"I came to see," he said, "what manner of man would turn his bonny daughter over to the keeping of a stranger."

Inwardly, she flinched. It was a question she would like to have answered too, but the only man who could do so was dead. And she had to escape this room now.

She tried to sidle around Lord Iolar, edging toward the door. "I do not believe that he did."

The marquess turned his head, watching her from beneath hooded eyes. "Ye have held his letter in yer own two hands, have read his words. Do ye doubt that I am yer legal guardian?"

"I meant only that I believe your father was known to him." She inched closer to the door.

In one leisurely motion, he effectively positioned himself between Gillian and freedom. "Do ye doubt that I am yer legal guardian?" he repeated.

She glared at him. "What do you truly ask, my lord? That I doubt your authority? Or that I accept it?"

"I would have an answer to both questions."

She lifted her chin defiantly. "As you wish. I do not doubt that you are my guardian. But I do not want you. I want no one."

He regarded her for a moment. "How many years have ye?"

Gillian struggled with her indignation over the impertinent question. As her guardian, he had a right to know and clearly her father had not seen fit to enlighten him. "Twenty," she snapped, her cheeks burning. Twenty years old and desperate for a husband. "How old are *you*?"

"Seven and twenty." His lips curled up. "Twenty, eh? Seems I have an auld maid on my hands."

Her temper snapped. "Old maid!" She brought her heel down on his bare toes.

Sharply, he sucked in his breath, making a strangled sound. He hopped about on one foot, kneading his injury with both hands and swearing in a language she could not understand.

"I will have you know I am *not* an old maid, sir! I plan to wed and—and quite soon." With a toss of her head, she swept by him, cloaked in righteous indignation. Out she went, into the anteroom, toward the door to the corridor.

"Oh, no, ye don't, ye little hellcat." He hobbled after her. She broke into a run. He caught hold of her arm.

Startled, she whirled around to face him and backed into the edge of a settee. With a squawk, she stumbled and tumbled backward, onto the carpet.

Already off balance, the marquess fell too, landing on top of her. With a grunt, he bore the weight of his fall on his elbows.

In the darkened room, illuminated only by the moon's silver light shining through the windows, she lay panting beneath him. His masculine body pressed against hers in unnerving intimacy.

With strong slim-fingered hands he clasped her wrists, pinioning them over her head. He lowered his face to hers.

"Now," he said softly, his breath warm against her cheek, "I'll have yer apology."

4

He was heavy and solid, all muscle and bone, and she sensed the power in him.

Moonlight trailed melted silver across his forehead and high cheekbones. His eyes were pools of black shadow beneath his brows. In the dim illumination, his mouth was etched clearly enough for her to see that he was not smiling, yet the line of his lips lacked the hardness of anger.

An urge to reach up and touch that precisely cut mouth seized her. It held a beckoning promise of warmth, which seemed at odds with what she knew of him.

Appalled at her thoughts, Gillian firmly squelched the urge. She attempted to buck him off but found she could barely move beneath the weight of his body.

"Yer apology, lass," he reminded her softly.

"I have nothing for which to apologize," she snapped.

"But ye do. 'Tis considered rare poor manners to stamp on a man's bare foot."

She glared up at the mysterious mask the night made of his face. He smelled faintly of sandalwood. "Your feet should not be bare," she informed him. "They should not even be here."

"And I've told ye, I'll go where I please. As yer guardian, I have the responsibility of yer safe-keepin'."

Gillian did not like being reminded of his legal power over her. "You, sir, are naught but a cad!"

His mouth hardened. "And ye, *Lady* Gillian, are naught but a spoiled brat."

Her eyes widened with indignity. "Spoiled?"

"Aye. And I'm givin' ye fair warnin', I'll no be tol-eratin' yer tantrums."

"Tantrums?"

She saw his jaw tighten and knew he still expected her to apologize. Confound the man, unless he got his way he would keep her here all night. That she could not afford. She was already late to her father's funeral.

"You have my apology, Lord Iolar," she said, spit-ting out the sour words before she could choke over them.

"Charmingly spoken," he drawled as he rose lithely to his feet and held out his hand to help her up. "Though I must confess I've never heard an apology sound so much like a curse."

She forced herself to take his hand, unwilling to antagonize him and thus run the risk of further delay. "Good night, sir," she said, jerking her bodice straight. She started toward the door.

"I will see ye to yer room, madam."

" 'Tis not necessary. I know my way," she replied, sweeping out into the hall, trying to ignore the lop-sided situation of her cap.

He walked beside her all the way back to her room, apparently unaffected by her stony silence.

"Sweet dreams to ye, Lady Gillian," he said politely at her door.

"May you rest well also, Lord Iolar—assuming that you've satisfied your curiosity about my father and have finished roaming the house."

His lips curved in a slight mocking smile. "I think I've learned much about the father through the actions of the daughter." Inclining his upper body in the sketch of a bow, he turned and strode silently away.

Gillian watched until the glimmer of his candle's flame vanished in the dark and then closed the door. Zerrin looked up from her seat by the bed.

"Where were you?" the young woman breathed.

"Detained. I'll explain in a moment. First, what happened with Papa?"

"When you did not come, I went to the crypt to inform the others. My lord Molyneux has been returned to his place in the icehouse." She shook her head. "Everyone is most nervous over this matter of conveying him back and forth. It is not good to delay."

At the thought of her father's body being hauled from icehouse to crypt and back again, Gillian's stomach knotted. She had never wanted him to be subjected to such irreverence as he now endured. She sent a silent prayer asking forgiveness for failing so profoundly in her filial duty to arrange a dignified burial.

"I wanted to see if anyone had thought to remove Papa's clothing and toilet articles from his room—as they would have been had he actually departed for Istanbul—and discovered everything still there. The trunks were set out, only half packed."

Over her veil, Zerrin's dark eyes widened in alarm. "This is terrible!"

"There is more to tell," Gillian said grimly. "The Scottish lord also came to Papa's chamber. He picked the lock to the door. Then he demanded possession of my keys."

"Your keys? But this also is not good."

"We must get them back. If we can substitute Mrs. Withecombe's keys for mine, I doubt he would know the difference. With so many keys on the ring, he would not notice the loss of two." But those two keys would allow him access to ledgers and papers that would reveal that she—a mere woman and a minor to boot—had conducted business and signed contracts without proper legal authority. Whoever found the documents of the estate's everyday transactions would soon see that there was no legal guardian, not even a permanent chaperone, but only Gillian and the people of Treymoor.

"What did he do when he saw the half-packed trunks?"

For the first time since her father's demise, Gillian found cause to smile. "He saw nothing of importance. I was able to conceal all." In her excitement over her discovery, she hugged a startled Zerrin. "You will never guess! I discovered a most amazing thing. A secret room!"

Zerrin leaned back to search Gillian's face. "Secret room?" she echoed.

"Yes. In truth, I believe it is a passageway. Perhaps it leads through the entire house."

Delight twinkled in Zerrin's eyes. "A secret passageway. How useful this will prove! Tell me how you discovered this wonder."

Quickly Gillian explained how she had stumbled upon the concealed door. "Tomorrow I will explore. Perhaps there are more doors," she said.

"And perhaps peepholes," Zerrin said as she began to unlace Gillian's bodice, pulling the ribbons through the eyelets. "It was said there were peepholes in every room of the Grand Seraglio. I have always thought it might be so, because the Kizlar Agasi—the Chief Black Eunuch—seemed to know everything."

Gillian knew that Zerrin had escaped from the Ottoman sultan's grand harem, and that her father had somehow played a part in it, but the how and the why remained a mystery. It had always been a subject neither seemed willing to discuss.

"I have never heard anyone mention hidden ways through this house," she said.

Zerrin shrugged, a graceful movement of her shoulders. "Perhaps they have been forgotten."

Gillian stepped out of her petticoat, and as Zerrin put the garment away she untied the ribbons holding her bustle roll in place. "Tomorrow night," she said, "we will have Papa's funeral. Same time as we'd planned tonight." She frowned. "We must be very careful of Lord Iolar. He is a dangerous man and not above stealth."

Zerrin's eyes turned up at the corners in a smile. "Nor are we, lady sister."

Gillian chuckled. "No, we are not, are we? And we shall outwit that Scottish interloper and his unhappy kinsmen."

After Zerrin departed to her own chamber, Gillian snuggled deep within the bedclothes of her high tester bed. Despite her brave words to Zerrin, she knew Iolar posed a real threat to their plans and thus to their well-being.

With the thought of him came the unwanted memory of his powerful body pressed intimately against hers, of his warm breath touching her cheek, and of the mingled scents of laundered linen, sandalwood soap, and vibrant male skin.

Her fingers tightened on the quilts as she fretted that her awareness of him was the pitiful desperation of an old maid. Oh, how she despised that status! Then she recalled that she had been in the presence of tall handsome men before—even recently on a visit from a neighbor—and she had not noticed any exceptional perception of them.

But then, none of them had held her home and her happiness, and that of her people, in the palm of his hand.

Gillian stared at the sliver of moonlight that shone through a crack between the window draperies. Iolar was a dangerous man. Until she was wed and held a son in her arms, she would do well to remember that.

"I shall outwit him," she whispered, needing to hear the words, even if they were only her own. "I *must* outwit him."

Calum stood in the dark and watched her door, but it remained closed.

She was up to something. It was as plain as the wee turned-up nose on her face. But *what* was she up to? The excuse she'd given for being in her father's room was plausible. From what little he'd learned about the Earl of Molyneaux, the man seldom stayed home. It would be natural for her to miss him sorely. Still . . . some sixth sense, some mysterious communication to which he could not quite set his finger, nagged at him.

He looked at her door. There was light showing beneath, but that was not necessarily significant. She might sleep with a candle burning. He shook his head. Just more evidence of the shameful extravagance that surrounded her. Spoiled she was, and no mistake. But then, what father wouldn't wish to shower every advantage on such a lovely daughter?

Every advantage, it seemed, but a husband. Calum's foot throbbed faintly. A lack she clearly resented.

Any man who took Lady Gillian to wife would need a braw strong will, of that there could be no doubt. He would have to establish immediately who ruled. The man would have a vixen on his hands.

He would also have at hand a woman with dark silk hair, soft gray eyes, and sweetly formed lips. Calum remembered how she'd felt beneath his body.

So slender. So female. Moonlight had glimmered in her wide, startled eyes. Her mouth had looked so inviting. . . .

Calum frowned. It was unseemly for a guardian to think of his charge in such a manner. The responsibility for her had been thrust upon him, but he would carry it out with honor.

Deciding he was wasting his time standing there, he cast one last glance at his ward's door, just in time to see Zerrin slip out of the room and hasten down the corridor. Her fluttering white veil shone starkly in her candle's glow. Far down the hall, she entered another chamber.

Quietly, Calum followed her. Did she visit someone within? Was she a messenger for her mistress?

After several minutes, the light in the room went out. The maid might just have been waiting up to assist her mistress in retiring for the night and then had sought her own bed, though from what he knew of English great houses, it struck him as odd that the maid did not stay in the servants' wing. But perhaps not too odd, considering that the little exotic must be at the beck and call of her demanding mistress.

Calum padded silently down the hall in the direction of his own chamber. Perhaps he was wrong. Lady Gillian might be innocent of any scheming.

But he doubted it.

Gillian rose before dawn as was her custom. She dressed and went downstairs by the light of her single-dipped candle, used to the unpleasant tallowy smell. Long years of scrimping and just getting by had made frugality second nature. Without giving them a second glance, she swept by the unlit costly beeswax candles in the wall sconces and girandoles. They were for show.

As a matter of survival, she'd learned early that appearances were all-important. Since the age of fifteen, she had depended on illusion to keep her people, her home, and herself safe from the clutches of scoundrels and do-gooders. She expected that it should serve her until the day she died—preferably as a contented woman full of years, surrounded by children and grandchildren, rather than as a felon in some miserable prison.

She ate her breakfast of oat porridge in the kitchen, but this morning the cook and her helpers bustled about the large, lofty room, busy with preparations for a morning meal befitting titled guests. This uncommon activity came as no surprise to her. Everyone was well acquainted with the steps necessary to keeping up the charade of being the household of a wealthy earl and his pampered only child.

Lucy Kendrew, a short, pleasantly plump woman of thirty-four years, labored at a long pine table worn smooth by generations of cooks. At the moment, her workplace was equipped with crockery bowls and wooden spoons, a heavy marble mortar and pestle, a cone of white sugar, and sundry other ingredients and implements. Behind her, in the enormous fireplace, caldrons and griddles heated on the open range. On the wall hung a battery of well-tinned copper pots, pans, and molds essential to Mrs. Kendrew's art.

"You be sure to come back and dine with your

guests, now," the rosy-cheeked woman told Gillian. "No sense in just eating porridge when there's to be all this food."

"I will, Mrs. Kendrew," Gillian assured her. "But first I have work to do."

The cook set a bowl in one arm and with a wooden spoon began to stir the thick mixture inside. Not for the first time Gillian marked the strength in the older woman's arms.

"Don't you always?" Mrs. Kendrew asked cheerfully. " 'Tis a hard-working lady you are."

Gillian smiled. "We all work hard."

Mrs. Kendrew's spoon swirled faster and faster. "That we do. But it's a good life we have here."

"Yes. Yes, it is."

"I know this is a tricky business we have here now, m'lady, what with them Scotchmen and"—she cast a quick glance toward the door—"all," she concluded cautiously. "Do you tell me if there be any way I can help."

"Depend upon it, Mrs. Kendrew."

Gillian set aside her empty dish and, rising to her feet, thanked Mrs. Kendrew for the porridge. Then she hastened to her father's room. She estimated that she had about an hour before Lord Iolar and his clansmen could respectably present themselves to break their fast.

Under her probing fingers, the carved acanthus leaf gave way. She heard a soft *click*. She pressed firmly in the middle of where she thought the door should be, and the panel opened inward.

Her candle cast flickering light into a chamber as dark as the pit. Her father's belongings still filled the space, and the trunks were still locked. It seemed Iolar had not discovered the secret door.

Gillian knew she could not leave the door into the passage open, but the thought of being trapped inside these cold spider-inhabited walls sent a shiver through her. Who knew what she might come upon?

Maybe peepholes. As she remembered Zerrin's suggestion, she brightened. Yes, peepholes might prove quite advantageous. But she would never find them if she stayed glued to this spot like a witless ninny. She straightened her shoulders and set about locating a latch on the inside of the door, which she found immediately. Unlike the one on the outside, this latch was not concealed. She worked it several times, to determine that it still functioned; then, taking a deep breath, she swung the door back into place.

She stood alone in the long-forgotten room. Suddenly the halo of amber light around the candle flame seemed pathetically small. Fumbling inside her apron pocket, she felt the narrow-edged steel and flint, the reassuring smoothness of the extra candles, and the ball of rough twine she had brought.

She tied the end of the twine to the handle of one of her father's trunks and turned away, feeding out the line, ready to explore.

Cobwebs hung like pale draperies that stirred as she passed. The light of her candle danced upon stone walls, revealing patches of mildew. A mouse scurried for its hole.

Not far from her father's room, she found another door mechanism. She estimated that it led into the suite next to the earl's apartments, which had remained unoccupied for years. Gillian laid her fingers on the latch. Although the maids regularly dusted and swept and polished in there, guests were never offered these apartments.

The door opened easily, and she stepped into quarters that had a distinctly feminine air about them, all soft colors, delicate furniture, and dainty porcelain figurines.

She looked around. She did not come in here anymore, though there had been a time when she'd visited often. Then the sound of laughter had rung often within these walls.

Her mother had died in this room. Pym and Odgers and Jenkins had borne her broken body here after that terrible carriage accident. Mrs. Withecombe had gently cared for her, but there was naught that could be done. In less than an hour, Gillian's mother had passed from this mortal world, leaving behind her an anguished sister, a bewildered child, and a household of grieving servants. Gillian's father, as usual, had been far from home.

As Gillian stepped back into the passageway, closing the door behind her, she was glad she had found no peepholes to this room.

She headed toward the wing of the house where she'd quartered her unwanted guests. Although the very idea of spying on visitors was repugnant, she told herself that what she planned to do was necessary. Her father had made a mistake. It was up to her to correct that mistake before it brought down disaster on all their heads. Surely his intention had never been to displace servants, tenants, and daughter. No, Benjamin Ellicott, fifth Earl of Molyneux, was not—had not been, she corrected, with a catch in her throat—a cruel man. Merely careless. And, as always, it was left to her to find the remedy.

Reeling out the twine, she wended her way through the narrow tunnel. She found two more hidden rooms like the one next to her father's bedchamber. Both were empty, and for that she gave silent thanks as her imagination supplied numerous horrid objects she might have encountered, not the least of which were the bones of some previous explorer.

A pennant of spiderweb caught in the ruffle on her mobcap, and when she tried to bat it away, it entangled her fingers and then her hair. With a strangled squeak, she swatted frantically at the sticky stuff, tearing it loose from its mooring on the ceiling. It floated down, trailing her, attached by a slender thread. A mouse chose that moment to dart across the passageway, scrambling onto the top of her foot. Instantly, Gillian recoiled, shaking her foot like a madwoman. The web followed her like a bouncing tail. The mouse clung to her stocking. Gillian swiped wildly at the rodent with one of the candles from her pocket. The beast leaped from her foot and scurried off into the dark.

Breathing rapidly, Gillian managed to brush off the last of the cobweb, then looked up to make certain she did not run into any more. A tiny, faint patch of light on the wall above her head caught her attention.

She backed to the other side of the passage, peering up through the gloom. The light came from a small hole in the wall. The aperture was no defect in the masonry, for its rounded shape testified to its having been carefully bored.

A peephole! She had not thought to look so high. Perhaps there were others she had missed. If only she could see through it! She gave a few experimental hops, trying to catch a glimpse through the hole, but to no avail. It was situated too high.

She hurried on to find other doors and other peepholes before she marked the wall with charcoal and turned back. The secret passageway, it seemed, ran throughout the house.

To her delight, she found the door into her own bedchamber and quickly closed it behind her. Upon reflection, she shoved a small chest of drawers in front of it. She felt great relief when her search disclosed no peepholes in the walls of her rooms.

Her looking glass revealed black smudges of mildew on her bodice and overskirt. Bits of old spiderweb clung to her cap, her hair, and her clothing. A harried glance at the mantel clock revealed that she had little time to clean up and change her clothes.

Soft taps on the door sounded a well-known code, and Zerrin breezed in. "What did you find?" she asked immediately.

"Doors and peepholes."

"Did you see anything of importance?" Zerrin asked as she began to help Gillian to undress.

"The holes are too high. Next time I shall take a stool." Gillian wrinkled her nose at the memory of the cobwebs and the mouse. "As well as a broom and one of our best mousers."

Rapidly the two women cleaned Gillian of dirt and

spiderwebs and dressed her hair in a simple arrangement with a few long curls at the back of her head, ignoring, as usual, the popular preference for extravagant hairstyles. Gillian had neither the time nor the taste for what she considered wasteful ostentation.

Dressed in a white dimity Levite, Gillian left her room and went to face the intruders. Aunt Augusta had insisted she have this pale confection of a gown made because it was so fashionable and because Gillian was an earl's daughter and therefore should be conscious of all who might be watching her. Plain garb would cause comment and, possibly, breed questions—a circumstance Gillian most ardently wished to avoid. So she had acquiesced to her aunt in the matter of wardrobe.

All three men were seated at the table breaking their fast when she arrived. Judging from their plates, they had almost finished their meal, which meant they had come down considerably earlier than she had expected. When they saw her, they stood.

"Good morning, gentlemen," she said with assumed cheerfulness. "Do, please, be seated. Is everything to your satisfaction?"

A chorus of voices rumbled assent as the men resumed their seats. Jenkins appeared at her back and drew out her chair. Pym went to the sideboard and dished up a plate for her of hot rolls, creamy butter, ham, and eggs. He also served her a cup of chocolate. It was a great deal more food than she was accustomed to in the morning, but its heavenly fragrance made her mouth water.

"Where are your chaperones this morning?" Lord Iolar asked as he cut a piece of ham.

Her hands paused in their task of buttering a roll. She did not miss his mild emphasis on the word *chaperones*.

"It is early yet, my lord. I am certain the Reverend Appleyard and his good wife will be down in a timely fashion. They always exercise the courtesies."

The youngest of the trio shot her a sharp look. "They'll be eatin' cold food, then. Calum had word sent to them, as he did to you."

But of course, she had not been available to receive a message. Mr. and Mrs. Appleyard, she knew, sometimes went out to watch the sunrise, seeing that as one more sign of God's goodness. Perhaps they had not received the message either.

Lord Iolar lifted an auburn eyebrow at his younger kinsman, who flushed and subsided.

She knew what time breakfast was to have been placed on the sideboard. The kitchen staff must have served the meal early to accommodate her guardian.

"It is only that we are used to rising early, Lady Gillian," the marquess said mildly. "Habits, ye understand, are sometimes verra difficult to break." He laid his knife and fork across his empty plate. "I hope ye'll forgive the earlier omission, but I dinna believe my cousins were introduced to ye."

"Indeed," Gillian said. "I have been most curious." Cautious might be a better word. She didn't trust the marquess's cousins any more than she trusted him—which was not at all.

Introductions were completed just as the Appleyards entered the room and so had to be repeated, a necessity which only served to fuel

Gillian's impatience to be done and away on her day's work.

Harvest was approaching, and she must make certain everyone was ready to do his share. Unless there was an untimely heavy rain, this year's crops of oats and barley would be the final push that tipped Treymoor into prosperity. The small flock of sheep had thrived this past year, as had the new breeds of pigs and chickens she'd introduced over the last four years. The bees had outdone themselves in both honey and wax. The tenants and their farms had done better every year, and this one promised to be no different. Even the kitchen garden blossomed with abundance. The end to years of deprivation was in sight.

"What a lovely gown, Lady Gillian," Mrs. Appleyard said admiringly. "My sister in London has written me that Levites in white dimity or muslin are quite modish as morning dress."

"You are too kind, Mrs. Appleyard."

The older woman's eyes twinkled. "I believe I see your aunt's fine hand in this selection."

Gillian laughed. "Yes, indeed. Aunt Augusta is more conscious of fashion than any other woman I know."

"Speaking of yer auntie, she'll be arrivin' today, will she no?" Iolar asked.

"Yes, of course," Gillian lied smoothly. "She would have been here earlier to greet you, but like the rest of us, she believed Papa was to depart for Istanbul today. I do not doubt but that she'll be here in time to rest and refresh herself before dinner."

"From where in Scotland do you and your kinsmen

hail, Lord Iolar?" Mr. Appleyard inquired politely, diverting the conversation in another direction.

"The Highlands, sir." If he was expecting some reaction from them, he received nothing but courteous attention. "I am from Iolar Glen. My cousins come from Aberdeen."

"I've heard Aberdeen is a fair town," Mr. Appleyard said.

"Aye," Hugh said. " 'Tis a fine place."

Ian nodded his agreement.

"I do not believe I've heard of Iolar Glen, Lord Iolar, but perhaps you will pardon my ignorance. I fear my sense of geography is somewhat lacking."

"Not at all, Mr. Appleyard. Iolar Glen is the bonniest glen in all of Scotland. 'Tis nestled high in the mountains. Forest is thick on the slopes, the crops and livestock are plentiful, and a river crowded with trout runs its length."

The rector smiled. "You make me almost wish to live there. How can you stand to be parted from such a garden?"

Gillian did not miss the glance exchanged between Hugh and Ian. They would know of Iolar's heinous reputation.

The marquess cut Gillian a brief hooded look. "We do what we must, sir. I have had a charge laid upon me and must now execute it to the best of my abilities."

Mr. Appleyard's color heightened. "I see," he said, and turned his attention to the plate before him.

Gillian ground a portion of ham between her teeth. So she was a burden, was she? One he wished quickly to execute? Well, she was not precisely delighted with the arrangement herself. Nor was she pleased to hear of him executing anything in her vicinity. Prison, transportation to the colonies, and hanging had been too much on her mind of late.

Lord Iolar pushed his chair back and rose. "Lady Gillian, please have your father's steward attend me in the library immediately."

She swallowed the bit of meat with a gulp. "What?"

"I wish a tour of this estate. You will accompany me. Mr. Appleyard, would you and your good wife do me the honor of coming with us?"

Gillian stared at him. "Now?"

The tall Scot sketched a bow, then straightened. "Now is as good a time as any." He turned and strode from the room.

She set her jaw. Of all the insufferable arrogance! She had tenants to visit, livestock to inspect. One of her best breeding cows was ailing. She did not have time to traipse along with Iolar. Gillian took a slow breath and let it out. At least she would be able to keep an eye on him. She must also set someone to keep watch on Hugh Drummond and Ian Gunn.

She excused herself from her guests and went to the morning room, where she tugged the bell cord. Then she wrote a note explaining the situation to her steward, William Harland. He was a dependable fellow, and she knew he would play his part. The work would get done after all, if in a roundabout way. When Jenkins arrived, she gave him the note to deliver to William and instructions to have Iolar's cousins observed. Also, someone must make certain that no one but Mrs. Withecombe entered the icehouse.

Then she went to her chambers and changed into

her riding habit. Zerrin fussed over the waistcoat, unhappy to find the patched places in the cream silk fraying at the edges.

" 'Tis in the back, Zerrin. The coat will cover it."

Muttering under her breath, Zerrin helped Gillian into the claret superfine petticoat, then into a frock coat of the same color. "I have heard that evil dreams disturb the Lord Iolar."

"I've no doubt."

Zerrin set a jaunty hat upon her head and stood back with an air of approval.

"He will find you attractive," she said.

Gillian did not have to ask who *he* was. "You are mistaken. He thinks me an old maid." She walked by Zerrin and out the door. "I do not care one whit what that person thinks."

Zerrin followed her. "If you make yourself pleasing to him, perhaps he will be distracted enough to think all is well. You have done this before many times."

"Yes, I know," Gillian admitted grudgingly.

"He is a most handsome man, is he not?"

"I've taken no notice."

Zerrin's knowing chuckle grated on her nerves.

"Handsome is as handsome does," Gillian said irritably, "and thus far, handsome has been stealthy and arrogant. Do not forget, Zerrin. He is a threat to us."

"I do not forget, lady sister. But a woman must be blind not to admire such a man. And it does no harm to have him admire you."

Gillian descended the stairs. "That likely will not happen. He believes me a spoiled child."

Zerrin followed. "But this is what you wished him to believe, is it not?"

"Yes, of course," Gillian said. For the first time, however, having an outsider think she was naught but her father's pampered darling bothered her.

When she entered the library, she found Lord Iolar and her steward deep in conversation.

"My lady, I understand you are to be joining us on this tour," William said smoothly, falling into his role of polite man-in-charge.

She slipped into her own part with practiced ease. "Yes. You know how tedious I find such business, Mr. Harland, but Lord Iolar will insist on my accompanying you."

Iolar straightened from where he'd been bending over a map of the estate, which was spread across the table. He lifted a dark red eyebrow but said nothing.

When the rector and his wife arrived, they all went out to the stables. As little as Gillian liked the thought, she was forced to admit that the tall Scot cut an impressive figure. He had the advantage in height over William by several inches, and he moved with the confident grace of a well-bred stallion.

As the group waited for their saddled mounts to be led out, Iolar moved closer to her.

"I much regret that ye find such matters dull," he said in a voice pitched only for her ears.

She pretended to adjust her riding gloves. "Then go on your tour without me. I assure you, we shall both be the happier for it."

"No doubt. Still, yer father's estate is a large one and will require time to see it all. I'd feel better knowin' that ye are . . . safe."

Her fingers stilled upon the buttery kid leather.

"Really, Lord Iolar. One might think you didn't trust me."

"One might."

She looked up sharply at him, but he was turning away to listen to something Mrs. Appleyard had said. Gillian studied him a moment. He wore the riding clothes he had arrived in, though they had been given a thorough brushing. He looked lean and powerful standing there in his riding boots, his buckskin breeches stretched tightly over long, muscular thighs, his rust waistcoat and somber brown riding coat covering his powerful torso and broad shoulders. He leaned over slightly, as if to catch the good wife's words. Sunlight gleamed in his bright hair, glinting on bronze and amber, cinnamon and gold. Gillian suppressed an urge to reach out and touch it.

With a small jolt, she realized someone was speaking to her.

"Your horse, Lady Gillian," Danny Ingleby, the groom, repeated softly.

She smiled. "Thank you, Danny." As she moved to accept his assistance up, she found herself face-to-face with Lord Iolar.

"I'll see to Lady Gillian," he said. With a nod, the groom moved off toward Mrs. Appleyard.

Gillian found herself unwilling to look into those startling green eyes. As if the act required her entire concentration, she looked down as she fitted her foot into the palm of his leather-gloved hand. A summer breeze caught the edge of her petticoat and lifted it, revealing the top of her half-boot and the length of her calf, covered in dark blue stocking. As she quickly smoothed the garment back into place, she felt ridiculously glad she had not worn one of her mended pairs of stockings.

"Nay," he muttered as he boosted her up into place, "ye are assuredly no bairn."

"I am thankful we have at least established that fact, Lord Iolar," she said crisply, privately pleased at his reaction. "Although I am an 'auld maid,' perhaps I am not yet a wizened hag."

He looked up, and their gazes collided with an impact that left Gillian breathless. She could not make herself break that connection.

"I think ye ken yer worth quite well," he said in a low, intense voice, "ye with yer hair like midnight and skin more lustrous than the very pearls about yer throat."

She blinked in surprise. Hair like midnight? Skin like pearls? No man had ever said such things to her before.

His face hardened. "Dinna worry for yer virtue. I'm yer guardian, and no matter what ye may think of me, I'll carry out my duties with honor."

"And I am naught but another duty to you." Unaccountably, she felt sad.

"Aye, madam, that is all."

He left her then and swung up onto his own saddle. He gathered the reins lightly in his hand and sat on the horse as if he had become one with it on contact.

"I believe we should start the tour by the river," he said. "At the icehouse."

5

Gillian's heart slammed to a stop. Mr. Appleyard turned pale.

It was to William's considerable credit that he managed to maintain a bland facade. "Might I inquire why my lord has chosen that as the starting point? Surely one icehouse is much the same as the next. I would have guessed you would wish to see the tenants' farms first. Or Lord Molyneux's prize sheep or cattle. We are all quite proud of them."

"As ye are no of the icehouse," the Scot said dryly.

William shrugged. "What can be said of the thing? Like all icehouses, it is dark and cold."

As a tomb, said a small accusing voice at the back of Gillian's mind.

No one spoke for a few seconds. To press the undesirability of visiting the ice house might serve only to make her guardian suspicious. And certainly if *she* said anything, he would decide he must see the cursed place if for no other reason than to show her who was master.

"Mrs. Appleyard, what do ye think?" Iolar asked politely.

Mrs. Appleyard sat lightly atop the bay mare she'd been loaned from Gillian's stables. "I have seen the icehouse, my lord. While it is a very fine icehouse, I cannot think my lord will find it diverting. But perhaps you do not have them in Scotland?"

"We have them, madam, even in Scotland. But perhaps prize sheep would prove more educational for us all. Unless Lady Gillian has a desire to visit the icehouse?" He turned a languid green gaze on her.

"I have no interest in such things, sir."

"I bow to the will of the ladies, Mr. Harland."

They went first to view the sheep, of which Gillian was enormously proud. Although, for the benefit of their guest, William now gave all credit to her father, she had begun the breeding program five years ago, while under the tutelage of the old steward. She'd read everything she could find on animal husbandry and spoken to many men who raised sheep. Then she'd imported a splendid ram and three ewes from Spain. Today the sheep in her small flock were hardier, and their wool more abundant and of a finer quality, than even the original stock.

"I'm no an authority on sheep," Iolar said to William, "but even I can see these are bonny beasts. Ye've a right to be proud, man."

"Oh, no, my lord. The credit must go to Lord Molyneux."

"Well, they are most excellent sheep and no mistake. Does the earl send ye detailed instructions on what must be done with them, then?"

Color rose up William's neck. "No. Yes. Er, that is to say, he does send some instructions. He's very particular, very particular indeed."

"Aye. Well. I'm certain ye've had a hand in the success."

Gillian's fingers tightened fractionally on her riding crop. *She* was the one responsible for these sheep. Then she realized the foolishness of her annoyance. In convincing her guardian that it was William who was responsible for Treymoor's blossoming prosperity, she had succeeded in maintaining the all-important ruse upon which her whole life seemed based. If Iolar knew she was the person he should be congratulating, he would no doubt be surprised. Then curious. Curious enough to investigate. No, Iolar must be shown what he expected to see, what everyone usually expected to see: a male steward overseeing the estate.

"You are too kind, my lord," William said.

From there the riders went to see the milk cows, and while William explained the breeding details of the herd, Gillian managed to sneak away and consult with the man tending the animal over which she worried.

"I done what you said to do, your ladyship." He gently stroked the cow's neck. "Margaret, here, she's sommat better."

Gillian smiled. "I am pleased to hear that. Continue the treatment. Mrs. Withecombe will supply you with all the onions you need."

"Right you are, your ladyship." He cast a squint-eyed look out the window of the cool stone byre to where William still occupied Iolar. "How's things coming along with the foreigner?"

"He's not precisely foreign, Nat."

The old man hawked and spat. "Scotch."

"Well, as you can see, I've not managed to get rid of him yet."

Nat gave her a gap-toothed grin. "You'll manage somehow, missy. You always do. I remember when you took the reins of Treymoor. A slip of a girl, you were, still taking your lessons from that teacher Mr. Pym hired. And you've managed ever since, for all of us."

Gillian gave his arm a small, grateful squeeze. "Oh, thank you, Nat. I needed to hear that."

As the tour proceeded, she recalled Nat's words and took heart. She *had* always managed. And she would this time, too.

The day wore on as they stopped on a hilltop to look out over the fields of oats and barley rippling in the summer breeze and went on to visit the orangery, the glasshouses, and the various domains of every kind of livestock kept on the estate. Finally, they stopped at the house of a tenant.

A short, wiry man in his forties sat on a stool near the yard door of a well-kept cottage, applying a whetstone to the blade of a scythe. When he saw the riders approach, he set the tool aside and rose to greet them.

He went directly to Gillian, his weathered face breaking into a smile. "How good to see you, m'lady! Alice, come out," he called toward the cottage. "Lady

Gillian is here." He gave William a nod. "A pleasure to see you too, Mr. Harland."

"And you, Mr. Varley."

A woman hastened outside to join them, attired, like her man, in homespun. "Lady Gillian, it has been too long since we seen you." It had, in fact, been only a week.

Careful to stay between her party of riders and her tenants, Gillian leaned down and clasped the hands of her tenants. "I wanted to warn you," she said in a low voice, "but there was no opportunity to do so."

Mrs. Varley's eyes grew large. "So that be the fellow."

"Yes," Gillian said. "That is the fellow."

Varley strode over to William. "Had to give my greetings to Lady Gillian," he said loudly—too loudly. "You know how seldom we see her. Now, sir, what business have you come on?" Gillian sighed. Dear John Varley was a far better farmer than an actor.

"We come strictly on pleasure today, Mr. Varley. Lord Iolar desired a tour of Treymoor."

Gillian caught the worried glance that passed between the farmer and his wife and wished she had something with which to reassure them, but she held her tongue.

"Mr. Harland has told me about yer bonny farm," Lord Iolar said, "so I am curious as to what improvements ye've made to the land. And, if ye would be so obliging, I should like to see yer livestock and anything else ye would care to show me."

Gillian looked at him. Oh, he was cunning, that one, appealing to the success of a hardworking man.

"If you wish, m'lord, though I do think there isn't much you can learn from a tenant farmer."

Iolar dismounted. "A wise man learns from everything around him." He smiled, and Gillian was so drawn in she almost smiled too. "I cannot claim to be wise, but I do try to learn."

The excursion of John Varley's farm took every long minute Gillian feared it would, but she was given no chance to conduct Treymoor's business.

Finally, as the visitors mounted their horses to go to the next farm, Mrs. Varley made an opportunity to speak briefly in private with Gillian, under the guise of giving her a small crock of chutney for Mrs. Kendrew.

"It's that Ralph Scarth," she said. "He's at it again. It's worried I am about Mary. He's . . ." her gaze fell away. "Well, you'll see for yourself. No woman deserves that, 'specially not one in a family way. And Mary, she's such a good soul." She looked back up at Gillian, her brown eyes pleading. "I'll never understand why she married that man, but she's my sister and I can't just keep silent. Will you speak to him, m'lady? He stopped last time you did. Didn't start again till only lately. The fiend gets angry because she's large now, and it's hard for her to get around, do you see?"

Anger and revulsion burned in Gillian's stomach. Ralph Scarth was the worm in the apple barrel of Treymoor. He was lazy and mean-spirited, and she still did not understand why her father had insisted she make a place for the creature. Supposedly, Scarth had saved her father's life and in the process incurred a debilitating wound. She knew someone had saved her father's life, but she did not see how it could have been Scarth, whom she knew to be a coward. But then, her father had once told her that fate sometimes made heroes of reluctant men. Only briefly, from what she could see of it.

"I will speak with him," Gillian said, "but if he chooses to ignore me, I do not see what can be done. Not when Mary continues to go back to him."

Mrs. Varley shook her head. "Mayhap not this time, I think. Before it was only her. Now she's got the babe to think of. It scared her good."

"I will speak with him," Gillian repeated, for want of more substantial comfort.

"God bless you, m'lady." She clasped Gillian's hands around the small clay pot of chutney. "You'll bring that monster into line, I know you will."

Gillian thanked the anxious woman for the chutney and wished she could be as certain as Mrs. Varley about Scarth's compliance.

They stopped at two more farms before Scarth's. At both, Gillian was warmly received, and William and the Appleyards were greeted with pleasant civility. The tenants regarded Lord Iolar as warily as if he were one of those tigers the earl had written about in his rare letters. With Iolar's red-gold coloring, his powerful lean body, and his watchful green eyes, Gillian thought he could easily bring to mind an exotic predator ready to spring and devour its prey.

As they rode up to Scarth's rundown cottage, Gillian frowned. Of all her tenants, only this man allowed his home and his outbuildings to fall into disrepair. She could cite that as reason enough to put him off her property. Only her father's request saved Scarth from a rapid eviction.

He lounged in a shady spot under a half-dead tree. A scrawny boy scattered meal for the even scrawnier chickens.

When Scarth saw the riders, he rose and stretched, then strolled toward them, his expression guarded.

"Lady Gillian," he said, clearly begrudging even that bit of acknowledgment. His glance flicked over the rest of the group, but he said nothing.

Gillian surveyed his unkept leasehold with distaste. "Mr. Harland and I would have a word with you, Mr. Scarth."

The tenant's thin mouth turned down. "You've been over to the Varley place, ain't you?"

Gillian dismounted. Accompanied by William, she strode up to the thin man, who never took his small dark eyes off her.

"I have warned you not to let your buildings go," she said evenly in a low, controlled voice. "This time, you shall be charged for the cost of repairs. And believe me when I tell you that repairs *shall* be made."

"Wouldn't need no repairs if this place were better made!" he whined indignantly. "It all but falls on our heads, it does."

She didn't deign to answer him but, instead, walked around the corner of the house and into the dirt yard, where she found his pregnant wife laboring over a tub of laundry. When the young woman saw Gillian, she quickly turned her face away.

"Please look at me, Mary," Gillian said gently.

Hesitantly, Mary did as she was asked, and Gillian caught her breath. Dark, purple bruises covered Mrs. Scarth's face and arms. Gillian read the shame in those once-pretty eyes, now swollen almost shut, and it sickened her. Before Mary had wed Scarth, a newcomer to Treymoor, she been given to laughter and teasing. Gillian couldn't remember the last time she'd heard Mary laugh.

Out of the corner of her eye, she saw William stiffen at the sight of Mary's battered face.

"Good God, Scarth, what possessed you to do something like this?" William demanded.

"It were the gin," Mary said.

Gillian glared at Scarth. "We have discussed this before."

"Several times," Scarth said sarcastically. He smirked at her, clearly aware that Gillian could do little about the way he chose to treat his wife.

"Mary, go pack your things," Gillian said. "You and the children are coming to the manor with me."

"You can't take my wife away from me. Who'll cook an' wash? I got my rights!"

Gillian whirled around to stand almost toe to toe with him. Scarth towered over her. "And what right would that be?" she said coldly, pointing toward Mary, who tried to hide her abused face. "The right to brutalize someone smaller and weaker than yourself? The right to be a bully and a vicious coward?"

Hatred twisting his face, Scarth drew back his arm to hit her.

A large hand caught hold of his wrist and jerked it back, causing Scarth to cry out in pain.

"No true man ever strikes a woman," Lord Iolar said, his deep voice hard-edged with warning. He shot Gillian a pointed look. "No matter the provocation." His gaze reached Mary, and his nostrils flared with disgust. "Ye are lower than a coward, Scarth. No one should beat even a dog like that."

Scarth flailed out at Iolar. With a swift motion, the marquess twisted Scarth's arm behind him, rendering him helpless to move without pain.

"Do ye wish to come with us, Mrs. Scarth?" he asked kindly.

Mary looked uncertainly at Iolar, then at her husband. Her arms slipped around her large belly in protective gesture.

"Hitting me is one thing, Ralph, but you struck our babe. You promised you wouldn't."

"You made me, woman! You got above yourself. You talked back. Umph!" He winced as Iolar twisted the arm higher.

"That dinna sound like an apology to me," Iolar said. "Does it sound like one to ye?" he asked William.

"No, indeed."

"She argued with me!"

"Och, well, if every woman who argued with her man were beaten, all married women would be bruised."

"I—!"

But Lord Iolar had run out of patience. "If I find out that ye've hit her again, I'll come lookin' for ye. An' if I'm forced to do that, I might be inclined to do a bit of hittin' myself." His voice lowered slightly. "Do I make myself understood?"

Sullenly, Scarth nodded.

Iolar released the tenant's arm and grabbed the back of his shirt neck, hauling him up until they were face-to-face. Scarth's feet dangled half a foot above the earth.

"And if ye ever again threaten the Lady Gillian," Iolar said softly, "I will make ye wish ye'd been smothered at birth."

Gillian shivered. Iolar's threat was all the more terrifying for the gentleness of his voice.

The marquess looked at Mary. "Should he raise a hand to ye again, send word to me."

"Yes, your lordship," Mary said meekly.

He turned a sharp look on William. "Is yer business here finished?"

The steward flushed. "Yes, my lord."

Iolar placed his large hand at the small of Gillian's back and, jaw set, firmly ushered her to where Mr. and Mrs. Appleyard waited with the horses. She all but had to trot to keep up with his pace.

He did not offer his hands to boost her up, but rather took her by the waist and plopped her onto the saddle like a sack of oats. She straightened her hat and glared at him.

He glared back. "We'll speak when we return to the house."

On the way to the manor, the rector and his wife doggedly kept a flow of conversation going among the riders, as if polite discourse would ease the tension between guardian and charge.

"Lady Augusta is due to arrive, isn't she?" Mr. Appleyard finally asked, as they reined in their horses at the foot of the front stairs and dismounted. Without a word, a groom led the beasts away toward the stables.

"Yes," Gillian said. "She may be here already."

A lie, of course. At this very moment, Aunt

Augusta was probably being jostled about inside her carriage, decrying the condition of the roads. Very soon now, a "messenger" would "arrive" here to announce that a wheel had broken on that very same carriage, necessitating an overnight stay at an inn while the damage was repaired. In truth, Aunt August would break her journey by spending the night at her comfortable estate in Northhamptonshire before continuing on to Treymoor the next day.

"Mr. Harland," Lord Iolar said, "a word, if you please." Without waiting for an answer, he took the portico steps in a brisk stride and disappeared through the front doors.

"Good luck, William," Gillian said.

William gave her a forlorn half smile and followed the marquess.

Fifteen minutes later, Jenkins brought the summons from Iolar to her room, and Zerrin conveyed it to Gillian, who was washing off with water from her ewer.

"That was certainly quick," Gillian said, accepting the linen towel Zerrin handed her.

"It does not take long to dismiss a steward," Zerrin observed.

Gillian stared at her, alarmed. "Oh, no. Surely Iolar would not do that. He seemed to admire the improvements to Treymoor, and since he gives all the credit to William, I cannot think he would so easily send him away."

"I hope it is not so," Zerrin said simply, and helped Gillian into a fresh gown.

All the way to the library, Gillian seethed. This was *her* house, and the library was *her* domain, and the running of Treymoor was up to *her*! Or, at least, if the world were a better place, that was how it would be. But she had never been one to deny the realities, and one of the more annoying ones was that men were in charge. Most of the time.

She entered the library to find Iolar standing by one of the tall windows, drumming his fingers on the casement.

She dropped him an exaggerated curtsey. "You summoned me, my lord?"

He turned to her, his eyes revealing anger and something else she could not quite read.

"What ye did was reckless," he said bluntly. "Reckless and foolish."

She straightened abruptly, lifting her chin in defiance. "What do you know of it? I'll wager you've never been beaten by such scum as Scarth. You are large and strong, but Mary is not. I cannot tolerate what Scarth does to her—I will not!"

"I dinna like what Scarth has done anymore than ye do! But Mary is his wife, and in the end she must be the one to make the decisions. Ye gave her a choice, and she chose to stay with him. Ye gave *me* no such choice."

"What choice did I fail to give you?" she asked, confused.

"Ye pushed Scarth, and had he harmed ye I would have had no alternative but to kill him."

She found it difficult to breath. "Kill him?"

"Aye, Gillian. Ye are mine to protect, and protect ye I shall."

"But to *kill* him?" The punishment seemed severe.

"There must be no doubt in any man's mind that

to touch ye will bring immediate and deadly reprisal." His face might have been carved of stone for all the emotion he revealed.

What kind of man was this Scotsman, who would kill someone for striking her? Where had he learned such a harsh code? It frightened her a little.

"What . . . what did you speak to William about?" she asked, not wanting to think about Iolar killing anyone because of her.

"Dinna fash yerself over Harland."

"You were angry with him, I could tell. But I don't know why. You didn't dismiss him, did you?"

Iolar strode over to stand in front of her. "Ye dinna ken why? He allowed ye into danger! As steward, he knows what kind of man is Ralph Scarth, the fact that the bastard is a wife-beater. Yet he allowed ye not only to go to that farm—if that wasteland can be so called—but to provoke the man."

Indignation bubbled up inside her. "*I* provoked *him*?"

"Ye did. Ye called him a coward."

"He is!"

Iolar nodded. "Of course he is. That was plain for all to see." His expression softened. "But do ye not know, Gillian, that 'tis always the craven man who most resents being called what he is?"

Her name spoken in his deep, lilting voice affected her like an intimate caress across her skin. Unexpected, audacious, it shimmered over her senses. She stood motionless for a second, faintly disoriented. Then she remembered he'd asked her a question. Like as not he was unaware he'd even spoken her Christian name twice without her courtesy title.

"Uh, no. No, my lord. I-I was not aware." Her maladroit attempt to cover her lapse brought the heat of a blush to her cheeks.

Iolar seemed not to notice her awkwardness as he turned to the walnut library table where she usually sat to go over the ledgers. She saw a pile of his opened correspondence alongside a fresh sheet of stationery bearing the crest of the Marquess of Iolar. Automatically, her eyes went to the signet ring on his finger. The ruby gleamed in the sunlight from the windows.

His correspondence, his writing paper, his seal—at her table. She smothered a flash of resentment.

"What about William Harland?" she asked.

"What about him?"

"Did you dismiss him?"

"Nay, I did no such thing, though it was perhaps warranted."

"What did you say to him?"

Iolar raised an eyebrow. "Dinna worry yer lovely head over it. Harland understands what I expect of him. And if he doesna abide by my wishes . . ." He shrugged.

Gillian knew without asking that William would receive only this one chance from Iolar. "I'm certain my father would not wish to lose William. He is an excellent steward."

"As I've told ye before, yer father appointed me yer guardian. I'll do what I think necessary to protect yer interests."

Before she could press for her cause, a knock sounded at the door.

"Come," Iolar said.

Sammy Blenkin entered the library. To her surprise the eight-year-old page looked spotless. His cowlick had been slicked down with water and his clothing had not one smudge mark or tear that she could see.

He walked directly to her and bowed stiffly. "Lady Gillian, I bear a message from the Lady Augusta."

Gillian concealed a smile at Sammy's effort to do everything properly. Life at Treymoor was more casual when there were no guests in the house. "Pray give me the message, my good fellow."

He thrust out the folded piece of paper, and she soberly took it. Then, as if he could not bear this formality one more minute, Sammy leaned forward and eagerly confided to Gillian in a loud whisper, "I would have worn my wig and livery, but 'twas too small for me. Mrs. Withecombe says I'm growing like a right weed and that soon I'll be as tall as Mr. Pym." His blue eyes sparkled with pleasure at what he had surely taken as a great compliment, for everyone knew Sammy idolized Pym.

Gillian smoothed the fabric of his frock coat over his shoulder. "Well, Sammy, we must have you fitted at once for new livery, a suit more man-sized, as befits Treymoor's page." She estimated the cost of the frivolous suit of clothes and repressed a sigh. Perhaps if it were cut a bit full it would give him room to grow and thus last longer.

"What about a wig?" he asked, gazing up at her eagerly. "One just like Mr. Pym's?"

"Perhaps we should just powder your own hair for now." She hated having to deny Sammy the wig. The boy never asked for anything.

Sammy bravely tried to hide his disappointment, but his expressive face gave too much away. "I guess wigs are expensive, aren't they?"

"You have such nice hair," she said. " 'Twould be a shame to squash it flat with a wig." She was painfully aware that Iolar listened to every word they spoke. "When you aren't growing as quickly, we will buy you one."

Sammy looked down at the floor, but he nodded.

She gave his hand a quick little squeeze of assurance. "Thank you for the message."

"Oh!" He cast a quick glance at Lord Iolar, as if he'd forgotten the man's presence and straightened immediately.

"Thank you, Sammy," Gillian said again.

"My pleasure, your ladyship." He winked at her and marched out of the library, shutting the door behind him.

"Are wigs so dear, then, that the Earl of Molyneux's daughter canna afford to buy one for the lad?"

She turned around to find Iolar regarding her, his handsome face an expressionless mask. She tried to conceal the hurt, frustration, and anger that boiled inside her.

"The boy is growing yet. Why spend good pounds and pence on a wig that shall soon be useless to him?" she asked with feigned indifference.

He said nothing at first but regarded her from beneath hooded eyes. "Why indeed?"

She turned away from him, toward the door, wanting nothing more than to escape his unreadable gaze.

"The note, madam. What has Lady Augusta to say?"

Gillian had forgotten about the piece of paper in her hand. Now she broke the seal and read aloud the words she knew Zerrin had penned. As planned, they told of a broken carriage wheel and Aunt Augusta's delay.

Iolar frowned. "Was anyone injured?"

"I'm certain she would have mentioned it."

He nodded absently. "I have business of my own to attend, so the sooner yer chaperone arrives the better."

"Oh?" Gillian asked, a spurt of hope racing through her. "Will you be leaving us?"

6

Calum's mouth curved slowly into a smile. He'd known the little vixen was eager to be rid of him, but never had she been so open about it. "Dinna grieve so, Lady Gillian. I'll no be leavin' ye."

"Oh."

She had yet to accept who was master here, he thought. In an odd way, her resistance to a new authority in her life appealed to him. He understood it, that familiar instinct to fight the tether. But he could not indulge her. She was far too spoiled already.

He looked down at the stack of correspondence on the table. Coming to Yorkshire had played havoc with his own affairs. After twenty years away from Iolar Glen and Dunncrannog Castle, he'd hated to delay his return to make this trip. He wanted to see for himself that the ridiculous rumor had no truth behind it, that his clan, the castle, and the glen fared as well as he remembered.

He tried to make his dismissal sound gracious. "Until dinner then?"

She lifted her chin. "Until then." With a whisper of skirts, she strode from the library.

Calum looked at the closed door for a moment. Her elusive scent remained in the room to tease his senses. Finally, determined to return to his work, he sat down and drew his chair to the desk.

No sooner had he picked up his quill than Ian and Hugh entered the room. Ian dropped into the nearest seat.

"How was yer grand tour?" Ian asked, lounging against the back of the settee. "Did ye learn if those fields we passed belong to Treymoor?"

With an inward sigh, Calum abandoned hope of finishing his own work that day. "Aye, they do. As well as a large orangery, five glasshouses, and countless sheep, cows, chickens, and pigs. And not yer ordinary beasties, mind ye. These have all been special bred. They are better producers and less likely to sicken. The most is made of the land here, yet 'tis no overworked. Trees: they've planted a forest of trees." He shook his head. "This place is a marvel of efficiency."

"Almost as marvelous as Iolar Glen, cousin?"

Hugh pulled a leather-bound volume from its shelf and carefully turned the beautifully printed pages. "How would ye know, Ian? Ye've never been there."

Ian grinned. "Nor have ye. But I listen to Calum and think it must be the most wonderful place in the world."

"It must be a bonny place indeed, to rival this holding," Hugh acceded.

"Even though I've no seen the glen since I was seven," Calum said, "I remember how green it was. The wind would sigh through the pine forest on the mountains. The marquess never allowed the trees to be cut like the other landowners. When the heather in the glen bloomed, it looked as if it had been painted by God's own hand." Now how had he gotten into that? He sounded like some sighing poet. He straightened in his chair. "What did ye do today? Were ye able to find out anything?"

Hugh shook his head. "Nay. If there is something afoot, no one here will speak of it. Oh, they're civil enough, but not what ye'd call friendly."

"All they'd talk about was the Lady Gillian," Ian said. "To hear them tell it, ye'd think she was the Blessed Virgin's sister, so bonny and sweet and patient is she."

Calum absently toyed with the end of his quill, puzzling over the apparent dichotomy his ward presented. He recalled how warmly the tenants had greeted Gillian. Yet she behaved so indifferently toward the workings of Treymoor. "She seems to take no interest in the estate itself, yet the people adore her," he mused aloud.

"Perhaps she aids them, like noble ladies are supposed to," Ian suggested. "Vistin' the sick, bringin' food for the poor, and the like."

Hugh closed the book and slid it back onto the shelf. "If that's so, she'd have made some lord a fine wife."

"I've been wonderin' why she's no married," Ian said. "She's comely and rich."

"Aye, Ian, and she's got the devil's own fiery temper," Calum said, remembering their encounter in her father's bedchamber.

Ian grinned. "Ye ken what they say about women with hot tempers."

Hugh chuckled.

"Nay, I dinna ken what they say about women with hot tempers," Calum said, knowing full well but inclined to humor his earnest young kinsman. "Will ye enlighten me, cousin?"

" 'Tis said they make passionate lovers. Or wives," he added, the tips of his ears going bright pink.

"Perhaps ye should find the lass a man, Calum," Hugh suggested. "It canna be easy for her, seeing all the others her age with weans and bairns. Anyone can see 'tis past time she wed."

"What do I look like? A matchmaker?" Calum asked, suddenly feeling irritable.

"Ye could wed her yerself," Ian declared, as if he thought this a brilliant idea. "Ye're a man of property and 'tis past time ye, also, were wedded."

Calum shot Ian a dark look. "How would ye like a trip to India in the cargo hold of one of my ships?"

"Aye, ye're right," Ian said hastily. " 'Tis no a good idea. She's English."

"Damn right. Now leave me. I've got work to do."

As his cousins closed the door behind them, Calum jabbed the tip of his quill pen into the inkpot. Wed with Lady Gillian indeed. What a ridiculous idea.

*   *   *

Dinner went smoothly, with all parties making an effort to be civil, even pleasant. Calum learned precisely nothing of value, except that his ward seemed to have an unending wardrobe and that she was as glowingly lovely in violet silk as she was in white dimity. The realization annoyed him. The fact that he had thought about it enough to come to a realization annoyed him.

Now the guests had dispersed to their rooms for the evening, and Calum found himself restless, unable to sleep. He decided to take advantage of Treymoor's excellent library.

The house was dark and quiet as he made his way downstairs. When he arrived at the library, he discovered a wedge of light under the closed door. Quietly, he turned the knob and entered.

Gillian stood across the room, wearing the violet dress she'd worn at dinner. One by one, she withdrew books, briefly glanced at their covers, then put them back. It struck Calum that she was looking for a particular book.

On silent feet he crossed the room to stand behind her. She continued what she was doing, apparently so involved with her search that she remained unaware of his presence.

"Lookin' for a good book?" he asked.

She whirled to glare at him. Her hand went to her pale throat, where he saw her pulse beating wildly.

"I see it is your regular custom to sneak around at night," she snapped.

"I dinna exactly sneak. I'm just such a quiet, unassuming fellow it's easy for ye to miss me."

She shoved the volume in her hand back on the

shelf. "I might call you many things, my lord, but unassuming would not be one of them."

Calum grinned. "Aye, well. Ye dinna know me well, ye see? Perhaps ye'll think differently as time passes."

She moved away from him, drawing out another book and opening it. "It seems unlikely we shall have *that* much time."

"Pray, tell me what makes you say that."

With a thump she shut the tome. "I plan to marry."

He folded his arms over his chest. "Do ye now?"

"Yes."

"Who is the lucky man?"

"I don't know. That is to say," she added quickly, color blooming in her cheeks, "I haven't decided yet."

"Ah."

She thrust the unfortunate book back into its slot but didn't reach for another one. Instead, she stood with her back partially to him, her head bowed. Her fingers went to the strand of matched pearls at her throat.

"Have ye so many offers then?" When she didn't answer, he took a step to the side, so that he could see her face.

Moisture glistened in her eyes. Suddenly he felt ashamed. He had no right to taunt her over her unmarried state. Her father might have been unwilling to part with his darling daughter, or maybe he had not found any man worthy of her hand. Perhaps she'd had no say in the matter.

"Och, I'm sorry, lass," he murmured. Without thinking, he drew her into his arms for comforting. "'Twas not well done of me to tease ye so."

At the first touch of his hand, she stiffened, but

under his gentle coaxing she came into his embrace without further resistance.

"If it's a husband ye want, than it's a husband ye shall have," he said, though he knew the earl must have his say on the subject. Perhaps a man could be found that would please both father and daughter. Calum stroked Gillian's back. She seemed so small, so fragile in his arms.

"I don't need your pity," she mumbled into the front of his shirt. Her breath warmed his skin through the linen.

He raised a hand to the dark silk of her hair. "Sometimes life deals with us unfairly." He knew just how unfairly.

She lifted her head and met his gaze with her mist-colored eyes. "Has it dealt so with you?" she asked softly.

He found himself drowning in a cloud-gray sea. Suddenly he felt the need to put distance between them. "Dinna concern yerself with me," he said briskly.

She looked away and stepped back. As much as he wanted to hold her a little longer, he forced himself to let her go. His empty arms dropped to his sides.

Gillian picked up her candle and made for the door. "It is late. I bid you good night."

He picked up his own candle. "I'll see ye to yer room," he said. But at that moment the last thing he wanted was to stay near her. He needed space to breathe.

She paused at the door without turning to face him. "Thank you, Lord Iolar, but I know the way."

He watched her leave, damning himself for a fool. The sooner he married her off, the safer they'd both be.

*   *   *

Gillian's heart raced as she headed toward her bed-chamber. She tried to tell herself the close call of being discovered had caused it, but the wretched little voice at the back of her mind kept insisting that was a lie.

She'd been searching for her father's journal—or something, anything, that would reveal the identity of the rightful heir of Treymoor. What she'd found was how safe and warm it felt in the arms of the Marquess of Iolar. And for a moment she had beheld another side of him. But like the white flash of a winter bird glimpsed through a clear spot on a frosted pane, it had been visible for only a second, leaving her to wonder if she had really seen anything at all.

She would think of the matter later. At this moment he was in the library. If she went to his room by the secret passageway, she might be able to switch the keys he took from her for Mrs. Withecombe's bunch, thereby reclaiming the key to the hidden compartment in the library where she kept Treymoor's ledgers and journal. It was in those books that she kept the contracts she had illegally signed, the agreements she had no real authority to make, though she had honored every one of them.

Gillian hiked up her skirts and flew to the servants' wing, to Mrs. Withecombe's room.

"Quickly!" Gillian panted when the older woman opened the door. "Give me your keys! If I hurry I may be able to switch them for mine."

Mrs. Withecombe frowned sternly as she handed

over the impressive collection. "Be careful, child. Maybe I should go with you."

"I'll be all right," Gillian said over her shoulder as she hurried out the door. "Go detain him in the library."

Once again inside the secret passageway, she easily located Iolar's room. Stepping up onto the stool she'd brought with her, she peered through the peephole in the wall. Good. The room was empty. She located the door latch and opened it.

Nimbly she moved around the washstand that stood directly in front of the door. She scanned the room, trying to imagine where Iolar would have put the keys. They were not on the the bedside table or the mantel. Dear Lord, what if he had them with him?

She went through the chest of drawers, then swung open the towering wardrobe. There they were on a hook. Almost weeping with relief, she quickly exchanged the two bunches, quietly closed the wardrobe, and dashed across the room to the open door into the passage.

A knock sounded at the door into the hall, and Gillian almost tipped over the porcelain ewer. Instantly she grabbed the pitcher and held it still, not daring to breathe.

"Pleasant dreams, cousin," came a low male voice that Gillian identified as belonging to Ian Gunn. The thud of his booted footsteps faded down the hall, and Gillian took two rapid, deep breaths.

As she inched around the washstand, she heard footsteps again approach the door. This time someone turned the knob.

She darted through the hidden door into the

passageway and pulled the door silently closed behind her. Her heart pounded in her throat as she eased the bolt home.

For a moment she leaned against the stone wall. What would he have done if he'd caught her? The prospect sent a shiver through her. She climbed onto the stool and looked to see who had entered the bed-chamber.

It was Iolar, and from the way he moved about the room, she thought he must intend to retire for the night. Good. Considering her plans, she'd feel safer knowing he was asleep in his room.

Gillian hurried through the passageway, intent on returning to her room, but as she passed the narrow stairs that served as access between floors, she hesitated.

The identity of the heir to Treymoor still remained unknown to her. She'd just finished her search of the library for her father's journal, which she hoped would name the man. She'd already examined her father's rooms from floor to ceiling. She'd looked everywhere she could think of, everywhere but the most sensible location—his trunks.

She judged she could go through the cases in less than half of an hour, which would give her time to return to her room and meet Zerrin.

In the room to which she'd dragged her father's personal possessions last night, everything remained as she'd left it. For a moment she stood there, looking at the large trunks, all with their lids in place, all locked. She knew why she'd put off searching here. These cases contained such items as shoes and smallclothes, coats and shaving gear—things that had been dear to him. He had touched them, seen that they were cared for. He had always taken them with him. It had seemed, sometimes, that these inanimate objects meant more to him than she did. Even so, she hesitated to rifle through them. Could nothing of his be left unprofaned?

"I'm sorry, Papa," she whispered, and unlocked the first trunk.

She found the battered, stained journal at the bottom of the third case. Scanning the pages of precise handwriting, she saw he had carefully documented supplies, recorded adventures, and made notations as to the sums he'd drawn on his London account, the account that Gillian had labored to keep in the black. At first there was little mention of Treymoor or of her. Then she found the entry for which she'd been looking. First her father detailed a letter he'd received from his distant cousin, Robert MacFuaran, Marquess of Iolar. MacFuaran had revealed to her father that he planned to acknowledge the son he had repudiated so many years ago. The marquess had no other heirs to which he could leave his title and sole estate, and he did not want his brother to inherit. Then, in short bald sentences, her father had recorded the fact that his own title and estate would, in the event of his death, go to Robert MacFuaran or his successor.

Now Robert MacFuaran was dead. Rather than leave his marquessate to his own brother, he had acknowledged his bastard son. How he must have hated his brother!

Gillian began to shake so badly she almost dropped the book. It was unfair. Unjust. Why had God done this?

Calum MacFuaran, new Marquess of Iolar, was the rightful heir to Treymoor.

The man's unforgiving nature was legend. If he had stripped his beloved Iolar Glen for revenge against his father, what would he do to Treymoor when he learned she had tried to withhold it from him?

To that terrifying question she had but one answer: he must never learn the truth. Now, more than ever, it was imperative that she wed. She must have a son for Treymoor!

With trembling hands, she returned the journal to its hiding place. It was safer here than in her rooms. She could not bring herself to destroy her father's private journal, but neither could Iolar find it. She locked the trunk and slipped the cool metal key into her bodice. Later she would find a hiding place for it. For now, there was a funeral to attend.

She hurried through the secret narrow corridor, climbed the stairs, and exited into her room.

"At last," Zerrin said. Her dark eyes reflected her relief. "Come, come, come." She shooed Gillian out the door, into the hall. "Pym and Jenkins expect us at the icehouse. Mr. Appleyard, blessings upon him, awaits our arrival at the tomb."

Mrs. Withecombe joined them just outside the kitchen door, and they made their way down through the gardens to the small building by the river, keeping to the shadows as they went.

Inside the icehouse, Pym and Jenkins stood by the improvised litter bearing the shrouded body.

"Are you certain a nice horse and wagon would make too much noise?" Jenkins asked, his voice vaguely plaintive.

"I am sorry, Jenkins," Gillian apologized, "truly I am. I just feel it will draw less attention if the five of us carry Papa than if we use a horse and wagon."

In the candlelight, Pym cast Jenkins a shaming glance. "And right you were, Gillyflower. Never you worry. Jenkins and I can manage. You have more than your share to fret about as it is."

The two men hefted the litter and its burden between them, and the funeral procession began its march to the church graveyard. They trudged up the long slope from the river. Instead of going through the gardens, they took the long route around, lumbering from shadow to shadow. The farther they traveled, the slower their pace.

The half-moon provided their only light, painting the familiar landscape of trees and hedges, rolling lawn and paths with a trickster's hand.

Jenkins stumbled, shoving the litter forward into Pym's back. Pym staggered as he struggled to regain his balance and hold on to his burden at the same time. He crashed into a hundred-year-old boxwood hedge, sending a shower of tiny leaves over everyone. Pym shot Jenkins a quelling look before they continued along the path that led to the cemetery.

Moonlight lent the headstones, crypts, and statues in the ancient graveyard of Saint Agnes an eerie quality. Gillian shivered.

" 'Tis said the spirits of the unhappy dead rise up at night," Jenkins whispered. " 'Tis said they look for victims."

"Rubbish," Mrs. Withecombe said. Then, "What kind of victims?"

"People what shouldn't be in graveyards at night."

"People not on honest business," Pym muttered.

Zerrin reached for Gillian's hand, shooting her a worried sidelong glance.

Pale long-shadowed monuments to the dead rose from the earth like desperate fingers reaching for heaven. Many of these weathered, moldering stones had far outlasted even the memories of those buried beneath, Gillian thought. Is that what would happen to her? Would she leave no children behind to remember her?

A prickle at the back of her neck had Gillian quickly turning to see who watched, but the only eyes she found belonged to a snarling gargoyle hunched on the corner of a nearby crypt.

She couldn't shake the feeling that the small procession was being observed as they made their way over sacred ground. Maybe spirits really did return to haunt their burial places. Out of the corner of her eye, she saw Zerrin draw her wrap more closely around her. Mrs. Withecombe looked to either side. Everyone walked a little faster.

The tomb of the Earls of Molyneux stood dark and austere in the center of the cemetery. Its entrance was guarded by twin griffins, their weathered marble wings outspread as if to shield those who lay within.

Finding the wrought-iron door unlocked, Gillian pushed it open. The metal gate creaked shrilly as it swung on its hinges. Beyond the antechamber, in the vault, the glow of candlelight was visible.

Mr. Appleyard peered around the doorway of the vault. When he saw who had entered, he breathed a sigh of relief and stepped into full view. He wore the somber vestments of his office. "We were beginning to worry about you," he said, leading the way back into the large interior room where the sarcophagi of the Ellicotts lined the walls. Gillian swallowed hard when she saw the open empty one.

Although Mrs. Appleyard and William greeted them in hushed tones, each word struck a hollow echo.

"Careful now," Mr. Appleyard cautioned as Pym and Jenkins tried to maneuver the litter between pillars and statues.

He spoke too late. With a thud, Jenkins backed into a twelve-foot-high statue of a knight.

Jenkins glanced up at the serene black marble face. "Sorry, your lordship," he quipped, a nervous edge to his voice. But in an attempt to align the litter with the open sarcophagus, he knocked into the statue again.

There came a gravelly cracking sound, and the knight's heavy stone shield broke away from the statue, tumbling down from its height. Pym leapt out of the way, taking a startled Jenkins with him. The rock shield crashed to the paved floor.

As the echoes faded, stunned silence filled the burial chamber. Then Jenkins's worried voice rang abnormally loud in the room.

"This ain't a good omen."

Gillian felt the prickle at the back of her neck again. She spun around, but no one stood in the doorway. This place and their deception made them all jumpy.

"Say no more about omens, George Jenkins," Mr. Appleyard said sternly.

Gillian was sick with regret as she knelt beside her father's fallen body. She watched as they lifted him into his stone coffin; then she gently smoothed his hair and crossed his hands upon his breast. It took William, Jenkins, and Pym to heave the lid into place, and as her father departed from her sight, she swallowed hard against the loss. She stared at the smooth surface where her father's name and dates should have been inscribed. His sarcophagus looked no different from the closed empty ones lying in their niches, awaiting future generations of earls and their families.

During the brief funeral service, there was much shuffling of feet, and Gillian noticed that there was more than one uneasy glance toward the door. Mr. Appleyard's soft voice droned on.

Finally, all the prayers had been said and the intercession asked, and Gillian knew she must leave her father to his eternal rest. 'Twas just his husk sealed in that stone, all alone, she reminded herself. His soul would already reside with the angels. Still, she added a special little prayer of her own for him.

"I will send someone to repair the statue," Mr. Appleyard said to her.

As the mourners filed out of the mausoleum, the chilling howl of a dog stopped them short in their tracks. Gillian's heart beat a little faster. Behind them, the rector secured the vault door and blew out the candle, casting them into darkness. With a shriek of hinges, he closed the wrought-iron gate and locked the access to the antechamber.

"Look there!" Zerrin pointed toward a row of headstones not far from them.

A dark figure flitted between the monuments as if caught up in some macabre dance.

Gillian stared, horrified. Pym muttered something under his breath.

Horrible, high-pitched laughter rose from the creature.

With a cry, Jenkins bolted, dashing away toward the mansion.

The laughter grew louder and more terrible.

Pym grabbed Gillian's hand and ran. Zerrin and Mrs. Withecombe followed.

They pounded out of the cemetery, across the road, and through the fields, sending leaves flying, ignoring the whipping branches of hedges and trees. The thud of their feet, the crashing of leaves, the tearing gasps of their breathing were the only sounds Gillian heard as they raced toward the great house.

Once inside the safety of the kitchen, she hastily locked the door and they scattered to their rooms. In silence, Zerrin quickly helped Gillian undress and hurried off to her own bed.

Her heart pounding, her mouth dry, Gillian huddled beneath her quilts, clutching them beneath her chin with icy fingers. What had darted among the headstones, making that terrible laughter? Were there indeed hellish spirits ready to extract a penalty from the living who trespassed after dark? Had she and the others been lucky to escape with bodies and souls intact?

Slowly her breathing eased and her heart resumed a more normal beat. Likely the question should be *who*, not *what*, had seen them leaving the crypt. The thought of being watched from the dark sent a small shiver through her.

She was thankful to have finally given her father a decent, if clandestine, burial and was relieved that the ordeal they had all endured to provide that observance was over. The funeral had not been elegant, but it surpassed the ignominious burial he probably would have received had he died in the course of one of his adventures. Still, knowing that did not banish the sense of loss that hung over her.

With a heavy sigh, she rolled onto her back and stared up at the bed's shadow-filled canopy. The question came back to her like the echoes in the crypt: Who had seen them?

She knew they weren't safe yet.

7

Birds sang in the fields. The leisurely, muted thump of the horses' hooves on the well-traveled earthen road beat an annoyingly repetitive tattoo that further frayed Gillian's nerves.

"I simply do not see why you insist on accompanying me," she said again, and then caught herself. She was beginning to sound like the whining brat Iolar already thought her. But she really *truly* did not want him with her for this morning's social calls, which were, in fact, a husband hunt.

"I told ye, since yer auntie has no arrived, and since Mr. Appleyard and his good wife could no longer put off their duties, ye need a chaperone. A fine-bred English lady canna go harin' about the countryside alone."

"Am I to believe you an authority on the behavior of English ladies?" she demanded, incredulous with indignation.

He turned his head to look at her. One auburn eyebrow lifted. "I'm the only authority that matters, as far as ye are concerned."

"This is outrageous! It's ridiculous and-and unfair!"

Lord Iolar laughed but offered no comment.

"I could have brought Zerrin with me," Gillian insisted. "I have before, you know."

"Zerrin is naught but a lady's maid. Not good enough."

"She is not just a lady's maid," Gillian denied hotly. The man was too provoking!

"Then what is she?"

"Why, she's . . . she's . . ." Gillian groped for a word that would accurately describe the relationship. "She's family."

"Och, family, is she? From what side, I'd be interested to know, yer mother's or yer father's?"

Gillian felt the warmth of color move up into her cheeks. "Well, she's not family, precisely. Not blood family."

"Then what is she? Precisely."

"She's my teacher."

Iolar's roan picked its way around the far edge of a large puddle. "And what, pray, does she teach ye?"

She had no intention of telling him *that*. "Languages. She's quite fluent in several tongues."

"Is she now?"

"Yes, and if you must know, so am I."

Iolar made no reply. He looked ahead, toward the large manor house they were approaching. His body swayed with the smooth movements of his horse.

"Did yer father send her to ye?" he asked.

"Yes, he did," she said softly, remembering how Zerrin had arrived all alone on a winter's night, drenched to the bone and sick with the ague.

"So we call on Mrs. Latham this morning," he said, changing the subject.

"Yes, though I'm certain you will find our conversation quite tedious."

He smiled lazily and looked at her from beneath hooded eyes. " 'Tis certain I'll survive."

"And that's not the only call I make this morning," she cautioned. "It has been too long since I've minded my social obligations."

"Why is that?"

"I haven't felt like it," she lied. In truth, she'd had no time to spare.

He looked at her a minute without speaking, his expression unreadable. "Ye are no what ye seem," he said quietly.

A stone dropped in her stomach, but before she could think of a reply, they entered the manor's paved courtyard. A young boy ran out to take the reins of their horses. Before Gillian could dismount, Iolar was there, lifting her down.

His warmth penetrated the leather of his gloves to imprint the shape of his hands and fingers upon her skin with unnerving intimacy. She looked up, startled at the effect of his touch. Her gaze collided with his, sending a shock through her body. The green of his eyes deepened. Her pulse quickened.

He set her down and turned away. Flustered, she made much of smoothing her skirt and straightening her hat.

The front door opened suddenly. "Well, by George,

I thought Markum said 'twas you!" Captain Latham roared. "It's been too long, much too long. Who is your escort here?" he demanded with good nature as he turned to Iolar. Behind his back, Gillian signaled to Iolar, pointing to her ear.

Iolar nodded almost imperceptibly and smiled. "I'm Gillian's guardian," he began loudly.

"The Marquess of Iolar," the captain bellowed. "By George! You're much younger than I thought."

Gillian was not surprised the captain had already heard about her guardian. The whole parish probably knew by now. Perhaps having a guardian of consequence might aid in her husband hunt. Or hinder it, she thought glumly, realizing how intimidating Iolar might be to a would-be suitor, how frustratingly inflexible he might be about her choice.

Before any introductions could be made, a woman appeared at the front door. She wore a yellow silk polonaise, and on her neatly styled hair perched a cap of linen lace. Younger than the captain by several years, the quiet Lady Sabina had always seemed perfectly content with her husband's ways.

Smiling, she took Gillian's hands in hers. "We received your note and were delighted you had decided to be social for a while, Lady Gillian."

"I realized it had been overlong since I returned the favor of your delightful visit four months ago."

They walked into the house, where the introductions were made, and where Markum, the butler, brought them jasmine tea and almond cakes. They chatted for a while, covering the small pleasantries, exchanging harmless gossip. Captain Latham, in his own way, interrogated Iolar, who bore the process with good humor. Finally, Lady Sabina spoke the words Gillian had been wishing to hear.

"Quentin should be here any moment. He has been out with our game man, checking for poachers."

Quentin Latham could be considered a candidate for matrimony. His father held this goodly estate, and his mother was the daughter of a baron. Quentin was presentable enough. Not what she'd imagined as a husband when she was growing up, but a desperate old maid in a bind, Gillian told herself, couldn't be too particular.

Iolar excused himself from the room and returned shortly after. A call of nature, Gillian thought, but gave it no more notice when Quentin made his entrance.

He was tall and robust, she told herself, and tried not to consider that his fleshiness suggested he might turn portly as he aged. He had thick straw-colored hair and eyes the loveliest shade of blue. Regrettably, one of them turned somewhat off to the side, making it difficult for anyone talking with him to know which eye to meet.

He was first introduced to the marquess, to whom he gave a curt nod. Then he smiled at Gillian and bowed over her hand. "A decided pleasure to behold you again, madam." His lips did not quite brush the back of her hand, as was proper.

"Only my responsibilities to my household have kept me away, Mr. Latham, else I would never have denied myself the pleasure of your company or that of your cordial parents." She opened her fan and leisurely fanned herself, smiling at Quentin, the captain, and Lady Sabina, who beamed back.

"More tea, Lady Gillian?"

"Thank you, Lady Sabina, that would be most agreeable. A quite delicious blend."

"You have brought the sunshine with you, Lady Gillian," Quentin declared. "Your long absence has devastated us."

Gillian lowered her eyes and fluttered her fan. "Oh, la, sir, how you flatter me." She glanced up coyly through her lashes, and met his eyes—or tried to.

Another cup of tea, a further gush of compliments, and it was time for Gillian to say good-bye to the Lathams, who came out to see her and Iolar off.

The two of them rode for several minutes without speaking.

"Pleasant people, are they not?" she finally asked, to break the silence that brooded between them.

Iolar continued to look straight ahead. "Aye. Verra pleasant."

"Their son is quite interested in the hunt."

"So I noticed. And it seemed he was no the only one interested in a hunt." He gave her a sidelong look.

"I'm sure I don't know what you mean."

"Och, I thought I'd sicken, so sweet was the adulation." He fluttered his eyelashes and said in an exaggerated falsetto, "Oh, la, sir, how ye flatter me."

"What would you have me reply to such a courtly compliment?" she demanded, her face burning with embarrassment.

"He said he'd been devastated without yer sunshine, for the love of heaven! What drivel. Ye should have given him that cold eye ye're always givin' me, is what ye should have done. Let him wonder where the sunshine had gone *then*."

Her cheeks burned hotter. "Well, thank you very much, sirrah! A lady does *not* consider the gallant efforts of a gentleman 'drivel'. And I-I don't give you any kind of eye, much less a cold one."

"Ha!"

"Ha yourself!" She turned up her nose and glared at the road ahead.

"Ye're courtin' the bastard."

"I'm doing no such thing."

Oh, what vile act had she committed to bring down on her head the curse of this man's presence? Gillian wondered self-pityingly. Her mission required delicacy—delicacy and great fortitude—which would have been more easily summoned were she not under the eye of a critic. She didn't want Quentin Latham for her husband anymore than she wanted any of the other so-called eligible men in the parish. But she was a desperate woman.

When he said nothing else, she sneaked a glance to see if his expression gave a clue to his thoughts.

His face looked as if it had been carved from stone.

The flame of defiance leapt in her heart. She would find a husband no matter how nauseating or humiliating she found it. She would get a husband and then Calum MacFuaran, Marquess of Iolar, would be sorry!

Gillian's next call took them to a small estate with a small manor. They were immediately shown into an elegant room furnished with expensive French imports. A minute later, a stocky woman of some forty-odd years rustled in, afloat in Italian silk. Two servants bearing trays of refreshments followed.

Gillian introduced Iolar to Mrs. Clough, their hostess. To her astonishment, he executed a flawlessly courtly bow and accepted the hand the older woman offered him, bringing it almost, but not quite, to his lips. "Enchanted," he murmured.

The white lead makeup and rice powder that covered Mrs. Clough's face failed to conceal her blush. "Oh!" Her smile grew so wide Gillian feared the woman's beauty patch would fall off.

Gillian snapped open her fan to gain Mrs. Clough's attention before the woman made a complete fool of herself.

In an officious rush of orders, Mrs. Clough instructed her servants regarding the placement of the trays and the laying out of refreshments. When the two had withdrawn through the paneled door, the mistress of the house turned back to her guests.

"I was delighted when I received your note, Lady Gillian." She poured the tea. "Mr. Clough is in London for a fortnight. I know he will be disappointed to have missed your visit."

Gillian murmured the appropriate regrets over having missed Mrs. Clough's husband. "I suppose now I shall have to wait to extract my revenge for the trouncing he gave me at whist."

Mrs. Clough nodded enthusiastically, a movement that threatened to dislodge her towering arrangement of powdered hair. " 'Twas a victory that has given my husband much pleasure. You were too kind to have allowed him to win."

Gillian feigned surprise. "Allowed him? Madam, Mr. Clough is simply too adroit a player for my poor abilities."

Apparently Mrs. Clough knew better. Over the edge of her cup, as she sipped her tea, her eyes twinkled.

"But where are your daughter and your son?" Gillian asked.

"They shall join us soon. They would not miss one of your visits."

As if they had heard themselves mentioned, Lydia Clough, twenty-five years old and seemingly content to live the rest of her life with her parents, came into the room with Kenward, her older brother.

Kenward had spent three months in London recently and had returned to the parish a new, more fashion-conscious man. His bright green frock coat was ludicrously long and bore buttons that were so large they looked silly. His wig was higher than his mother's. Instead of knee buckles on his breeches, he wore yellow rosettes. His rouge marked two round circles on his cheeks. Gillian tried to tell herself that his presentation was undoubtedly the height of elegance in London.

Introductions were made, tea was poured and passed, and the five settled down to exchange news and pleasantries. Kenward sat a bit too close to Gillian. The strong smell of his perfume, mingled with the stench of his unwashed body, made her feel queasy. She inched away.

Kenward eyed Iolar's conservative garb with barely concealed disdain. "Do you go to London often, my lord?" He produced a silver snuffbox, which he opened and offered to Iolar.

Iolar declined the snuff. "Only when my business takes me there. I dinna much like the place."

The dandy applied a pinch of tobacco to each nostril, sniffing loudly each time. Then he raised a delicate eyebrow. "Not like London? How can one possibly not have a passion for the town? One finds such refinement there, such culture."

Iolar took a sip of his tea and set the cup in its saucer on his knee. "One also finds stink an' filth. 'Tis a matter of personal taste."

Kenward frowned, as if unsure whether or not he had just been insulted. "One learns to overlook those things in favor of the more refined life London offers."

Iolar regarded Kenward with a bland expression. "Perhaps I dinna stay long enough."

Gillian hid her smile behind her fan. *Touché*, Iolar.

"It would seem not." Kenward did not appear to know he'd been bested in that exchange.

Iolar turned to Lydia, who had been sitting very quietly next to her mother. "And what do ye think of London, Miss Clough?"

Her plain, scrubbed face pinkened at being the center of attention. "It is noisy."

"Aye, so it is." He smiled.

Miss Clough's fan began to flutter more quickly. "I suppose I like the quiet of the country."

"Everyone should have at least one country house," Kenward said absently. "Do you like London, Lady Gillian?"

Gillian felt her cheeks grow warm. She'd wanted to spend a spring season in London. Then she might have found a suitable husband, instead of now pursuing what was left in Saint Agnes parish for an unmarried woman of her age. She looked at Lydia, who quietly grew older at her mother's side. No man of her own. No children. No life.

"I've never been to London," Gillian said, struggling not to drown in the desperation that swamped her. She didn't want to spend the rest of her life like Lydia, but did she want to take someone like Kenward as husband to avoid that fate? She looked at the grime around his neck and under his fingernails and tried not to breathe too deeply. Swallowing hard, she told herself she had no choice. She must keep Treymoor and her people safe.

"Never been to London?" Kenward echoed stupidly. "How can that be?"

"I've always wanted to go," she said, "but with Papa gone so much . . ." She let her words trail off, hoping Kenward would appreciate the wistful quality of her voice and respect her reluctance to talk about the matter.

"Then you must let me show you the town. There is so much to see and do. You will love the shops." He seized her hand and pressed a wet kiss to the back of it.

Instantly, Iolar rose from his chair. "Release her," he said. His words were quietly spoken, but the violence of the threat that underlay them sent a shiver down Gillian's back.

Kenward's mouth fell open, and he stared at Iolar in surprise. He dropped Gillian's hand as if it were a hot stone.

"I-I beg your pardon, my lord," Kenward stammered. "I fear I was swept up in my enthusiasm over the prospect of showing London to Lady Gillian."

"Aye. Well. There will no be any trip to London with my charge, d'ye hear me, Mr. Clough?"

"Aye. I mean, yes! Yes, my lord. But of course I would never dream of taking Lady Gillian to London without a proper chaperone."

"I'd no allow Lady Gillian to go to London with ye unless I went, and I dinna have time now." He regarded Kenward with a glacial stare.

Kenward wilted back into the cushions of his chair. "Oh."

Gillian seethed with frustration. She had no desire to spend another minute in the company of Kenward, but she most strenuously wished to avoid even the merest whisper in the rumor mill that Iolar was a difficult man. What prospective groom would wish to undertake negotiations with an ogre?

Conversation grew increasingly stilted after that, and Gillian was thankful when she could decently bid farewell to the Cloughs. As soon as the front door shut behind them, she swept forward and accepted the groom's help up before Iolar had time to so much as hold out his hand to her. Just as he fit his left foot in a stirrup, she nudged her mare with her heel and was off, cantering toward Fox Briar and her last and most important call.

Iolar caught up with her with no apparent effort. "Dinna ever leave me like that again." His voice was deep and rich and smoky, but there was steel in his words.

"Don't you threaten me!" she snapped, her temper flying at full flag.

His light-green eyes, his high, elegant cheekbones, his straight nose, and finely chiseled mouth were composed in a handsome, unreadable mask. Gillian, who out of necessity had become an expert at extracting information from people's expressions, found his unreadability unnerving.

"I never threaten," he said.

"It certainly sounded like a threat." Atlanta sensed Gillian's high emotion and nervously sidestepped. Gillian smoothed her hand down the animal's satiny, dappled gray neck and murmured soothingly.

"If it wasn't a threat," she said stiffly to Iolar, "what was it?"

"An order."

At Gillian's command, the mare leapt into action. Long slender legs stretched out to eat up the hard-packed road. Powerful muscles moved beneath her. Gillian leaned over the horse's neck, and for a time-less moment rider and mount melded into one and took flight.

Wind streamed by her, gliding over her skin, pushing at her clothing, tugging at her hair and hat. She smelled the rich earth and the ripening oats waving in the fields. For this brief instant, she was free. Free of everything.

She heard the thundering of hooves behind her and knew her taste of freedom was at an end.

"Halt," he commanded, his face tight with anger. "Halt, damn ye."

Gillian reined in before he could grab her mount's bridle. They stood there a moment. The sides of their horses heaved. Gillian and Iolar glared at each other, breathing heavily.

"Why?" he asked. "Why do ye fight me at every turn?"

"Because I don't want someone to rule my life!" she flared. "You, a stranger, arrive on my doorstep and bully your way in, taking over, changing everything. You show me no regard!"

He looked surprised. Then thoughtful.

When he finally spoke, he made no mention of her defiant race, of her display of temper. "We have one more call to make," he said.

There was a strange note to his voice, a kind of weariness that pierced Gillian with regret, that made her want to reach out to comfort him. Instead, she tightened her fingers around Atlanta's reins. She must not forget that he was the enemy.

They rode in silence, settling into an undeclared truce.

"This Clough fellow—do ye like him?" Iolar asked.

Gillian sighed. Everything would be so much easier if she could like Kenward Clough. "No."

Iolar nodded. "Good."

Puzzled, she asked, "Why is it good?"

"Well, to tell the truth, I found him a wee bit fragrant."

Gillian laughed. "A wee bit," she agreed.

Iolar smiled, and she felt her heart skip a beat. He was a remarkably handsome man, and when he smiled she was certain no angel could rival his beauty. But it was more than that, some other element that she could not quite define.

"He would no make ye a good husband."

"I—" She broke off. What could she possibly say? She had humiliated herself in front of this man. For the safety of her people, of Treymoor, she had simpered and flirted with two distasteful men. She would crawl on her belly and beg Kenward to marry her if that would ensure the happiness and security of those she loved.

"Did yer father no make arrangements for ye to join the other lassies in a London spring season?"

Her first impulse was to lie, to protect her father's memory. She'd been lying for him so long that it came now as second nature. Then she realized there was no memory to protect. Her father had not taken the time with her to create any.

"No. He was gone." He'd always been gone.

Iolar looked up, his gaze following a wheeling bird. "Could ye go now?"

Gillian stared at him. "Now?" she echoed. "Do you mean for me to have my coming out now, with eighteen-year-old girls?"

"Perhaps it was a dimwitted idea," he muttered.

"Were you proposing to send me to London, my lord?" she asked, surprised.

A deep scarlet crept up his neck. "Aye."

At that moment, she felt like throwing her arms around him and kissing him. No one—with the exception of Aunt Augusta—had ever made her such a generous offer.

But she couldn't accept it. Now, more than ever, there wasn't time.

"Thank you," she said. "I appreciate your kind offer, but it's far too late for me."

He nodded slowly. "I dinna ken about such things as the annual rush to London by young ladies looking for husbands, but . . ." He frowned, seeming to have thought better of what he'd been about to say.

He'd tickled her curiosity with his confession that he did not know about every subject under the sun. "But what?" she prompted.

A breeze teased a red-gold tendril away from the mass of his neat queue. "It seems to me that it must lead to much unhappiness."

She suppressed her urge to tuck that bright strand back with the rest, to smooth her hand across his cheek. "A woman of property does not expect to find happiness in marriage."

"What *does* a woman of property expect to find in marriage?"

She considered a moment. "To come under the rule of a man who might well be a stranger to her. To bear his children. If she is blessed, she may also find respect and honor."

"No fairy-dust dreams for the woman of property," he said dryly.

Gillian smiled. "Ah, now, dreams are a different matter entirely."

"What are yours?" he teased.

"Oh," she said airily, "the dreams of every old maid, I suppose. To be swept off to a castle by a handsome prince who loves me with all his heart and cannot bear to live without me."

Iolar's eyes twinkled. "Is that all? Only the heart and soul of some fairy-tale prince?"

"No, there's more. We must live happily ever after."

"Of course."

"Now tell me your dream."

"Oh. Is that the manor up ahead?" he said, peering down the road. "We dinna have time for me to tell ye."

"Yes, that is Fox Briar. We're on the estate now. And there is plenty of time for you to tell me. 'Tis only fair."

He surveyed the vista Fox Briar provided. A flock of sheep grazed in the pasture to the left of the drive. A field of rippling oats awaited harvest in the field to the right. The only sounds were the soft rhythmic thud of hooves, the creak of saddle leather, and the occasional jingle of a bridle.

"I dream of going home," he said simply.

"To Iolar Glen?"

"Aye. And to Dunncrannog Castle, which guards it."

"You have a castle?" she asked, embarrassed now.

He bowed at the waist. "Shall I sweep ye away, milady?"

"Toad."

He smiled. "But a prince of a toad, all the same."

She couldn't help but laugh. And he looked so rakishly charming.

"Who will we be callin' upon here?" he asked.

"Mrs. Leake."

"Who, of course, has an eligible son."

His comment stung her. She found this scouring of the parish's leftovers in her search for a husband mortifying beyond words. Every forced flirtatious glance, every calculated pleasing phrase spoken was a lash to her pride. She hated that Iolar had witnessed it all. She hated it more that he found it amusing.

"You are unkind, sir," she said lightly, refusing to allow him to see that he had hurt her.

"And where is Mr. Leake the elder?"

"Dead these past ten years."

"Who now owns this estate?"

"The son, Maynard Leake."

Iolar said nothing as he dismounted and tossed his reins to the waiting young man. Then he came around and placed his hands around Gillian's waist. They were large and strong. Their eyes met and held as he lifted her down.

"That really isn't necessary," she said, finding herself slightly breathless as his touch vibrated through her. "I can dismount on my own."

He didn't acknowledge her feeble protest, but rather turned and led the way to the modest front door, which opened before they stepped onto the porch.

They were ushered into a somewhat austere room. The wood floor lacked carpets. The walls were bare of all but one large painting in a gilded frame, which hung over the small fireplace. Gillian knew the woman in the painting: Caroline Leake, Maynard's mother.

The paneled door opened and that woman entered, leaning on her son's arm.

"Good morning, Lady Gillian," the widow said primly.

"You look radiant this morn, Lady Gillian," Maynard said, his thin face lighting at the sight of her. He smoothed his free hand over the top of his thinning hair.

Gillian greeted them both and performed the introductions. That done, everyone settled down into damask-upholstered wing chairs.

Mrs. Leake eyed Iolar, her withered lips pursed as

tightly as usual. "A bit young to be a spinster's guardian, aren't you?"

"The Earl of Molyneux doesna think so," Iolar said.

"Huh. Much he knows. He's never paid attention to the important things, like his estate. And she"— Mrs. Leake gestured toward Gillian with her cane— "should have been married off a long time ago."

Maynard went bright scarlet. "Mama, I'm certain that Lady Gillian's reasons for not marrying are none of our concern."

"Fiddlesticks. She has a responsibility to produce an heir for Treymoor, since her father was foolish enough not to remarry."

"Will yer wife be joinin' us?" Iolar asked Maynard with pointed innocence.

"I have no wife," Maynard replied as he darted a longing glance at Gillian. He'd made it clear two years ago that he would come calling if he received from her the least bit of encouragement.

"My son is as yet unmarried, Lord Iolar," Mrs. Leake snapped. "We've not yet found the right woman for him. He is a man of some wealth, you understand. It will not do for him to marry the first baggage to throw herself at him."

Gillian could have laughed. With Mrs. Leake keeping her constant keen-eyed vigil, few women could get near Maynard, much less throw themselves at him. Only Gillian's status as the daughter of the parish's only peer gave her the necessary prestige to permit her to socialize with Maynard. But there was little time for such things in Gillian's schedule, and in the past she'd never considered him prime husband material. She'd always wanted a man she could look up to, a man she could respect. But now she needed a manageable man, and Maynard—polite, spineless Maynard—would do very well.

"One must be so careful where marriage is concerned," she said, adopting Mrs. Leake's pretentious tone. "It's so important to chose from the right sort. Breeding does tell. And of course there is the matter of land and chattel." She sighed delicately. "But still, one wishes for a certain compatibility in one's chosen. A respect for the finer things. I'm sure *you* can understand what I mean, Mrs. Leake, having certainly gone through this yourself in your tender years."

The widow's face softened somewhat. "Yes. Yes, most certainly."

"That is why I've not yet chosen to marry. That is why my dear father has not forced the issue. But I am hoping my search is at an end." She cast a coy glance at Maynard from under her lashes and curved her lips into a shy smile. She squashed her twinge of guilt when she saw his smitten expression.

"Well, you certainly will not wish to act on your decision with unwise haste," Mrs. Leake said, her eyes narrowing.

Gillian sedately waved her fan. Out of the corner of her eye, she saw a muscle flex in Iolar's set jaw.

Maynard furtively glanced at his mother, then smiled again at Gillian.

"Her guardian will have something to say in the matter," Iolar said flatly.

Gillian felt a knot form in her stomach.

"Yes, of course," Mrs. Leake agreed. "Where in Scotland is Iolar?" she inquired politely.

The conversation drifted from subject to subject, all of an impersonal nature. Tea was brought—the cheap blend Mrs. Leake served all her guests—and shortly thereafter Gillian and Iolar took their leave.

As they rode home from Fox Briar, Gillian told herself that the visit had gone well. Maynard still wanted her. She would help him break his mother's tenacious hold and establish her own, more gentle grip. Mrs. Leake was as avaricious as she was cheap, and Gillian had discovered long ago that greedy people were easily manipulated.

Iolar's mouth was set in a hard line, and he hadn't spoken since they'd left Fox Briar twenty minutes ago. She supposed she should be glad he remained silent, but she sensed he was brooding, which might spell trouble later. With the intention of trying to coax him into conversation, she turned to look at him.

Abruptly, he snapped his head around to scowl at her. "How can ye even think of marryin' that whey-faced nidget? 'Tis clear who rules in *that* house! The auld trout would make yer life miserable, I'll lay gold on it."

Gillian stared at him, wide-eyed with surprise. "You didn't have such adamant objections to the other two, and neither of them was as suitable as Mr. Leake."

"I could no actually believe ye would consider a slimy sort like Latham! I've seen his kind before."

"Oh, and what sort might that be?"

"He's no a gentleman, and that's a fact."

" 'Tis a serious accusation, my lord."

"Aye."

"And how would you know that Mr. Latham is not a gentleman?" she demanded, having harbored just that uneasy suspicion for years.

"So sweet and full of honey for ye is the man, but he doesna hesitate to force his attentions on an unwilling serving girl. The poor lass was terrified."

Gillian's fingers unconsciously tightened on the reins, causing Atlanta to toss her head with displeasure at the additional restraint. Instantly, Gillian eased her grasp.

"When did you see all this?" she asked, but even as she spoke the words she knew what he said was true. The Lathams and the Ellicotts had been neighbors in a small parish too long for her not to have heard rumors. Many sons of the gentry felt it their right to sport with the female servants. If a girl or woman proved uncooperative, she usually lost her employment. Faced with a choice of starvation or degradation, servants often chose to survive.

"When I went to the privy."

She remembered he'd excused himself before Quentin had arrived. "Does he know you saw him?"

"Oh, aye. 'Twas hard for him not to, since I interrupted his little game long enough for his prey to escape."

She felt inordinately pleased that Iolar had stepped in to save the girl. "What did you do?"

He squinted up at the bright blue sky. "Nothing really. Just strolled up to him and told him he was expected in the parlor."

"I imagine having a strange Scotsman interrupt him was a surprise." A tall, strong, fiercely intimidating Scotsman.

"I'm no a strange Scotsman. I'm quite normal."

Gillian couldn't help but smile. "All Scots might seem strange to me, since you and your cousins are the only ones I've ever met."

"Well, ye'll have the opportunity to meet many Scots when yer auntie arrives."

"What?"

"I'd fear that swine, Latham, would mistreat ye when ye crossed him. And cross him ye would. Should he prove injudicious enough to come askin' me for yer hand, I'll no give my consent."

Gillian knew Iolar's high-handed refusal should have annoyed her, but instead she felt a sense of relief at no longer having to consider Latham as a prospect for matrimony. "I don't believe I ever said I wished to wed him. *You* said that."

He fixed her with a knowing look, and she felt her face go warm.

"You mentioned something about my meeting many Scots," she said, hoping to divert him.

"I did."

To her annoyance, he did not elaborate. She tried again. "What did you mean?"

"As soon as yer auntie arrives, we'll be doin' some traveling."

8

Calum and his charge did not have a chance to continue their conversation because, as they entered the cobbled courtyard in front of the stables, an elegant carriage pulled by matching grays was brought around from the front of the house. Lady Augusta had arrived.

As they entered the entrance hall, they ran into a mountain of trunks and hatboxes. A stream of servants—both Lady Augusta's and Treymoor's—hurried about, carting luggage and fetching hot tea. In the middle of all the activity stood a petite, fashionably attired woman who looked to be in her mid-thirties.

She held a china cup and saucer in her hand and, between orders, occasionally took a sip of steaming tea.

"No, no, Jenkins, the one with the red leather handles. Yes, that's it. *That's* the trunk that should have been brought in first. That way Barbara could have already begun unpacking."

"I would have been happy to, your ladyship, but your man stacked it at the bottom of the pile. The others had to be moved first."

"So you've said before. Well, there's no help for it now." She looked over at a short woman of matronly appearance who was sorting through the smaller cases. "Barbara, please show Jenkins where the trunk ought to be set. Mrs. Withecombe"—the newcomer turned to the housekeeper—"has my usual room been prepared?"

"Yes, Lady Augusta, and I've put fresh-cut white roses in a vase for you, just as you prefer."

Lady Augusta smiled brightly. "You are a jewel, a positive paragon among housekeepers. I told my sister that engaging you was quite the cleverest thing she ever did."

To Calum's surprise, the ever calm and collected Mrs. Withecombe flushed with pleasure.

"You are too good, m'lady," she said.

"Nonsense. Now where is that niece of mine?" Lady Augusta looked around as she absently handed the empty cup and its saucer to Mrs. Withecombe.

"Here, Aunt Augusta." Gillian swept forward, and the two women embraced warmly. "Aside from the difficulty with your carriage wheel, how was your journey?"

"As good as can be expected, dear. You know how I abhor travel."

Now that the two woman stood together, Calum saw a certain familial similarity, despite the disparity in their ages. Lady Augusta also had an oval face, dark hair, and fair skin, though her large eyes were not the mist color of Gillian's but rather a dark gray. They were the same height, as they stood there, daughter and granddaughter of the ninth Earl of Swanton. The earl had died, leaving no sons behind him to inherit, so his title and estate had passed to a distant male relative who had badly mismanaged the property. Calum smiled faintly. The servants of Treymoor were cautious about what they told him and his cousins regarding Gillian, but they had proved willing to discuss the family history.

Lady Augusta seemed to notice Calum for the first time. "And this gentleman, I presume, is your new guardian." She held out her hand to him. "I am Augusta Turville," she said, before Gillian could make a more formal introduction.

Calum liked her straightforwardness. He gently clasped her small warm hand and bowed, noticing her exquisite jeweled rings before he released her. "An honor to meet such an exceptional lady," he said. "I am Calum MacFuaran."

"Marquess of Iolar," Gillian added.

Augusta stood back and surveyed Calum. "But you're so much younger than I expected."

It was getting damned annoying, the way people kept saying he was younger than they expected, Calum thought. Just what had they expected? Some bent graybeard? "I'm twenty-seven, madam. I've been out of leading strings for some time now."

"I meant no offense, Lord Iolar, but to own the truth, I find it worrisome that Gillian's father should have chosen a man so close to Gillian's age to be her guardian. It . . . well, it hardly seems proper, if you will excuse my saying so."

Calum lifted a eyebrow in warning. There were two things in life that he could not, *would* not, tolerate: liars and any aspersions against his honor.

"In what way does it seem improper?"

"Well, you're still young enough to be hot-blooded with passion."

Calum regarded Lady Augusta coolly. The woman certainly did not mince her words. "Och, and at what age does a man's passion dissipate?"

Augusta thought for a moment. "Sixty would be a decent age for a guardian."

Thus she neatly sidestepped his question.

"Well, I am the man her father appointed, but I shall endeavor to contain my hot-blooded passions in her presence," he said dryly.

He looked at Gillian, who inspected the pile of her aunt's cases. Her shining dark hair framed a face of such intriguing beauty that he could not help but think the men of Saint Agnes parish must all be blind or stupid to have left her a spinster. Yet he knew behind her lovely visage lay a mind he had yet to understand.

Last night he dreamt she'd come to him in his bedchamber, her lovely face pale in the dark, a diaphanous mist of silk floating about her body. The exotic fragrance that seemed to be hers alone teased his senses. Her eyes had been heavy-lidded with desire, her delectable lips slightly parted, soft and moist. . . .

Lady Augusta's voice reached him. "Lord Iolar?"

With a start, Calum realized that he'd been

caught staring. "Lady Gillian is safe in my care," he said stiffly, feeling awkward and foolish and annoyed with himself. "I will not abuse Lord Molyneux's trust."

The older woman regally inclined her head. "I will accept you at your word, sir. You understand my concern, of course; my niece is precious to me."

"I am pleased ye feel so, Lady Augusta. That's as it should be." He smiled. "Now, if ye'll excuse me, I'll be leavin' ye to yer reunion."

He strode toward the library. His own business could no longer be put off. He sat down at the table, dipped the tip of his quill into the inkpot, and began to write. His first letter went to Oliver Farnum, the steward of Dunncrannog Castle and Iolar Glen, a man who had worked for Calum's father, according to the solicitor. Knowing that, Calum had decided to keep the steward on. His father, who had loved the castle and the glen, had apparently been satisfied with the man's work, and until Calum arrived at Dunncrannog and took stock of the situation he would keep the status quo. He penned the date that he, his cousins, his ward, and her chaperone would be leaving for the castle. The steward was to make the place ready to receive them. Calum pressed his signet into the hot sealing wax and rang for Pym, to have the letter taken immediately to Poppleton for posting.

Then he answered the pile of correspondence from his cousin, Balfour Drummond, whom he'd left in charge of the successful trading company Calum had built from the concern his maternal grandfather had left him. The deal with the merchant in Java must be decided upon if he was to beat out his fiercest competitor, Bell Mercantile. Success now would effectively close off that market to Bell, at the same time opening one to Drummond and Company.

Calum leaned back in the chair and frowned at the wall. He'd given much thought to the three ships and their cargo that his contact in Java wanted. There were buyers there, desperate for the goods. His ships would return to Edinburgh laden with silks from the Orient, with porcelain, tea, ivory, and spices. It was risky, yes, but it was a singular opportunity, one not often given a man. *If* the ships arrived in Java intact, *if* the imports arrived undamaged in Java and were loaded into his ships, and *if* they made the perilous journey back to Scotland unscathed, he would be a very rich man. His business would increase. He would have something to leave his sons. Something more than a legacy of rejection, lies, and dishonor.

It was a gamble he would take.

Dipping his quill pen back into the India ink, he scrawled out his instructions to Balfour. The ships were to be loaded; the goods were to go out. Money would be tight for several months, but he would survive.

After sealing those letters, he set about answering the rest of his mail. By the time he finished, it was almost time for dinner. He gathered his letters and carried them upstairs with him, intending to take them to the village the following day. In his room, he quickly washed with the fresh water in his ewer and changed his clothes. As he finished tying his neckcloth, there was a knock at the door.

"Come," he called, shrugging on his frock coat.

Hugh and Ian entered, dressed for the evening meal.

"Did ye meet Lady Augusta?" Hugh asked.

"Aye, I did," Calum said. "An interestin' woman."

Hugh inspected the deep cuff of his coat sleeve. "I thought so too."

Ian laughed, a teasing twinkle in his eyes. "Hugh thought she was interestin', and that's a fact."

Calum opened the door of his bedchamber. "Then most certainly we dinna wish to keep the ladies waitin'." He waved the other two men out into the hall, winking at Hugh, who, much to his surprise, pinkened.

They arrived in the drawing room a few minutes early, which allowed Gillian and her aunt to make an entrance. Augusta breezed through the towering doors first, a vision in ice-blue satin brocade. Gillian followed, immediately commanding Calum's attention. He barely noticed her rose silk polonaise, with the darker rose petticoat, or the fact that her embroidered shoes had been dyed to match.

Instead, he saw how her large gray eyes were framed by long, thick, slightly curled lashes. How her imperious little chin, which seemed to spend so much time in the air when she was around him, had the power to make him smile at the recollection. How her white throat curved down to a vulnerable pulse point, framed by the pearl necklace she always wore. He lifted his gaze and found her staring at him.

She lowered her lashes and looked away, bringing her silk and mother-of-pearl fan up to flutter against her cheeks like a moth's wing.

After an exchange of greeetings between Augusta, Hugh, and Ian, they all went into the dining room, where Jenkins and another footman in full livery waited. Calum sat at the head of the table, with Hugh and Ian on one side and Gillian and Augusta on the other. While he didn't hold with the promiscuous seating so popular in London, which seated men and women alternately, he found he liked having Gillian next to him at their meals.

As a bowl of venison broth soup was set in front of Calum, he was surprised to hear the first voice was Hugh's. He couldn't remember quiet Hugh ever initiating a mealtime conversation.

"Lady Augusta, do ye come to Treymoor often?"

"Of course, Mr. Drummond. My brother is often away, so I stay with Gillian. I'll be her chaperone until she weds."

Both Hugh's and Ian's eyebrows shot up. "Weds?" Hugh echoed. "I dinna know Lady Gillian was betrothed."

Calum sliced Gillian a sharp look. She met his gaze evenly and then lowered her eyes to her soup and lifted her spoon to her lips, silently dismissing him.

"She is not precisely betrothed, sir, but it is a matter of some delicacy, so you will appreciate my reluctance to discuss the particulars. I can only say that my niece will wed by spring."

"Please accept my felicitations, Lady Gillian," Hugh said with solemn sincerity.

"Thank you, Mr. Drummond." Gillian regarded him consideringly.

"And mine."

"Thank you, Mr. Gunn." Ian received the same look. It was as if she were reexamining her opinion of them.

Not for one moment did Calum believe Gillian had an engagement pending. If he asked her, he doubted she could even give him the name of her mysterious intended. "As Gillian's guardian, Lady Augusta, I will be most interested in hearing the details of this . . . arrangement."

"I cannot—"

"Soon," he said, mildly but firmly.

Augusta frowned slightly. "Of course."

Of course. Why did he have the feeling that he'd just been put off?

"Lord Iolar," Gillian said, "earlier today you mentioned that I would soon have an opportunity to travel. May I inquire what you meant?"

Pleased to move promptly to a topic dear to his heart, Calum smiled. "Yes, the matter of travel. Now that Lady Augusta has arrived so ye have a proper chaperone, we can leave. Pack yer belongings. Warm clothing. We leave tomorrow."

"W-where are we going?" Gillian asked, looking thoroughly rattled.

"Scotland."

"*Scotland*?" cried the women in unison, their eyes wide with alarm.

A loud clatter of dishes drew all their attention to Jenkins, who had just gathered their soup bowls to carry away. He stared at Calum, clearly horrified. "Scotland?"

" 'Tis not as if I'm proposin' we set out for the edge of the earth," Calum said, annoyed by their reaction. "Scotland *is* considered part of the civilized world, ye know."

"By some," Jenkins muttered, as he rebalanced the bowls and stalked to the sideboard. Then he went to the warming table next to the hearth where a small fire burned, from which he brought a platter of trout from the river that flowed through Treymoor.

Calum shot Jenkins a quelling glare, then turned to the women. "I have matters of business to attend in Edinburgh, and I've no been home to Iolar Glen for twenty years. Now it's come to me, and, while I've been assured the holding prospers, I wish to see for myself." For nearly twenty years he'd been banished from his home. He'd left a repudiated child. He had endured loneliness, hardship, and scorn. Through determination and strategy, he had wrested success and wealth from a hard world. Finally, as a man—some said a hard man—he would return home to the glen. But he would return as master. And, by God, no one would ever drive him away again.

"You can't go!" Lady Augusta exclaimed. "I mean—er, *I* can't go. That's it. I can't go. I was . . . uh . . ." She looked over at Gillian as if seeking help. "I was planning to return to London and take my niece with me. A girl her age and no time in town behind her. Really, her father has been so absentminded about such things."

"Yes," Gillian piped, "I've been looking forward to going to London."

"But ye said—" Calum began, only to be interrupted by Lady Augusta.

"Oh, yes, my dear! Why, I'll take you to my mantua maker and have you fitted for a complete new wardrobe. That way everything shall be ready in the spring, and you can have a gay season among Society. A positive *must* for a young girl," she added to Calum.

"A must for a young lassie, but not for Lady Gillian," he said bluntly. "She'll be comin' with me."

Lady Augusta quickly picked up the dish of sweeting pudding and offered it to Calum. "She can't."

Without thinking, he took it from her. "What do ye mean, 'she can't'?"

"I can't," Gillian volunteered promptly.

"She can't," Jenkins concurred from his place by the fire.

Thoroughly exasperated with this nonsensical rebellion, Calum said, "If someone doesna give me a reason—a *good* reason—why Lady Gillian canna leave for Scotland tomorrow, she'll be on her horse and on the road come sunup, if I have to hobble and gag her."

"It—it's the harvest," Gillian said. "We can't leave before the harvest."

"And the ball! Don't forget the ball, dear. It would be unthinkable."

"*The ball?*" Calum stopped abruptly, realizing from the shocked faces of Gillian and her aunt that he was shouting. He drew a long breath and silently counted to twenty, trying to put things into perspective, struggling to be accommodating—something he found he wasn't used to.

"Ye have a steward to attend to the harvest," he

said in what he thought was a reasonable tone. "And I dinna think a ball is a necessity."

"Oh, but it is," Lady Augusta assured him. "Most necessary. Why, people would think there was something desperately *wrong* if a harvest ball wasn't held at Treymoor. Until they found out you were Scottish, of course."

"And just what is that supposed to mean?" But he knew perfectly well what she meant.

"Means they'll know you're Scotch," Jenkins explained, with too much satisfaction for Calum's liking.

He could just imagine all those smug Englishmen clucking over their port to one another about the niggardly ways of the Scots. But then what did the Sassenachs know of sensible frugality? "Do ye have food to serve, man?" he asked in a warning tone.

Jenkins stiffly drew himself up and went around the table, gathering up the dishes from the first course and replacing them with those of the second.

"And what is yer reasoning for staying until the harvest is in?" he asked Gillian and Augusta, expecting another bit of bizarre reasoning.

"I can't go because I must be present during the harvest," Gillian said quietly.

"Why? Ye have a reliable steward."

" 'Tis bad luck," piped Jenkins. "For the farmers."

Calum scowled at the obstinate, interfering servant. This was the most ridiculous thing he'd heard yet. "Ye expect me to believe that?"

" 'Tis true," Gillian said.

Hugh looked faintly skeptical. "The farmers think ye bring them luck?"

"The mistress of the house. It is . . . it is—an ancient belief," she ended in a rush.

"Extremely ancient," Lady August agreed, nodding, her ostrich plume bobbing.

Calum's eyes narrowed. "It canna be too ancient if it involves the mistress of the great house."

Gillian waved her hand airily. "A mere adaptation of an older tradition."

"Oh? How old?"

"Who can say?" Lady Augusta said.

"I heard tell it started with the Druids," Jenkins volunteered.

"The Druids, eh? I dinna know there had been Druids in this area."

"Oh, they traveled a great deal," Gillian assured him. "They loved to walk."

Calum turned to Hugh and Ian for confirmation. Ian shrugged. Hugh raised his eyebrows and shook his head, indicating he did not know. Calum found the story hard to swallow, but he'd heard of stranger things that had proven true.

"So the farmers think ye bring them luck?" he asked dryly.

Gillian lifted one slim shoulder and let it drop. "Who can say why? Their lives depend on the elements. The harvests have been good since I was fifteen and began to ride with the old steward as he went about his business on Treymoor. He was an amusing fellow, you understand, and I liked his company. During the harvests, I would go out into the fields and bring the workers food and drink and visit with them. It was so much more entertaining than sitting in the house, jabbing at my needlepoint."

There it was again, Calum thought. That discordant note. The apparent boredom that did not quite fit with the other things he observed. The warm affection and protectiveness the tenants and the house servants displayed toward Gillian. Her concern for them, which showed despite her attempt to conceal it. Why would she wish to conceal something so admirable? And all this business about a mysterious husband-to-be. There was no betrothed, no man intending to step forward to claim her, Calum was almost sure of it.

"I've never seen ye just sittin' around workin' at stitchery," he said, studying her face. Under his gaze a faint blush tinged her cheeks.

Then he turned his attention to the ragout of veal on his plate. He felt her gaze upon him and almost smiled. Let her fret, the little vixen. She was hiding something from him. Whatever her real secret was, he planned to uncover it.

"Do we stay for the harvest and the harvest ball, Lord Iolar?" Lady Augusta asked.

"How long?"

"Two weeks. The invitations went out almost two months ago."

The muscles in Calum's jaw tightened. Damn bloody Molyneux to hell.

"The oats will soon be ripe," Gillian said quietly. Her fingertips moved up and down the stem of her wine glass. "Everyone knows there can be no ball until the harvest is in."

"Quite," Lady Augusta agreed. "The ball is to celebrate nature's bounty. But this year we shall have the opportunity to honor Lord Iolar. And his two charming kinsmen, of course," she added, smiling at Hugh and Ian.

Calum calculated what business could be put off a while longer. He and his cousins would need more clothes than the ones they'd brought with them. Since he'd already dispatched his letter notifying the steward of Iolar Glen that they'd be leaving tomorrow, Calum made a mental notation to send the new date of departure.

Damn and blast! He disliked altering his plans to indulge anything as frivolous as a ball, but he would not willingly embarrass Gillian or her aunt before their friends and acquaintances by making them cancel the thing. Nor did he wish to cause the tenants hardship. As suspicious as the story Gillian had given still sounded to him, he understood superstition. The men aboard the *Bonnie Gail* had been a superstitious lot. Sometimes clinging to a belief in the impersonal caprice of unknown powers made it easier to bear the personal cruelties and neglect of mortal authority.

"We'll stay," he said.

"Excellent!" Lady Augusta exclaimed. "We are most grateful to you, Lord Iolar, are we not, my dear?" she prompted her niece.

Gillian gave him a pale smile. "Ever so grateful."

Jenkins removed the dishes, brought new plates and utensils, and then laid out the dessert, which consisted of fruits, jellies, orange cake, and glasses of whipped syllabub.

Lady Augusta regaled them with stories from her sojourn in London. The lady had a wit that teased even Gillian to laughter. Calum had never seen

Hugh so attentive to a woman before. And the more attentive he became, the more vivacious Augusta grew.

Finally, after Ian had scraped the last bit of syllabub from his dish, Gillian leaned over and touched her aunt on the arm. "Perhaps we should retire."

"Oh." Augusta suddenly seemed to realize that the hour had grown late. "Yes, of course. You're entirely correct."

The men stood, and everyone said good night. The ladies glided out the door.

Calum caught himself watching until the last glimpse of Gillian disappeared down the hall.

"How did ye fare with the social dragons of Poppleton parish?" Ian asked.

"Poppleton is the village, Ian. Saint Agnes is the parish."

"Saint Agnes, then," Ian said good-naturedly.

"We made only three calls, and there was but one real dragon. I'd say she made up for the other two."

"Did ye get a glimpse of Lady Gillian's intended?"

Calum led the way into the salon. "Nay." He wasn't willing to speak of his suspicion that there was, indeed, no intended. That Gillian had been looking for one today.

They poured themselves each a few drams of whisky and sat in overstuffed chairs in front of the empty fireplace.

"What have ye to say about the matter?" Hugh asked.

"I'll no be handin' her over to someone I dinna approve of," Calum said, then wished the words had come out differently, less pompous. But he would not let her throw herself away on the likes of a Quentin Latham or a Kenward Clough. Not even on a milksop like Maynard Leake. She needed a strong-willed man. And, of course, a man of title and property.

Abruptly Calum tossed back the remainder of his drink. He didn't want to think about Gillian getting married.

Hugh shook his head. "Och, lad, 'tis easy enough for ye to say now, but what if she loves the man?"

9

"Aunt Augusta, did you really send out invitations to a ball two months ago?" Gillian asked, as she and her aunt swept down the hallways to the suite in which Augusta customarily stayed when she was at Treymoor. All the candles in the sconces and girandoles had been lit, on orders of her extravagant aunt, no doubt. The pleasant scent of melting beeswax floated on the air.

"Of course not, Gillian dear. I know how you abhor the cost of festivities."

Gillian frowned. "I can't afford the enormous expenditures."

"Likely you could now, with things so improved here," Augusta said, leading the way through her antechamber into her bedchamber. "But I shall pay. I can better afford it than you."

Augusta's maid, Barbara, dozed in a wing chair, snoring lightly, apparently awaiting the return of her mistress. Augusta touched the woman's shoulder. Barbara started from her slumber with a small snort.

"Go to bed, Barbara," Gillian said. The woman was clearly exhausted. "I will help my aunt with her clothes."

Barbara looked to her mistress for consent and, when Augusta nodded, thanked them both, curtseyed, and hastened away.

Augusta laid her fan on her dressing table. Together she and Gillian set about unhooking and unlacing the elaborate garment.

"As I was saying, you can afford to have a ball now. You're not sending every hard-earned shilling to your feckless father."

"'Tis unkind to speak of him so," Gillian said, easing the polonaise from her aunt's ivory shoulders.

"He all but deserted my sister, leaving her to manage everything on her own until the night she died—alone. He honored none of his obligations to you, his daughter and only child, yet was only too willing to have you toil like a slave on his wretched estate so he might have all the money he wanted to do heaven-only-knows-what in one far-off heathen place after another. I'm sorry to speak ill of the dead, niece, but when it comes to Benjamin Ellicott, I feel most unkind."

"Mama wasn't alone when she died, Aunt Augusta," Gillian said gently. "She had you. And me. And everyone here at Treymoor. We all loved her." Gillian held the ice-blue satin gown in her arms and remembered that night.

Moisture welled up in Augusta's eyes, and she blinked rapidly. "You're quite right, dear."

"I think Papa was really the one who was alone."

Augusta smiled sadly at Gillian. "Perhaps."

Carefully, Gillian put away the polonaise and helped her aunt step out of her petticoat. As she hung it in the wardrobe, Augusta sat on the bed and rolled down her stockings.

"Now, about the ball. I'll send out invitations immediately," Augusta said. "It just so happens I brought my best writing paper with me."

"Of course."

"I know you think Maynard Leake is your best chance at matrimony, dear, but I must disagree. He's much too young. What you need is an *old* man. Old and rich. Even better would be *sick*, old, and rich."

Gillian smiled. "Really, Aunt Augusta, I need a man who can give me a son."

"Yes, I suppose you're right. Perhaps not ailing, then, but definitely well advanced in years."

"Your husband was young."

"More's the pity! It looked as if the lout would see me to my grave and live to make another woman miserable. If it hadn't been for that fortuitous hunting accident I'm certain he would have gone on to pluck another child bride from the bosom of her family. No, an old man is better. More appreciative of little attentions. He won't live long enough to become truly annoying, so as you enjoy your widowhood in luxury, you can remember him with a certain fondness."

"What woman could resist such a delightful prospect?"

Attired now in her night shift and dressing gown, Augusta kissed Gillian's cheek. "We've been through many trying times. We will get through this one. Leave all the arrangements of the ball to me. You have enough to occupy your attention."

Almost as soon as Gillian arrived in her room, Zerrin tapped and entered, closing the door silently behind her. She assisted Gillian in undressing. "The people of the Lady Augusta, they do not seem so competent as the people here. Always they wait for her orders." She tapped her temple. "They do not *think*."

"Households differ, Zerrin."

"You are too kind, lady sister."

Gillian chuckled. "Treymoor is not like most great houses. Here, we are like a family. We *are* a family. We protect each other, care for each other."

"Then I am happy that I am here."

"I, also, am happy you are here."

Zerrin pulled back the coverlet and quilts on the tester bed and absently plumped the pillows. "You have not had a lesson since before my Lord Molyneux arrived. You would not have me fail him—or you— in this matter?"

"No. I shall be your rapt student evening after next."

Zerrin nodded her assent. Then she picked up her candle. "May you be preserved through the night, lady sister."

"God keep you, Zerrin. Sleep well."

When Gillian was alone again, she sat on the edge of her bed and thought about what had transpired at dinner. Iolar wanted to return to Scotland. He said he wanted to see Iolar Glen, which he described as a kind of Highland Eden. Why did he speak of it so, when the sheep trader had told Gillian that the new marquess had already destroyed the place, stripping it in revenge for his having been repudiated? The trader had sworn he'd seen the miserable remains of the estate with his own eyes, and he'd never given Gillian cause to doubt him. Well, the estate was Iolar's now. He could go back and gloat. In the end, the bastard son had triumphed.

Only she couldn't envision him exulting over Iolar Glen's destruction. She remembered too well the note of wistful yearning in his voice, the far-off look in his eyes, as if he saw something the rest of them could only imagine. Something he found beautiful. Something, someplace, he loved.

She understood that feeling. Treymoor held the same power over her. Each time she walked the lush cultivated fields or beheld a wobbly legged newborn lamb she felt a kind of renewal. Each time she shared grace with Zerrin and Pym, Mrs. Withecombe and Odgers, Jenkins and Sammy, and the others of her family as they sat together around the long table in the servants' hall, she experienced it.

Now Calum had delayed his reunion with Iolar Glen. He had done it for her and her people—based on a lie.

Not all of what she'd told him was untrue. She did need to be home at harvesttime, and her people would be uneasy if she were not. They believed she brought good luck, owing, no doubt, to the fact that out of the five years she'd been mistress of Treymoor, all but one had produced bountiful yields. Every year she had gone out to the fields to provide food and drink for the workers and to work beside them.

Even to her, the superstition sounded a bit silly. Certainly the tenants' belief seemed insubstantial when compared to the many more venerable superstitions abounding in the area.

Gillian crawled beneath the covers, snuggling under the comforting weight of the coverlet, her cheek upon the goosedown pillow. What was one more lie, she reasoned, when it involved a guardian she'd never wanted?

Unbidden, the image of Iolar's savagely beautiful face floated into her mind. His thick red-gold hair was pulled back into a queue that hung down between his shoulders. His light-green eyes glittered with determination, and his high cheekbones were flagged with color. *Ye are mine to protect, and protect ye I shall.*

For the past several years, she had been the protector: of her people, of Treymoor, of her father's source of funds. Now came a man, willful and confident of his power, who informed her that he would protect her come what may.

He was the man she'd always dreamed of as her husband, but the dream had turned into a threat to all she loved.

Oh, why hadn't he come years ago, when she'd prayed for him? Instead of now, when it was too late?

"Is this the last of it?" Gillian asked, eyeing the hillock of heirloom silver and gold plate. Candlesticks, tureens, platters, statues—the list went on, all valuable, all handed down through generations of

Ellicotts. The pile included gifts from monarchs and ambassadors. Any piece here, or in the other two caches she and Mrs. Withecombe had established in the secret passageway, would have brought the price of a winter's fuel for many families. There had been two years when she'd had to sell off some of Treymoor's valuables to feed and warm her people. It had hurt, parting with some of her heritage, things she planned to leave her hoped-for children. But gold and silver do not weaken from lack of food, nor do they suffer from the cold. The choice was clear.

"This is all," Mrs. Withecombe said, as she dropped a holland cloth over the treasure to protect it from dust.

"I really can't imagine Lord Iolar or his cousins taking anything, much less something costly."

"You don't know Scots, m'lady. They're a thieving lot of scoundrels. Best to take no chances."

Gillian knew Mrs. Withecombe came from Northumberland, where raiding from each side—Scottish and English—had grown to be a way of life. "You don't think they'll notice the absence of the silver candlesticks or serving dishes?"

"I've substituted pewter and porcelain. If they're honest men, I doubt they'll notice."

"Then I suppose we'd best return to our work before they get back from the village." Gillian didn't feel right about hiding every silver spoon and salver from Iolar and his kinsmen. Never had they indicated any interest in such things. Besides, Aunt Augusta had told her Iolar was wealthy. He would have his own silver and gold—perhaps much more than comprised Treymoor's dwindled trove. Mrs.

Withecombe, however, had worried and fretted over the matter, distrusting the Scots, and eventually Gillian had given in. Now the valuables were hidden within the secret ways that honeycombed the house.

"You realize, of course, that Aunt Augusta will want most of these things back in their places for the ball," she pointed out, as she and Mrs. Withecombe began their trek back to the secret door Gillian had discovered in the stillroom.

"They'll be safe until then."

Gillian sighed. There was no convincing Mrs. Withecombe it was unlikely that Iolar and Messrs. Drummond and Gunn had any designs on the valuables.

Over the past two days she had seen little of Iolar, who had either been in Poppleton, being fitted for additional suits of clothing, or closeted in the library.

Hugh Drummond and Ian Gunn had accompanied Iolar to the tailor's shop, but, shortly after, Ian had ridden out of Treymoor's drive, on his way back to Edinburgh.

Abandoning good manners, Gillian had questioned her guardian about Mr. Gunn's departure.

Iolar had raised an eyebrow in that maddening way, a silent comment on her nosiness. Then, to her surprise, he'd answered her. "He's gone back to fetch something important." More than that, Iolar would not say. Gillian wished he'd remained silent on the matter, for now curiosity and worry both nibbled at her.

On the third day, Iolar elected to ride with Gillian, effectively altering her plans to carry out the work needed to run Treymoor. Under pressure to accomplish as much as possible before her departure in less than two weeks, Gillian chafed at this enforced leisure.

"Most inconvenient of him. Now I must play the chaperone," Aunt Augusta grumbled, as Zerrin assisted Gillian into her riding habit. "I had planned to show Mr. Drummond the orangery. Do you know, he's never seen one?"

Gillian and Zerrin exchanged knowing smiles.

"Perhaps what the esteemed Mr. Drummond meant was that he has never seen an orangery in the company of such a pretty lady," Zerrin suggested, her dark eyes twinkling.

Augusta toyed with a small enameled box on Gillian's dressing table. "Yes, of a certainty, but I do believe he truly hasn't seen an orangery."

Gillian's and Zerrin's smiles grew in the face of Augusta's acceptance of her allure for the opposite sex. And why not? Gillian thought. Aunt Augusta was lovely and elegant and clever. Any man with his wits about him would find her attractive.

A tiny frown creased Augusta's brow. "Do you truly need me to go with you, Gillian dear? Iolar is, after all, your guardian."

The last thing Gillian wanted was to spend the day alone with Iolar. It went beyond the fact that she found herself sometimes forgetting that he was the enemy, it was because he disturbed her. Like the moon drew the tide, his presence never failed to tug at her awareness. She wanted to ignore all but the threat he posed. Instead, she found herself noticing how his eyes looked in the sunlight. He was altogether too arrogant for her liking. Too virile. Too male. He was outside her experience, and she didn't know how to handle him. He'd immediately seen through the tactics she'd used on the others. No, Calum MacFuaran, Marquess of Iolar, was most definitely *not* a manageable sort of man.

"Yes, he is my guardian," she told her aunt, "but—"

"I knew you would agree with me, my dear. I wouldn't want to smother you, after all." Augusta flipped open her fan and idly moved the painted chicken-skin-and-ebony affair back and forth, stirring the air. "All this business with chaperones is so . . . so *Mediterranean*, don't you think? I have every confidence in your sense of propriety, and Lord Iolar has given his word that your virtue is safe with him."

A spurt of desperation shot through Gillian. "Yes, but—"

"Do hurry now. Your guardian is not the sort of man who tolerates waiting at all well. Have a lovely afternoon!" Augusta swept out of the bedchamber, closing the door behind her.

Gillian felt as if she'd been abandoned.

"The Lady Augusta, she is sometimes difficult to understand, is she not?" Zerrin asked, stepping back to assess her handiwork.

"She's consorting with the enemy!"

"Is she?"

"Of course she is," Gillian muttered, glaring at her reflection in the looking glass. What cod's head had come up with the idea of sticking ostrich plumes in ladies' hats?

Zerrin lit the ball of incense and placed the perforated top on the hammered silver incense burner. Perfumed smoke wafted up, curling in languorous tendrils. As she had almost every morning since she had arrived at Treymoor, Zerrin set the incense burner on the floor. "Perhaps," she said, "the Lady Augusta knows that making herself agreeable might bring her what she wants."

The room filled with the fragrance that Zerrin had devised for Gillian alone. Notes of jasmine, orange blossom, costly vanilla, and amber resin combined to create a sensuous yet elusive scent.

Automatically, Gillian took a step and stood over the incense burner, moving so that the pale fine smoke touched her petticoat, her shift, her stockings, her thighs, and the more intimate regions of her lower body. Then she stood back and Zerrin placed the burner on the dressing table. Gillian bent over, allowing the incense to scent her clothing, hands, neck, face, and hair.

Then Zerrin extinguished the burning ball of resins and oils and returned the silver burner to its place on the chest of drawers.

"What do you think she wants, Zerrin?"

Zerrin raised her shoulders and dropped them in an eloquent shrug. "Who can say what thoughts move through her head? Perhaps it is better to remember that she has come from her beloved London whenever you have called, that she keeps your secrets for you. I think sometimes you are to her the child she never bore."

A pang of guilt stabbed Gillian. She'd never stopped to consider that her aunt might yearn for children. The thought made her sad.

She turned to Zerrin. "Do you want children, little sister?"

Zerrin looked surprised. "Of course. What woman does not?"

Gillian took her friend's hand between her own. "You do know that you're free to go to any man of your choosing? I know father extracted some kind of promise from you, but I free you of it. Your happiness means much to me."

"I have not yet found the man of my heart."

"But how will you? I fear you've had no opportunities to meet him."

Zerrin smiled. "He will come."

Minutes later, Gillian descended the staircase to find Lord Iolar waiting for her in the marble-paved entry hall.

His gaze moved down the length of her, and her heart tripped a little faster.

Without a word, he opened the front door for her. As she passed in front of him, he breathed in deeply. "Ye look bonny," he murmured.

She turned and met his light-green eyes. They held her like a mystic spell for several beats of her heart. "Thank you," she said softly. Unexpected shyness welled up inside her. Quickly, she looked away and finished passing by him. Her petticoat brushed against his legs. A vibration shivered through her.

Out on the portico, she discovered Maynard Leake handing the reins of his horse to one of her grooms. He looked up and caught sight of her.

"Lady Gillian," he said and beamed with pleasure. His smile faded somewhat when he caught sight of Iolar, who strolled over to stand beside her. "Lord Iolar," Maynard acknowledged.

Iolar inclined his head.

Maynard looked back to Gillian. "I fear I've come at an inconvenient time."

"No," Gillian said promptly, hoping to cut off anything her guardian might say. "Of course not, Mr. Leake. We are always pleased to see you."

"You were not just leaving?"

Gillian waved airily. "A pleasure ride only. Will you join us?"

Sunlight glinted on his pink scalp through prematurely thinning hair. "I would not wish to intrude."

"Intrude?" Gillian laughed, then prayed neither man heard the forced edge in that sound. "We are delighted with the prospect of your company, are we not, Lord Iolar?" She turned to Iolar so Maynard could not see her expression and narrowed her eyes warningly at her guardian.

Iolar regarded her a moment, his handsome face unreadable. Just when she was certain he would refuse, he said, "Of course." The inflection of his deep, lilting voice gave no indication of either pleasure or disapproval.

The groom returned Maynard's horse to him. At the same time, another groom led out Atlanta and Iolar's roan.

Once the three were mounted, Gillian suggested they take the path that hugged the river's shore. In silence, they rode toward the ribbon of water. As the silence stretched, Gillian grew more desperate not to lose this opportunity to allow Maynard to court her, regardless of Iolar's dour presence. She would not think of all the work she needed to do around the estate, or how Iolar's proximity sent a simmering under her skin. The man riding so close beside her was capable of heinous deeds. He'd already destroyed one estate; she must ensure he'd not have the chance to repeat the offense at Treymoor. And in order to do that, she needed Maynard.

She turned to her neighbor with a smile. "This has been a good year for the crops, don't you agree, Mr. Leake?"

He bobbed his head in agreement. "Of a certainty. 'Tis a pleasure to look out at the fields. Our animals, also, have done exceedingly well. More of the lambs and piglets survived."

They shared something in common, Gillian thought. If there could be nothing else between them, there would always be their interest in their estates. And, of course, there would be children. . . .

As the three of them rode along the path, she surreptitiously studied Maynard. He was tall. Not so tall as Iolar, of course, but few men were. Maynard was fair-skinned, with thinning brown hair. He was slim. Very well, to own the truth he was scrawny. For all the world, he reminded Gillian of an underfed white chicken. Rooster, she corrected. A hen-pecked skinny white rooster.

Her chest constricted at the thought of shackling herself to him for life. What would their children be like? Would they have that pasty hue to their skin? Would they look like starvelings? Would her sons cling to her apron strings after they had grown to manhood? Worse, would they be so very dull?

Without wanting to, she glanced at Iolar. His children would be nimble-minded. Perhaps they would also inherit that gleaming hair and those startling eyes. They would be beautiful. And probably naughty. She smiled, thinking of little boys with frogs and little girls smuggling kittens into the nursery. She quickly caught herself. In that direction lay danger.

No, it appeared her only choice was Maynard, unless one of the men she met at the ball proposed immediately. That prospect appeared unlikely, so she turned and smiled at Maynard again.

"Did you go to the dance last month?" she asked, referring to the gathering in the Poppleton Assembly Rooms. As usual, she had not found time to go, though she had wanted to.

"No. Mama didn't wish to go."

"Oh."

"Does yer mother no like to dance, Leakes?" Iolar asked, emerging from his silence.

"Leake," Maynard corrected. "No, sir, she does not. She feels it is naught but an unhealthy display that provides the devil opportunities for mischief."

"And how do ye feel about dancing?"

"I agree with my mother, Lord Iolar. 'Tis most unwholesome. Such contact between the sexes is bound to incite bodily lust."

"Och, a terrible thing is bodily lust," Iolar said solemnly. "But do ye think the mere touchin' of hands is sufficient to enflame a man?" To Gillian's annoyance, the question was asked in a tone of innocence that she instantly recognized as false but that Maynard apparently accepted as genuine.

"Beyond doubt, my lord. Lust is always present in the hearts of men and women. It is liable to explode at the least provocation, turning gentlemen and ladies into slavering beasts intent on degradation. One must be constantly on one's guard against it."

"Ah," Iolar said and nodded sagely.

"Another temptation is cards," Maynard declared, clearly warming to a favorite subject.

"I am forced to admit, Mr. Lack, that I've no heard of bodily lust being connected with a game of whist before."

"Leake. Just think of it, Lord Iolar. A man sits at a table, holding his cards. Across from him sits a woman, holding her cards." He awaited their response with the triumphant air of a man who has proved his point.

Try as she might, Gillian could find nothing in the image Maynard painted that might enflame one to indecorous behavior.

Iolar wore a blandly polite expression. "I fear, sir, the danger in the situation quite escapes me."

"Pray enlighten us, Mr. Leake," Gillian said, with more enthusiasm than she felt.

"Don't you see?" Maynard asked. "A woman's gown exposes her bosom. The man will see it. He will see it for as long as their card game continues. The sight will befuddle his mind until he is consumed with lust for her."

"And then what happens?" Gillian asked, her curiosity aroused by the bizarre reaction Maynard described. She had played whist while attired in a gown that partially exposed her bosom—what gown worn at assemblies or other evening social gatherings did not?

"Why, he might be prompted to sweep her off into the dark garden and—er . . ." Maynard's words died out and his face flooded with crimson.

"Have his evil way with her," Iolar supplied help-fully.

Gillian frowned. She had never witnessed such a sight from the card table. Had she often missed it?

"Precisely," Maynard said primly. "What man of character would allow his wife to disport herself in such a manner?"

"I cannot conceive," Iolar said, and Gillian felt like unhooking a leg from the horn of her sidesaddle and kicking him when she saw the amusement gleaming in his eyes. *I told you so,* they said to her.

When Maynard wasn't looking, she cast a glare at Iolar, who answered with a smug smile.

"What form of entertainment do you favor, Mr. Leake?" she asked, feeling a little desperate.

"Reading is good."

Gillian seized on the latest item she'd read. "Have you read Crompton's treatise on the eradication of tapeworm in sheep? 'Tis quite excellent—so I've been told," she added hastily, aware of Calum's presence.

"No, I have not, but I should like to. Might I ask to borrow it from you?"

Calum grinned.

Gillian favored him with a frosty look and then, wearing a smile, turned to Maynard on her other side. "I shall borrow it from my friend for you and send it over this very day." This day which seemed to be dragging on forever.

She knew she hadn't seen Maynard at any of the assemblies in the village, but she had thought he was simply shy. Never had it occurred to her that he was a prig.

As the mare daintily picked its way down an incline in the trail, Gillian swallowed hard against despair as she thought of what life with him would be like. It stretched before her, year after long year. No games. No dancing.

No love.

10

"*Mrs. Withecombe,*" *Calum said,* "*this house has rats.*"

The housekeeper stood just inside the library door, as if she had neither the time nor the inclination to present herself before him at the desk. Hands clasped in front of her, she leveled a cool gaze at Calum. "I'm aware of that, m'lord, and I'm attending the matter."

Damn it, how could the auld harridan always succeed in making him feel like a bairn caught stealing a fresh-baked bannock? Calum thought. He tolerated her impertinence because she was amazingly efficient and because he would soon be gone. Treymoor would need her.

"The place must be overrun with the beasties. I can hear 'em at night, rustlin' around," he added, then realized how defensive he must sound. Blast. Somehow, the woman reminded him of one of the

Bonnie Gail's captains. The third one, Old Poker Spine, who'd not been like the others, the sots and the martinets.

"Yes, m'lord."

"Has anyone been bitten?"

"Not that I know of, m'lord."

Calum reined in his impatience. "Please keep me informed of yer progress," he said in dismissal.

"As you wish, m'lord." Her tone was impersonal as always. She dropped a brief curtsey and left the room.

With a sigh, Calum shoved back his chair and rose to his feet, stretching the kinks out of his back muscles. For three days, ever since he'd accompanied Gillian and that codless clunch, Maynard Leake, on the ride along the river's edge, Gillian had been avoiding him. What was worse, he found himself seeking her out. Thoughts of her stole into his brain when matters of importance should have occupied him: his investments, his business, his responsibilities.

Responsibility. The word almost made Calum flinch. She wanted to marry Leake. If that sorry fellow could not see it, Calum certainly could. Probably the whole of Saint Agnes parish could see she wished to wed her neighbor.

It had been easy eliminating Quentin Latham from her pitiful list of prospects. The man was a bounder. And that slimy wee worm, Kenward Clough—as if Calum would let him escort Gillian to a local fair, much less London. Ha! But then there was Leake.

Why did she want that mother's little darling anyway? Oh, he could see why Leake would want *her*. What man wouldn't? Her, with skin so soft and fragrant and hair like jet silk. Her lips were as red as summer berries and promised to taste as sweet.

Abruptly, Calum straightened. He had seen with his own eyes that she believed the worst of him. The way her face had changed that first day, when she'd realized he was not his father but the once-repudiated son. Then she'd lied to him. When he handed her the earl's letter, she'd recognized it as her father's yet had denounced the document as a fraud.

Calum could tolerate almost anything but a lie. His family had been torn apart through the evil of a lie. False words had stripped him of everything he'd valued, everyone he'd loved.

He restlessly prowled the confines of the library, but after a few minutes he gave up trying to concentrate on correspondence and finances and strode out the door with the intention of locating Hugh. Perhaps he'd learned something from the Lady Augusta that might help Calum discover what the beguiling Lady Gillian was hiding.

At that moment, Sammy Blenkin came tearing around the corner. He collided with Calum and would have landed on his backside if Calum hadn't caught hold of his shoulders and steadied him.

"Begging your pardon, m'lord," the lad said breathlessly, clutching a powdered wig in place on his head.

"What's the hurly-burly over? Is this yer new wig, then?"

Sammy's eyes danced with excitement. "Yes, m'lord. Mr. Jenkins just brought it from town. 'Tis just like the one Mr. Pym wears," he confided. "Exactly as you told the wigmaker."

"Och, let me see this wonder." Calum took a step back and studied the wig. Mostly he enjoyed the glowing young face below. " 'Tis a fine wig and no mistake. I'll wager there's no a finer wig in the county."

"Except Mr. Pym's, of course," Sammy said loyally.

"Of course."

"I knew she'd get one for me if she could."

"She? Meanin' Lady Gillian?"

They began to walk down the hall together.

"Oh, yes," Sammy said reverentially. "I knew she would try."

Try? How much effort would it have taken her to order the lad a wig? Again he sensed that off note, that veiled discordance humming below the surface of Treymoor.

"Ye seem verra confident of that, Sammy," he teased.

The boy's cherubic face grew solemn as he considered the question. "Lady Gillian, she takes care of us. We're all family, you see? And I know she was sad because she thought she couldn't get me my wig. But it's more important that we all have food and warm clothes and coal for the winter, isn't it? So I pretended the wig really didn't matter to me."

"That was brave of ye. I've known grown men who've not shown such good judgment." It seemed there had been harder times here at Treymoor. Perhaps that was what he'd been sensing all along. To the eye, the splendor of Treymoor defied frugality.

Sammy brightened. "Really?"

"Aye. Really."

The child seemed to mull over what Calum had told him, and as they continued down the corridor, Sammy's thin shoulders gradually straightened.

"What do yer mother and father do?" Calum asked. "Are they farmers here on Treymoor?"

The boy shook his head. "No. They—they died when our cottage at Frampton Park burned down. After the old lord died, the estate went to a terrible relative who let everything tumble to the ground. Tenants moved away. All my da's relations were gone. There was no master living in the great house, so Lady Gillian came and got me."

"And ye were placed with another family at Treymoor?"

"Everyone at Treymoor *is* my family."

"I don't understand, Sammy." What was all this business about everyone being his family?

"I live here, in the house."

"Who cares for ye now?" Calum asked.

"Everyone here in the house," Sammy said, carefully touching the side of his wig.

"Ye dinna have a new mother and father now?"

"No."

"Ye're no just left to find a bed at night?" Calum didn't believe Gillian would be so careless.

"I have my own bed. And a bedtime."

Something that was beginning to tighten in Calum's chest eased. "Ah."

"Sometimes Mrs. Withecombe tells me a story and tucks me in. Sometimes Zerrin or Lady Gillian does it, or Mr. Odgers, or Mr. Pym. Or one of the others here in the house. They all care for me."

"Sounds as if ye're a lucky fellow."

"Aye, m'lord, for an orphan," Sammy said, and laughed delightedly when he saw Calum smile.

"Be off with ye, ye wee fiend," Calum said good-naturedly, recognizing the pent-up energy in the boy.

Sammy raced off, hurtling down the hall and around a corner.

"Be careful!" Calum called after him. A moment later, he heard the rattle of jarred dishes on a tray and a short soprano exclamation of exasperation. Then the faint sound of Sammy's "Sorry!"

Calum continued on his way to look for Hugh in the glasshouses, which seemed to fascinate the older man. Sammy's words repeated themselves in his mind. The more Calum considered all he'd learned about his unwilling ward, the more he wondered: Who was the real Gillian Ellicott? What did she hide from?

In the orchid glasshouse, Calum found Hugh deep in discussion with the old man who tended the plants. Calum thought there must be hundreds, maybe thousands of orchid plants in this warm, humid place, many in various stages of fantastic bloom. Those that were not flowering looked, in his opinion, rather uninteresting.

"Yer spendin' quite a bit of time in these glasshouses, Hugh. Are they that fascinatin' then?"

Hugh looked around them, smiling. "Och, aye. 'Tis like nothing I've ever seen before, though I'd heard of glasshouses. Did ye know, Calum, that they could eat pineapples all year long, what with their pinery?"

Calum shook his head. "A whole building with nothing but pineapples? What can they do with them all?"

"They sell them," Hugh said. "All the glasshouses produce food or plants for sale to the great houses throughout Britain, Scotland, and Ireland. The gardeners tell me there have even been orders from France and Norway."

"I thought they were producin' all these things for their own use. 'Tis what most estates do."

"Aye, so I've heard. But not at Treymoor. Here they make money."

The trader in Calum came alive. " 'Tis damnable clever," he said slowly, his mind working. "Perhaps Molyneux is no a complete ass."

Hugh laughed. "Considering what the man has tangled ye in, 'tis a generous observation."

"We could do this at Iolar Glen." Calum surveyed the myriad wondrous blooms. " 'Twould require more heat than at Treymoor, and fuel would no be as easily obtained. Still . . ." It would bear looking into.

"Are ye still plannin' to build a Turkish bath, lad?"

Calum smiled as they filed through the narrow walkway toward the door. "It spoils a man, does it no? I've enjoyed my baths here so much I'm certain it must be a sin."

The men exited the steamy glasshouse, and Hugh closed the door behind them. " 'Tis a bit of heaven," he agreed.

"If my ships to Java make it through, I'll be able to build a field of glasshouses and a Turkish bath the sultan himself would envy."

Calum glanced at his pocket watch. "We might as well go into Poppleton to finish with our suits."

They headed toward the stables.

"Dunncrannog Castle will be needin' a wee bit of

work too, I'm thinkin', to make it more comfortable," Hugh said.

"Aye. It will probably need a few modern improvements." Calum looked off into the distance. Pale gold fields of grain bowed in the breeze. Those fields were keeping him here. But in less than a fortnight they would be harvested.

Calum remembered riding with Gillian past those same fields as she'd made the cursed social calls on her neighbors. Was he the cause of the deep unhappiness he'd sensed in her ?

The candles in the library burned low, and the shadows grew bolder, crowding in to make it difficult for Calum to distinguish the words in Balfour Drummond's cramped handwriting. There was no help for it, the candles needed to be replaced. He walked over and tugged the bell cord.

Fifteen minutes later, no one had responded. Calum stalked out of the library, toward the servants' wing. Where *was* everyone? Hugh had retired to his room with a tome on flowering plants. He hadn't seen Gillian or her aunt since dinner.

The halls were empty of people. It was too early for everyone to be abed. Calum's impatience grew with each stride. All he wanted were some bloody candles! He would have gotten them himself if he'd known where they were kept. Why had no one answered his summons?

When he reached the servants' wing he discovered why. No one was around to hear the bell ring.

Surely everyone had not gone off to their beds. It

wasn't that late. Had Gillian let them off this evening? Without telling him? Why? And just where was *she*?

His impatience vanished, replaced by suspicion. What were Gillian and her people up to?

He made his way quietly through the house, searching for signs of life. From a window, he saw the night-darkened form of a man hurrying toward the bathhouse.

The bathhouse. Of course! What more perfect place could they have selected for a clandestine meeting? The building had no windows.

Quickly, Calum left the mansion and glided soundlessly down the path the man had taken.

The door was locked. He heard voices from within, men's voices. He identified them as belonging to Odgers and Pym.

Calum scowled. Something was going on in there, and he was damned well going to find out what. He could pick the lock or go back to his room for the keys he'd taken from Gillian.

He returned to the house and found the keys just where he'd left them, in the wardrobe. He'd half expected to find them gone.

As he retraced his steps through Treymoor's halls, he saw Jenkins. Quickly he concealed the keys and called to the footman.

"Good evening, your lordship," Jenkins answered, walking over to him.

"Where is everyone this evening?"

"Abed, m'lord. What with the harvest and the ball to prepare for, everyone is sore tired."

"Is there no one, then, to respond to the bells?"

"Oh, yes, your lordship. 'Tis my night, tonight. Last night Mr. Pym stayed up. Tomorrow night 'twill be Mr. Odgers's turn."

The story was almost believable. It did not, however, explain why, if everyone was so fatigued, Pym and Odgers were in the Turkish bath with the door locked. Tonight was not bath night for the male servants. "Sounds a good plan if the man on duty stays alert."

Suddenly Jenkins seemed to catch the drift of the conversation. "Did you ring, sir? I was just coming back from . . . er . . . answering nature's call."

Calum privately conceded that Jenkins did look tired, but that didn't explain why his trip to the privy had lasted so long. "I called for someone nigh on to half of an hour ago."

Even in the gloom of the hallway, Calum could see Jenkins's face flush darkly. "I . . . uh . . . fell asleep."

"In the privy?" Calum was well acquainted with the extremities of exhaustion, but tonight he was inclined toward suspicion.

"Yes, your lordship."

"Am I the only one remaining up who might require attention?"

"Yes, m'lord."

"Go to yer bed, Jenkins. But on the morrow make certain the candles in the library are replenished."

"Very good, m'lord. I will, m'lord."

"Good night to ye."

"Good night, m'lord."

As soon as he was certain that Jenkins had gone to his room, Calum returned to the bathhouse. When he listened at the door, he could not hear

Pym's or Odgers's voice, but there was someone in there. They were not close to the door, though, so their words were indistinguishable.

Quietly, carefully, he tried keys in the lock. His luck was holding and he found the right one on the fourth try. The door swung silently open.

Calum slipped inside and closed and locked the door behind him. Two lighted candles glimmered in the changing room. Someone was still here.

He saw clothing folded on a shelf as he crossed the room. Now he heard the voices more clearly, though the acoustics of the high-ceilinged, tiled room created eddies of echoes that made words difficult to discern. He listened intently. A burst of feminine laughter fell like a shower of crystal notes. Calum scowled. What exactly were Pym and Odgers doing in there? Was this foray doomed to reveal nothing more than the midnight trysting place of Treymoor's butler, valet, and their light o' loves? Calum cursed under his breath. It would explain the clothing on the shelf.

As distasteful as the prospect was of interrupting the lovers, Calum resolved that, as Gillian's guardian, he had a duty to enforce discipline among the staff.

Still hoping he was wrong and that he would discover something more valuable than amorous servants, Calum quietly looked around the corner.

His breath stuck in his throat.

Gillian sat on a stool next to the basin closest to him, naked.

She was beautiful. Sweet Jesus, she was beautiful! Her skin possessed the pure white luminescence of pearls.

Twinkling candles reflected on the jewel-like tiles

that covered the walls of the room, casting a glow over the only occupants. A fully clothed Zerrin tipped the steaming contents of a brass bucket over the slender nymph who lifted her arms to welcome the downpour, clothed only in her single strand of costly pearls with its ruby pendant.

Water cascaded down Gillian's body, slicking heavy midnight hair to slim shoulders, arms, and back. A stray dark lock drew Calum's mesmerized gaze to breasts that were high and round and perfect, with rosebud tips.

Her lithe body tapered down to a willow-slim waist that he could all too easily envision his hands encircling and then drifting lower, smoothing the soft curve of hips and a lushly rounded backside.

His gaze continued lower, to long shapely legs and narrow elegant feet, then back up, to a triangle of jet curls. . . .

Calum squeezed his eyes closed, engulfed by the blaze of his need. His breath came quick and shallow. *Gillian.* Spirited, saucy, fearless.

He wanted her. Christ's blood, a stone saint would want her, seeing her like this! So innocent of restraint, unfettered by decorum and arousingly sensual, she was a beauty of mythical proportions, like a silkie rising from the sea in woman's form, come to tempt some mortal man. And in this moment, Calum felt desperately mortal. Knowing he must not, yet unable to stop himself, he opened his eyes.

Her long inky lashes formed crescents on moist heat-flushed cheeks, and her enticing lips were slightly parted.

He knew he should leave this instant. No gentleman

spied on a lady at her bath, particularly if that lady were his ward.

It was degrading for them both.

It was inexcusable.

It was impossible to leave.

He hungrily drank in the sight of her, memorizing all the details he knew he had no right or claim to. This moment must last him a lifetime.

A small ringlet of wet black hair clung to her temple. Her skin glistened with water. Her slim fingers curled around the edge of the stool. Her breasts rose and fell with sensual ease. A small mole crested the dimple above her left buttock. Around one prettily turned ankle she wore a fine gold chain. An Eastern adornment, certainly. Odd that something so simple should be so excruciatingly erotic.

Hot blood pounded through his veins, and his body trembled with the force of his desire. *Gillian.*

He staggered to the door through which he'd entered the bathhouse. His hand shook as he fumbled the large key from the heavy bunch and inserted it into the lock. With a soft click, the lock opened. The door gave way before him. Somehow he managed to secure it behind him and make his way directly to the river, ignoring the moonlit gardens that extended all the way down the terraced slope to the water's edge.

Fully clothed, Calum plunged into the cold water. Welcoming the shock, yet hating it, he dove twice more, losing the black ribbon that bound his queue. Finally, he came up to gasp for air and shake the water from him. With chilled hands he skimmed his hair off his face.

He cursed himself roundly for a fool and a voyeur and a betrayer of trusts. Despite his curses and the cold water, his body still pulsed with his desire for Gillian.

Calum had seen beautiful women naked before. Not a few of them had come to his bed. With Gillian, what he felt was somehow different. Stronger. Maddening. Different. Why? Sloshing up onto the bank, he considered the question: What made her unique?

This was the woman, the "sweet child," he had once wanted nothing to do with. This was the woman who had denied and subverted his authority at every opportunity. This was the woman who had told him her dream.

As silly as her fantasy had sounded, he knew it had cost her something to tell him. And he suspected that her pride had been cut at having him witness her flirting with those poltroons they'd visited.

Why had she done it? Why would a lass with the wit and beauty of Gillian Ellicott throw herself at the likes of those three? Desperation for a husband? But hadn't she told that old trout, Mrs. Leake, that she'd simply not yet found the man of her dreams? The prince with the castle? Leake had no castle, and he was in no measure a prince. But Gillian appeared to prefer him over the other two. And Leake clearly had a fondness for her. Hugh's words came back to Calum now, as he stood dripping on the grassy bank of the night-blackened river.

But what if she loves him?

"No." Calum spoke the word aloud, as if that were enough to make it true. She couldn't love

Leake. She couldn't. Could she? The thought tightened a knot in his chest.

He scowled up at the moon. If she wanted Maynard Leake, why had she visited those other two? Had they been no more than the social calls that she'd claimed? But why Leake, when she could do better? And why now, when they had lived in the same parish all their lives, yet had not so much as courted?

Suddenly, he remembered her with Sammy Blenkin. The way her face had softened when he'd appeared at the door. The way she'd listened carefully to him. Her hands had smoothed over his shoulders, reassuring, maternal. What must she feel, knowing she was full twenty years old, still unwed and childless?

Was Leake her choice out of desperation or love?

Calum started back up the slope, toward the house. His shirt and breeches clung wetly to him and his shoes chafed.

He, Calum Gregory MacFuaran, was her guardian. Not her sweetheart, not her lover, but her guardian. And he would fulfill his duties as such, as an honorable man must.

If Leake was the one who she wanted, and the man's character, pedigree, and financials withstood scrutiny, then Leake she would have.

True to his word, Jenkins had already replenished the candles in the library by the time Calum arrived there the following morning.

Calum spent the day poring over Treymoor's ledgers, which he'd finally managed to extract from the steward. By evening, his head throbbed. When it came time to dine, he closed the book he was working on. Everything looked to be in extraordinarily good order. William Harland seemed a most excellent man of business—knowledgeable, demanding of quality, yet careful with a guinea. Calum only hoped the steward of his own estate was as responsible.

After the meal, Calum decided to withdraw to his room. He'd had little sleep the night before. It seemed everyone else had the same idea, for when he wished everyone a good evening, his cousins decided to retire too, as did the ladies.

In his room, he read awhile, but the subject of ulcerous cow udders and the treatment thereof did little to keep his eyes from growing heavy.

Finally he stood and stretched, trying to work out the kinks in his muscles that came of sitting over books all day. His mind wandered for a minute, going over things that yet required his attention. As he thought, his gaze idly roamed over the patterns in the wallpaper.

With a jolt, he realized that what he'd thought a rather odd acorn was actually a single long-lashed eye peering out at him from a small hole he'd never noticed before.

So *that* was the true source of the noises Calum and his cousins had been blaming on rats. There must be hidden passageways honeycombing the walls of this house. Many old houses had secret rooms and passages. They had been useful in hiding priests and smuggling goods—and now, it would seem, in spying on unwanted Scotsmen.

Calum carefully schooled his features not to give away his discovery. He'd be willing to lay gold that the pretty eye watching him belonged to one Lady Gillian Ellicott.

Casually, he began to undress for bed, removing his shoes, pulling off his stockings. The eye widened. When he unfastened the first button at the front of his breeches, the eye blinked, then abruptly disappeared.

Instantly, Calum rushed to search the wall for an entrance. Rapidly, he pressed and twisted every carved leaf and piece of fruit. When he stabbed his finger against a grape behind the washstand, a door opened.

He grabbed a lighted candle and swooped into the passageway. Beneath the hole in his wall he saw a stool. Faced with choosing which direction to take, he decided in favor of going toward Gillian's room on the other side of the house.

Quickly, quietly, he made his way through the narrow tunnels. There were no cobwebs, no mice or rats that he could see, but up ahead, in a niche, loomed a tall mound covered by a holland cloth. When he reached the niche, Calum paused to lift the dustcover to see what lay beneath.

Candlelight glimmered on silver and gold, on platters, bowls, and statues. Valuable heirlooms. Calum frowned. Why put it in here? Unless . . . was this what Gillian and her people were hiding from him? The wealth of the household?

His fingers tightened on the candlestick. He tossed down the edge of the cloth and strode rapidly toward Gillian's room. His steps quickened into a jog, hoping to catch the spy while still in the tunnel.

When minutes passed and he saw no sign of the culprit, Calum wondered if he might have been too hasty in thinking the eye belonged to Gillian. Maybe it was a servant.

Just as he considered turning back toward the servants' wing, he saw the dim glow of candlelight ahead. He hugged the wall and peered around the corner. The retreating light revealed a woman's silhouette.

Calum hurtled headlong down the passageway, toward the fleeing spy.

She must have heard his footfalls, because she broke into a run. She was fleet, he would grant her that, but it was only a matter of minutes before Calum reached out and caught hold of her arm, forcing her to halt in a flurry of skirts.

Panting, Gillian rounded on him. "Unhand me," she gasped.

"What are ye doin', sneakin' round, spyin' on me? On my cousins too, were I to venture a guess."

Dark color tinged her cheeks. "I . . . I wanted to see. I mean—"

"Ye wanted to *see*?" he demanded incredulously. "Ye wanted to watch me take my clothes off?"

Her blushed deepened. "No! 'Tis not what I meant."

"Och, but ye *did* watch, did ye no?"

"I did *not*. Well, I mean you only took off your shoes and stockings. And I've seen you bare-legged once before, if you will remember. Then *you* were the spy."

"But I was no peerin' at ye through a bloody wall, now, was I? Like some disgustin' Peepin' Tom."

"No, *you* were going to pick the lock of my father's bedchamber door. Every bit as low, if you ask me."

"I'm not askin' ye, for I know ye'll just say me a

lot of nonsense. Now, I want to know why ye were slinkin' round, spyin' on me, instead of tucked up in yer wee bed."

She cast him a furious glare, then looked away. "I just wanted to make certain *you* weren't slinking around the house."

"So ye watched me take off my clothes."

"I did not! I left before you uncovered anything . . . er . . . indelicate."

"Tonight, perhaps, but what of other nights?"

"Nothing, I saw nothing."

"Well, I'm greatly relieved," he said sarcastically, "for I'd no wish to offend yer maidenly eyes by unwittingly revealin' my indelicate parts to a peephole in the wall."

She had the grace to blush again.

"And what of my cousins? Ye've spied upon them as well, I've no doubt. Have ye seen any of *their*—"

"No! Of course not."

Calum realized he hadn't relinquished his hold. Her arm seemed so fragile in his hand. So feminine.

"Get us out of here," he ordered.

She directed him to the nearest door and instructed him on how to open it.

They stepped into an unused bedchamber. Holland cloth shrouded the furniture like pale ghosts. Draperies at the tall windows were drawn shut. Their candles created a sphere of golden light, surrounded by crowding shadows.

He took her taper and set it with his on a covered side table, trying not to remember how she'd looked in the Turkish bath. But the image of Gillian, so gloriously nude, so arousingly female, burned in his mind.

If any of her self-appointed guardians here at Treymoor suspected that he'd seen her unclothed, Calum had no doubt he'd be called into stern accounting. God, to be treasured by her as she treasured her people! If she had no concern for the workings of Treymoor, she made up for it in the care she took of those who lived and labored within the estate's boundaries. It seemed that not so much as a motherless child or an ill-treated wife went unattended. In return, she was given respect and devotion he'd only heard tell of between a Highland chief and his clansmen. A Sassenach and her tribe.

He reminded himself that he'd caught her spying on him and he damned well knew she'd lied to him. Curse her for the conniving female she was! And damn his own blind stupidity for wanting her despite everything.

Calum reached out a hand to touch her hair. With a flare of willpower, he curled his fingers closed against the urge and dropped his hands to his sides. "Ye lied to me," he said chokingly.

Her lips trembled but she made no denial as she stared at him, her mist-gray eyes wide. In the candlelight they glistened with moisture.

Gillian's latent tears succeeded in piercing through the heavy armor he'd layered over his heart year after lonely year for almost a lifetime. Even as he reached for her he was filled with a stunned wonder that this woman could move him.

She hesitated, searching his face, then moved into his gently coaxing arms.

He cradled her against his chest and she stilled, the tension running out of her body. He felt moisture against his chest. "Och," he murmured. "Dinna weep, lassie. 'Tis over now. Just dinna ever lie to me again. I canna tolerate lies." He stroked her slender back. The warmth of her skin permeated the fabric of her clothing. The crown of her head felt like silk against the underside of his chin. Her elusive, exotic fragrance swirled around his senses. Gradually, his hand stopped.

She lifted her cheek from his chest to look up at him. And he was lost.

Calum lowered his head, his heart hammering in his chest. Softly, he brushed his lips back and forth against hers.

Gillian's eyelids fluttered closed as a whirlwind swept her into dizzying flight. As her moorings pulled free of her known world, she clung to him, to the bone-and-sinew burning strength of him. His mouth moved with deepening hunger across hers, firing a kindred blaze within her. No other man had ever kissed her like this, held her like this. She would never have allowed it. Only Calum. She wanted only Calum.

She parted her lips under his coaxing, and his satin tongue greedily glided over her teeth to stroke against her.

Her breasts grew tight and feverish. In the low center of her body, heat pulsed.

His hand moved up her back to palm her nape, threading his fingers through her hair.

Calum raised his head and looked down at her. He cursed himself for a fool. He did not trust this woman, yet her response to his kiss stoked in him a jubilant satisfaction. The sweetness of her passion ensnared him. He was a twice-damned fool.

There, hidden in the sea-green depths of his eyes, Gillian saw doubt, shattering the magic of her wonder. He did not trust her, she thought, almost choking on her bitterness. Wise man. If anyone in this world should not trust her, it was Calum MacFuaran.

Nor could she trust him. Determinedly she called up the words of the sheep trader. *The poor beasts were starving and riddled with parasites. Not fit for meat nor wool. 'Twould have been a mercy to shoot them.*

Calum had done this. He had laid waste to a valley, leaving its inhabitants to suffer. She would not allow him to do the same with Treymoor.

As if sensing her change in mood, he released her, dropping his arms to his sides.

"Are we finished here?" she asked coolly.

His eyes narrowed. "In the passages I passed piles of silver and gold plate, costly bowls, platters, and vases. I saw a epergne I recognized as one that was on the table in the entrance hall when I arrived at Treymoor. 'Tis a great silver thing with leapin' dolphins. It was replaced shortly after with a bowl of flowers. I thought 'twas being cleaned. Now I dinna think so. Why have ye hidden yer valuables?"

Here it was, the opportunity to cleave a safe distance between them. Calum would never be tempted to kiss her again. He would never want to hold her.

He would hate her.

Gillian swallowed hard against the regret that filled her throat and weighed on her heart.

"Why," she said, trying not to let her voice crack, "I should have thought that would be obvious."

"Tell me anyway." His voice was low and harsh.

"I don't trust you."

His voice grew lower, harsher. "And why, pray, is that?"

Defiant against her traitorous heart, she raised her chin. "I'd heard about thieving Scots and worried about my valuables, so I concealed everything. Until you came, there was no need to count the silver after meals."

Calum stiffened. "So ye've all but buried yer paltry collection of silver." He moved toward her and, despite her resolve not to give ground, she moved back, away from him, until she bumped against a post of the draped bed. Seeing him so coldly furious, she could easily believe Calum capable of ruthlessly stripping an estate.

When he spoke, his voice held the chill and hardness of ice. "Yer treasures are quite safe from me and from my cousins. We've no interest in yer spoons and bowls. I've silver of my own in my house in Edinburgh." He took her chin firmly in his palm. "Ye've nothing that I want, Gillian. Nothing."

He let go of her and strode to the door into the hall. He held it open.

"Now get ye to yer bed."

She quickly brushed by him, every nerve in her body tingling with apprehension.

"Gillian."

She stopped short at that one word, which bore a tidal undercurrent of dark promise.

"Dinna enter the passageways again."

Fury, regret, and caution warred inside her. Not trusting herself to speak, not certain of his reaction, she responded with a single short nod.

"Good night," he said.

She walked away, toward her bedroom, forcing her stride to a dignified pace, not giving in to the desire to run.

Calum watched Gillian disappear around a corner at the end of the hall, the halo of her candle's light vanishing with her. Now he knew what she and her people had been hiding from him.

The knowledge gave him little comfort.

11

Gillian watched Maynard ride away down the drive, toward the road, and released a sigh of relief. He was always so serious. Clearly he was courting her, but he didn't have the knack for flirting or charming that might have made the ordeal easier to bear.

Aunt Augusta, still attired in her fashionable riding habit of green and blue embroidered silk, came to stand beside her. "Thank God he's finally gone," Augusta said. "Really, dear, he's too tedious."

Gillian smiled. "I thought you were going to doze off while we were riding. I feared you might fall off your horse."

"Unconsciousness would be a blessing where Mr. Leake is concerned. I cannot credit your desire to marry the man."

"He has not yet approached Lord Iolar to ask for

my hand." The fact worried her. Time was running out. In five days Iolar planned to drag her off to Scotland, and she had no confidence in Maynard's strength of will without her there to prompt him.

Aunt Augusta yawned. "Probably afraid of that troll he has for a mother. What a prize she shall be when you wed her son. I'm sure the three of you shall be very happy."

"I am willing to consider any alternatives you may offer, Aunt Augusta."

They walked up the portico stairs and entered the cool, polished marble entry hall.

"Excellent, for I have invited many such options to the ball. If you are the engaging hostess I know you can be, you shall have several proposals before the evening is out, of that I have no doubt."

Gillian stared at her. "Are the men you invited so desperate?"

Augusta laughed lightly, her voice a tumble of musical notes. "Rather I would say that they are men who know what they want and are not afraid to act." She led the way to the blue drawing room.

Casting Augusta a doubtful look, Gillian pulled off her riding gloves and rang for tea to be brought. "I must have a proposal before Lord Iolar takes me to Scotland or I know not what I shall do."

"Simply do the same thing with the men I have invited to the ball, Gillian, that you do with dull Maynard Leake, and you shall have enough offers that you may pick and choose."

"And what, pray, do I do with Maynard that will prove so alluring to the gentlemen of your acquaintance?"

"Why, flutter your eyelashes and smile, of course. What all courting women do."

Realizing she was doing exactly that brought a bloom of heat to her face. What bothered her most was knowing that if her behavior was so obvious her aunt could see it, then so could Iolar—and for some reason she felt reluctant to try to fathom, she wanted his good opinion. She wanted . . . Gillian frowned. It was best not to think in such terms. What she wanted could not matter.

With her usual grace, Augusta spread her skirts and sat down on the settee, effortlessly managing to look portrait perfect. "And why do you insist on addressing your guardian so formally? Lord Iolar indeed. He is Calum. An odd but rather nice name. And his cousins are *not* Mr. Drummond and Mr. Gunn, they are Hugh and Ian."

Gillian picked up a porcelain figurine of a spaniel. The artist had rendered the subject in a playful pose, with pink tongue lolling and hindquarters up in the air. The observer could almost see the tail wagging. "They have not indicated that they wish such familiarity," she said, evading the fact that she felt safer keeping a formal distance—especially from Iolar.

"I must admit, Calum is extremely intimidating. There is something quite fierce about him. But he's so very handsome. He will breed beautiful children on the woman he chooses for his wife." Augusta's delicate eyebrows drew down in a thoughtful frown. "'Tis a shame he is such a barbarian and cannot be trusted with the welfare of Treymoor. I think he would make rather a good husband for you." She smiled suddenly. "Certainly an interesting one."

Gillian abruptly set down the figurine. "Sometimes your fantasies are quite extraordinary, Aunt Augusta."

"Perhaps. But my point is, these men are living in your house, eating food you have grown. You are entitled to call them by their Christian names. Besides, I am certain they enjoy being addressed so. It is much friendlier, don't you think?"

A single knock sounded at the door and Jenkins entered, bearing a large pewter tray with their tea and biscuits. He smiled broadly and set about arranging the service for their convenience. "Did you have a pleasant ride, m'lady?"

"Yes, thank you, Jenkins," Gillian said, answering his smile with one of her own.

"What do *you* think of Maynard Leake, Jenkins?" Augusta demanded.

The footman blinked in surprise. "I . . . well, he—"

"Exactly!" Augusta was triumphant. "Just as I said. Gillian can do better."

"Most assuredly," Jenkins agreed emphatically. "That sod's not nearly good enough for you, Lady Gillian. Why, he ain't even tried to kiss you yet!"

Gillian sighed. "Is there nothing that escapes the notice of my household where I am concerned?"

"And Lord Iolar." Jenkins shook his head. "These days he fair snaps the head off a body what disturbs him."

Gillian sat down. "I cannot help it if Lord Iolar dislikes Mr. Leake. My only concern is that he give his approval when Mr. Leake asks for my hand in marriage."

Jenkins looked at her for a minute. "You're a real

lady, you are. Don't think we don't all know you're sacrificing yourself for us."

Embarrassed, Gillian pretended to give her full attention to pouring the tea. "Be off with you, Jenkins, before Pym takes exception to your extended absence. Tempers are short enough as it is, what with all the work to be done for the harvest and the ball."

"And the packing," Augusta added.

Jenkins went to the door and opened it. He turned back to face Gillian across the room, his hand still on the knob. "Don't think we don't know, Lady Gillian. We do." Then he left, quietly closing the door behind him.

As she sipped her tea, Gillian felt her aunt's gaze on her.

"Are you absolutely certain this is what you wish to do?" Augusta asked softly. "'Tis no shame to make the best marriage you can and let the dice fall where they may concerning this estate. It was never yours anyway."

Gillian set her cup carefully into her saucer and looked her aunt full in the eye. "Treymoor has always been mine," she said, her voice equally soft. "It was never Papa's because he did not love it: not the land, not the people. But I do. This place—the fields, the river, the gardens—has ever been my comfort and my solace. These people, the servants of this house, have been my family."

She found herself leaning forward intently and so eased back. "To raise me as they thought a proper lady should be raised, they risked prison and the loss of all they owned and exercised the powers my father neglected, to hire teachers and governesses, dancing instructors, and even the old steward, so there might be something left for my dowry when the time came for me to marry. The tenants have been my army of conspirators, closing ranks around me and those in this house, to present a united front in this web of deceit that has kept us all safe."

Gillian carefully selected the words she hoped would make her aunt truly understand. "They have all risked much for this home of ours. Can I do less? Once, they protected me. Now I must protect them."

Augusta reached out to Gillian, who went to her instantly, clinging to her aunt as her aunt clung to her.

"I was remiss in my duties to you," Augusta said, tears in her voice.

"You were assailed with problems of your own. A brutish, greedy husband."

"At least you were not foolish enough to wed at sixteen. How wrong I was about him! Men can be such deceivers, Gillian. Behind a noble facade can lie a treacherous, cruel devil."

Gillian stroked her aunt's back comfortingly. When she gained her freedom as a widow five years ago, Augusta had been a mere ten years older than Gillian was now. Release from the tyranny of father and husband had proved to be a heady draught. The subject of remarriage had never come up, though Gillian knew that there had been proposals aplenty from wealthy, powerful admirers.

"Still," Augusta finally said, straightening, "there must be someone better for you than Maynard Leake."

If you
have a passion
for great
historical
romance,
here's an offer
you'll love...

4 FREE NOVELS

Reader Service.

Yes! I want to join the Timeless Romance Reader Service. Please send me my 4 FREE HarperMonogram historical romances. Then each month send me 4 new historical romances to preview without obligation for 10 days. I'll pay the low subscription price of $4.00 for every book I choose to keep--a total savings of at least $2.00 each month--and home delivery is free! I understand that I may return any title within 10 days and receive a full credit. I may cancel this subscription at any time without obligation by simply writing "Canceled" on any invoice and mailing it to Timeless Romance. There is no minimum number of books to purchase.

NAME		
ADDRESS		
CITY	STATE	ZIP
TELEPHONE		
SIGNATURE		

(If under 18, parent or guardian must sign. Program, price, terms, and conditions subject to cancellation and change. Orders subject to acceptance by HarperMonogram.)

With a sigh and a last pat, Gillian released her aunt then sat back against the cushions. "If there is, he has not presented himself, and I have almost run out of time."

Augusta smiled. "I know the ball will yield some-one. I was most particular about the men I invited," she said confidently.

There were two brief, impatient taps at the door; then it opened. An unsmiling Iolar regarded them from the doorway.

"Have ye ladies begun yer packing? The harvest is tomorrow, and the ball the night after."

An increasingly familiar vibration rushed through Gillian. The intensifying awareness she had of this man never failed to disturb her. To cover her agita-tion, she spoke sharply. "A fact of which we are well aware, Lord Iolar. After all, you have reminded us almost hourly for over a week."

Dark cinnamon-bronze eyebrows lowered. "I think ye exaggerate, madam."

"Ha! If I hear one more time when we are going to leave for Scotland I believe I shall go mad."

Augusta stood and swept out the door. "If you will excuse me."

Gillian barely heeded her aunt's defection. Iolar seemed to notice not at all, merely stepping aside for her to pass, his gaze still locked with Gillian's.

" 'Tis only that I've seen no evidence of yer makin' ready for the journey," he said, his deep voice rolling around her, touching her like warm silk.

As she struggled against its pull she rose slowly from the settee. "I hope, sir, that you have not tres-passed into the sanctity of my boudoir."

His eyes widened. "Sanctity of yer—" They narrowed. "Ye sound as if ye might have something to hide in yer . . . *boudoir*."

She sniffed in what she hoped sounded like disdain. "Certainly not. *Some* of us are above reproach." The words slipped out before she could stop them.

Iolar stiffened. "And what do ye mean by that?" he said, his tone as deadly as a naked rapier.

Horrified at her carelessness, Gillian clung despairingly to her pose. She suspected any attempt to temporize would meet with failure. This man was spoiling for a fight.

She straightened her shoulders. "What do you *suppose* I mean?"

He stood several feet away, yet his presence seemed to cast a net about her that held her helpless in his thrall. Green eyes darkened to the wintry cast of a storm-ravaged sea. She felt as if he were trying to strip away her protective layers, her dearly constructed armor, to look deep into her thoughts, her heart, her very soul.

Half afraid of what he might find, more afraid of what she would discover if she dared to look, Gillian broke free of his silent hold. She tried to appear unconcerned as she picked up her cup and took a sip of cold tea, but her hand trembled.

His mouth hardened into a grim line. "Ye think me a black-hearted bastard."

She almost dropped her cup. Quickly she set it down. In the heavy silence of the drawing room, it clattered loudly against the china saucer. "You are quite wrong, sir," she snapped. "I meant no such thing." Certainly she would never say it.

In an instant he was across the room. He grasped her upper arms in his hands, and she felt the steel in their sinews. "Liar!" The word struck her like a lash. "I thought ye might be different, but ye're not. Ye're like all the rest."

She heard a sobbing breath and realized it was her own. The fire of his pain seared her.

"*I am a man of honor*! Ne'er once have I told ye false! Can ye say the same to me?" Now his heaving breath mingled with hers.

Suddenly he released her, as if contact with her might contaminate him. "So ready to believe the worst of me." He stalked to the door, where he turned back to face her.

"Ye believe me to be a bastard and the devil to boot, so I make ye this promise, Lady Gillian—I shall not disappoint ye."

Gillian stared at the empty doorway where Iolar had just stood. Her chest felt tight with her rioting emotions.

She knew she should be trembling with fear that he would carry out his promise. The small sampling of his wrath she'd just received, coupled with the knowledge of what lengths the man could go to exact revenge, would have had any intelligent woman quaking in her shoes or running for safety. There was no denying that she was afraid. The man was dangerous.

But more than his rage, she'd felt Iolar's pain. It had blazed through him, into her, with a force that stole her breath. Tears gathered in Gillian's eyes. She ached for him. Had the world wronged Iolar in blaming him for the destruction of his father's home and lands? Worse, had she?

Or had the pain she'd experienced with him been remorse over what he'd done?

She wiped her eyes with the heels of her hands and drew in a long, steadying breath. Then she rolled her shoulders back. There was much to be done to ready Treymoor for harvest day tomorrow, the ball the following night, and her departure three days away. Also, she reminded herself, there was her lesson with Zerrin tonight. She'd tried to persuade her tutor to postpone instruction for a while, but Zerrin had been adamant. This had been Gillian's father's wish. Besides, Zerrin had said implacably, Gillian's acquired knowledge would soon prove important.

As Gillian hurried down the hall to compare notes with Mrs. Withecombe regarding the preparation of food and drink for the workers in the fields tomorrow and the subsequent harvest feast, her stomach clenched at the thought of leaving her home, friends, and family for the first time in her life. They needed her! She pushed open the door into the kitchen. The sweaty faces that turned toward her broke into smiles of greeting, and Gillian felt her heart lift. Oh, how she needed them too!

After locating Mrs. Withecombe and finding everything in that lady's domain in hand, she sought out Odgers, who was delighted with the prospect of having duties as a valet. While many of the gentlemen guests would bring their own men, some would not.

"And are you ready for our journey north?" she asked. Odgers would be accompanying them. Pym and Jenkins would be required at Treymoor.

"That I am, m'lady. 'Twill be an adventure."

She managed a smile. *She* certainly did not see being dragged off to a remote corner of Scotland as an adventure.

"Not meaning to talk out of turn," he said, "but your aunt, she's a poor traveler. Complains and moans as long as she's on the move. You might consider bringing along a nip of strong spirits. For nerves, you understand."

"My aunt seldom imbibes strong spirits, Odgers."

Odgers shook his head. "The spirits is for *our* nerves, not hers."

"Oh, dear."

"As I say, Lady Augusta makes a sorry traveler."

Gillian bit her lip. "Please make certain that Atlanta and a horse for my aunt accompany the carriage. We may wish to ride outside sometimes. For the sunshine and fresh air, you understand."

Odgers's eyes twinkled. "Right you are, m'lady."

A few minutes later, as she made her way toward the stables to check on their readiness to receive the horses and vehicles of their guests, Sammy Blenkin caught up with her, out of breath.

"I've delivered all your messages, m'lady," he told her eagerly.

She smiled at him and reached out to smooth back his silky blond hair. "Treymoor is fortunate to have such an excellent page."

Sammy beamed proudly. "What can I do now?"

"Ask Mrs. Withecombe if you may help her. She is excessively busy now and will likely find your aid most beneficial."

He ran off to find Mrs. Withecombe, and Gillian watched him until he turned the corner. She hoped her son would be as sweet-natured as Sammy. She sighed. First must come a husband.

She had told Maynard she would be going to Scotland and did not know when she'd return, hoping to prompt a proposal from him. None had been forthcoming.

Suddenly she felt tired, as if the weight on her shoulders was growing too great to support much longer. The only hope left to her was the ball. She must depend upon a stranger to ask for her hand.

Dinner was served before the usual hour, to allow everyone to complete their work and retire early in preparation for harvest day. Conversation was subdued, which Gillian attributed to fatigue.

Still embarrassed and confused over her encounter with Iolar, she directed her attention to her aunt, to Hugh, and to Ian, who had just returned from wherever his business had taken him.

Tonight desert was simple, a variety of fruits and cheeses. As soon as it was served, Jenkins trundled the dirty dishes from the first courses of the meal away to the scullery.

"Are ye expectin' many people to attend the ball, Lady Gillian?" Iolar asked politely, addressing her directly for the first time since that morning.

"My aunt is in charge of the guest list," she said, looking to one side of his face.

"There is bound to be quite a crush," Augusta informed him. "There always is."

"I see. And do ye always attend to social matters for yer niece, Augusta?"

Now he had them both trapped, Gillian thought. A glance at Augusta's expression assured her that her aunt would exercise caution.

"Not always. As far as social gatherings go, Gillian is quite capable to arranging them. But we lead a relatively quiet life here in the country. Not like the whirl I imagine you're used to, living in Edinburgh as you do." Not from Augusta would he learn that Gillian rarely had a chaperone.

Gillian ventured a surreptitious glance at Iolar through her lashes and saw his mouth move slowly into a smile. She didn't dare meet his eyes, unwilling to chance one of those breath-stealing, heart-stopping meetings of gazes that seemed to happen between them. Such occurrences always unsettled her. She found them exceedingly . . . disturbing.

"I suppose yer keepin' to yerselves explains why the neighbors we called on claimed not to have seen ye in a goodly while," he said to Gillian.

She could feel his eyes upon her and knew she could no longer avoid them. If naught else, it was a matter of pride. She would not back down to this man. But even as she raised her lashes a voice in her mind kept asking, Have I wronged him? Might Iolar be the target of some evil-tongued gossip?

As her gaze met his and awareness of him quaked through every fiber of her body, she felt certain this man could be no one's pawn. As she stared into his eyes, she thought no person would dare to cross him. No sane person. She was not feeling particularly sane at this moment.

Time slowed. Everything around them seemed to recede into the distance and fade away. There was only Iolar, only the heat of him, only the longing in his sea-storm eyes, only the fierce beauty of his hard-planed face. Only Iolar.

Dimly she heard a voice. It spoke again, more insistently this time. Something cool touched her wrist.

"Gillian, dear, we really must leave the gentlemen to their port and their conversation," Augusta persisted. This time she thumped Gillian's wrist with her closed fan. The mother-of-pearl sticks clicked faintly.

Gillian blinked. "Oh. Yes. Yes, of course." Mortified heat rushed to her face as she realized what she'd been doing. She discovered Iolar had laid his fingertips over hers, where they'd rested on the table. Quietly he withdrew his hand. She fumbled with her fan.

"I quite believe my niece has consumed too much claret," Augusta confided laughingly to Hugh and Ian, who looked concerned. "No head for spirits, I'm afraid." As she stood, she directed a covert glare at Gillian and with a slight motion of her head indicated that they both should leave the room immediately.

"'Tis an admirable thing in a lady," Hugh said gallantly, as the men rose to their feet.

Augusta smiled at Hugh and Ian, standing across the table from her. "Good night, gentlemen. I believe we should retire for the evening. Tomorrow will be a strenuous day. Rest well." The cousins wished her and Gillian a pleasant sleep. She turned to direct a pointed look at Iolar. "Good night, Calum."

He gracefully inclined his head, his expression unreadable. "A peaceful rest to ye both."

Gillian was eager to escape, and every step of their dignified walk from the long dining room seemed to drag. Finally, they passed through the doorway into the hall.

When they were out of sight and hearing of the men, Augusta stopped abruptly. "What were you doing back there? I thought you'd been seized by a fit and were unable to move or hear."

Gillian stared down at the fan she held. "I apologize, Aunt Augusta. I have disgraced myself."

"Nothing of the kind. I was simply worried. I've never seen you do that."

"I should hope not! This has never happened before."

"Most unfortunate, dear. A lovely girl like you should have stared deeply into many a handsome man's eyes by now."

"By now," Gillian echoed bitterly. "You mean now that I'm an . . . an old maid." She choked out the last two hated words.

"Quite. But not for long," August said firmly, as she placed her arm around Gillian's waist and guided her down the dimly illuminated hall. The scents of candle wax and rose-petal potpourri mingled in the air. The towering, shadowed ceilings and marble floors echoed Gillian's and her aunt's steps and turned their words into a murmurous river of whispers.

"It is unfortunate that this particular handsome man is unsuitable," Augusta said.

Gillian searched her aunt's face. "Oh, but are you

certain? I know I heard it from a sheep trader I trust, but perhaps he was mistaken. What if Iolar is, in truth, innocent? How can we be certain he is guilty of such a terrible thing?"

Augusta smiled sadly and patted Gillian's waist. "I had it from a reliable authority—Fanny Kilvington. The lady is no gossip, I assure you."

"But did she actually *see* that Iolar Glen has been left devastated? Perhaps it's all just a wicked rumor started by an enemy. You know the damage a well-placed word can do to a reputation."

"There is more than just a word damaging Calum MacFuaran. Did you know he is not accepted in the better houses in London?"

Gillian frowned as they climbed the curved staircase. It hurt her to think he might have been shunned over something as elusive and unprovable as gossip. "Would they close their doors to him over hearsay?"

"There are some who might, some who are so concerned with their so-called good names that they reject on the least evidence. But there are others who are more just."

"Like your friend Fanny Kilvington?"

"And her husband." At the top of the stairs, Augusta turned to Gillian and clasped both of her hands between her own. "Dearest niece, Michael Kilvington has seen Iolar Glen and the castle with his own eyes. He went there to look over some sheep—which turned out to be wretched creatures indeed. The valley was in terrible condition. The beasts were being sold off. Crofters and tacksmen were being evicted daily, and the name of Calum

MacFuaran was a curse upon their lips." Augusta shook her head. "What your guardian has done to that estate is a sin against God, man, and animal. What his father did to him was terrible, but this is unforgivable."

Gillian could not give up yet. "How would he have managed to do this?" Mr. Foley, the sheep trader, had told her that Calum had the steward under his thumb. Blackmail. But she hoped her aunt's report would differ, thereby casting doubt on *all* reports.

"Michael said he'd been told that Calum was blackmailing the steward."

A tight knot grew in Gillian's chest. "How long"—she wet her lips—"how long ago did your friend's husband see Iolar Glen?"

Augusta thought a moment. "Almost a year."

Gillian's last hope shattered. Iolar had told her that he'd only learned of both his uncle's and his father's deaths in India a few days before he'd received her father's letter appointing him her guardian. It seemed the rumors were all horribly true. Calum MacFuaran had exacted his revenge on his father while that man was still alive. Iolar Glen had been viciously stripped. The act had, perhaps, brought considerable satisfaction to a man who had been cast out of his home as a bastard, but in the process of obtaining that eye-for-an-eye price, harm had been done to innocents. The people of Iolar Glen had suffered, as had the animals and the land itself.

Knowing this, Gillian saw his recalling the beauty of that valley as darkly sinister, a Visigoth recounting the grandeur of Rome. Well, that Scottish Visigoth would never get his hands on *her* Rome, even if it meant proposing to Maynard herself!

Renewed determination swelled within her, mingled with fear—fear of failure, fear of being caught. But, like the lingering fragrance of a trampled flower, a wistful yearning haunted her.

Gillian shook her head. People she loved, people who had put themselves at risk for her, needed her protection. She would not fail them. She must remember: Calum MacFuaran was a dangerous man.

Augusta walked with Gillian to the door of her chamber. "Good night, Gillian, my dear. You are very brave. Your mother would have been proud of you."

Gillian embraced her aunt. "Thank you, Aunt Augusta. For coming when I asked, for your help with the ball, for . . . for everything."

Augusta smiled and kissed Gillian's cheek. "Sleep well." She turned and left, her petticoat and overskirt rustling.

Gillian opened the door of her chamber and stepped inside to find the room illuminated with myriad tiny candles. Flames danced inside small glass bowls specifically designed for the purpose of holding a lighted, perfumed candle. The air in the room was redolent with the scents of gardenia, frangipani, and cedarwood.

"We must not forget your lesson," Zerrin said softly.

"I have not."

Zerrin helped Gillian undress. "We will take only a little time tonight. You must be rested for tomorrow.

Perhaps there will be more time when we arrive in Scotland."

Gillian waited for Zerrin to unfasten the hooks in back that she could not reach. "I pray I can prevent us from going to Scotland, Zerrin, for once we are there I may never find a husband. I will propose to Maynard if I must."

Zerrin's fingers hesitated, then continued with their work. "We shall hope for better from the gentlemen the Lady Augusta invites." Under her veil, she wrinkled her nose as she made a face. "Your Maynard, he is not a man of passion. He fears the shadow of his mother."

"Well, it *is* rather a lengthy shadow." It seemed to follow Maynard wherever he went.

"A she-dragon, that one."

After Gillian pulled the white linen night shift over her head, Zerrin went to the trunk at the foot of the bed and lifted out a small carved harp. Years ago, Zerrin had settled on this portable harp as the instrument Gillian would learn to play. It mattered not one whit to her that Gillian already knew how to play the harpsichord. Zerrin saw that as useful only for English social gatherings. Instead, searching for a Western musical instrument of a more intimate nature, she had been delighted when she heard the music of this harp and located a teacher.

By now Gillian no longer needed an instructor. She loved this sweet-toned harp. Plucking the strings sent a sensual vibration through her that melded with her pleasure in the ethereal sound that issued forth. Faerie music, she thought, as she caressed first the smooth walnut, then the intricately carved knots and herons. It was an old harp, lovingly cared for by its previous owners and by Gillian.

Zerrin walked across the room and regarded Gillian with the critical eye of a teacher. "Play for me the 'Greensleeves'."

Gillian complied, pouring her feelings into the music of spurned love. She breathed in the heady perfume that surrounded her. Pinpoint flames reflected subtly in the mellow gloss of the harp's wood. When the last echoes of the lament hung on the air, her fingertips tingled.

It had been weeks since she'd played. She waited for Zerrin's pronouncement.

"Good. Very good, my lady sister," Zerrin finally said. "I had feared you would forget. But there is in your playing tonight a quality I have never heard before. Your audience will be pleased when the time comes."

"Thank you, Zerrin."

"There are no new lessons, only, perhaps, reviews. But for now such things must wait." Zerrin walked around the room, blowing out candles. Gillian returned the harp to the trunk and helped Zerrin until only two lighted candles remained. One of these Zerrin took for herself. The flame reflected in the liquid darkness of her eyes.

"Sleep well, lady sister. You will need all your strength for tomorrow."

12

"*Hi-ho, Mable, you must* go faster!" Gillian laughed as she called to the old horse. The creaking wagon was loaded with kegs of ale, crocks of porridge, smoked hams, loaves of freshly baked bread, and homemade cheeses. "Come along, girl, we can't have our workers hungry."

Zerrin, who sat next to her on the seat of the roughly built wagon, joined in her laughter, and Gillian's spirits lifted even higher. On the horizon, the sky glowed faint with pink and gold and gray. Morning birds flitted black against the still-dark sky. Larks warbled their song, and roosters from every farm around heralded the new day.

Mable plodded on at her steady pace, the same pace the sturdy mare had kept last year, the year before, and years before that. Gillian had adorned Mable's mane with a chain of late-summer daisies, and Zerrin had woven circlets of the flowers for Gillian and herself to wear in their hair. They had both donned their work clothes and now drove the wagon that carried breakfast for the workers, who would spend the day going from field to field, harvesting the oats until everyone's crop was in, tenant and landlord alike.

They arrived at the meeting place—a fallow field—to find the cooking fire already going. Quickly Gillian and Zerrin poured the porridge into the heavy iron pots waiting to heat the cereal. Other women, wives and daughters of the tenants, greeted them, adding their specialties of preserved fruits and rich butter to what the great house provided. In minutes they were all chattering and laughing as they worked together to slice the hams, cheeses, and loaves of bread. They worked on planks set across trestles, which would also, when they were finished, serve as sideboards for serving the food.

As the sun rose, men began to arrive, carrying their scythes and rakes. The women dished out the hearty breakfast to those moving through the line that formed. There was much good-natured teasing and flirting. Both men and women speculated on the prospects of the day. Mild weather had combined with carefully tended soil and hard work to yield a rich abundance of oats.

"It looks as if the luck of Treymoor's lady is workin'," said a deep voice with a soft Scottish burr behind Gillian.

Surprised, she turned away from her place at the serving board to find Iolar holding a wooden plate heaped with healthy portions of breakfast in one hand and a mug of ale in the other. He was dressed like most of the other men, in a rough-spun linen shirt and breeches of everlasting. Only he did not look like any of the others. His height and rare good looks set him apart.

"A pleasant morn to you, Lord Iolar," she said politely. "I had not expected to see you here."

He arched an eyebrow. "Did ye think the Scots would no do their fair share o' the work, then?"

A quick glance told Gillian that another woman had already taken her place serving, so she started down the line, collecting empty pitchers and refilling them from a keg. "Truly," she said, "I have not thought on it at all."

"Well, my cousins and I are all here, ready, able, and willing to swing a scythe or tie a bundle."

"'Tis William's place to say," Gillian fibbed, trying hard to keep her gaze from wandering to his broad shoulders. With his long muscular arms, Iolar would be an asset with a scythe. She'd felt those arms around her and could testify to their strength.

Quickly she turned her thoughts in another direction.

"Have you spoken to William?" For this harvest, with outsiders present, she had put her steward in charge of the crews. The tenants knew the situation and played their parts. William was a competent man, one, who, if she could not find a husband by tomorrow night, could take care of Treymoor in the full capacity of his office. The thought of turning over the reins of this estate to someone else made Gillian's stomach tighten into a knot.

"Aye, we talked yesterday." Iolar raised the mug to

his lips, and Gillian watched his throat work as he swallowed. The ordinary yet somehow sensual movement reached into her and trapped her breath. With a will, she tore her gaze away, paying close if unnecessary attention to every detail of filling the ale pitchers.

"He asked us to wield scythes." He smiled. "And what will ye be doin'?"

"I'll bundle," she replied. The sheaves would then be stacked in the field to dry.

"So the lady works in the fields as well?" His smile was infectious.

"Och, aye," she said, with a smile of her own.

He laughed. "Ye sound like a true Scots lassie."

"I do?"

"Well," he admitted, "perhaps more like an English lassie tryin' to talk like a Scot, but I'll wager a guinea that no one here would know the difference."

Now she laughed. "Your money is safe, Lord Iolar. There's not a soul here, save Zerrin, William, and Ralph Scarth, who were not born and bred to this land."

"Why do you do that?" he asked.

"Do what?"

"Insist on calling me 'Lord Iolar'."

She stared at him, hating the hot blush that moved up her face. "Because it is proper."

"Propriety has been served. Even yer auntie now addresses me by my Christian name, as she does my cousins."

Her mind raced, seeking another excuse. "I'm merely showing you respect."

"Nay, lass, I think not."

She snatched up two filled pitchers and marched them over to the board where she had removed the empty ones. Gillian knew why she continued to use his title. The formality encouraged remoteness. Speaking his Christian name demolished that much-needed distance.

As she considered this, Gillian saw for the first time that by continuing to insist on addressing him by his title she might be issuing an insult. One could easily interpret the continuing formality as her lack of faith in her guardian or, worse, her dislike of him. It could open him to ridicule.

She smiled bitterly. While she might be willing to lie to him, to cheat and steal from him, she flinched at the thought of hurting him. Even though it seemed clear that the man had savaged his father's estate with no thought to the people living there, there was still a tiny spark of doubt in her. She'd spent time with this man. They shared a roof and table. She could easily believe that he was dangerous—but not vicious.

She returned to the place where he'd been standing, only to find he had finished his meal and was taking the empty plate over to the pile that would be hauled to the scullery at the house. Noon meal would not require plates, but the feast would.

Gillian heard him thank the goodwives overseeing that chore for the delicious meal. Then, with a smile, he added something else she couldn't quite hear, but the women's pleased laughter was entirely audible. Gillian frowned and turned away, to discover Hugh leaning against the side of the wagon, almost directly in her path.

"Dinna be impatient with him, lass."

"I cannot understand him," she admitted.

Hugh smiled, and she realized she hadn't seen this quiet man smile much, except perhaps when her aunt was nearby. Gillian had seldom spoken with him, but she'd always found merit in his infrequent observations on life and human nature.

"Och, ye're not alone in that," he said. "But he's had to keep his own counsel from an early age, do ye see? His life's been a rare hard one. Hardship shapes men. Some are broken and become tools for others to use as they please. Some rear up and fight back. They take their lashes with a stiff jaw and never cry for mercy. I leave it to ye to determine which is Calum."

Gillian couldn't imagine the stiff-jawed Lord of Iolar ever being a pawn. But what she said was, "Thank you for offering your help today, Mr. Drummond. We always welcome extra hands at harvesttime."

"Hugh," he corrected. "As little as ye like it, lass, it seems as if we're fated to spend time in the same house. 'Tis not the Scots way to drape ourselves in formality—unless, of course, it serves our purpose." He lifted an eyebrow. "Does it serve *yer* purpose?"

Gillian managed a smile. He couldn't know. He was fishing. Wasn't he?

"What purpose would that be, Mr. Drum—" She caught herself. "Hugh?"

"'Tis for ye to say."

"Then I say this. Until you and your cousins arrived at Treymoor, I had never heard of you. I do not know why Papa said naught to me of your cousin, I can only assume—"

"Calum. My cousin's name is Calum."

"—that he planned to tell me, but that the message was lost in the haste of his departure." She tried not to think of the silent stone sarcophagus.

"Aye, well, if it lightens yer mind any, yer father's letter appointin' Lord Iolar yer guardian came as a surprise to Calum."

An unwelcome surprise, Gillian thought. She sighed. "I regret Lord Iolar—I mean Calum—had to postpone his return to Iolar Glen." Though, privately, she couldn't understand why he wanted to go back. Was it a matter of triumph? Self-punishment?

William Harland leapt up onto the bed of one of the wagons. "To harvest!" he shouted.

The time-honored response of the workers roared in the morning air. "To harvest!"

Men took up their scythes and rakes and piled into the waiting wagons, helping the women up alongside them.

Zerrin climbed onto the wagon bearing the empty food vessels and dirty plates and mugs. She waved before she clucked to Mable, and the old horse started back toward the house.

Gillian enjoyed the talk and laughter on the wagon around her. Through the years these people had been her friends and staunch allies.

When the drivers brought the horses to a halt, everyone clambered down from the wagons and took their places. The men with the scythes formed two lines, the spacing of the workers staggered.

The first line went into action, keeping far enough apart to avoid harming one another with their deadly blades. They moved with the rhythm and precision of a well-made clock as they sliced through the sea of golden stems. Behind them, the second line started. After these men had swept their scythes through the rows of oats left behind, the rakers and gatherers began their work.

Along with several other women, Gillian tied the raked piles into neat sheaves and stacked them. The summer sun climbed higher. When they finished one field, they went on to the next. Gillian's hands were raw and bleeding by the noon meal break.

"Here, what's this now?" John Varley exclaimed as he scooped her hands into his weathered ones. "You promised to wear gloves," he scolded. "We can't have our mistress of the manor mistreating her hands. 'Tis how you tell a lady, you know: by her hands." He clucked disapprovingly.

"I know I promised, but gloves are too awkward. They make it difficult to tie the sheaves and they slow me down." She tried to win her hands back from his hold, so everyone couldn't see them.

A bigger hand caught her by the wrist. "What is this?" her guardian demanded, scowling as he examined the hand she tried to close. " 'Tis foolishness," he said. "Ye injure yerself needlessly."

She tried to close her hands, tried to tug them from his unrelenting grip. "I want to work. It is my place," she said, lifting her chin.

By now several people had gathered. She heard more tongues clucking at the condition of her hands, but she also saw ominous looks directed toward Iolar, who still had not released her.

"I dinna say ye could no work, Gillian. I said only that ye're foolish for abusing yer hands like this."

With his free hand, he reached up and whipped off the kerchief he wore around his neck like most of the other men, then refolded it to expose a clean white side. This he wound around her palm, the worst part of her injury.

Ian, who stood behind at his shoulder, immediately handed over his own kerchief, and his bossy cousin wrapped her other hand, which Varley released for the purpose. A murmur of approval went through the now-larger cluster of workers.

"This will allow ye to work, if ye wish it. Ye can move yer fingers better than ye can in gloves, but the rest is protected." Her guardian looked down, and their eyes met.

Her stomach fluttered. "Thank you . . . Calum."

He smiled. Despite the sweat and the field dirt that etched his face, and the bits of leaf and stem caught in his hair, his warrior beauty stole her breath.

Calum gazed at her. Slowly his smile faded. "Ye're verra welcome, Gillian."

She found herself caught in a green net that pulled her through a light-and-shadow tumble of emotions.

"Let's eat," Ian said.

Calum turned aside to his cousin and spoke to him in a low voice. Ian nodded once. When he noticed Gillian watching them, he gave her a mischievous wink. Then he strode off through the throng of workers.

"Where is he going?" she asked, as Calum guided her over to the line waiting to be served.

"An errand."

"I must help serve," she said, easing away from his disturbing proximity.

Gently, he caught her arm and pulled her back. "Let these other women do it. They are no workin' in the fields as ye are. Ye need to rest a bit if ye plan to finish out the day bundlin'."

The farmer in line in front of them turned around. "He's right, your ladyship. You need to have a care for yourself."

"Ye've already done more than any other lady of the manor would do," Calum said, and several people around them nodded agreement.

"But what about you?" Gillian asked. "You've been wielding a scythe all morning, which I know is most strenuous." A few understanding chuckles and nods down through the line showed the general agreement. Men, she noted, who had been cutting oats.

"Och, dinna fash yerself over me, lass. I'm used to hard labor."

The moment he'd walked into the library at Treymoor, Gillian had noticed that his body was in splendid form, but she had supposed he kept it that way through gentlemanly sports. "May one ask the nature of this hard labor?"

All noise seemed to cease, as if everyone present in the clearing awaited his answer.

Ruddy color crept under the bronze of his high cheekbones. "I have no always been a lord, ye ken. I've labored for my bread."

Out of the corner of her eye, Gillian saw heads nod. "Yes, but what kind—"

"Ships," he said shortly. "I worked aboard ships.

One thing led to another, and today I am a trader, a merchant. For the last few years, the only ships I've worked on have been my own."

Apparently he felt disinclined to elaborate on precisely what "one thing led to another." Still, she'd learned more about him in the last five minutes than she'd learned since he had arrived at Treymoor.

"A trader with his own ships," she said, genuinely impressed. "I had no idea." She sensed those around them returning to their own conversations as the muted babble of voices resumed.

"Ye never inquired."

She looked away. In the near distance stood the great house of Treymoor. She loved the patina of years that softened the gray color of the stone. Each familiar column, pediment, and window was dear to her. How could she bear the loss if this man took Treymoor from her? "I do not think I wanted to know," she said softly.

She turned back to find him studying her. Then, without a word, he lifted his gaze over her head, viewing the line in front of him. She felt as if a door had been closed, shutting her out.

To her consternation, the feeling hurt. Dear Lord, when had Calum acquired the power to hurt her? When had she given him the power?

Perhaps, she thought, remembering the touch of his fingertips at the dinner table last night, just perhaps that power was a double-edged sword. She curled her tender hands around Calum's kerchief.

They completed their trip through the line in silence and went their separate ways.

She was just finishing the last bite when she

looked up from where she was sitting to see Mrs. Withecombe marching toward her, armed with what Gillian knew to be the housekeeper's box of remedies.

"Hello, Mrs. Withecombe, I didn't expect to see—"

"You took off your gloves," the older woman observed crisply, setting down the brass-latched wooden box and settling on the ground next to Gillian. "We've spoken of this before, have we not?" She reached for Gillian's hands, examining them with a concerned frown.

"Yes, Mrs. Withecombe," Gillian said meekly. As the older woman unwound the kerchiefs, Gillian caught sight of Ian, standing in the last remnant of the line to be served. He grinned at her, and she realized what had happened.

Calum had sent Ian for Mrs. Withecombe.

Gillian tried to spot Calum, but to no avail. A group of workers who had finished their meal stood in front of her, blocking her view.

"Hold still, child," the housekeeper scolded. "Just look at your hands. How will you dance tomorrow night?"

"The damage looks much worse than it truly is."

Mrs. Withecombe swabbed the lacerations with a moist piece of linen. Instinctively, Gillian jerked away from the sharp sting.

"Ow! What have you on that cloth, lye?"

"Och, buck up, lass," Ian said as he sat down cross-legged next to her. "Ye dinna want yer people to think ye're a wean, now, do ye?"

She didn't miss the twinkle in his eyes. "Informer," she accused. "Calum sent you, didn't he?"

"Aye, he did," Ian said. "Someone had to show some sense."

"Oh, that's right. Stand up for him. Well, I'll have you to know that the people of Treymoor know I am not a wean—whatever *that* is."

"A babe," Mrs. Withecombe translated. She opened a jar and began applying a pale gold ointment to the cleaned wounds.

"A babe!" Gillian glared at him indignantly. "Anyone can see I'm no babe. *Ow!*"

Mrs. Withecombe proceeded in her efficient no-nonsense way to wrap Gillian's hands with clean linen strips, leaving the thumbs and fingers free.

"I cannot cover the fingers if you insist on using them, but as soon as you have bundled the last sheaf, Mr. Gunn will attend again to your hands, and your fingers also." She cast a stern eye on Ian. "Did you take notice of what I did, so that you may treat her?"

Ian's eyes twinkled. "Aye, Mrs. Withecombe," he said with false meekness, and as Mrs. Withecombe repacked her box of medicinals, Gillian thought she saw the corners of the housekeeper's lips twitch.

"I'll leave sufficient supplies with Mrs. Smith," Mrs. Withecombe said. "She will return to help with the feast."

"Feast?" Ian asked, instantly alert.

"After the harvest there is a feast," Gillian said, wondering how a man so interested in food remained so trim.

Ian stood and, with helping hands, assisted the ladies to their feet. "What are we standin' about for, then? There's work to be done."

It was then that Gillian noticed the workers heading toward the wagons. "Thank you, Mrs. Withecombe, for coming all the way out here. I know you are busy with preparations for the feast and the ball." The small speech sounded stilted to even Gillian's ears. Ordinarily, she would have hugged her dear friend and substitute mother, but today the Scots were present, so she continued the fiction of being the uninterested daughter of the lord, though it was becoming more and more difficult. Before, she'd only had to keep up the act for a day, two at most, but she'd been doing it for two weeks, now, and she felt the strain like tightly drawn harp strings strung through her shoulders.

" 'Twas my pleasure, Lady Gillian," Mrs. Withecombe said. Gillian almost expected her to curtsey. The housekeeper turned and strode to a dog cart hitched to a pony that stood munching grass.

Ian placed his hand at the small of Gillian's back and nudged her into motion. "Come, Gillian, or we'll be left behind."

All of the wagons but one had already left. Ian boosted her to a strong pair of hands that caught her about her waist and lifted her onto the crowded bed.

Gillian looked up to find Calum holding her. Her breath stopped as the potency of his presence closed around her. He smelled of fresh-cut oats, warm earth, and musky male sweat. His shoulders seemed impossibly broad under the loose linen shirt. She hardly noticed Ian hoist himself up beside her feet.

The wagon jerked as the horses began the trip to the next field. Calum caught her shoulders to keep her from tumbling to the ground. His palms and fingers seemed to sear through the flimsy cloth of her bodice.

She labored to draw breath into her lungs. Slowly, inexorably, she felt her gaze drawn up to his.

Sunlight shone on thick cinnamon-gold lashes and turned the color of his eyes lighter then usual, but as she watched, the crystal green grew darker, more opaque. From the edges of her vision, she saw his nostrils flare. A faint tremor went through his fingers, and for a moment suspended in time she thought he might never let her go. In that same moment, she hoped he would not.

Then he looked away. "Make way," he called, and eased her back into the greater safety of the wagon, away from the edge.

She tried to glimpse him over her shoulder, but those who had made way for her returned to their places, blocking her view. The tenants cheerfully included her in their conversation, forcing her to refocus her attention.

When they reached the new field, many hands helped her off the wagon, as if she were incapable of getting down by herself, and she smiled and thanked them all. She walked to where the women were standing, waiting to start their work.

The men with scythes spread out and went into motion. Calum and Ian worked next to each other, but her eyes were only for Calum. The billowing sleeves of his rough-spun shirt, now stained by dirt and grass, had been rolled up well above his elbows, revealing his long muscular arms. Sinews rippled under golden sun-bronzed skin with every rhythmic swing of the scythe. His height and power and grace marked him among the other men.

Gillian began gathering up the piles of mown oats, tying them into sheaves. Her hands smarted and the dressings caught on oats and stalks, but she persevered. Like the women with her, she moved swiftly and efficiently, years of experience guiding her hands. But every so often she found her gaze wandering back to Calum.

"He is the handsomest man I ever did see," Mary Scarth said. "Like a prince he is, or a king. Not like the other men."

"He's a lord," her sister Alice said. "O'course he ain't like other men."

"I seen lords afore," another woman, Jane Yarrow, said. "Didn't look nothing like Lord Iolar." She shook her head. "Too bad he's a Scotsman. Everyone knows you can't trust 'em."

Other women nodded sagely. "Savages, most of 'em," another woman stated.

"Too bad he's not English," Alice Varley said. "And honorable, of course. That would have made a good match for you, Lady Gillian. Oh, your babes would have been lovely."

There was a general murmuring of assent, and Gillian wished the earth would open up and swallow her. All these women were married, all had children, and most seemed generally content with their husbands. She had none of those things, but she did not want pity.

"Children make life bearable," Mary Scarth said. "They need you. They trust you."

Jane Yarrow chuckled. "They keep you awake at night and fret you near to death when they're sick or hurt."

"Which is almost always," Alice Varley said, her hands busy with their task.

"But they're worth it," Mary insisted.

Gillian thought that with a husband like the brutal shifty-eyed Scarth, Mary especially needed someone to love, someone who loved her.

But Gillian wanted more than that. She wanted the man of her dreams to sweep her away to his castle in the clouds, where he would love her, and cherish her, and not expect her to solve every problem by herself.

But unless that dream man arrived by tomorrow evening, she would have to make do with Maynard the Manageable . . . or worse.

13

Candles blazed in the grand saloon, where ladies and gentlemen, attired in glittering jewels and glimmering silks, danced, sipped wine, talked, and flirted.

Jenkins, outfitted in satin livery and powdered wig, stood at the saloon's entry door. A short plump man past his middle years walked into the cavernous room and told the footman his name. Without changing his impassive expression, Jenkins thumped his gold-topped staff three times and loudly announced, "His Grace, the Duke of Mulvern!"

Augusta, gorgeous in green satin and tissue of silver, her powdered wig flawlessly styled, flowed out of the crush to greet their noble guest. From her vantage point several feet away, Gillian couldn't hear what her aunt was saying to the duke, but from the way they were laughing and kissing cheeks, they must be old friends.

Old being the defining word.

The saloon was heavily populated by old men. Once again, her aunt had determined to have her own way. As she had told Gillian countless times, she was wiser in the ways of the social world than her niece. Gillian did not doubt that observation for a second. After all, she had never left the parish in her life, seldom even left Treymoor, while her aunt had been married, had traveled, and now moved among a circle that, while not the highest, at least nudged into rarified air. Perhaps that very air was responsible for Augusta's addled brains. Wasn't it abhorrent enough that Gillian must accept—no, desperately *need*—a husband who was even remotely suitable, so long as he was manageable? Must her aunt press senility into the bargain as well?

When she saw her aunt look around, as if seeking someone, Gillian knew only too well whom she sought. Quickly she stepped out of sight behind a man with an enormous wig. She snapped open her ivory-and-lace fan and hid her face behind it as much as she reasonably could.

"Lady Gillian?" a reed-thin elder standing on her other side inquired. The rice powder he wore emphasized every line and wrinkle in his face—which were considerable in number. He smiled, revealing several missing teeth. "I would know you anywhere from the description your most celebrated aunt gave."

Gillian began to fan herself, hoping to dissipate at least some of his foul breath. Where was Maynard? And her guardian and his cousins? If she must have a guardian, then let him guard her! For the past twenty minutes she had been eluding the paws of eager old men who clearly ignored the social imperative not to handle the hostess.

Thump-thump-thump, went Jenkins's staff. "Mrs. Josiah Leake and Mr. Maynard Leake!"

Relief lessened the tight knot in her stomach, and she managed a smile for the old gentleman next to her. "Yes, I am Lady Gillian. I do not believe we have been properly introduced." A ploy, one that had worked well these past twenty minutes, since the first guest had entered the saloon doors.

"Ah," he said. "True. Wait right here, my dear, and I shall retrieve Augusta to make the introductions."

Gillian graciously inclined her head, but as soon as he departed from her sight she headed in the opposite direction, threading her way through the press of guests, smiling and nodding, speaking a few words here and there with those she knew and those newly introduced. Finally she reached Maynard and his mother, whose greeting from her aunt, Gillian had observed, had been pleasant, if brief.

Maynard's face lit up. "Lady Gillian, you look radiant this eve. Er, that is to say, as radiant as ever. You *always* look radiant."

Gillian fluttered her fan slightly. "You are too kind, sir."

Mrs. Leake opened her own fan with a jerk of her wrist. "Were this *my* party, I would not allow some relation to greet my guests."

Gillian's fingers clenched on the ivory sticks. She forced herself to weigh the consequences of setting Mrs. Leake in her proper place here and now. Aunt Augusta was not merely "some relation." But then,

Caroline Leake was not just any old ill-tempered harridan.

Gillian knew that, if she were to attain her goal, she must exercise patience and subtlety. She resumed the slow movement of her fan. "My dear aunt also is hostess tonight, Mrs. Leake. Of course, I quite understand your confusion. Doubtless things were done differently in your day."

Mrs. Leake shot Gillian a black look but refrained from a retort, as her son moved to straighten her shawl.

"Do not distress yourself, Mother. I told you there would be a reason we were greeted by Lady Augusta. Lady Gillian would never do anything improper."

Mrs. Leake sniffed but offered nothing further on the subject. Her fan swept the air around them with near storm force.

"May I bring you a refreshment, Mother? Lady Gillian?" Maynard asked.

Coward, Gillian thought, frustrated with the prospect of being left with his petulant mother when it was Maynard with whom she needed time.

Just as Maynard fled toward the long damask-covered refreshment table, Gillian discerned a decided lull in the low roar of voices that filled the immense room. She turned in the same direction as those around her. A hush fell over the crowd.

There, standing on the threshold of the grand saloon, stood a tall man with red-gold hair, clad in full Scottish Highland splendor.

He wore a ruffled shirt of purest white and a waistcoat and coat of dark blue, over which was draped a brilliant plaid of red with dashes of blue, white, and yellow. His kilt was of the same tartan. Blue stockings came to his knees, and the buckles on his black shoes were polished silver. Behind him, wearing the same regalia in a different tartan, stood Hugh at one shoulder and Ian at the other.

Thump-thump-thump. "The Marquess of Iolar!"

Not one full year since the prohibition against the wearing of the plaid had been lifted, there stood her guardian on the threshold of an English gathering, fitted out in the barbaric splendor of a Highland lord.

Which, of course, he was.

But never had she expected him to flaunt his origins, and certainly not so outrageously. Did he have no care for what this might do to her chances of catching a husband? What man in his right mind would wish to approach this fierce Scottish peer to ask for her hand?

Even as she fretted and fumed, she found she could not take her eyes off him. If ever she had seen a prince, it was Calum. Arrogant and bold he might be, but no man of her acquaintance could compare to him. She doubted any man, anywhere, ever, could compare to Calum MacFuaran.

He seemed to be searching the silent crowd for someone. Then their eyes met, and the familiar shock vibrated through her body. Before Augusta could approach him, he descended the few steps into the room. Without taking his eyes from her, he passed through the throng. As if sensing in this Highland lord an unstoppable force, the crowd parted before him and he made his way directly to her.

Pride swelled in her, alien to all she knew she

should be feeling. His loyalty to his strange heritage
might enflame the anger of others, but she understood. In her life, heritage was the only thing her
parents had left her. She had known her mother for
such a short while, and her father almost not at all.
But together they had endowed her with a bloodline
that would never shame her and a place and people
who had filled her life with their love and caring. To
them she owed her loyalty. Without them she would
have been just another lost orphan.

And then Calum was standing before her, and the
rest of the world faded into nothing. His eyes roved
her hair and face and moved down over her gown.
"Ye are lovelier than ever," he said softly. "The pearl
of Yorkshire."

Gillian blushed with pleasure. "And you, my lord.
You are . . . magnificent."

With a graceful sweep, he gave her a bow that
Gillian was certain would have impressed the most
accomplished courtier. "My lady," he murmured.

Vaguely, she was aware that her guests had
returned to their own conversations.

"I have heard that each Scots family has its own
colors," she said, trying to maintain some semblance
of decorum. She fanned her face, hoping to cool its
warmth.

"Clan. Many clans have plaids of their own,
though many were wiped out by the English laws
enacted and enforced after the Forty-five."

"The Forty-five. Is that what the Scots call the
last Jacobite uprising?"

"Aye, 'twill do well enough now for an explana-
tion." His gaze moved over her face. "But for different

reasons, I dinna think I would ever have a right to wear this tartan. Most of the MacFuarans are gone now. Dead or scattered to the four winds." He smoothed a hand down a drape of his plaid with a kind of reverence. "There are still MacFuarans livin' in Iolar Glen."

"You are quite differently dressed from the other men tonight," she said, and felt foolish for making such an insipid observation.

He smiled. "I am that."

She moved her fan a little faster. "Few men here would look so . . . so"—manly? exciting?—"natural in a skirt."

Strong white teeth gleamed in a grin. "Are ye sayin' I should start wearin' women's clothin'?"

"No! I didn't mean—" Her fan blew a bit of powder off her wig, onto her bare shoulder. She snapped shut her fan, trying to ignore the powder, hoping Calum hadn't noticed. "To own the truth, I know the garment is not called a skirt at all, but the proper name escapes me." Much escaped her. Where had her sense flown?

"'Tis a kilt."

"Yes, quite. A kilt."

The musicians in the gallery struck up a new tune, and Calum took her hand and examined it. "Yer damage is no as bad as I'd feared." Then he bowed over her captive hand. She found herself hoping he would commit the faux pas of touching her with his lips. He did not.

"May I have this dance?" he asked.

"Yes." She held her breath when he set his fingers lightly on her shoulder. Against her bare skin, they were warm. With a small motion, he flicked away the dab of powder.

"My son has gone for our refreshments," Mrs. Leake said sharply.

Calum turned and looked at Mrs. Leake as if just noticing her for the first time. "Good evening, madam," he said politely, slightly inclining his head. "Ye look well."

"Thank you, Lord Iolar," the beldam said, lifting a hand to pat the back of her outmoded wig.

"Since your son has not returned yet, perhaps he will not mind my stealing Lady Gillian away for a dance."

"Well, I—"

"Excellent. Your servant, madam." He again inclined his head and then turned to escort Gillian to where the guests were taking their places for a popular country dance.

As she lined up with the women, facing the row of men, she felt a small stab of guilt. She didn't want Maynard having to stand around holding the beverage she had requested. On the other hand, he had left her stranded with his abominable mother.

She found it difficult to consider Maynard while she danced with Calum. He possessed such virility that she could think of nothing but him: of how tall he stood, of the breadth of his shoulders, the strength in his arms. Yet she knew his strength had been used to comfort her. He had held her with a tenderness that haunted her.

The dance ended too soon, and to her distress she was immediately claimed by a portly gentleman of perhaps fifty years, whom her aunt had introduced as the Earl of Fendleton. She looked at Calum in time to see Lydia Clough place her hand on his arm and speak to him.

As Gillian lined up with the other women, her aunt cheerfully excused her way into place next to her.

"Henry would make you a fine husband," Augusta said in a low voice, reminding Gillian of the true purpose for this gathering tonight.

Throughout the dance, the earl's face grew red with his exertion, but he never failed to smile when Gillian looked his way. Although his teeth were a trifle crooked, they were all in place and all his.

Her eyes combed the room for Calum. She finally saw him bending over that creature Lydia's pale hand. Seething, Gillian returned her attention to her dance partner with a vengeance.

He was richly dressed, and she could not help but notice that his clothes fit him properly, unlike so many of the other men she had met this evening, who had clearly gained weight since the last time they'd squeezed into their embroidered suits. She'd lost count of all the waistcoats that looked as if they would pop a button. The glint of small diamonds on Lord Fendleton's shoe buckles caught her eye. Hmm, she thought. How manageable was this fellow? Of course, he could not compare to Calum, but as much as she might wish it otherwise, Calum could not be the quarry in her husband hunt.

She fretted over Maynard's disapproval of dancing. What if she received no proposals? She would be faced with asking Maynard to marry her.

"Do you much enjoy dancing, Lord Fendleton?" she asked as they hooked arms and skipped in a circle.

"Don't do it as often as I used to, m'dear," he replied, "but if I had a pretty young thing like you as a partner, p'rhaps I would find more occasion."

She laughed prettily. "Oh, la, sir, you are a terrible tease."

He laughed too, a pleasant baritone sound, but she did not miss the glint in his eyes. "I own you make me feel like a lad. Dance with me again."

"I fear I cannot now, sir, for I have promised to take refreshment with another gentleman."

"Later, then," he persisted. "Soon."

"I look forward to it," she said. The music ended and she fluttered her fan in front of her face, ostensibly to cool her heated cheeks, but she saw that he caught the tiny flirtation by the faint widening of his smile.

She made her way back toward Maynard, who did indeed still hold her cup of punch. As ever, his mother was with him.

Gillian accepted the cup with a smile. "Thank you. I do hope you have not been waiting long."

"Dancing, I see," he said primly.

She sipped the milk punch, letting it slide slowly down her throat before she answered. Then she took a deep breath and called up her will to please.

"Yes," she said. "I have it on the best authority that dancing is excellent for the humors. The movement, you see."

"What authority?" Mrs. Leake asked suspiciously.

"A journal I read," she lied airily.

"Humph. Humors indeed. The only thing dancing is excellent for is bodily lust."

Maynard nodded solemnly.

"Ah, there you are, you naughty girl!"

Gillian turned to see the thin old fellow who'd gone off to find her aunt making his way through the crush, smiling his gaping smile, Augusta in tow.

"By the time I found Lady Augusta, you had gone. But I have found you again." He looked so pleased that Gillian felt a little guilty over her escape—an escape that had been only temporary.

Augusta made the introductions smoothly, including the Leakes. Mr. Nesling politely acknowledged them, then turned to Gillian and asked her to dance. Over his shoulder she saw her aunt nodding emphatically. Summoning a smile that she hoped looked more genuine than it felt, she accepted Mr. Nesling's invitation.

As they passed her aunt on the way to the dance area, Augusta whispered, "He owns several glass manufactures and numerous estates."

As Gillian and her partner executed the steps and turns of the dance, she listened to the story of his life: how his late wife had failed to bear him children and how he was certain a new, healthy young wife would correct that omission.

"You look healthy," Mr. Nesling observed.

Gillian thought she knew now how a cow on market day must feel. She curtsied, then rose and touched fingers with him as they moved in a small circle. "I am." Dear Lord, what had she done to deserve this?

He tweaked her waist.

"Oh!" she exclaimed in surprise, and when he cackled with glee, she slapped him sharply on the hand with her closed fan.

Mr. Nesling blinked in surprise. "That hurt," he complained. His expression changed to a sly smile. "I like a chit with spirit." The dance came to an end, and the other dancers wandered away. He looked her over boldly. "A good breeder, I'll be bound."

Gillian felt a presence close around her and knew who had arrived to stand just behind her before he spoke.

"Ye'll no be speakin' to Lady Gillian in such a manner. Not if ye enjoy breathin'."

Mr. Nesling went pale. He had to crane his head back to look up at Calum. "I meant no offense."

"Ye sounded damned offensive to *me*. If ye lay a hand on her again, ye'll have no more use for it, that I promise ye."

Gillian took a step backward, moving deeper into the aura of Calum's warmth. His protectiveness filled her with a singing glow.

"Ye owe the lady an apology."

"I-I am most profoundly sorry if I have offended you, Lady Gillian," Mr. Nesling stammered as he bowed.

"I accept your apology, Mr. Nesling. 'Twas only playfulness on your part, I am certain, but pray remember, I am unused to gentlemen employing such informality with my person."

Calum offered her his hand, and she laid her palm upon it, allowing him to lead her away. Behind them she heard Mr. Nesling murmur, "A true lady."

When they were out of earshot, Calum gave her a stern look. "Yer makin' a sight of yerself."

Gillian's eyes widened in surprise, and she withdrew her hand from his. "Do you wish to explain that comment?" With a flick of her wrist, she opened her fan. By steel discipline she kept the rhythm of her fanning slow, leisurely, unconcerned.

"Yer simpering up to every auld fogram in the place," Calum said tightly.

Indignation and not a little guilt filled her breast. "I do not simper!"

He snatched her hand back and with a glare dared her to remove it. When she did not, he led her through the mob and out the door, past a startled Augusta. He did not stop until he turned into a small deserted drawing room where he closed the door. When he turned back to her, his face was set.

"I'll no have ye flirtin' with every man in that saloon. 'Tis a disgrace."

"Every man in the saloon? My, how my accomplishments have expanded in the short distance from the dance floor to this room! Before 'twas only the *old* men!"

Crimson tinged his high cheekbones. "And that's another thing. Why are there so many auld men at this ball? There are damned few of any other age."

In her agitation, Gillian's fan fluttered faster and faster. "That, sir, you will need to ask of my dear aunt. 'Twas she who made the guest list and sent out the invitations."

His eyes narrowed. Without warning, he snatched her fan out of her hand. "And *this*! Ye're entirely too flirty with this thing. Twitterin' it back 'n' forth, makin' cow eyes over it at some poor sod so taken with ye he canna think straight. I'll no have it!"

Her control broke. She took a step forward. "You'll not have it? *You'll* not have it? What gall! What unmitigated nerve! I saw you making over Lydia Clough. All but drooling on her. It was disgusting!"

His eyebrows rose. "Making over Lydia Clough, was I? All I did was ask the lass to dance. I brought her a cup of lemonade, but I most assuredly did *not* drool. Ye've an evil mind, and no mistake."

"*I've* an evil mind? I merely conduct polite conversation with a few gentlemen and you accuse me of being a strumpet."

Calum looked shocked. "I dinna—"

"Oh, yes, you did!"

He scowled at her. "Ye'll no be puttin' words in my mouth that were never there. And ye'll no get away with tryin' to change the subject. I saw what I saw." He took a step forward. "Dinna tell me ye have no idea what those men were all thinkin' as ye waved this fan and gave 'em those looks."

She glared at him. "What 'looks'?"

"Ye know damned well the looks I'm talkin' about! The kind that fire a man's blood. The looks a woman gives a man that makes him think of gettin' her to his bed!"

Furious at the unfairness of his accusation, Gillian took a step closer to him. "I saw you kiss Lydia!"

He bent nearer until they were nose to nose, his face a thunderhead of anger. "I never did!"

Gillian could feel his warm breath on the skin of her cheeks. "You kissed her hand!"

"Nay, I dinna kiss her hand. I dinna even want to!"

Their gazes locked.

Lightning passed through Gillian. She did not know who reached for whom first, but suddenly they were in each other's arms and Calum was crushing his lips against hers.

The soft wool of his plaid brushed her cheek. His body was solid and warm, and his freshly shaven face smelled faintly of sandalwood soap.

Her heart soared as Calum's mouth moved on hers. She slid her palms up the front of his coat, to his shoulders. Her fingers curled into hard muscle. His arms tightened around her. She felt his heart pounding hard and fast.

The room and the world outside faded away. In that moment there was only Calum, strong, fierce Calum, whose skin invited her lips, whose gleaming hair tempted her fingers. Once his hands had gently stroked her back in solace. She pressed closer to him, yearning to absorb some of his strength, some of his warmth, so that she might keep a part of him with her, tucked away inside her heart, forever.

His kiss grew more demanding, dragging her into a maelstrom of unfamiliar sensations. An ache built inside her, dull but tingling, distant yet insistent.

Calum wrapped his fingers around her upper arms and tore his mouth from hers. So heavy was his breathing, he might have been running for miles. A wild light burned in his eyes. "'Tis no honorable thing we do here. Holdin' ye in my arms, kissin' yer sweet lips—'tis foul wrong of me. Ye've been given into my care. I should be protectin' ye, not wantin' ye for myself. And ye! Thinkin' of me as ye do, holdin' me in such low esteem, how could ye stand to have me touch ye so? Are ye so easy with yer affections, then?"

Gillian felt as if she'd been slapped. She stared at him for a moment, stunned at his cruelty. Then she jerked her arms out of his grasp, burning with shame and humiliation. She had forgotten her first duty, her goal, and thrown herself into the arms of the enemy. She struck back at him, seeking to hurt him as he'd hurt her.

"You are right, of course." She straightened her shoulders. "A lady should be particular about the company she keeps. After all, the manners of the baseborn are bound to soil those around them."

Color drained from Calum's face, and instantly Gillian regretted her poisoned words. But she could not relent. She needed protection from what she felt for him. His hatred would be her armor against her own traitorous heart.

The shutters closed over his emotions. His face became an expressionless mask. Flicking away a strand of her hair from his plaid, he said coldly, "There are those of us who are, by many, counted baseborn. And then, madam, there are the true bastards." He strode to the door and opened it. Without turning around to face her, he said, "Both can be vicious."

As soon as she heard the door close behind him, Gillian sank down on the harpsichord bench and expelled a sobbing breath. Tears swam in her eyes. Well, she thought, she'd succeeded. Calum hated her.

She sat there for a minute, trying to gather her shattered emotions. Pulling her handkerchief from her sleeve, she dabbed at her eyes, then released an uneven sigh. Hiding here would solve nothing. She must return to the ball and continue her quest for a husband.

Slowly, Gillian left the quiet of the music room

and walked down the hall with the heavy step of a mourner at a funeral. Just outside the door into the ballroom she stopped and straightened her shoulders. Head up, a smile glued to her face, she swept back into the grand saloon. She paused when she felt a gaze searing into her. Calum stood ten feet away. He watched her, unsmiling. Then he turned away and continued his conversation with a young woman Gillian knew to be a widow from Poppleton. The woman fluttered her fan outrageously. Hadn't anyone taught her how to use it properly? Gillian thought pettishly.

Calling up another artificial smile, she moved into the mob of her guests. She listened and sympathized, chatted and laughed. It's all a lie, she thought, feeling hollow inside. Only a lie. Like her life.

Augusta introduced her to what seemed like a never-ending stream of men, all rich, all old. Lord Fendleton returned for another dance. He fetched her a glass of lemonade and told her amusing stories of his adventures in India. He seldom traveled these days, he confided, except for the occasional trip to London. A retired adventurer, Gillian thought. She couldn't recall ever having met one before.

Maynard stepped up to join their conversation— a bold move for him. His mother, of course, remained affixed to his side. Gillian performed the introductions, then puzzled over Maynard's unusual behavior as he launched into a tale of how he'd almost been cheated by a horse trader at the fair several years ago.

She felt a tug at her overskirt and discovered Sammy Blenkin with the silk of her gown still wadded in his small fist. She raised an eyebrow and he guiltily dropped his hold on her clothing.

Tonight he too was decked out in his livery. To her surprise, he wore a new powdered wig. It had been made to look exactly like Pym's, and it fit Sammy perfectly. Excusing herself with her companions, she bent down and said in a soft voice meant only for Sammy, "Your wig looks just like Mr. Pym's, Sammy."

He beamed up at her. "It does, don't it?" His brow wrinkled. "Does it not. Oh! I forgot. Thank you, Lady Gillian."

Confused, she asked, "Thank you for what, Sammy?"

His large blue eyes were filled with trust. "Why, for my wig, o'course. Lord Iolar, he took me into town and had me fitted. He said you wanted me to have it."

Gillian's throat closed with emotion. She lifted a hand to the child's new wig. *He said you wanted me to have it.* Even in so kind an act, Calum had refused to lie. He could not know why she had not purchased Sammy the wig, yet he must have sensed that she truly did want the boy to have it. She swallowed hard. Curse the man. Curse him.

"Do you have a message for me, sir page?" she asked, maintaining an untroubled facade for Sammy's sake.

"Oh! I almost forgot! Mrs. Kendrew says to tell you dinner is served."

Her aunt led the ladies into the state dining room and the Duke of Mulvern led the men. This was the first time Gillian had taken a meal in this room. Now, as everyone was about to take their places at their proper side of the long tables, Gillian saw the small handwritten cards. Each bore a name. As she read them, it dawned on her that her aunt had rearranged the seating to the promiscuous style, alternating a female diner with a male. Quickly she glanced at Calum, knowing his feelings on the subject. He directed a stony stare at Augusta, then moved out of the way of a woman who was trying to pull back one of the heavy chairs. Graciously, he drew out the chair for her and pushed it back in when she seated herself. It seemed he would not cause a scene. Aunt Augusta had gotten her way.

"I had to do it, don't you see, dear?" Augusta told her in a low voice at her ear, startling Gillian from her speculations. "It would never do to have you wasting precious time in polite chitchat with women when you could be spending time with *eligible* men. You will notice that I arranged Mr. Leake's seat beside that of his dear ma-*ma*—far from you. Next to you I've placed two gentlemen I'm certain you will find quite diverting."

Finally, everyone settled into their assigned chairs. Conversations filled the imposing room with a constant low roar that echoed against the high coffered ceilings.

Gillian listened to her elderly dining partners, trying to look attentive even as her eyes scanned the faces of the others at her table. Her gaze abruptly halted on Calum's. He was talking to the pretty girl sitting next to him, who looked entranced by his words—or by him.

What woman would not be entranced by the Marquess of Iolar? Gillian thought, trying to breathe

around the ache in her heart. The memory of his kiss
still burned in her.

As if he sensed someone watched him, Calum
turned. His gaze went right to her, stunning her with
its impact. He held her in thrall for a long moment,
then turned back to his pretty companion. Whatever
he said made the girl laugh, a coy feminine trill that
cut through Gillian like shards of crystal.

After that, Gillian devoted herself to intriguing and
ensnaring the men around her. She employed every
lesson she had ever learned about being a pleasing
woman and about the nature of the opposite sex.
Shamelessly, she traded on her beauty. When the meal
ended and everyone returned to the grand saloon to
dance or to the blue drawing room to play whist or
loo, men vied to dance with her. Later she lost charmingly to three gentlemen at a game of cards.

Maynard surprised her when he asked to speak
with her a moment. Her surprise increased when she
discovered that his mother was nowhere in sight.

He led her into a deserted section of corridor
down from the saloon. "Where is your mother?" she
asked, unable to contain her curiosity.

"Asleep on a settee in one of the drawing rooms."
He took Gillian's hands in his. "Tomorrow I leave
for Leeds. When I return, I will have something to
ask you."

Gillian's weariness vanished. "You know that we
depart for Scotland in three days. Lord Iolar will
wait no longer."

"Can you not put him off awhile?"

"I am certain he will brook no further delay. He is
eager to return to Iolar Glen."

Maynard frowned a moment; then his face cleared into a smile. "I shall return before you must leave."

Gillian's heart beat faster. This was what she'd been hoping for . . . wasn't it? She wanted to wed Maynard, yet she did not. The thought of spending the rest of her life with this man—and his mother—depressed her. Still, she needed a husband. "Could you not ask me your question now?" she coaxed.

"No, no. It would be unthinkable."

Abruptly, Maynard leaned forward and kissed her full on the mouth. His dry, narrow lips remained tightly closed. Gillian found the experience less exciting than adding a column of figures in Treymoor's ledger.

"I shall be back before your guardian can carry you off," he reassured her.

At his expectant look, she fluttered her fan in front of her face and lowered her eyes in what she hoped passed for maidenly shyness. "I am already breathless with anticipation."

Maynard beamed. "Well, I must go wake Mother, and then we'll be on our way home." He hesitated, and for one awful minute she thought he would kiss her again. Instead, he wished her a good evening and strode off down the hall.

Twenty minutes later, the last guest had retired. Gillian and her aunt wearily wished each other pleasant dreams and went to seek their beds. Tomorrow packing would begin in earnest, and there were still the overnighting guests to entertain.

Gillian blew out candles along her way. This ball had cost a fortune, she thought. Why, at least seventy pounds for beeswax candles alone would have been squandered by the time the last guest departed tomorrow. Of course, her aunt was financing the ball.

As her footsteps echoed in the dark corridors, she thought perhaps her aunt might be right. A rich old husband might be the ticket. At least Gillian wouldn't have to endure a lifetime of dry, dull kisses. If the fellow wasn't ancient he would still be able to father children, though she didn't want to think what those children might be like.

When she reached her room, Gillian struggled out of her clothes, having sent Zerrin off to bed hours ago. With a sigh of relief, she let the soft linen of her night shift slide over her skin and slipped into bed.

She couldn't sleep. There in the darkened room, illuminated only by the sinful luxury of one sweet-smelling beeswax candle, its golden glow dancing upon the silk-lined walls, Calum's kiss came back to her. The texture of his lips. The warm strength of his arms. The pounding of his heart.

Their harsh, hurtful words came back to her too. And the way he had all but ignored her for the rest of the evening.

With a deep, uneven sigh, she turned on her side and stared at the wall. She deserved his anger, of course. Hadn't she wanted it?

No.

In truth, she did not want his anger, and especially she did not want to hurt him. She wanted . . . what? His admiration? Yes, but if she were being honest, she must also own that his admiration was not enough.

She wanted his love.

A hiccup of laughter that was more a sob escaped

her throat. Oh, what a hopeless mess her life had become!

For a small eon she lay in her bed, gazing up at the canopy overhead. Finally, she sat up and pushed the covers back. She pulled on her slippers and dressing gown and took up her candle. At the wall of her chamber, she pressed what looked like just another carved berry in the gilded frieze and then pushed open the door into the secret passageway.

Restlessly she prowled through the house. She checked to make certain Treymoor's original and incriminating log books were still where she had locked them away in the library. Moving silently through the passages, she found herself at Calum's room, as if she had been inexorably drawn there. She eyed the stool under the peephole. What if he had not returned to his room? What if he'd spent the night with one of the women to whom he'd been so attentive? Something twisted painfuly inside her at the thought. She had no right, she told herself sternly. The company he kept was his own affair. Only to her was he forbidden, by his own code and for the sake of her people.

She had turned away and started back toward her room when a shout from Calum's room stopped her. She ran to the stool and peered through the peephole, but the chamber was dark. Perhaps it was naught but the bad dreams she'd heard plagued him. Certainly not cause enough to warrant her concern. She stepped down from the stool and turned to go.

From his room came another cry, raw with fear. The chill it sent through her convinced Gillian that such a sound could not possibly be the product of a mere nightmare. Instinctively, she went to the secret door. He must have taken ill. The thought of him suffering spurred her quickly into Calum's chamber.

The light from her candle revealed his still form. He lay amid twisted sheets. Bare arms and shoulders rose above the quilt. His hair spread across his pillow like gleaming red-gold silk. His face appeared no softer in sleep than in wakefulness, the dark red eyebrows just as flared, the cheekbones just as high and sculptured, the fine mouth just as sulky and sensual. Perspiration beaded his forehead.

Gillian frowned. Perhaps he'd caught a fever. "Calum?" She spoke his name quietly.

He did not stir.

She came to the side of the tester bed, setting her candle in its brass holder on the table. To reach him, she had to boost herself up onto the mattress. Then she laid her palm upon his forehead. He was warm but not feverish.

Leaning closer, she listened for congestion in his breathing. There was none.

His body suddenly tensed and he tossed from side to side, as if struggling against some restraint invisible to her. A sound so piercingly heartrending that she feared for him tore from his throat.

Someone pounded on the door. "Calum!" Hugh called. "Are ye all right, man? Calum!"

As if the sound of the pounding reached through to him, Calum's eyes opened.

14

Calum's eyes widened when he saw her.

Hugh banged on the door again. "Calum!"

"I'm all right, Hugh," Calum called, never taking his eyes off Gillian. "Go back to bed."

"Are ye sure, lad? Was it one of yer nightmares, then?"

"Aye." Calum's voice was still thick with sleep. " 'Twas just a dream."

"Perhaps they'll stop when ye return to Iolar Glen. Good night to ye."

"Good night, cousin."

Gillian heard the sound of Hugh's footsteps fade down the hall. She tried to scramble backward off the bed. Instantly Calum's hand grasped her upper arm and pulled her back.

His sleep-tousled hair tumbled down over his shoulders and back. The quilt fell to his waist, baring his upper body.

Gillian knew she should avert her gaze from his nakedness, but she could not take her eyes away from him, away from his broad shoulders, his powerful chest with its mat of curling red-gold hair, light against his darker, sun-bronzed skin.

"What are ye doing here?" he demanded in a low voice.

"I heard you cry out."

His eyes narrowed. "Ye heard me cry out, all the way across this great pile of stone, in yer own bed-chamber?"

"Uh . . . well . . ." She cleared her throat. "Not precisely."

"Ye were spyin' on me again." He tugged her closer.

"No." It was the truth, after all. She hadn't looked through the peephole until she'd heard his shout.

"I told ye to stay out of the passages."

"I go where I choose," she flared.

"Nay, ye do as *I* say." He pulled her closer. Their faces were so close together that in the dim illumination from the candle she could see the striations in the shadowed green of his eyes. "Like it or no, I am yer master."

Furious, she tried to yank free of his hold. "Well, I *don't* like it. I don't like it at all!"

"Nay, ye'd rather have a whey-faced weed like Leake as yer master, or that toad Fendleton. I'm no good enough for ye."

Her eyes widened. "That's not so!"

"Aye, 'tis so and well ye know it." His deep, fierce voice vibrated through her. His warm breath burst upon her face. "I'm naught but a bastard to ye, a low, conniving whoreson unfit to touch the hem of yer skirt. Ye'd give yerself to any man in a marriage bed, as long as that man was not *me*."

"Not true," she whispered hoarsely. "Not true!"

He gave her a small shake. "Aye, damn ye, it *is* true."

Gillian heard the torment in his voice. It ripped through her, merging his pain with her own. She reached out and cupped her palm against his cheek.

He stared at her, as if trying to fathom her thoughts, trying to see the truth. Then, slowly, he covered her hand with his own. His eyes closed as he rubbed his cheek against her palm. She felt the scratch of the night's growth of beard.

In that moment, it all became too much for Gillian: the long struggle, the unceasing weight of responsibility, the years of inner loneliness. She needed someone. Someone to love her.

She needed Calum.

Hesitantly, she lifted her other hand to his mane of fire-gold hair. He went still.

"'Tis not true," she whispered.

He made a animal noise in his throat as he surged around her in a fierce embrace. His lips moved on hers in a wild kiss of possession that ignited an answering blaze within her.

She laced her fingers through his hair, glorying in the feel of the heavy silk, in the power humming through the body of the man who held her, kissed her. *Calum.* At long last, Calum. She closed her eyes and yielded to the tide of desire that rose in her.

Her lips parted under his demand and his tongue invaded her, scouring the recesses of her mouth, sliding along her teeth before rubbing against her own tongue. The flame in her grew brighter, hotter. Her fingers tightened in his hair.

His hands roamed restlessly up and down her back. He rose up onto his knees, carrying her with him.

Her breasts ached. The linen of her night shift chafed her. She burrowed against his body, wanting to feel him, the deep solid chest, the crisp curling hair, the burning heat of his skin.

Without thinking, she reached for his hand and pressed it against her breast, as if that could relieve the fever mounting within her.

His fingers conformed to the shape of her, massaging her through the fabric of her dressing gown and shift. But that wasn't good enough. It felt . . . wrong.

Calum fumbled with the ribbons at the closure of her shift. One knotted. His eyes blazed as he gathered the neckline in his fists and tore it open. His hands moved down and finished the work until the garment was rent from neck to hem. Roughly, he shoved it off her shoulders, down her arms. Somewhere in her hazy brain she knew she should be alarmed, but she was not. She felt only relief at being freed of the restrictive covering.

He stared at her, a feral gleam in his eyes. His chest heaved with his short, shallow breaths. "Ye are beautiful," he said thickly. "So verra beautiful." He slid his palm down her side, dipping at her waist, coming to rest on the curve of her hip. His other hand lifted to her hair. "Ye canna know how I've wanted to touch yer midnight hair, yer soft white skin."

"Touch me now," she whispered, moving closer to him, unhappy with the distance of inches that separated them. "Touch me."

" 'Tis wrong." His deep, lilting voice grew hoarse. "Dishonorable."

She ran her hand down his ribs, his belly, his thigh. "Touch me, Calum."

He shuddered under her hand, his flesh burning as hers burned. "Aye." He groaned. He caught her by the wrist and pulled her up against him. "Ye are *mine*."

His mouth branded her with his passion, and she exulted in it. If she was his, he belonged to *her*.

Slowly, he lowered her onto her back atop her dressing gown and the remnant of her shift. He touched her: her breasts, the plane of her belly, the tender inner flesh of her thighs. Blinding pleasure sent her arching up as he took her nipple into his mouth. The wet heat of his tongue teased her. The edge of his teeth tormented her. She cupped the back of his head, wanting, needing. . . .

"Calum." His name tore from her throat in an urgent whisper.

On his elbows, he lifted his torso, spreading her legs with his knee. Slowly, he thrust into her—and halted. His breathing grew shorter, sharper. She saw the muscles in his arms and shoulders straining. Sweat beaded his top lip. And then he began to move.

"Forgive me," he murmured. "Forgive me. I canna stop. Dear God, ye feel so *good*." He thrust harder and harder, deeper and deeper.

She clung to him, meeting him stroke for stroke,

caught in a storm of spiraling sensations. Something eluded her, dancing just out of her reach. She moved faster.

Suddenly Calum tensed, the sinews of his body standing out in stark relief against his glistening skin. He shook with the force of his release.

He opened his eyes and searched her face. Immediately, Gillian did as Zerrin had taught her.

"You were magnificent," she said. "It was as if the earth shook beneath me." When she saw his skeptical look, she added in a rush, "Truly."

His face hardened. "I canna abide a liar, Gillian, and I'll no have it from ye, of all people."

Confused, Gillian didn't know what she should say. Zerrin had never mentioned anything about a man denying a woman's compliments, only that pleasure was up to the man. He would take his, naturally, but whether or not he chose to see to the woman's needs was his decision to make. Most men, Zerrin had informed her, did not bother. Calum, however, had given Gillian great pleasure. He had set her afire with it. No, this small, nagging feeling of incompleteness could only be her fault.

"I've failed ye," he said. He looked away. "I've failed us both." Raw emotion thrummed through his voice, reaching out to pluck an answering chord within her.

"I should have stayed in my room," she said miserably.

He rolled to his side, his mouth set in a grim line. "Ye're but an innocent. I . . . I knew better." He looked away. "We'll speak no more of it tonight. Tomorrow will be soon enough to face the consequences of what we've done."

Without another word, he crooked one arm beneath his pillow. With his other arm, he drew her nearer, tucking her snugly against his warm, imposing body, her naked back curving into his lightly furred chest.

It was a long time before his even breathing told her that he finally slept. Gillian knew from Zerrin's teaching that she was now expected to return to her room.

Quietly, she wriggled out of his embrace and off the bed. She eased the edge of her clothing out from under his heavy form. A bloodstain marred the white purity of the tattered shift where she had lain on it. This, too, she knew was natural. She had lost her maidenhood to Calum. Suddenly, realization struck her with full force as she looked at the stain.

She'd lain with the enemy.

Worse, she loved him.

Her hands shook as she bundled up the shift, then wrapped herself in her dressing gown. What had possessed her? How could she have been so foolish? Why had she allowed this to happen?

Entering the secret passageway, she slid the bolt into place, ensuring no one could enter from Calum's side. On the verge of tears, she ran all the way back to her own room. There, she struggled with a chest of drawers, trying to move it in front of the door into the hall. The chest's great weight resisted her efforts, and she gave up, leaving it standing a few feet inside the door.

Exhausted, miserable, and confused, Gillian curled up under her quilt and cried herself to sleep.

*   *   *

A sense of something amiss drew Calum up through cocooning layers of sleep. The pale light of early morning that sneaked through the crack between the draperies revealed the room as it was when he'd gone to bed for the night.

Suddenly, memory assailed him. He rolled onto his other side and stared at the empty pillow, the pillow where she had lain. His fingers curled into the white linen. It smelled of her, the sensuous, elusive scent that haunted him.

He'd dreamed again. That dream. The terrifying, sheet-twisting nightmare that had followed him through the years, over sea and land, mountains and moors. It had started shortly before his mother and he had left Iolar Glen. Always when he woke, he remembered only the panicked fear, never what had actually occurred.

Gillian had come to him. She had heard him and come to help him.

And he had seduced her.

Calum's hands clenched into fists. God, what had he done? In a matter of moments, he had broken every promise he'd made to himself regarding his responsibilities to Gillian. He had defiled the trust her father had placed in him. He had ruined any chance she had of marriage, not only to any of the rich, ancient men she'd met last night but most especially to Maynard Leake. Calum's chest tightened. What if she loved Leake? What then?

Calum sat up as he remembered how Gillian had responded to him. How she'd turned to flame in his arms. How he'd burned with her.

He'd dishonored them both.

Quickly he got out of bed and pulled on his breeches. Then he strode to the door into the secret passageway and pressed the carved grape. Nothing happened. He pressed again. The door remained in place. It had been locked.

Damn the little vixen!

Storming to the room's other door, he yanked it open and stalked through the house. On his way he passed several servants who stared at his state of undress. Calum ignored them. When he arrived at Gillian's room, he found the door locked.

His temper mounting, he pounded on it. "Unlock this door, woman!"

"Go away!" she shouted from the perceived safety of her chamber.

Why hadn't he anticipated this and brought the keys? He banged on the door again. "Open this door *now*!"

"Leave me alone!"

Calum hammered on the door, taking out his guilt and frustration on the barrier. "Nay, I will not. Like it or no, we have things to settle between us. Now *open this door*!"

He heard the click of a key in the lock. He flung the door open—and abruptly stubbed his bare toe on a heavy chest of drawers that blocked his path.

"Bloody hell, Gillian, are ye tryin' to kill me?" he demanded, glancing down at his throbbing toe.

"I find the thought has certain appeal." She stood in the middle of the room, looking defiant and unhappy at once. She wore a pink short-waisted gown with a wide blue sash. Her ankles and feet were bare, and she wore no cap. From one hand dangled a stocking.

To his annoyance, Calum wanted nothing more than to drag her off to bed again, where this time he'd make certain of her pleasure too. He'd never ignited like that before.

"Ye're up rather late this mornin'," he pointed out, pleased to see that he, at least, was not the only one suffering over what had happened last night.

She eyed his solitary garment. "There are guests in the house. I'd prefer they not see a half-naked man running about."

"I dinna gave a damn for what they see. I've come to settle things with ye."

Gillian dropped her gaze to the stocking in her hand, though she made no move to put it on. "Please leave me alone," she pleaded halfheartedly.

Calum shoved the chest of drawers out of his way and crossed the floor to her. "'Tis important that we settle the matter now. We canna put it off."

She looked up at him, and his heart clenched at the misery in her eyes. Had making love with him been so repugnant to her?

"Can't we just pretend nothing happened?" she asked.

He raked his fingers through his uncombed hair and struggled to rein in his agitation. "Nay, lass," he said softly, "because something *did* happen last night. And ye may have conceived."

Her mist-gray eyes widened. "I-I had not thought . . ."

Calum squared his naked shoulders and took a deep breath. God help them both. "I know what's right. We must wed."

Color drained from her face. "Wed?"

The desolate way she spoke that one word was a knife in Calum's chest.

A small metal click echoed in the chamber, and both of them turned to find Pym, Odgers, Mrs. Withecombe, and Zerrin gathered at the door. Pym held an old wheel-lock musket aimed at Calum's chest. Odgers clutched an ancient tasseled sword at the ready. All four scowled.

"Move away from her, Scotsman," Pym ordered.

Calum frowned. "What is the meaning of this?"

"Move. Now." Pym adjusted his grip on the musket and squinted down the barrel at his target.

Calum took a few steps away from Gillian. Pym followed him with his aim.

"Come here to us, Gillyflower," Odgers said. "You're safe now."

Gillian hurried over to them. "He wasn't going to harm me."

Calum straightened indignantly. "Of course I wouldna harm her."

"Ha! You already have," Mrs. Withecombe informed him. "You've ruined her reputation. No fewer than three guests saw you enter Lady Gillian's room. And you nearly naked! Oh, you made certain to attract the attention of every living soul in the house with your bellowing and your pounding on the door." She snatched Gillian into her maternal embrace. "Oh, my poor Gillyflower! I say shoot him, Mr. Pym."

At that moment, Lady Augusta arrived, brandishing a large silver ladle. "Make way!" she ordered. "Let me set my hands around the throat of that despicable varlet!" She elbowed her way to the front of the group and over to Calum. "You have cost my niece four offers of marriage. This morning all four gentlemen came to offer for Gillian. Early this morning, each trying to be the first. The offers were good, most generous. Gillian could have been a *duchess*! But you, you odious man, must parade around wearing naught but your articles and lay siege to her door. Then you entered the poor girl's bedchamber!" Augusta thumped the ladle against Calum's arm. "Wretch!"

Calum winced. Fury lent the lady strength, and clearly she didn't mind using it against him. He backed up a step, out of reach. "I—"

"There's no help for it," Pym announced. He narrowed his eyes at Calum. "You must wed our Lady Gillian."

Gillian looked at Pym, horror-stricken. "Do you know what you ask?"

Calum felt as if he'd received a sharp jab to the stomach. Gillian still held him in contempt. He carefully schooled his features to reveal nothing of his true, turbulent feelings.

"I know well what I ask," Pym replied. "But there is no help for it, is there? There have been too many witnesses."

"What of Maynard?" she asked.

"He will find out eventually. Would you wish to be bound to him when he learned? Living with him . . . and his mother?"

Gillian shook her head.

"You will wed her," Pym said, looking Calum straight in the eye.

"Aye."

At that moment, Hugh and Ian appeared behind the others, and expressions, first of surprise, then anger, crossed their faces when they caught sight of Calum facing Pym's and Odgers's weapons.

"What goes on here?" Hugh demanded.

"Lord Iolar is going to wed Lady Gillian," Odgers said, never taking his eyes off Calum or easing his grasp on the sword.

"What?"

"'Tis a long tale, Hugh," Calum said wearily. "I'll tell ye later. Meanwhile, prepare to leave for Iolar Glen at once."

Instantly, a clamor of protest arose from the English contingent.

"She'll marry here!" Pym roared. "As soon as a special license can be obtained."

"She'll marry in Iolar Glen, in Dunncrannog Castle, or not at all," Calum said coldly. "I'll no go to my own wedding surrounded by folk screamin' for my blood. I'll marry in my ancestral home, where my bride will live."

"And you think the people on your father's estate won't be howling for your blood after the way you've treated them?" Mrs. Withecombe jeered.

A hard iciness grew within Calum.

"Ye know nothing of it, woman," Hugh told the housekeeper sharply.

"*Every*body knows!" she snapped.

"How can we be assured that you intend to wed the Lady Gillian once you are in your Highlands?" Zerrin asked quietly.

Calum looked at Gillian and their gazes locked. "He asked me to wed him," she said.

"When?" Odgers asked.

"This morning. Just before you arrived."

Silence reigned in the room while the significance of Gillian's words sank in. Five sets of eyes moved first in the direction of Calum's near nakedness, then to Gillian's pale face.

"Despoiler of innocents," Mrs. Withecombe hissed, glaring at Calum.

Gillian blushed darkly. "It . . . it wasn't like that. He didn't seduce me. Everything just . . . happened."

Mrs. Withecombe hugged Gillian more tightly, rocking her in consolation. "There, there, child," she murmured.

"She is no a child, madam," Calum said flatly. "She's a woman full grown. And now she's *my* woman, like it or no. We leave tomorrow at first light."

He stalked across the bedchamber and out the door. No one tried to stop him.

The journey to Scotland was a miserable affair. Gillian was confined to the carriage with her moaning aunt and Barbara and Zerrin, while Odgers rode alongside, guarding her like a sharp-eyed hawk. Silent hostility bristled between the Englishmen and the Scots, and even among the latter Gillian sensed tension. While she never actually heard Hugh or Ian criticize Calum, she was certain sharp words had been exchanged.

Calum remained aloof from everyone. He spoke only when necessary and then with cool courtesy.

Gillian, who had never spent a night away from Treymoor, was appalled at the accommodations offered by the inns along the way. Poor food, filthy rooms, and bedbugs and other vermin appeared to be the regular lot of travelers.

Homesick, worried over Treymoor—though she knew William Harland to be a good steward— Gillian dreaded her wedding to a man who had become a stranger. To a man who had already destroyed one estate out of spite. If he knew her father was dead, she did not like to think what he might be capable of doing to Treymoor in his present state of mind. Oh, if only she'd stayed out of the secret passages as he'd ordered!

They left the carriage in Edinburgh, purchased a wagon and horses and more supplies, and proceeded north.

Up into the rugged mountains they rode. The days and nights grew cooler. Sometimes there were no roads to follow. A scarcity of inns meant they often slept upon the ground, under the stars, which Gillian thought preferable to most of the hostelries in which they'd stayed.

Until she heard a wolf howl. It was a wild, haunting sound that brought to her mind the night of her father's funeral and the creature that had danced among the gravestones. She shuddered under her blanket, despite the comforting sounds of even breathing and soft snores that surrounded her.

" 'Tis only a wolf," came Calum's low voice close to her. "He's far from here."

She turned her head to see his dark form sitting propped against the trunk of one of the Scotch pines that surrounded them. His rifle rested across his bent knees.

"How can you be certain that he'll *stay* far away?" she whispered back, ridiculously pleased that he'd finally spoken to her.

She saw his white teeth flash in the gloom. "I can no be certain of any such thing."

Gillian sat up in alarm. "You mean he could come here?"

"Unlikely, with the fire we have. And 'tis too early for a wolf to be desperate enough for food that he and his pack would tackle a group of men. That becomes more of a problem when the snow falls."

"Calum?"

"Hm?"

"I'm sorry."

He remained silent for a moment. "Go to sleep, Gillian. What's done is done."

A lump weighed heavy in her chest as she settled back into her blanket. What's done is done.

Four days later they rode single file out of a narrow pass to face a dark tarn, tightly encircled by high, rugged mountains. On the far side of the lake, Gillian saw another narrow pass. But it was what stood between that captured her attention.

Rising from the black lake, like a fantastical cathedral, stood a castle on an island. It looked like no castle she had ever seen in books, with its soaring towers, lofty spires, and crenelated battlements. Gillian thought the architect must have reached for heaven with his creation.

The imposing structure towered over the bridge that connected it to land and the cramped track that went around the lake. Gillian doubted anyone could have reached the far pass if the castellan did not wish it.

She nudged her horse with her heel and guided it over to Calum, who sat gazing at the sight before them.

"What place is this?" she asked. "It looks like it's been standing here alone for a thousand years."

A corner of his mouth twitched. "Not quite that long."

Immediately, Augusta joined them, followed by Zerrin and Odgers. Disliking horses, Barbara rode in the wagon. "Where have you brought us?" Augusta demanded. "The edge of the earth?"

"It is most unfortunate that you feel that way, madam," he replied coolly, "for this is Dunncrannog Castle."

Gillian stared at her new home. It was as far removed from the familiar symmetry of Treymoor as anything she could have imagined. Her eyes followed the lines of the chimerical citadel upward. "Was this where you once lived?"

"Until I was seven."

Hugh drew his horse up on the other side of Calum. "Do they expect us?"

"Yes."

"They have a peculiar way of welcoming their master," Odgers observed.

"Perhaps they have not yet seen us," Gillian suggested.

"It doesna look as if there's anyone about," Ian said, edging his mount up next to Hugh's. "Yet the drawbridge is down and the gate is standin' open."

Calum frowned, never taking his eyes off Dunncrannog. "Ian's right. I've no seen a soul."

Zerrin twitched the reins of her restive horse, bringing it back into line. "If they anticipated the arrival of their new lord, someone would have been watching."

"Perhaps my letters never reached the steward," Calum said.

He led the way across the long bridge. The hooves of the horses thundered against the wooden planking, and the wagon wheels rumbled.

As they drew near the castle island, Gillian noticed signs of neglect. The pennants flying from the tops of the spires were faded and tattered. When the party of riders passed beneath the jagged-toothed portcullis, flanked on either side by towers, she saw clumps of weeds growing here and there between the stones of the outer curtain wall.

At that moment, a figure appeared on the battlement around the inner ward. It waved to them. "Are ye the new laird of Iolar?" The crackling voice of an old woman echoed among the high stone walls.

"Aye," Calum answered. "Calum Gregory MacFuaran, Marquess of Iolar."

"Come, then. Ye're expected."

The outer ward was deserted as they entered. Tall grass and weeds swayed in the cool wind. Nowhere was there a sign of the sheep or cattle that would have kept such growth checked.

Only the thud of their horses' hooves on earth, the jingle of tack, and the bass vibration from wagon wheels broke the silence. Gillian's heart began to beat faster when she noticed Calum, and then the other men, reaching for their pistols.

The mounted party passed under another portcullis and clattered into a paved inner ward devoid of life. Doors hung open on rusted hinges. Moldering straw packed the floor of empty stables. A cart with a broken wheel stood in the middle of the courtyard. The kitchen garden had been ravaged. Broken windows, crumbling mortar, and rotten wood related a tale of long neglect. Gillian turned toward Calum with a scathing reprisal ready on her lips—and stopped.

Stark shock etched his face, a face gone pale beneath its tan as he looked around him. "My God," he whispered hoarsely. "What has happened?" The anguish in his eyes echoed in his voice.

The polished armor of her distrust, the shield of enmity she had carefully nurtured within her breast, crumbled away.

No one could feign such raw pain. The shock, the mounting grief she saw in him were real, horribly, fatally real. And Gillian could not stand against them.

She did not know why the home of the Marquess of Iolar had been stripped and ravaged, or who had committed the heinous deed. These things she might never learn. But with a certainty that flamed white in her heart, Gillian knew Calum was innocent.

The heavy door to the east gatehouse creaked open and out hobbled a crone, puffing for breath. "Welcome, my lord!" she gasped. "Welcome, and God bless ye!"

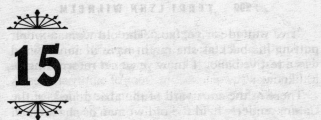

15

Wind moaned through the towers of Dunncrannog. Everyone stared at the scrawny white-haired elder as if she were an apparition.

"Do ye no recognize me then, laddie?" she demanded, turning faded blue eyes up to Calum. "Och, 'tis brokenhearted I am to think ye've forgotten yer auld Beathag."

The wind tugged at Calum's hair, pulling loose fine locks. His eyebrows drew down over the green of his eyes as he studied the ancient woman. "Beathag?" He pronounced the word as *Beh-hak*.

She gave a cackle of laughter and held out her arms. "Ye did not forget yer nursie after all!"

Leather creaked as Calum swung down from his saddle. His spurs jingled as he stepped onto the stone paving. He called out something in Gaelic as he engulfed the woman in his embrace.

"I've waited for ye, lad." The old woman wept, patting his back as she might have done when he was a restive babe. "I knew ye would return. I knew it. I knew it."

There in the courtyard of the abandoned castle, Calum tenderly held the old woman as she sobbed against his chest. He stroked her hair and crooned softly to her. Sore and weary though they were, the rest of the party sat quietly on their horses.

Finally she cried herself out. "Och, what ye must think o' me," she fretted, accepting the handkerchief he gave her. "And ye with all yer fine friends here."

"Hush now, Beathag," Calum said. "Dinna worry yerself." He gave her a wink. "Ye know ye stole my heart long ago."

"Och, get on with ye," she blustered, clearly pleased.

The moment had passed, and everyone dismounted, walking about to relieve the stiffness caused by long hours in the saddle.

"I dinna know how ye recognized me," Calum said.

A sadness passed over the nursemaid's face. "Ye've grown to be a braw bonny man, and I was no there to see it. My Seumas would no let me go with yer mother and ye when ye left. He was yer da's man, ye see, and could no verra well leave him."

"Well, I am back now."

Gillian wandered over to peer into the stables. The stench made her draw back, wrinkling her nose. She certainly would not put Atlanta in there, or any of the other horses, until it was cleaned out.

Calum called to her, and she walked over to join him.

"I would like ye to meet my betrothed, Lady Gillian Ellicott, daughter of the Earl of Molyneux. Gillian, this is Beathag, who tolerated me until I was seven."

Gillian looked up, startled to hear him speak of her as his betrothed. Nothing had been formally declared, only a marriage agreement signed, setting out financial arrangements. His words gave her a warm glow—until she realized he was merely showing courtesy.

"Seven years auld when he was taken from me," Beathag said stiffly. "Taken off to Edinburgh by his proud mother."

" 'Tis in the past and best forgot," Calum said. He scowled as he looked around. "What happened here, Beathag? Where is Oliver Farnum? He wrote me that all was well. That both Dunncrannog and Iolar prospered."

The old woman muttered darkly in Gaelic and spat on the ground. "A curse on his head! All was well here before *he* came. A letter arrived from your father in India dismissing the auld steward, ye see? A good man was the auld steward. Under his care, everyone and everything fared well. But the new steward, Oliver Farnum, was no the same kind of man. *He* destroyed Iolar Glen and let Dunncrannog fall to ruin. Said 'twas by yer orders, which I knew to be false. But by then, people were desperate. They could no think of a reason yer father would dismiss a good man and hire a fiend, why he should wish to bring destruction on the glen he held dear, so they accepted the lies Farnum told. They believe it still, the ones who stayed. 'Twas only me to say naught,

and the words of an auld woman bear little weight
against such misery as they've suffered. 'Tis no the
place it was when ye were here, lad."

The features of Calum's face had set into a hard
unreadable mask as Beathag related the tale of his
inheritance. "So it would seem," he murmured, as
he looked up at the deserted battlement. Blades of
grass growing between the large stones of the walls
waved in the breeze.

What was going through his mind? Gillian wondered. Was he filled with rage at having been
unjustly robbed of his heritage and then blamed for
the damage done? Remorse, for the years lost away
from his home? Indignation that an elderly woman
had been left behind to fend for herself in a remote
medieval castle? Gillian felt certain that he was
sorely in need of comfort, but as he stood there, gazing toward the mountain pass beyond which lay
Iolar Glen, he seemed to have set a distance between
himself and every other living thing.

Gillian tried to imagine what he might be feeling.
The very thought of losing Treymoor made her sick.
Hesitantly, she reached out and took the hand that
hung at his side. He did not look at her. Timidly, she
gave him little squeeze. He removed his hand from
her hold.

Her heart sank, and she withdrew from him. She
knew she had no right to his trust. She, more than
anyone, had flung the lie of his treachery in his face.
By disobeying him, she had damned them both to a
marriage neither wanted. His honor would settle for
nothing less. She could not blame him for hating
her.

Without a word, he strode to his horse. He leapt into the saddle and charged out of the courtyard. Moments later, they all heard the drumming of hooves on the bridge.

Instinctively, Gillian gathered Atlanta's reins in her hand, ready to race after him, but she did not mount. Something, some inner sense, warned her to let him go.

She looked at Beathag. "He's going to Iolar Glen, isn't he?"

The old woman nodded sadly. "Aye. 'Tis no a good sight that will greet his eyes, but he must see for himself."

He wouldn't want her there when he beheld his beloved valley for the first time in twenty years, Gillian thought. The moment would be too intimate, too filled with sorrow, to share with someone he despised. Yet she worried for him, should he encounter one of the inhabitants who blamed him.

She crossed the courtyard and went to Hugh. "Please ride after him. I know he needs to be alone now, but there is no way to know whom he will meet. I would not have him harmed."

Hugh met her gaze. She did not know what he sought, but perhaps he found it, for he nodded. "Aye." He swung into his saddle, wheeled his horse around, and galloped after his cousin.

"I'll go too," Ian said, fitting his foot into a stirrup, ready to mount.

"Please stay, Ian. We have need of you here." When he turned to her, a protest poised on his lips, she said, "Do you doubt that Hugh will know what to do?"

Ian sighed. "Nay. Hugh's a wise man."

Gillian laid her hand on his arm. "Perhaps we can make Dunncrannog Castle seem more welcoming. For a time, at least, 'tis our home."

She set about putting things in order. Ian and Odgers were sent to work in the stables. Gillian asked Beathag to show her the castle.

The place was filthy. Debris littered the interior. Gillian wondered if any improvements had been made since the late Middle Ages. In the great hall, tattered banners and tapestries sagged on soot-stained walls. Long, heavy benches and tables had been overturned. Mountains of cold ash filled the enormous fireplaces. After visiting the barren store-rooms and deserted kitchens and taking a brisk tour of the ground floor, Gillian, Zerrin, Barbara, and Augusta followed Beathag up narrow stone steps to the floors above. These rooms had served as sleeping quarters, judging from what little remained of furniture and stinking ticks. Gillian's nose wrinkled against the smell in the rooms. Beneath her feet rustled old reeds, the likes of which she knew had been used to cover floors long ago. She'd thought those days long gone, but at Dunncrannog Castle, it seemed, the past clung on with an unbreakable grip.

In the bower, they discovered two spinning wheels, some carding combs, and a simple loom. Apparently, the steward and his lot had found no use for this equipment. Gillian guessed Farnum had been a bachelor and a man of little industry. While she had purchased most of the cloth needed at Treymoor, the wool from her sheep had always been processed and woven on the estate for use there. Wool was a valuable commodity.

Gillian glanced out a leaded window at the mountains that surrounded the tarn. Here, too, the warmth of wool would be needed. She remembered what the sheep trader had told her about the state of the Iolar Glen sheep and sighed.

She grew increasingly worried about Calum and Hugh as the hours passed, but she could not stop so much as a minute to fret if everyone was to have a decent place to sleep and a warm meal tonight. They'd brought enough food with them for several days, but after that they must depend upon their skill and ingenuity.

For the first time, she noticed how painfully thin Beathag was. Righting an overturned chair in the great hall, Gillian sat the protesting old woman on it and gave her a hunk of bread and a piece of cheese.

"When was your last meal?" Gillian asked as she bound her own hair in a kerchief in preparation for housecleaning.

"I canna rightly remember," Beathag said between hungry mouthfuls. "It has been too long since anyone in the glen has eaten a proper meal, save the steward and his cronies." She shook her gray head. "Evil man. Evil, evil man. The devil's minion for certain."

Gillian said nothing as she bound a thatch of reeds to a stick of broken furniture with a strip of rag. Not much of a broom, but the best they would have for a while. This she handed to her aunt, who went to the far side of the hall and set to work sweeping.

It would have been easy enough for the steward to strip this remote estate and blame Calum, Gillian thought. If the state of the glen and its remaining inhabitants was as destitute as she'd heard, the funds to the old marquess would have trickled to nothing. Why, then, had Calum's father not written his lawyer in Edinburgh to investigate? Instead, he had recognized the son he'd repudiated twenty years earlier. Was the whole thing a cruel trick? Had the old marquess nursed such hatred of his son? Gillian found she could not believe that. It made no sense. But then, love and anger had no logic.

"Have ye heard what is being said of my dear laddie?" Beathag asked, hobbling along after Gillian, who wielded another makeshift broom against the rubbish and dirt.

"There is a rumor that he is responsible for the present condition of Iolar Glen," Gillian replied. She found she could not meet the venerable nursemaid's gaze.

"Aye. 'Tis a terrible lie. Calum always loved the glen. He loved Dunncrannog Castle. Who could believe he would ever bring harm to them?"

Guilt twisted inside Gillian, and she swept even more vigorously.

As if sensing there was something Gillian was not saying, Beathag demanded, "Ye dinna believe such a wicked untruth, do ye?"

Gillian ceased her sweeping and looked directly at Beathag. "No," she said softly, truthfully. "I do not believe it."

Beathag's faded blue eyes studied Gillian's face for a moment. Then she smiled. "Good." She returned to her chair to eat the last bite of her food and then began to bind a broom for herself. "Good."

"Did no one here write to tell Calum's father what was going on? Or his lawyer?"

"The schoolmaster wrote to both of them, but he went missing shortly after. 'Tis doubtful those letters ever made it past the castle."

"Just rest, Beathag. The rest of us can tend to this."

"Nay," the old woman said stoutly. "Ye'll need every hand to help, and I'll no be lyin' about like the Queen o' Sheba while others work."

By the time Ian and Odgers finished in the stables and saw to the horses, the great hall had been swept and the debris hauled away to the outer ward for later burning. When the men came inside, they were put to work helping the women place the heavy tables and benches in order, then given the task of gathering wood and cleaning the heaps of old ash from the fireplaces—a task that would require more than what was left of this day. The women rolled up their sleeves and plunged in to work on the filthy kitchens.

Gillian fretted over Calum's continued absence, glancing repeatedly out the windows at the waning light. Had he encountered some savage Highland beast? Been attacked by maddened tenants? Fallen from his horse? Where was Hugh?

Odgers came back to Dunncrannog at dusk, his packhorse carrying much less firewood than she'd expected.

"There's little wood to be found around here," he reported. "The trees have all been cut down. Tomorrow I'll leave earlier and go farther."

Finally she could delay the evening meal no

longer. She served a simple stew accompanied by bread and ale, which they ate sitting around the fire in the vast, shadowy great hall. As the sun sank behind the mountains, the temperature grew cooler.

"I should have gone after him," Ian said as he set his plate aside. He turned an accusing look on Gillian.

"Here now, let's have none of that," Odgers said sternly. "Would you have left the women with but one man to defend them when we know not what to expect?"

Ian sighed. "Nay."

"We're all tired and worried," Augusta pointed out.

A soft snore came from the direction of Beathag, who had fallen asleep in her chair.

"Perhaps it is time to take our rest," Zerrin suggested. Barbara nodded sleepily.

The extent of the wood supply settled the matter of decorum. There was only fuel enough for one fireplace, for one night and the morning's breakfast. Blankets were handed out, and everyone lay down in front of the hearth in the great hall. Ian and Odgers divided the watch shifts between them, with Ian taking the first.

Gillian couldn't sleep. Surrounded by the heavy, even breathing and snores of her fellow travelers, she felt isolated and alone. She stared up at the high fan-groined ceiling. It reminded her of a painting she'd once seen, of the interior of a cathedral. Only the ceiling in the cathedral hadn't been black with soot and grime and age.

She heard the soft tread of booted feet. "Can ye

no sleep?" Ian whispered as he squatted on his heels by her side.

She sat up. "No."

In the low glow of the fire she saw him lift an eyebrow.

"I'm worried," she admitted. "They ought to have been back long before now."

Ian smiled. "As I'm about to become yer kinsman, I should think there would be no harm to yer reputation to come keep watch with me until ye tire."

Gillian gathered up her blanket and stepped over a sleeping Zerrin to follow Ian through the hall and up the steps. He led the way into the bower, to a window with a clear view of the bridge across the lake. A full moon cast its silver light over the black water. The dark, craggy mountains encircling the tarn wore gleaming one-sided cloaks of argent.

"Earlier I went out and barred the gates," Ian said, as they settled onto the deep, stone window seat, looking out the many-paned leaded window. An intricate stained-glass coat of arms held the place of honor in the center. "We must watch for them so we may let them in."

Gillian nodded as she traced the red, blue, and green bits of glass with her forefinger.

"Is this the MacFuaran coat of arms?" she asked.

Ian leaned back against the side of the embrasure. He brought one foot up on the generous seat and clasped his hands around his bent knee. "Aye. Once—before the Forty-five—this was the seat of Clan MacFuaran. Dunncrannog Castle was the home of the clan chiefs. 'Twas a powerful clan. Verra fierce. Verra prosperous."

"Did the MacFuarans support Charles Edward Stuart?"

Ian shook his head. "Nay. But after Culloden, it scarce mattered. The English took their revenge on rebel and loyalist alike. 'Twas naught but their way of bringing all of the Highlands under their heel. The bastards stripped us of our language, of our faith, of the very clothes we wore. Tartans were outlawed. Thousands of clansmen dispersed to the four points o' the compass, robbed unjustly of their lands. The laird of Iolar had to journey to London to plead his case. He was lucky. The Crown returned his lands."

"Was that Calum's father?"

"His grandfather. A crafty auld fox, so I've heard."

Gillian's gaze was drawn back to the empty bridge over the black-diamond water as she thought about a man desperately struggling to hold together family and heritage, forced to witness the systematic destruction of his way of life. That man's grandson had just discovered that same valley had been ruthlessly raped—and the blame laid at his feet.

"Ian . . ." Her words faded in her throat. Would he tell her?

He looked away from the window, at her, expectant.

"Ian, what happened to Calum after he was . . . repudiated by his father?"

The radiance of the moon poured through the thick panes of glass, frosting half the dark, chilly bower with pale light.

Ian made no answer.

She turned her gaze back to the coat of arms. "I'm to be his bride, yet I know only what others say about his past."

"The past is no important."

She sighed. "That is untrue, and I believe you know it. The past is a trap that can snap shut on the innocent."

"Are ye claimin' to be innocent?"

She blushed hotly. "Perhaps ignorant is more precise a word."

Ian looked at her for a minute, then expelled his breath in a disgusted huff. "Och, lassie, I ask yer forgiveness. 'Twas ungentlemanly of me. I fear I'm no fit company now."

"Will you tell me?"

He hesitated. "'Tis no a happy story. At least, no till the end."

"I like happy endings."

The corner of Ian's mouth tugged up. "Perhaps ye are the happy ending for my cousin."

Something twisted deep inside Gillian. Ending. Where was he now, her prospective groom? *Please, dear Lord, please let him be safe.* She would deal with the unhappiness later, if only he was unharmed.

"I would wish our union might prove more a beginning than an end," she said and tried to smile.

"Aye. A beginning. He needs that, I think. But 'tis his story to tell, should he choose to say aught of his past. I will say only that after his father accused his mother of being unfaithful and announced that Calum was no son of his, Lady Iolar left this place and took Calum with her. They went to Edinburgh."

"Why did she not return to her own family?"

"There had been a row over her marryin' with Robert MacFuaran. Her parents had arranged for her to wed another man. They were no best pleased when she insisted on a wild Highland laird, but she would have her way. It was a love match. Mind, I'm tellin' ye the story as Hugh told it to me. I was no around at that time."

Gillian did smile then. "I would imagine not."

His teeth flashed in the dim light. "Aye, well. Hugh is a reliable historian. He said 'twas indeed a love match, and, when she wed Robert MacFuaran, her family refused to come to the weddin'. Nor would they answer her letters when she came to live here. So ye see, she had no one to turn to when her husband accused her of adultery. And she was a proud woman. As stubborn as her husband. So she took her son and left. Calum's no seen the valley since he was seven. He remembers it as a place where everyone prospered."

"A happy time in his life," she murmured.

"Aye. The last truly happy time, 'twould seem."

Gillian remembered the shock and pain she'd seen etched in his face when they'd ridden into the abandoned, long-neglected Dunncrannog Castle. For a moment she'd glimpsed a soul that had been stripped of its last hope.

She knew he'd been impatient to return to Iolar Glen when they'd been at Treymoor, but she had never credited the valley with the true importance it held in his life.

Now she felt she could more clearly see how he must have been longing to return to this place, home to his few fond memories. This castle and the valley beyond had always lived in his mind as a sanctuary, a destination that held the power to heal the ravages of injustice and malice. He might have ignored her father's letter appointing him her guardian and gone straight to his newly acquired estate, perhaps the only place he'd ever been content. But he had not. He had ridden to Treymoor, and there, spurred by his honor, the honor others refused to acknowledge in him, he had assumed a responsibility he had neither expected nor wanted. She wondered how many others would have undertaken a similar charge from a stranger.

Movement from the corner of her eye sent her bolting forward in her seat to peer through the wavy glass.

Two horsemen stood at the bridge, wrapped in shimmering moonlight and velvet black night.

"Ian!" she exclaimed.

"I see them!"

She leapt from the window seat and raced across the room, where Ian almost ran into the back of her as they fumbled to pull the door open. Down the stairs they plunged, then across the great hall.

Odgers sleepily lifted his head. "What . . . ?"

"They're back," Gillian told him, nearly hopping from foot to foot with impatience as Ian unbarred the door.

"Back?" Beatheg asked.

"Aye!"

Then Ian had the door open, and Gillian bolted through the space, sprinting through the alien landscape of towers and stone curtain walls. Behind her, she heard Ian's heavier footfalls.

"Wait," he said, "we must make certain."

Ian raced up the tower stairs to call down to the riders. "Who goes there?"

Hugh's fatigue-roughened voice came back across the water. "Calum MacFuaran and Hugh Drummond."

Ian joined Gillian in lifting the one portcullis Ian had earlier lowered. Then they eased down the drawbridge.

Horses' hooves pounded hollowly against the heavy wooden planking as the two horsemen crossed the final length to the island fortress.

Calum swung heavily down from his saddle. Slipping the reins through his fingers, he started back toward the courtyard.

"What are ye doin' up?" he asked, glancing at her, then continuing on the worn path, trailed by his horse.

Feeling suddenly awkward, put back by his apparent indifference to her, she muttered, "I could not sleep."

If he heard her, he made no answer. As they entered the cobbled courtyard, the hooves of the two horses clattered in syncopated rhythm, echoing against the high stone walls.

Gillian stopped and stared after Calum, the tallest of the three men. None of them spoke as Ian guided them to the stables. None seemed to notice her absence.

She went back toward the great hall, where she was met by a crowd coming out the door.

"Are they unharmed?" Augusta asked, a question that seemed to speak for everyone there.

"They appear to be, but it is difficult to tell with

only the moonlight to see by." Gillian ushered everyone back into the hall. "They will be in soon."

Beathag held her silence, her weathered face revealing nothing of what she thought.

"They will be hungry," Gillian said, relieved to find something to keep her busy. As she made her way to the largest of the kitchens, Beathag and Augusta fell into step with her.

Although she wanted to give them warm food to eat, she knew that would leave no firewood to cook the morning meal. She settled on bread and cheese, and Augusta added pieces of dried fruit. Beathag poured out only two cups of ale, a silent reminder of their limited food supplies.

When they carried the food into the great hall, Gillian saw Hugh slumped wearily in a chair by the fire, with the others gathered around him, listening.

"—dire straights," she heard him say. " 'Twas as bad as Beathag said."

"Where is Calum?" Gillian asked, more sharply than she'd intended. Everyone in the hall turned to look at her in surprise.

"He's no come in from the stables yet," Ian said gently.

"He must eat," she muttered. "I will see what keeps him." She walked out the door—and stopped short.

Calum stood alone in the courtyard, bathed in silver and jet. He looked out toward the mountains that surrounded the castle like a dark enchanted crown conjured by an ancient sorcerer.

He must have heard her footsteps, for he glanced briefly over his shoulder at her.

"They were right," he said, his voice flat and empty.

Slowly she approached him. When he didn't turn toward her, she stepped forward to face him. "Who was right?"

"Everyone. Ye."

She swallowed, not wanting to ask what he meant, yet afraid not to know. "About what were we all right?"

"Iolar Glen is ruined."

She saw his throat work in the pale moonlight, and shame washed through her. "What . . ." She swallowed. "What has that to do with me?"

He cut her a narrow look, then returned to his study of the distance.

"I had reason to believe you were responsible," she protested defiantly. "Reliable people said—"

"So many reliable people! So . . . many . . . good . . . *reliable* . . . people." He forced each word through clenched teeth. "Every one of them ready to believe I would destroy the most important thing to me in my whole bloody life."

"I'm sorry," she said humbly.

"Why? Why do people think I committed such a horrible deed? I'll no deny I wanted revenge on my father many times through the years, but I never acted on it. *He* was wrong, and I dinna intend to become like him!"

"I'm sorry," she whispered, tears burning in her throat.

A cool night breeze tugged at the many strands of his hair that had come loose from his usually neat queue. For the first time, she noticed the dried blood on his cheek.

"You've been hurt!" she exclaimed, reaching to his wound.

He caught her wrist before her fingers could touch him. " 'Tis nothing," he said roughly.

"Let me tend it," she said, but her heart pleaded for his forgiveness.

"I said, 'tis nothing." He dropped his hold on her as if he'd been burned.

"How . . ." Her throat closed. She drew a long unsteady breath and tried again. "How did it happen?"

Now he looked full at her, his beautiful face an otherworldly mask of silver and black. "Since ye seem so interested, I was struck by a rock."

"Was there a rockslide? You must have a care. These mountains are perilous." Gillian ached to hold him, to comfort him as he'd comforted her. But he would not have her touch him, and that knowledge twisted painfully inside her.

Calum laughed, a hollow, haunted sound rife with bitterness. "Aye! These mountains are perilous indeed for a man deemed to be a nameless bastard and a low, plotting thief." He swept his arm out in an arc that included the valley beyond the pass in the mountains. "It matters naught to the people remaining in Iolar Glen that my father recognized me before he died. They have heard the lie and they believe it. There was no rockslide. The stone that struck me was launched from the hand of a crofter. To my own clan, I am the enemy."

The full horror of his words penetrated Gillian's misery. One of his own relations was responsible for the wound. All Calum's waiting, his dearest memories of the Eden beyond the mountains, smashed to pieces through a lie.

She could remember receiving only love and loyalty

from the people who lived on Treymoor. The knowledge that a kinsman could feel so hostile toward Calum that he would commit an act of violence filled her with dread.

That Calum compared her to that very tenant hurt her immeasurably. Yet she knew she had given him cause.

"I was wrong," she said, her voice hoarse with regret. "So very wrong."

He looked away, over the moon-touched battlements and spires of Dunncrannog. He did not speak, and she could not fathom his thoughts.

Her slim hope for their future flickered and, like a flame when the candle has burned too low, began to die. She'd nursed her hope through the journey from Yorkshire, against all the odds of logic, against every sign that she was wrong. Now she came face-to-face with the barrenness that stretched before her. There could be no trust between them. He would never love her.

Unable to stand next to him a second longer as her dreams disintegrated into dust, Gillian whirled on her heel and ran across the courtyard, her boots ringing against the cobbles.

"Gillian."

Her name on his lips, spoken in that deep voice, had the power to stop her before she reached the door to the silent kitchens. She struggled for breath against her suffocating grief.

"Ye are to be my wife."

Her back to him, she hesitated, then nodded, unable to do more and still maintain any shred of dignity.

He crossed to her side, his long legs easily eating

up the distance between them. If only the distance between their hearts could be so easily traversed.

"Ye are to be my wife," he repeated. "Even now ye may have conceived our first child."

Hysterical laughter bubbled up against her throat and she struggled to squash it. He could not bear her touch, yet he anticipated making a flock of children with her. How could she survive the mating act as it would be with him in the future? Stripped of the searing passion they had shared, of the trembling intimate need? Would he expect her to obediently spread herself beneath him, biting her lip as he made the few required thrusts, then complacently to take herself off to her own bed, in her own room somewhere down the hall? A sob escaped her lips.

He stiffened beside her. "Does the prospect of wedding with me distress ye so?"

She looked up at him, tears spilling onto her cheeks. "Yes. I mean no." She shook her head. "Oh, 'tis hopeless!" Another sob threatened, and she drew in a sharp breath to try to dispel it. "I wanted . . ." The words died on her lips. If she must live without his love, at least she might draw the tattered remnants of her pride around her to help keep out the cold.

He lifted a hand to her shoulder, but he did not touch her. He hesitated; then his fingers curled into a fist, which he dropped back to his side. "Tell me," he said leadenly.

She tilted up her chin as defiance licked through her. "I had hoped for better for us. I had hoped we might work together as husband and wife and bring this—this pile of rocks and even Iolar back to what

you once knew. And perhaps even eventually—"
Suddenly her defiance deserted her, taking her
courage with it. "But I see you've already given up,"
she muttered. She started to continue on her way,
eager to gain a quiet sanctuary where she might cradle the shards of her dream in private.

His hand shot out and caught hold of her arm.
"Wait. What were ye about to say?" An odd note of
urgency penetrated his voice.

"Nothing."

"If 'twas nothing, then ye should no object to finishing what ye started to say. Eventually what? What
did ye hope?"

She tried to pull her arm from his grasp, wanting
to make her escape, but he seemed not to notice.

"Very well!" she snapped. "I hoped we might
eventually love each other."

Unable to face another minute of his stunned
expression, she snatched her arm from his slackened
hold, picked up her skirts, and ran.

In the pitch-black kitchen, she gave in to her
grief, her body torn by raw, heartbroken sobs. Hot
tears drenched her cheeks.

She heard footsteps outside the door into the
courtyard and choked into silence. The door swung
open with a creak and moonlight flooded the room.
Gillian pressed her back against the wall, trying to
make herself smaller.

Calum called to her softly. "Gillian?"

She held her breath.

"Will ye no speak to me, then?"

He couldn't see her, she was certain he couldn't
see her. She pressed more firmly against the stones,

wanting only to be left alone with her guilt, her humiliation, and her hurt.

"What took so long for me to return tonight was findin' a minister to wed us tomorrow," Calum said. "I know 'tis rushed, but we canna risk something happenin' to me before ye have my name. Hugh and I had to leave the valley to find him."

Gillian bit her lip, trying to stem a fresh tide of tears.

"Ye'll have until noon to prepare yerself." Was there a note of apology in his words?

With another creak, the door swung shut, leaving her once again in thick, inky gloom redolent with the smell of onions, porridge, and ashes.

Tomorrow, Calum would make her his wife.

16

"*Forasmuch as Calum Gregory MacFuaran* and Gillian Rose Ellicott have consented together in holy wedlock, and have witnessed the same before God and this company, and thereto have given and pledged their troth, each to the other . . ."

The minister's words, spoken in his lilting bass, rolled like thunder around Gillian, her icy hand held in Calum's.

She had taken Calum as her husband.

Always she had thought she would give her promise standing before Mr. Appleyard in Saint Agnes, surrounded by people she had known all her life. Instead, she stood before a bearlike travel-stained stranger in the neglected great hall of an alien castle, high in the Scottish Highlands.

Suddenly she realized that the minister had stopped speaking. Calum turned to her, still holding her hand. His eyes searched her face. Then, solemnly, he lowered his head toward her.

Gillian's eyes widened, then closed of their own accord, as the warmth of Calum's mouth touched hers. She lifted her face to his and felt his fingers tighten fractionally around hers. She leaned closer, losing herself in the elemental magic of his kiss.

It ended almost as soon as it had begun. Gillian wanted to protest when Calum drew away; then awareness of the others returned, and she nervously patted the long curls that Zerrin had painstakingly arranged that morning. Remembering how painstakingly, Gillian snatched her hand away, unwilling to ruin the effect. Like it or not, Calum was her husband now, and like it or not, she wanted him to think her pretty.

Everyone surrounded them, congratulating Calum, felicitating her. Ian and Hugh were hearty in their best wishes, slapping Calum on the back, each giving Gillian a robust kiss on the cheek.

Augusta wept as she enfolded Gillian in her arms. "I expected things to be different. I wanted you to wed in someplace pretty, not this wretched pile. Oh, well. Above all, I wanted you to marry for love." She dabbed at her eyes with a lace-edged handkerchief. "And"—she delicately blew her nose—"in a way, I believe you have."

Gillian stared at her. "Love?"

Augusta gave her a watery smile. "Yes, dear. I do believe that you're in love with your husband."

Quickly Gillian glanced around to make certain Calum was still talking with his cousins and the minister. "He does not love me," she said in a low voice.

"I would not be too certain of that," Augusta said.

"He bears many signs of a man besotted with a woman," Zerrin observed, her dark eyes crinkling at the corners as she smiled beneath her veil.

"Do you think so?" Gillian asked worriedly. *Don't be daft*, a small voice at the back of her mind warned.

The two women nodded. All of them turned to look at Calum. He seemed to feel their gaze, for he turned around, saw his observers, and gave them a dignified nod.

They nodded back and returned to their conversation.

"You have a better chance to make an agreeable life with Calum than most women have with their grooms," Augusta said.

Gillian wanted to believe that, but she knew better than anyone all the barriers that separated them.

The wedding party sat down to a simple meal prepared from their supplies, as the men had been unable to find any fresh meat. The ancient oak tables had been decorated with bouquets of wild-flowers that grew in the outer ward.

"There are neither deer nor boar nor grouse left," the traveling minister said. "After the livestock was either sold off or slaughtered last year, the people who managed to stay on in the glen were forced to hunt to put food on the table for their wives and wee ones. Now the game is gone." The traveling minister shook his head. "'Twill be a hard winter and no question. Many if not all in Iolar will die."

Augusta looked at the minister reprovingly. "Pleasant conversation for a wedding party."

The man shrugged. "Those newly wed must contend with the hard truth, just as we all do."

"The truth can wait until tomorrow, sir."

He sighed. "Aye, I suppose."

Gillian had been seated next to Calum at the head of the table. Though she tried to be a good hostess, little of her attention was not focused on Calum. She seemed to notice everything about him. The red-gold hair dusting the back of his hands. His dark-fire, slanting eyebrows, his high broad cheekbones and sensual mouth. The faint aroma of sandalwood and clean male skin seemed to her more heady than a thousand draughts of the eye-watering whisky with which they'd drunk toasts.

Calum was so tall, so powerfully built. And she knew well what he could accomplish with his potent male body, how he could make her feel. The thought brought a slow heat pulsing through her, an ache rife with need. Quickly she lowered her eyes to her untouched platter, but she feared the deep flush that warmed her skin must reveal her thoughts to everyone.

Finally the minister took his leave. There were two funerals, a churching, and another wedding he must attend to while he was in the area. The wedding party escorted him to the outer curtain wall, waving to him as he reached the shore side of the bridge, a big man on a sturdy pony. She watched him disappear over the horizon.

Quiet drew her notice to the fact that everyone had drifted away, leaving Calum and her alone.

"It appears we have an afternoon for our honeymoon," Calum said.

She nodded, feeling absurdly shy. What was wrong with her? She had lived under the same roof with this man, seen him unclothed, lost her maidenhood to him.

"Have ye something ye'd like to do?" he asked politely.

"If 'twould not distress you more, I would like to see Iolar Glen," she ventured hesitantly.

He stiffened beside her, and she wondered if he thought she was going to gloat or if she was afraid he was willing to expose her to danger.

"Your people are now my people, Calum," she said softly. "I would know what can be done for them."

He studied her intently for a moment, and gradually the tension ebbed from him. "Anything would be an improvement in their lot. Rarely have I seen such grievous misery."

In a silence filled with glances and shy smiles, they saddled their horses.

"Thank you," she said.

"For what?"

"For taking me into your glen."

" 'Tis our glen now."

Was he just being kind? she thought. Or was there something more?

When they told Hugh where they were going, he frowned. "Are ye certain this is wise, lad?" he asked Calum. "Takin' yer bride among hostiles?"

"The idea is mine, Hugh," Gillian said.

His brow eased slightly. "Aye. Well. What man could refuse such a bonny bride? But have a care. Yesterday 'twas a well-aimed stone. Today they may be bolder."

Gillian gave Hugh a cocky grin, casting back a glance at Calum. "I'll not let them hurt him again."

Hugh laughed, and the corner of Calum's mouth drew up in a crooked smile. "What man could ask for better assurance than that?"

Minutes later, their horses galloped across the bridge.

As they raced toward the gap that was the entrance into Iolar Glen, Gillian was filled with a heady exuberance that held her doubts at bay. For whatever reason, Calum had agreed to share his valley with her. The future stretched before them, filled with possibility.

He led the way through the narrow gap, which was wide enough for a single farm wagon to pass. She saw that a road had been graded from the gap to the valley floor, or no vehicle could have left or entered the glen because of the steep incline. To her surprise, Calum did not follow the road but, rather, edged his mount to the boulder-strewn side. She followed him.

He dismounted, then came to reach up for her.

She laughed self-consciously. "I am quite capable, sir."

His beautifully sensual mouth curved into a smile that was at once teasing yet uncertain. For the first time she realized he might be feeling some of the awkwardness and hesitancy she experienced. In the face of his gaze, her heart melted and she gave herself into his hands willingly.

Their eyes met and held as he lifted her from her saddle to stand close to him. She felt his warm breath upon her cheek. A bridle jingled as a horse tossed its head. High above, a golden eagle cried to its mate.

"I know ye think ye need no one's help, my lady," Calum said softly, "but do me the honor of letting me believe I might be of service to ye."

"Aye, my lord," she whispered, unable to do more.

A twinkle came into his eyes. "I like a biddable wife," he said, then lowered his head and claimed her lips with devastating tenderness.

Her fingers curled into the leather of his riding coat as the world spun away, leaving her dizzy and anchorless.

"I like an attentive husband," she said breathlessly, still clinging to his coat.

He laughed, a rich, masculine, heart-lifting sound. "I shall most definitely bear that in mind, madam."

He turned her around until her back was against his chest and, still in his embrace, she stood looking out over the valley.

The green of summer had given way to the amber and russet of autumn. Down the length of the glen flowed a glittering gold-brown river, past rocky banks. The stone huts of the crofters and their tilled squares dotted the land. Few squares contained any plants. Most were brown and dead. She noticed a marked absence of trees and saw that much of the forest had been stripped from the near slopes. Although she observed no sign of erosion, Gillian knew that, come spring when the snows melted, there would be no watershed to absorb and slow the flow and rich topsoil would be lost. As her gaze moved farther into the glen, she observed what must once have been a village. Now the buildings looked deserted and a few were tumbled and blackened, as if they had burned.

Nowhere did she see sheep or cattle. What she did see were empty pens and byres.

"I remember the mountainsides covered with ancient forest," Calum said. "There were elk and deer. Oaks grew along the river." A faint aching note underlay his words, and Gillian curved her hands around his forearms.

"It can't have gone on for too long, this stripping of the glen. We can turn back the tide, I know we can."

He sighed and nestled her more closely to him. "Dinna underestimate the task. 'Twill take much effort and gold."

She could see it would, but he was a wealthy merchant, was he not? As far as returning this valley to prosperity, where there was gold, there was a way. It would buy healthy livestock and pay the wages of men to replant the mountainsides. Once the country was not so overhunted, the game would return. With improved conditions in the glen, new tenants could be found to replace those who had been driven out. Over time, the village would be rebuilt.

"What better way to use one's fortune than to restore one's home and land?" she asked. She would be a part of that restoration. Their children would play in the great hall of Dunncrannog and run and fish in Iolar as their father had once done.

Their children. The thought warmed her heart.

"With that I am in complete agreement." His words were what she wanted to hear, yet she detected in them a faint note of reservation.

She turned in his arms and looked up at him in question. The muscles of his jaw tensed. He kept his eyes turned toward the valley. When he met her gaze, she sensed he'd just come to a difficult decision.

"I dinna wish for ye to worry. I will always find a way to provide for ye, but—" He clamped his jaw shut and looked away. She felt the tension in his muscles. His reticence pricked her nerves. "My money is tied up in a business venture," he said. "'Twas done before I knew I would take ye to wife, or I would no have taken such a risk. The steward had said . . ." His words died away.

A cold wave washed through Gillian. Calum would need money, a lot of it, to repair the damage and neglect to Iolar Glen and Dunncrannog. His money was beyond his reach. If he knew Treymoor was his, would he strip it for the sake of the place he loved? He had no ties there, no affection, as he did for Iolar Glen and the castle. Somehow, in spite of that, Gillian couldn't believe he would abuse Treymoor.

She thought about how Calum had handled Scarth when the man had threatened to strike her. About how he'd bought Sammy the much-coveted wig and told the boy she'd purchased it. And the harvest: he'd labored in the sun, alongside her and her people, when other men would have considered the hard work beneath them. He'd eaten the plain food and thanked the women who served it.

God help her, she believed in Calum Gregory MacFuaran.

She raised her hands and cupped his face, bringing it downward until their gazes joined. "I'm not worried," she said softly. "Together we shall work to make this the place you remember. We will find a way." She could not bring herself to speak of Treymoor. She did not wish to destroy her tentative chance for a successful marriage with an ill-timed revelation of her deceit. But soon. Soon she would tell him.

He held her close. "It will be a fine thing," he murmured, "havin' ye by my side here, when the place is restored."

Gillian smiled. Beneath her cheek, the cambric of his shirt was warmed by his skin.

He drew in a long breath and slowly let it out. "I was a fool. A stubborn, arrogant fool. I should have come straight here."

Gillian turned in his arms to face him, feeling the sting of guilt. "You came to Treymoor instead, didn't you?"

"Aye." She remained quiet, waiting, and he continued. "Did ye never wonder how I was supposed to have accomplished the ruination of my father's estate while he was yet alive?"

"The sheep trader I deal with, a man I've known for many years, told me that when he came to Iolar to look at some supposedly rare sheep, the steward confessed to having done it all at your orders. He said you were blackmailing him into it."

"Is that so?" Calum asked. "And did he say what hold I had over such a person?"

"Mr. Wilson said it was too unsavory to discuss with a lady."

Calum spat an oath. "It would seem that cursed steward must have had a convincing story."

"It convinced many."

"I believed him to be as innocent as I."

"But then, you are an honorable man," she pointed out.

A deep red flush moved up Calum's neck, into his face. "I try to be."

She ducked her head at the memory of their passionate lovemaking. Under normal circumstances, she would have joined him again in his bed this night. Instead, tonight they would curl up beside the hearth in the great hall with the others. She was caught between relief and disappointment.

He tipped his forefinger under her chin and nudged her head up. "I seem to have trouble with my honor where ye are concerned," he said. "For yer sake, I am verra sorry."

"My sake?"

"Ye wanted Leake, did ye no?"

"Did I?" she asked coyly, batting her eyelashes. "I quite forget."

Calum's mouth curved in a slow, sultry smile. His eyes darkened with promise. "I plan to help ye continue to forget."

Feverish heat pulsed through her veins. Her lips parted, ready.

"Nay, lass," he said, his voice rough, yet gentle. "Another kiss, and ye'll see no more of the glen than the ground between these rocks. I've been wantin' ye too long now."

"But—" Instantly she bit off her words, blushing hotly, remembering.

He placed his mouth close to her ear. "Aye. I know. And it only made me want ye more." His breath caressed her ear, and she shivered with desire.

Calum lifted her onto her horse, his strong hands firm against her waist, his gaze intense.

He turned to his own mount and with a creak of leather swung up into the saddle to lead their descent on the only road into Iolar Glen.

They traveled in silence past a burned-out shell of a hut. The picked-clean skeleton of a dog lay in the dirt near the front door. Gillian swallowed hard. Why had the dog not been buried? What had happened to the people who had lived here? Had the dog been killed while trying to protect them? She turned her eyes away.

They passed many burned remains of cottages, several with graves nearby, which were marked by mounded earth and twigs bound in the form of crosses. Here and there she saw the bones of a sheep or a cow.

"Who did this thing?" she asked. "The steward?"

Calum rode close beside her now, his eyes constantly surveying the area around them. "Beathag said Farnum had his men drive the crofters from their cottages. If someone refused to leave, the cottage was put to the torch. 'Tis also what happened to the village: people rousted from their homes, buildings burned."

"He should be hanged!"

"The people in this glen think I should be the one to swing."

Sorrow welled inside her. "Oh, Calum. They've been wronged and lied to."

His jaw tightened as he regarded an empty cottage, the door hanging open, the wind lazily shifting it to and fro. " 'Twould appear to be a MacFuaran legacy."

She longed to reach out to touch his hand, to offer comfort, but she sensed withdrawal in him. He was a proud man. Sharing his deepest feelings with someone after a lifetime of making his own way in a merciless world would not come easily.

"Eventually they will come to see the truth. But they are not your true family, Calum."

He turned to look at her, his expression unreadable. "Aye? And just who are my 'true' family, then? Have my parents returned from the grave?"

For an instant, Gillian recalled her midnight visit to the cemetery. Standing in the cool marble vault, surrounded by the dust and bones of her ancestors, she had consigned her father to a nameless stone coffin. Afterward . . . the shadowy creature with the blood-freezing laughter. Who had that been? No authorities had shown up on her doorstep to arrest her. She'd detected no rumors about mysterious circumstances surrounding her father's early departure for Turkey. Perhaps Jenkins was right. Perhaps instead of asking "who" had seen them she should be asking "what" had witnessed their deception.

She pushed those thoughts away to concentrate on Calum.

"I speak only of the living," she informed him, "and there appear to be a few of those. What of Hugh and Ian? And your other cousins in Edinburgh? I believe I've heard one mentioned who is seeing to your company while you are absent."

"Balfour Drummond."

"Yes. They are blood relations, are they not?"

"Aye, on my mother's side."

She pulled Atlanta up to his horse as closely as she

dared and placed her hand over his, urging him to halt. When he complied, Gillian leaned over to search her husband's shuttered face. "Calum, true family are not just those who share the same blood ties. True family are the people who protect you, who care for your welfare, sometimes at the risk of their own. True family are those upon whom you know you can depend."

His horse shifted its weight. "Are ye sayin' that the people in this glen are no my kinsmen?"

She shook her head. "I'm saying they are not your *family*. I own it is a peculiar distinction. Blood ties or no, you and the people of this valley are strangers now. You do not trust one another. There is no personal caring. Not yet. Once they realize they've been told lies, and they see you are an honorable man, that may change. But even if it doesn't, you are not without family. I stand with you."

He reached over and touched his fingertips to her cheek. "Ye are a wonder, Gillian. A rare wonder."

His softly spoken words set butterflies fluttering in her stomach. She could think of nothing to say.

He chuckled. "I've never seen ye speechless before."

To which she could think of no reply.

"Come," he said, and nudged his horse with his heels.

As they drew nearer the river, she heard the music of water flowing over rocks.

Where there were no boulders to send the swift water into turbulent white, the gold-brown river revealed stones jumbled together in the bed below.

Less than half a mile downstream, men, women, and children fished from the shores. Ragged clothing hung loosely on undernourished bodies.

"Iolar River is the sole remaining source of food," Calum said.

"For how long?" Gillian asked.

He nodded, and guided his horse away from the water.

A shout rang from the opposite bank. A man pointed in their direction.

"Stay close to me," Calum commanded in an undertone. He opened the flap of his saddle holster and rested his hand upon his thigh, within easy reach of the sheathed flintlock pistol.

To her relief, no one attempted to molest them, but from the strident quality of the voices that carried over the water Gillian knew they were not pleased to see them.

Calum and she continued up the valley at an even pace. Here and there they saw people. None threatened to harm the new laird or the woman with him, but their painfully thin faces reflected their distrust and blame.

The inhabited cottages looked in little better condition than the empty ones. Signs of long-term neglect suggested that the steward had been robbing the estate for more than a year. She saw churned earth where kitchen gardens should have been and suspected that hunger drove the crofters to harvest vegetables before they were ripe.

"Where are we going?" Gillian asked when it became apparent that Calum was leading them in a particular direction.

He halted his horse in front of one of the larger cottages. Like the others, its animal pens stood empty.

"We're here," he said, making no move to dismount.

Not two minutes later, a big Highlander ducked through the door. As he straightened, Gillian saw that he was lean and gaunt. She guessed him to be about sixty.

"Good day to ye, Fergus MacFuaran," Calum said, his face effectively masking his thoughts. A mild smile curved his lips.

The older man regarded him for a moment. "I heard ye had returned."

"Aye."

"As ye may have noticed, ye're no a popular fellow in Iolar Glen."

"I'm no responsible for what has happened here, Fergus. I canna say why the blame was laid at my door, but I've had naught to do with my father, or anything that was his, until his solicitor contacted me just above two months ago."

Fergus studied Calum consideringly, his arms crossed over his massive chest. "The man dinna even have the ballocks to recant to yer face, did he?" the crofter asked gruffly.

Calum slowly shook his head.

"The devil take him," Fergus said darkly.

"I imagine he did."

Fergus lowered his arms to his sides. "Come, lad. I havena much to offer ye, but what's mine is yers."

Gillian sensed relief in Calum. With his usual grace, he dismounted. He came directly to Gillian, swinging her down from her sidesaddle.

"And who is this bonny lassie?" Fergus asked, some of his reserve sloughing away.

"Gillian Rose Ellicott MacFuaran, my wife."

My wife. Those words on Calum's lips, the proud

way he said them, quickened Gillian's heart. She dropped the crofter a curtsey deep enough to have done honor to the king.

"Gillian, I'd like ye to meet the man with whom I spent many of my days and nights before I—uh, left Iolar Glen. My foster father, Fergus MacFuaran."

She offered Fergus her hand. "I am honored to meet you, Mr. MacFuaran."

He stared at her. "A Sassenach? Calum, ye wed with a Sassenach? Och, lad, this is no a good thing."

Fergus took her hand, but by that time Gillian felt inclined to snatch it back. Only her regard for her husband's pride kept her fingers in Fergus's paw.

Calum scowled. "I'll remind ye, Fergus, this is my wife ye speak of. Have a care."

Fergus patted Gillian's hand apologetically. " 'Tis not for me I'm concerned, Calum. I know ye were wrenched from the bosom of yer clan, dragged away from their lands by yer dear wronged mother. Anything can happen when a man's adrift. He gets lonely."

"Your flattery is overwhelming, sir," Gillian said dryly. "What woman does not long to be compared to some tavern doxy who has just ensnared a homesick sailor?"

Fergus's face went dark red. "I ask yer pardon, madam. It was never my intention—that is to say, I never meant . . ."

Calum laughed. "Ye've put yer great hoof right in it, man. Ye're on yer own now."

"I only meant to say—"

"Yes?" Gillian prompted sweetly.

"Never would I compare ye to a tavern doxy!"

"How very kind."

Fergus released her hand and tugged at the bottom of his shabby waistcoat. "I dinna mean to insult ye, Lady Iolar, but yer bein' a Sassenach will make it more difficult for Calum to win people to the truth. I know things have likely changed outside the glen over the years, but here memories are long. The English are hated still by many."

"And yerself, Fergus," Calum said. "Do ye hate the English?"

"I like to keep my feuds a bit more personal than that, though I dinna say I'd welcome the whole lot of 'em here. No, I try to judge a man—or woman—by their actions."

Gillian inclined her head in acknowledgment.

Calum tied the horses' reins to the top rail of an empty pen. "Have ye anything to drink, Fergus?"

The crofter ushered them inside his cottage. "Water is all I can offer ye in the way of drink. The *uisce beatha* was the first to go. Then the milk. We've not even had tea for nigh on ten months now."

"What of herbs?" Gillian asked.

"Gone. Perhaps in the spring some of the plants will come back."

"Water it is, then," Calum said. "Where is Rachel?"

Fergus paused in ladling out horn cups of water. "My Rachel died last year," he said quietly. "Taken by a fever."

Calum did not reply immediately. Gillian trained her gaze on the cups, trying to allow Calum a moment of privacy.

"I'm sorry to hear she's gone," he said, a slight roughness to his voice. "She was a verra good woman."

Fergus nodded, a wistful look passing over his craggy face. "Aye. That she was." He finished pouring and handed them their cups.

They sat in the cozy cottage and talked. Or rather, the men talked and Gillian listened, content to learn what she could of Calum's life after he left the valley, of what had passed in the glen in past years to bring about the present situation.

"What happened when yer mother took ye away?" Fergus asked. "In the dead of night, it was. It cast an unpleasant light on the matter. There was quite a stramash when ye both were found missin' the next morning. Everyone was sayin' as how she must have been guilty after all. Yer uncle was the only one in the castle to hold as how he thought yer mother was innocent of adultery. And Beathag, of course. She never believed Lady Iolar had been unfaithful."

Calum gazed into the bottom of his empty cup for a long moment. "Things werena good in Edinburgh. Employment for cast-off gentlewomen is rare. For a gentlewoman with a child there was none at all. She might have become the mistress of a wealthy man— she had offers."

"Yer mother was a true beauty." Fergus nodded. "A true beauty, and no mistake."

"Aye. And too proud to become any man's whore. So she found work in a tavern. 'Twas a low vermin-ridden place, full of cutthroats and smugglers. Her beauty became a curse to her.

"We lived in a dark, stinking place in the worst section of town. We supped on meat when I could kill a rat or two and bread when she could smuggle home crusts. I remember wishin' hard, so hard, that I was a man full grown so I could take her away to a clean sweet-smellin' place filled with sunshine. A place where she'd never again have to serve a stoup of sour ale to some slimy, leering—" He broke off, his jaw rigid. "Then one night, walkin' home from the tavern, she was set upon." His fingers tightened around his cup. "She was beaten . . . and violated . . . and left to die." Calum's knuckles turned white.

"When she dinna come home, I went out searchin' for her. I found her lyin' in the street where the bastard had left her. Her hair, her lovely hair, was all covered with mud and filth. Her clothes had been torn off her, and she was smeared with her own blood."

Gillian listened in horror. From the corner of her eye, she saw Fergus's ruddy face had grown pale.

Calum continued. "She was still alive when I found her. A neighbor helped me get her upstairs to our room." He took a long breath. "It would have been a kindness, I think, had she died . . . when it happened. 'Twould have spared her the pain. As it was, she lingered, burnin' up with fever. I had nothing to give her. Nothing for the pain. There was no question of her . . . gettin' better. She died two days after I found her. That afternoon they took her away from me. For burial. But no one could show me, for certain, *where* she was buried. She was poor, ye see. It dinna matter."

Tears hung in Gillian's eyes. Dear God, no wonder Calum had nightmares! She ached to turn back the years, to make everything right for him. She wanted to chase away his memories of that terrible time and replace them with happy ones. Foolish wishes, of course. No one could alter the past. But she would do everything in her power to ensure that he and his children lived in a clean sweet-smelling place filled with sunshine, free from hunger and fear.

"A week later," Calum said, "I went to sea."

"How old were you?" Gillian asked.

"Seven. Still seven. We were no in Edinburgh but five months."

She knew it was not unheard of for children to go to sea, but she'd read enough on the subject and overheard enough men's conversations to know that life aboard ship was brutal and dangerous. Many men did not survive, even fewer boys. Gillian could only imagine what his days had been like.

" 'Tis a miracle ye lived to return," Fergus said. He sucked thoughtfully on an empty clay pipe, tobacco a luxury of the past.

A corner of Calum's mouth turned up. "Sometimes it was that. Between the weather, the rotten food, the scurvy, and a few of the ship's officers, 'twas a miracle any man lived. But some did, and they signed back on, again and again."

"Did you?" Gillian asked.

"I did. Where else did I have to go? What else did I know to do? I stayed aboard the *Bonny Gail* until I was sixteen, when I received a visit from my mother's father."

Fergus's bushy eyebrows rose in surprise. "So the auld coof finally relented, did he? Took him long enough."

"Seems his wife had died, and he'd decided to make peace with his daughter. When he was informed she'd left the glen when her husband had accused her of adultery, the auld man combed Scotland. His search led him back to Edinburgh. Finally, he found the tavern where she'd worked, and he learned of her death. Many more years of huntin' led him to me. He offered to teach me his trade as a merchant. He was a stranger to me, one I resented for my mother's sake, but my desire to be part of a family again swayed me, and I accepted. Though I canna say he was a warm man, or even that he ever liked me much, he did honor his word to me, teachin' me the ways of a merchant. When he died, he left me his establishment. Over the years I've expanded it and bought ships to carry my goods. Then a letter arrived from my father's solicitor informin' me that I was the new Marquess of Iolar, and here I am."

Fergus smiled. "Ye're leavin' out the wee matter of acquirin' a bride."

Gillian restrained herself from casting an uneasy glance at Calum. His unexpected bride. A woman who had come to him in the night.

"My lady's father made me her guardian while he is Turkey." He smiled at Gillian, and she found herself wanting to believe he was not just being considerate. "We found we were well suited." He held out his hand to her, and she took it. When his fingers gave hers a slight squeeze, she looked at him, surprised. He winked at her.

Silly, lightheaded bliss flooded her. She feared it would not last, but she could not bring herself to dispel it with reason. She smiled back at Calum.

"We must leave you now, Fergus, if we are to be back at Dunncrannog by dark." He rose to his feet, retaining his hold of her hand.

The three of them walked outside, and Calum helped Gillian up into her saddle before he swung into his.

" 'Twas a pleasure meetin' ye, lass. I much regret ye could no have seen Iolar Glen in its former days. A grand place it was."

"Somehow," she said, "we shall find a way to make things better here."

Fergus looked up at her, and she sensed that behind those brown eyes worked a keen mind, undiminished by age and hardship. "I hope ye shall, Lady Iolar. I hope ye shall."

Calum bade his foster father good evening and led the way out of the empty yard.

"Once there were chickens there," he told Gillian, as they headed back toward the castle. "And goats."

"There will be again. We must find a way."

Calum laughed shortly, a hollow, sad sound. " 'Twill require a mountain of gold and a deal o' backbreakin' work. The work I'll do, and gladly. The gold is something else." His fingers tightened briefly on the reins. "If only I had known before I committed my fortune on this Java venture."

Guilt gnawed at Gillian's insides. *If only I had known before. . . .* Before he'd come to Treymoor. Before he'd received the letter from her father. Before he'd been trapped by his honor. Then he could have come straight to Iolar Glen, where he would have witnessed the steward's handiwork, caught the man in the act of treachery. Then Calum would have committed his wealth to save Iolar and Dunncrannog.

Compared to the starving remnants of his clan, her own people enjoyed untold abundance. Treymoor's fields yielded plentiful crops. The sheep and cattle she'd so carefully nurtured and managed were in demand by those who sought to improve their own flocks and herds. The products of her glasshouses found ready regular buyers. Surely Treymoor could share some of its newly acquired wealth with Iolar Glen.

But how would she explain it to Calum? How would he take the news that she was carefully doling out funds from a property that had been his since before he'd even set eyes on it? That the death of the Earl of Molyneux, a peer of the realm, had been criminally concealed from the authorities by his daughter, her household servants, the parish minister, and his wife in a plot to defraud the rightful heir? Would he understand her desperation to keep her home and the people who were her only family safe from the evil clutches of . . . the man she now called husband?

17

"I'll be up shortly," Calum told Gillian quietly as she rose from the wildflower-bedecked table in the great hall. They'd returned from the glen to a modest meal of travelers' rations that their friends had done their best to make festive.

Now the moment had come for Gillian to prepare herself for her wedding night.

Zerrin slid off her bench and went to Gillian's side. "Come. I will show you to the room I have prepared," she said, her dark eyes alight above her veil.

Gillian followed her up the stairs and to a closed door.

"A moment, please," Zerrin said. Opening the door only wide enough to slip through, she disappeared into the room. Minutes later, she allowed Gillian to enter.

The newly laid fire in the massive fireplace reflected

on scrubbed stone walls and a pallet of blankets that had been laid out on the wood floor in front of the hearth. By one side of the pallet Gillian saw her harp and the silver incense burner. Just beyond, deeper in the shifting shadows yet within reach, were a bottle of wine, two glasses, and the familiar shapes of bottles and jars she knew contained perfumed oils and unguents.

"I can't believe you brought all this with us." Gillian's throat closed with emotion, turning her last word into a rasp. "I didn't think Calum and I would have a chance to be . . . alone together."

"But you did not think I would have spent so many years preparing you for this moment, for the many moments you will share with your handsome husband, only to forget you on the night of your wedding?"

Gillian blinked rapidly. "No, of course not."

Zerrin lowered her eyes. "I feel as if I am losing my sister," she murmured as she began to unhook Gillian's dress.

"You are losing no one, Zerrin," Gillian said stoutly, turning to face her friend. "Now I will need you more than ever."

Zerrin's soft laugh sounded vaguely unsteady. "I think that now you will need your husband. And he will need you. This is as it should be. The harmony between you will give me happiness."

Gillian's stomach tightened. She wanted there to be harmony between Calum and her. Dear heaven, she wanted more than that. Maybe too much more.

She wanted his love.

Today, he had behaved differently toward her. He

had been . . . gentler. More loverlike. And she had found herself responding like a flower opening to the sun.

She must not lose that! More than anything, she wanted him to continue to court her as he had today.

What if it had been naught but an act? A man's effort to please his bride on her wedding day? But . . . she chewed her lip. His pleasure in her company had *seemed* quite real.

Zerrin resumed undressing her. "You are nervous."

"Yes."

"You are no ignorant girl, lady sister. You come prepared to your lord's bed."

"I know. And for that I am thankful."

Moisture glimmered in Zerrin's sloe eyes. "I have fulfilled my promise to your father. You do not go to your husband filled with fear of what happens between a man and a woman." She shook her head. "Such secrets your people make of natural things."

Gillian stood a minute, looking down at the toes of her shoes without really seeing them. In her mind's eye, she saw Zerrin reverently touching her forehead to Gillian's father's hand as he lay dying on the coping of the fountain. "Zerrin. You and my father . . . ?"

Zerrin carefully laid Gillian's bodice in a corner of the room. "You wish to know what passed between my lord Molyneux and me."

"I confess I do."

Straightening, Zerrin did not meet Gillian's gaze. Instead, she untied the ribbons that fastened the skirts at Gillian's waist. "I was one of the great sultan's women, a gift from my father, who was head-man of our tribe. It was thought I might impress the sultan with the goodwill of our people, thereby gaining additional grazing rights." Her fingers nimbly unknotted the slender ties. "I was nothing to the sultan, of course. A twelve-year-old girl, her hands, feet, and face carefully hennaed, wearing the coins of her dowry stitched to her *abayeah*, a gold ring in her nose. The other women of the *harim*, they laughed at me. I was taken in and trained, just another slave in a hidden city of slaves, one among hundreds. Years passed as I served, well out of the sight of the sultan. One day, I was called upon to sing for the Sultan Validé, the sultan's mother. Then she invited her son to dine with her. She had me sing again."

Zerrin shrugged. "Who can account for the moods of the mighty? The sultan became enchanted with my voice. Jealousies arose among certain of the other women. One was caught poisoning my food. Another marked my face as I slept. Ah, but one woman succeeded where the others failed. She accused me of having a lover. She was sly, that one, and I was judged guilty. My punishment, death.

"I was tied in a weighted bag and thrown into the Bosporus Sea."

Gillian gasped. "How barbaric!"

"Your father saw what had happened from his boat. He was on his way to a ship anchored off the coast. I cannot say why he was allowed to pass so close to where I was thrown. Perhaps the executioner was eager to return for his payment. Perhaps it never occurred to him that someone would dare to interfere. It is enough for me that your father leapt from his boat and dived down to intercept my sinking prison. He cut the bag and carried me to safety. Had he been caught, it would have meant his life."

Not for many years had Gillian envisioned her father as a hero. To discover he had risked his life to save Zerrin gave her pause.

"Were you acquainted?" Gillian asked.

"No. I was a stranger to him."

Gillian plucked at the pale blue ribbon on her corset. Her father had risked his life to save someone he had not known.

"After I told my lord Molyneux my story, he took me aboard the ship. He treated me with respect. He protected me from the lust of the sailors. In return, he made one request."

Gillian remained silent, waiting.

"He asked me," Zerrin said slowly, "to come to you. To instruct you in the arts of love, as they had been taught to me, so that when the time came you would not fear your husband's body as your mother had feared his."

"He said . . . he told you that my mother had . . . feared him?"

Zerrin nodded. "It saddened him."

Gillian could remember nothing of the relationship between her parents. She had been a small child when her father had left for the first time. After that, he'd seldom returned. And his rare visits had always ended sooner than he'd promised.

Now Zerrin had shown her a glimpse of another side of her father. Had he loved her mother? Had her mother turned away from his touch? Gillian thought about how Calum had made her feel, and her stomach fluttered with anticipation. She could not imagine turning away from him.

"Perhaps Papa was not gentle," she said, then remembered that Calum had not been especially gentle with her, yet he had inflamed her. She had not drawn away. Rather, she had wanted to be closer to him.

Zerrin moved around to unlace Gillian's corset. "There are women who cannot bear such closeness," she said gently.

Gillian stared down at the time-smoothed wood plank floor. "Zerrin, did you . . . did he . . . ?" Her question died away, too impertinent to voice, even of her dear friend.

"No. My lord Molyneux never touched me. It was your mother he loved."

Neither spoke while Gillian finished undressing and donned her linen night shift. Zerrin brushed out Gillian's long hair and lit the incense. As the scented smoke curled up through the piercework in the hammered silver, Gillian stepped over it absently, her mind filled with sadness for her mother, her father, for Zerrin.

Moving back, Gillian bent low, allowing the airy tendrils to perfume her arms, the top of her night shift and the tops of her breasts, her throat, her face, the dark drapery of her hair. Now she must set aside her sadness. This was her wedding night, her long overdue wedding night. The wedding night she did not have to share with Maynard Leake! She had been given her prince in his castle. Now she must endeavor to keep him.

"I hear your husband approach," Zerrin said. "It

is time." She embraced Gillian, who hugged her back tightly. "You will remember all I have taught you?"

Suddenly, cold anxiety swept through her. "I-I will try."

Zerrin kissed her on the cheek and slipped silently out of the chamber, taking the incense burner with her.

Seconds later, Gillian heard a light knock on the door. She nervously smoothed her hair, then her night shift. She noticed that her feet were bare and thought about finding her slippers, but it was too late. The door opened.

Calum stepped into the room and quietly shut the door behind him. He wore only his kilt and his plaid. He stood for a moment, taking in the fire, the pallet, the decanter and glasses, the collection of fragile stoppered bottles and jars. At last he turned his gaze on her. The heat of it seared away her agitation.

She filled her eyes with the sight of him. Tall and strong, he was a man like no other. His fierce masculine beauty pierced her with longing to tame him, to hold him to her and make him hers in heart and soul, so that he would never want to leave her.

She caught glimpses of deep chest, narrow waist, and hard ridged abdomen between the draped folds of tartan wool.

He pulled off the plaid and easily looped it behind her shoulders. Slowly, he drew her to him, until he cradled her body with his.

"Ye're lovely," he said softly.

She could find nothing to say. Desperately she

tried to remember what Zerrin had taught her, but she couldn't seem to think.

He lowered his head and lightly brushed his lips across hers. "Och, a silent woman," he whispered, his eyes shining with a teasing light. "A jewel more precious than pearls." His fingers caressed the tender skin beneath her necklace, around the base of her neck. His fingers moved up to follow the line of her throat, then her jaw. His lips touched her there, sending shivers of desire through her. "Pearls suit ye."

Gradually, the years of lessons slowly filtered back, and Gillian thought how pleased Calum would be when he realized his bride did not come to him ignorant and afraid. She eased from his embrace and took his hand. "Will my lord have wine?" she asked, leading him to the pallet and indicating that he should be seated.

"Wine?" he asked, gracefully stretching out upon the quilts. He crossed his bare ankles and leaned back on his elbows. "Where did ye find wine?"

She smiled as she poured the dark aromatic liquid into two glasses. "Zerrin brought it for our wedding night."

"A resourceful woman is our Zerrin," he said, his gaze meeting Gillian's as she gave him the glass. He accepted it from her, never breaking that simmering connection. The tips of his fingers lightly brushed hers. Dazzling heat scored through her.

Drawing in a long, unsteady breath of cooling air, Gillian removed herself from his reach, concerned that she might forget everything permanently if he touched her again. She took a deep swallow of her wine, then placed the glass on the floor and picked up the harp. She sat down on the pallet, careful to maintain her distance from Calum.

She played several melodies and sang with a few. As usual, she regretted that her voice was not high and clear like so many accomplished ladies she had heard. In songs from England, Wales, Ireland, and France, she sang of undying love, and when the last note faded away there was only the intermittent crackle of the fire.

"Yer voice reminds me of port wine," he said, gently removing the harp from her unresisting hands and setting it aside.

"Port?" She couldn't keep her eyes off him, off his gleaming gold-fire hair. His sensual mouth. She wanted another kiss.

"Aye," he said, as he moved next to where she sat on the edge of the pallet. His voice was deep and low, more a vibration that thrummed through her body than mere sound. "Sweet and rich and full of body."

He was close—too close! She would never remember what to do if he kept looking at her like that.

Quickly, she picked up a small bottle and moistened her fingertip with the perfumed oil.

Calum leaned over her, slanting his mouth across hers. His lips were supple. They coaxed and persuaded. With a small plaintive sigh, she parted her lips. His tongue moved in to reclaim previously won territory, gliding over her teeth, stroking her tongue. Heat curled low in her belly. She reached up and drew his name on his cheek with the oil that carried her fragrance.

He drew back a little. "What is it ye do?" he asked. "It feels . . . different." He breathed in. "The scent reminds me of ye."

"You wear my brand on your cheek, Calum. I've written your name in the oil with which I scent my body."

Desire flared in his eyes. "After ye bathe?"

"Yes," she whispered.

His lips hungrily claimed hers, his large palms cupping her head, his fingers entangled in her hair.

Gillian untied his queue and laced her fingers through his hair. "Like fire," she murmured. "Like bright, gleaming fire."

He caught the hem of her night shift and impatiently tugged it up, over her head. She shivered slightly as the cooler air of the room licked her flushed body.

"Ye're so verra beautiful, Gillian," he said, his deep voice gone slightly husky. His gaze moved over her. He dipped his head and brushed his lips along the tender side of her neck in several soft kisses. "Like the pearls ye wear about yer lovely throat. Perfect. Beyond price." His mouth moved to the curve of her shoulder. "Smooth and warm to my touch." He stroked her breast, leaving it tight and tingling. When Calum dipped his head and took her nipple into his mouth, pleasure seared through her body, driving a breathless moan from her lips. She arched back. Her fingers curled into the warm, smooth strength of his shoulders.

For a second time, Gillian learned his skill with teeth and tongue, until she thought she might burst from her skin. The low, aching throb in the core of her beat stronger, more insistently, with his every touch. If she was to employ any of her skills she must do so now, while she could think.

Surprise flickered in Calum's eyes when Gillian eased away. She replied with an enigmatic smile.

Her fingers fumbled open the buckles that fastened his kilt. Carefully, slowly, she peeled away the overlap of colorful wool. Her mouth went dry at what she found beneath.

She slid her palm over his warm flat belly and felt his muscles contract.

His breathing grew more rapid. He grasped her wrist.

"Dinna do that, sweetheart. I would no have a repeat of our last time together."

Gillian drew back, hurt. "You didn't enjoy our last time together?"

He kissed her palm. "Aye, I did. Too much. I neglected ye shamefully, and I intend to make it up to ye tonight."

Neglected? Gillian stared at him in confusion. "I-I had pleasure."

His silken mouth curved up. "There is more."

"More?" The thought that there might be even more than the wonder she had experienced intrigued her.

He kissed the inside of her wrist. She felt the warm wet tip of his tongue on her skin. A shimmer of sensation sped down her arm and through her body. The ache throbbed more insistently.

"Much more," he said.

She was tempted—oh, so tempted!—to give herself over to him. But years of instruction blocked her way. His pleasure must come first.

"The night is yet young," she said. "Will you not let me have my way with you first?"

Calum's eyes widened. "Have yer—? And just what way would ye have in mind? Ye, an innocent?"

She leaned closer to him, brazenly brushing her breasts against his chest. "Indulge me." She heard his breath stop momentarily.

Then he lay back down. "I'm yers to command, my lady."

Firelight flickered along his hard, muscular body, stretched out in its full magnificence against the background of Clan MacFuaran tartan. Tall, golden, and heart-poundingly virile, Calum was a force to be reckoned in the full light of day, completely clothed. Here in this shadowed room, with a very naked Calum reclining before her, Gillian felt as if she'd stumbled into the lair of a hungry tiger.

His mouth curled up at one corner. "Have ye changed yer mind, then?"

Gillian thought of her father's concern for her, of Zerrin's promise and her devotion in keeping that promise. And Gillian thought about her own wish to bind Calum to her.

If he desired her enough, perhaps his love would follow.

"No, my husband. I have not changed my mind." She smiled as she leaned over to kiss him.

She toyed with his ear, gliding her fingertip over the outer edge, softly, oh, so softly. Her lips followed. Beneath her, he shifted restlessly. She nibbled at his earlobe, then moved down to his neck, his shoulder. Her fingers brushed lightly over his chest.

"Touch me," he said, and grasped her hand.

When he tried to guide her to where he wanted her hand, she slipped it loose of his hold.

"Not yet," she whispered. "You aren't ready."

"Ye may witness for yerself if I'm ready or no." He wrapped his arms around her and pulled her on top of him.

Breath caught in her throat as she felt him against her. Hard. Hot. Oh, so very ready.

"You said you were at my command," she said, the words nearly sticking in her arid mouth. Dear Lord, she wanted him.

"Aye."

She touched him then. Touched him as she'd been taught.

Calum bowed up from the pallet, a strangled sound trapped in his arched throat. Gillian worried that she had done something wrong.

"Christ in heaven!" Calum panted. His body moved against her, silently urging her for more.

Encouraged, she touched him again in the same manner. Again, he responded, muscles straining. Sweat broke on his forehead.

Before he had time to recover, her hands moved upon him again, this time differently. His eyes squeezed closed. A long gut-deep groan tore from him. His chest rose and fell rapidly. His fingers clenched handfuls of plaid.

"Shall I stop?" she asked uncertainly.

"Nay! Dinna stop. Oh, God, dinna stop!"

A sense of power flooded into her. She could please him—and he wanted that pleasure. He wanted her hands on him. With new enthusiasm, she applied herself to the practical application of her lessons.

Gradually, she found herself ensnared by his wild passion. As his breath came more rapidly, her own hastened. With each gasp or moan that escaped his lips, her body quickened. When his eyes squeezed shut, their dark lashes skimming his cheeks, the ache inside her pulsed more heavily, more demandingly.

Abruptly, Calum dragged her down to him. He rolled them over until she lay on her back. Firelight gleamed on his moist body.

"Enough," he said hoarsely. He found that she was ready, then pressed into her.

Driven by the hunger deep within her, she arched to meet the power of his strokes with increasing urgency.

The spring that had coiled tighter and tighter within her burst free, flinging her into buffeting, blinding, heart-stopping release. Distantly, she felt Calum's body tighten, then shudder.

She lay savoring the feelings. The luxurious glow. The sweet exhaustion.

Calum rolled away from her, depriving her of his weight and warmth. A quilt settled over her.

"Calum?"

"Go to sleep, Gillian."

She lay on her side, staring into the room, wadding and unwadding the edge of the quilt in her fingers, under her chin. Calum lay quietly at her back. Why didn't he put his arms around her? She turned on her other side.

He lay on his back, his arms folded beneath his head.

"Calum, is there something wrong?"

He continued to look at the ceiling. She searched his face for a clue to his thoughts but found none.

"Go to sleep," he repeated in the same low, level tone of voice. "'Tis been a long day."

Gillian felt as if she were drowning. She desperately needed a lifeline, one only Calum could throw. But he lay unmoving, his face turned away from her. She ached for him to hold her, but his arms made no move toward her.

She sat up, clutching the quilt around her, suddenly ashamed of her nakedness. Perhaps he waited for her to leave. Isn't that what Zerrin had taught her to do? Now she understood why. The thought of being away, out of Calum's remote presence held sudden appeal. Had a separate room been prepared for her? Someplace where she could go to nurse her hurt, to solve her confusion?

She rose, balancing precariously on bare feet as she tried to keep her cover completely in place. It dragged on the floor as she crossed the room, to the door.

"Where are ye goin'?"

"I-I'm leaving now," she said. Why must he always confuse her and make her feel so awkward, so unsure? "To my room." She looked back to see that he had rolled to his side. His tousled hair framed his beautiful face, his powerful throat, and shoulders. His body, his glorious long-muscled body, glowed in the light from the ebbing flames. Yearning twisted within her. She had let herself believe that he might care for her, so badly did she want his love. Her life had been filled with lies for so long, she had come to confuse them with truth.

"Yer place is here. Ye sleep here."

She grasped the quilt more tightly around her. "But—"

"Ye are my wife." His voice was more a growl than a statement. "Now come to bed."

Wearily, Gillian returned to the pallet. Without another word, she curled up on her side and closed her eyes. She heard Calum get up and toss another log on the fire, then the rustle of covers as he lay down. The fire crackled as it grew.

Now wasn't the time to think about anything important, she decided. For all she knew, Calum had many eccentricities, and this sudden shift in mood was one of them. Time. Everything seemed to require time.

Burned wood collapsed in the fireplace sending up a spray of embers, startling Gillian from her slumber.

She knew without looking that the other side of the pallet was empty. With a heavy sigh, she rebuilt the fire, then lit a fresh candle from the budding flames. Absently, she noticed his kilt still on the floor. His plaid was gone.

She found she could not credit Calum with being an eccentric. No, his change in mood had something to do with her. It must have been something she'd done wrong, because until they'd made love he'd been thoughtful and tender. Loverlike. Of course, she admitted, her experience with lovers was severely limited, but she'd learned to read human nature well.

She had done something wrong. But what?

Gillian combed her memories for a clue. Had she not given him pleasure after all? Had his reaction to her touch been indicative of pain rather than pleasure? The more she thought on it, the more it seemed to her he might have been suffering from excruciating agony. There had been no smiles, no sweet sighs.

Gillian covered her face with her hands. Dear God, she had given him no pleasure at all! Was it any wonder he had no wish to get close to her? Poor man, she had brutalized him, and he had borne the torment in near silence.

She thought of all Zerrin's lessons. For practical reasons, there had been no men on which to experiment. Everything had been learned on paper, through gestures, or on a model of a man's essential parts. The placement of the fingers, the amount of pressure—all so exacting. Zerrin, had, of course, instructed her carefully. But what if Calum was somehow different? What if Scottish men were not the same as Turkish men?

Gillian glared down at the floor. Was she just to sit here and let Calum believe he was doomed to life with a fiend? No! She was not wicked, merely inept. And perhaps if he knew that, if she vowed to learn the correct ways to touch a Scotsman, they would have a better chance of happiness together. That hope flicked to life in her breast.

Bundled in her quilt, her candle lighting her way, Gillian went first to see if he had joined the others. She did not find him among the sleepers in the great hall.

She searched room after empty room but found

no sign of him. Finally, she dropped down on the bower window seat. Defeat formed a heaviness in her chest as she laid her cheek against the cold glass. With a fingertip, she traced the leaded outline of the MacFuaran coat of arms. A single tear dropped to wash against the stained glass emblem.

Movement out of the corner of her eye claimed her attention. She turned her head to find a solitary figure standing on the battlement. Moon-kissed hair whipped about his face. One end of his plaid snapped in the night breeze.

Gillian bolted from the window seat. She raced out of the bower. When she came to the stair into the great hall, she slowed, her bare feet taking each step silently. She eased across the room to the door, only to find it bolted. How had Calum managed to bolt the door from the inside?

Masculine hands settled on the timber across the door, and Gillian looked up. Ian lifted an eyebrow in query. She brought a finger to her lips, and he nodded. Then he opened the door, and she slipped out.

She ran through the courtyard and the ward and came to a stop at the foot of the stairs in the gatehouse, as she recalled what she would have to say to Calum. It would leave her pride in shreds. Her pride—her only remaining defense against his rejection.

What if she was wrong?

What if she was not?

Taking a long breath of cold night air, Gillian slowly mounted the stairs to the battlement.

His back was to her when she came out onto the high guard walk. He stood gazing out over the black-and-silver lake below. Moonlight gleamed on the crown of his head and on his one bare shoulder.

The breeze tugged at her ungainly quilt, pulled through her hair.

She came quietly to his side.

"Ye should be in bed," he said.

"I came to talk with you."

"There's naught to talk about," he said flatly.

For an instant, Gillian clung fiercely to her pride, wanting only to turn around and march back to the room. But she knew that if she did, they would never have a chance for happiness as husband and wife. Never again might she be able to remedy the grievance. Over time it would grow more poisonous. In their stubborn silence, each of them would nurse new grievances, until neither could forgive.

If Calum cloaked himself in his pride, Gillian understood. For much of his life, pride had been all that was left to him. But she'd had more, much more.

"I'm sorry," she said.

He whirled to glare at her. "Ye're sorry? *Sorry?* When I think of all the times I burned for ye, of how I wanted ye so badly I could all but taste it—but no! I wouldna touch ye, because I believed ye an innocent." He tilted his face to the starry Highland sky. "God, what a fool!"

Gillian could make no sense of what he was saying, so she concentrated solely on what she'd come to tell him. "I know you must be surprised—"

"Surprised? Ha! Shocked, more like. Damned well stunned."

"—and disappointed—"

His eyes widened. "I felt like a bloody idiot!"

"—but please believe me, I never meant to cause you pain."

Calum stiffened. "What did ye expect?" Swathed in his plaid, bare-armed, bare-legged, and barefoot, his red-gold mane dancing on the breeze, he made a breathtaking sight.

"I expected to give you pleasure. I swear to you, that was my sole intent. To please you. But . . ." She chewed her bottom lip as she tried to chose her words. So much rode on her eloquence. "Please understand, I'm new at being a wife. But I know I can bring you pleasure," she added hastily, "if you will be patient. There's a difference between Scottish men and Turkish men, you see. I'm certain that's what's actually at fault. Of course, Zerrin can't be held to blame, not really—"

"Stop." Calum's single word cut through her concentration like a heavy sword.

She looked up at him, her heart in her throat.

"What the *hell* are ye talkin' about?" he demanded.

"Why, I'm trying to explain the reason for what happened—or *didn't* happen—when I . . . when we . . . that is to say—"

"I take yer meaning," he said shortly. "But I still dinna understand what you've been sayin'."

Her fingers clenched around the edge of the quilt. "I am saying that I thought I was pleasing you. Instead, I hurt you, possibly injured you. I was almost certain that I had got the position and the pressure right, but it's difficult for me to tell."

"What?" Calum asked through a set jaw.

"My lessons."

His eyebrows drew down. "Lessons?"

"The lessons my father asked Zerrin to give me, so that I would not be fearful of my husband's body."

"Ye've no seemed particularly fearful of my body either time we've made love."

"Yes, well, some women are not. But it had been his experience, and it created much unhappiness for him. For my mother too, perhaps. He did not want that for me. So he sent Zerrin to teach me."

"And I'm expected to believe all this?"

His accusation struck Gillian harder than a blow. She stared at him, speechless with hurt and disbelief. Then she whirled and quickly walked toward the staircase. The bottom of the quilt slipped down to drag and catch on the rough planking. Tears blurred her vision, tears she desperately did not want to shed.

"Gillian, wait." A large hand grabbed hold of her covering, effectively halting her.

She averted her face. "Let me go."

"Gillian, please." He moved closer, shielding her from the wind. "Gillian." She heard him release a sharp huff of breath. "Will ye look at me, wife?" When she did not, he gently nudged her face toward him with his fingertip on her jaw. She closed her eyes, but to her chagrin, two fat tears escaped her lashes to roll down her cheeks.

"Och." Regret vibrated in his voice.

She opened her eyes to the face of an embattled archangel, a beautiful warrior engaged in an unfamiliar war. His hair streamed around his head. His night-shadowed eyes studied her intently.

"Trust doesna come easily to me," he said gruffly. "And I have found ye in a lie before."

A chill passed through her. "Lie?"

"Ye said ye would marry, that ye had an intended. But there was no such man, was there? 'Twas no more than a bare-faced lie."

She drew a ragged breath. He did not know about her father, or he would have mentioned it now. Yet he had caught her in a lie.

"I lied to you then. I scarcely knew you, and I was desperate."

"Desperate? How could such a bonny lass, with what I imagine is a generous dowry, ever be desperate? 'Tis a mystery to me why ye were not wed years ago."

"My father was gone much of the time. There were few opportunities for me to meet eligible men."

"Were there no parties and such in Saint Agnes parish? Did yer friends never invite ye to their homes? I canna credit that ye received no invitations. I met a few of yer neighbors, remember? Ye seemed popular enough."

She studied Calum a moment, debating the wisdom of revealing a risky secret she'd held closely for so long. He was her husband. Their happiness, their very future was at stake.

Gillian wet her dry lips. "I received invitations, but . . ." Her courage faded.

He gently cupped her face. "But what?"

She restrained herself from leaning into his tender touch. "I had no time. You see, I was in charge of Treymoor. All of Treymoor."

"The house?"

"And the lands. The tenants. Everything."

His eyebrows climbed. "The sheep, the glass-houses?"

"All of it."

"Why?"

Dear, God, what had she gotten into? Her secrets, so strenuously guarded for years, did not come easily to her lips. "My father was an adventurer, not a farmer or a landlord. He needed money for his expeditions, and his only source was Treymoor. If it were not entailed, he would have sold it off long ago. Instead, he bled it nearly dry. The people there, they were my real family. My mother died when I was so young I can barely remember her. My father stayed abroad. I could not see my loved ones turned out of their employment, off their farms, so"—she nervously cleared her throat—"I learned to do it myself. I read voraciously. I corresponded with experts. I talked to anyone who might have information that could help me. I had the wisdom of the old steward; then, later, the sound advice of William. Everyone on the estate worked, and worked *hard*. We scrimped and did without."

"And Treymoor has finally flourished," he said, his voice low, considering.

"Yes." Tension burned in her stomach.

"Then why did yer steward give all the credit to yer father? Why did ye act as if ye had no interest in the running of the estate?"

"You were a stranger. We wished to protect ourselves."

He regarded her a long moment. "What were ye hiding?"

Oh, God, oh, God, she had gone too far! She had revealed too much. He would hate her now for what he knew, as he would have loathed her before for what he did not.

"William had no authority to sign contracts. I signed them."

"*You* signed them? Not your legal guardian? But why?"

"I had no legal guardian," she replied dully.

"Bloody hell! No legal guardian?"

Numbly, she shook her head. It was all over now. All that she'd hoped for . . . gone.

"The ledgers I went over?" he asked.

"Adjusted."

He turned his head, looking off toward the mountains that bounded Iolar Glen. Silence blew on the wintry breeze. Gillian realized numbly that her feet and hands were cold.

"So yer life has become but one lie after another."

Misery swamped her, aching in her chest, clutching in her throat. The love she'd yearned for had turned to ashes, seared away by truth.

Calum faced her again. "If yer father were here now," he said quietly, "I would make him pay."

"What?" She could not believe she'd heard aright.

"The bastard all but cast ye to the wolves! Damn him! How could he be so careless with his daughter?"

"He knew what I was doing. And he never interfered."

Calum paced. "Never interfered? How magnanimous of him. Considerin' how he profited from all yer hard work, I dinna find that a recommendation for his character! His greed and neglect placed ye in jeopardy. Placed yer very soul in danger, forcin' ye to lie, to deceive." His eyes narrowed. Fists opened and closed, opened and closed. "Wait until I meet him. He'll pay for makin' yer life a misery." Black promise rumbled through his voice.

Gillian stared at Calum, unable to take in his unexpected reaction to what she'd told him. "You *believe* me?"

"I—" He stopped. His brow furrowed in a puzzled frown. "Yes," he said slowly. "I believe you."

Hope surged within her. She reached out and grasped at their future, taking one last risk.

"You accused me of playing you false, of coming to you a woman of the world, not as an innocent."

Even in the dim light, Gillian saw deep color move up Calum's neck, into his face. "Ye shamed me," he muttered.

She blinked. "Shamed *you*? How could I have possibly done that?"

"I wanted to show ye I was no the great, slaverin' beast I behaved the first time we were together. I wanted to pleasure ye the way a man should pleasure his woman. Instead ye made me a slave to yer touch. I longed to hear yer sweet voice cryin' out for me. But 'twas *I* who cried out." One corner of his mouth curved up slightly. "I canna say I like the sound of my own voice beggin'."

"It felt good?"

Calum cleared his throat. "Aye. A man could die of feelin' so good. But, I wanted to make *ye* feel good, do ye see?"

She laid her hand on his bare arm. She filled her gaze with Calum. In that moment, nothing else mattered. "I hurt your pride. But you see, I only wished to please you. I want to be a good wife to you, Calum."

His throat worked a second. Without speaking, he dragged her into his arms, cradling her against him. Joyfully, she rested her cheek against his partially clad chest and listened to the rapid beat of his heart.

"I'll make ye a good husband, Gillian, I swear I will. But we must make a promise to each other."

"Yes. Anything," she agreed, happiness bubbling up inside her.

"There can be no lies between us. Only the truth."

The bubbles dissolved, a heavy stone taking their place in her. No lies. Calum was asking for her promise.

For the first time in either of their lives, happiness was within their grasp. This was the husband she had always dreamed of but had feared never to find.

She could imagine Calum's reaction if she were to tell him that her father lay dead, entombed in unmarked stone, his death unrecorded in the parish register. If she told him that she had committed a crime to make certain Treymoor did not fall into his hands. That she'd planned to rob him of his inheritance.

Oh, she could imagine his reaction quite clearly.

Gone would be their happiness. Gone would be her husband, her future children. There would possibly be prison sentences. But worst of all, she would have Calum's undying contempt and hatred.

If she simply held her silence, he would still come into control of Treymoor and their eldest son would inherit. Her father's "letter" could arrive just as originally planned. Perhaps sooner, if she could find a way to arrange it.

One last lie.

"I promise," she said.

"And I make the same promise to ye."

Calum guided her along the battlement, his arm around her shoulders, tucking her close to his body. "Now, let me show ye the other stairway, the one not far from our chamber. Then *I'll* do the touching."

18

On the horizon, the setting sun streaked the winter sky with amber, carmine, and deep blue-purple. Calum looked at his wife as they rode back to Dunncrannog from the glen. Though they'd been married three months, he still marveled that this lovely, spirited woman who rode quietly next to him was indeed his wife. No other could have brought him such hope for the future.

She had labored beside him to improve conditions for his kinsmen. In this, her skills had proved more valuable than his, and he had swallowed his pride and listened to her.

Although his clansmen had finally, grudgingly accepted him, they had not liked her. She was foreign. Worse, she was English. Yet she had continued to work on their behalf, doggedly chipping away at their hostility, until she'd won their respect. Eventually, he thought, these tough Highlanders would come to love her.

But never as he loved her. Calum was certain no woman could ever have been loved as much as he loved Gillian.

He drank in the sight of her as their horses took the familiar track. The lowering light gleamed upon her dark hair and touched her fair skin with a golden tint. The dark circles of fatigue beneath her eyes fretted him.

"Ye work too hard," he said, realizing even as he said the words that they would do no good.

She looked at him, and her smile shone softly. Dear God, he was a lucky man!

"We all do our part," she said. "But, Calum, I fear it may not be enough. We have not yet repaired all the cottages. The people are eating what livestock we could afford to replace. Their dire hunger drives them to it, I know that. But if they eat the beasts, there will be no milk for the children, no cheese, no eggs, no wool. Were they to slaughter and smoke every beast, 'twould not be nearly enough to see them through the winter. Once slaughtered, there will be nothing with which to begin rebuilding the flocks and herds."

Calum nodded, the welfare of his people weighing heavily on him. "Aye." He knew the problems were legion. Unless they could repair the cottages, the snow would collapse many of them. And what of the seedlings they needed to replant the forests? There had been no time even to start them.

Though he'd sold his house in Edinburgh and all his silver and gold plate, it had not been enough.

"Well, there is no help for it," she said with forced cheerfulness. "We shall just have to find a way. But now all I wish to think of is a bath and dinner. I wonder what Augusta has prepared for us tonight."

Calum tried not to grimace at the prospect of another meal by Gillian's aunt. "Likely turnip soup again."

Gillian laughed. "She was taught to manage a large house and an army of servants. The preparation of fine cuisine was not among her lessons. But then, we have not the ingredients for fine cuisine. Our shelves are almost bare. In truth, I am amazed that she has not fled back to England."

Calum smiled knowingly. "I'm no amazed at all."

"Ah, yes, the admirable Hugh. Why does he not just ask her to wed him and be done with it? He is a good man, and Aunt Augusta would make him a fine, certainly an adoring, wife."

They crested the road and entered the gap through the mountains. Before them, the castle on its island loomed in silhouette, a fantastical dark form against purple mountains and a brilliant gold-and-red sky. Calum absorbed the sight with deep pleasure as they guided their horses along the narrow road that rounded the lake. The world was still, save for the soft thud of hooves.

"Hugh will no marry until he can offer his lady a measure of security," Calum said. "Though he's a master mason, he doesna feel 'twould be a grand enough life for Augusta. But he's invested in the cargo my ships carry to Java. So has Ian. If the voyage is successful, we will be rich men. If it is no successful . . . well, we'll all be poor."

Gillian made no reply, but he did not miss the tiny furrow between her eyebrows or the way her lips pressed together.

"Dinna worry, sweetheart. We canna be any poorer than we are now," he teased, knowing it for a poor lie.

Her face cleared. "Oh, I am not at all worried. I know that somehow, some way, we shall all pull through."

They crossed the bridge, and as they approached the castle, Zerrin came onto the battlement. She waved at them.

"Mr. Odgers and Ian have arrived," she called, excitement in her voice. "They have returned in triumph!"

At Gillian's suggestion, precious trees had been cut in a desperate attempt to raise money. Denuding more of the mountainside had gnawed at Calum until Gillian had pointed out that they could replant trees but they could not resurrect the MacFuarans who would surely die of hunger or exposure when the heavy snows came. Odgers and Ian had taken the timber to be sold in Inverness.

A familiar sound greeted his ears. He and Gillian looked at each other as recognition struck. They raced their horses into the outer ward, where they were forced to come to an abrupt halt.

Baaing sheep and lowing cattle filled the wide area between the stone curtain walls. Their number seemed to extend around the entire castle.

Calum stared. "Sweet Mary," he murmured, stunned by the great number of beasts. "Our prayers have been answered."

"Yes." Gillian's voice held a peculiar roughness to it. "Yes, I believe they have."

Calum reached out and took her gloved hand in his. She continued to gaze around her, but he saw the corners of her mouth tremble. Then she smiled.

They eased their horses through the crowd, into the inner ward. There they found stack after stack of crates filled with squawking chickens and honking geese. Bags of milled wheat and tea formed a small mountain range, and crates of dried fish might well have served as another curtain. Oats. Hay. Kegs of nails and kegs of ale. Tools had been laid out, and tanned hides, and iron ingots.

Calum frowned. "'Tis hard to believe that two wagonloads of timber brought all this."

"Ah, but this was not just any timber," Gillian said. "This was timber from ancient trees grown high in the Scottish Highlands. Perhaps the merchant found that our timber possesses some special properties."

"I dinna think the cedars of Lebanon could bring such a price."

"Well, he found something about them he liked," she pointed out. "Mayhap 'tis the time of year. A shortage of lumber. Or a ship needed cargo. Pray, let us not question our good fortune."

He smiled. "Ye're right. We've had a stroke of rare good luck. Enough said on the matter."

They proceeded into the courtyard, where they found more goods stacked and Odgers and Ian coming and going, toting the boxes, bags, and barrels to those places Augusta specified. Gillian went to see what she could do in the kitchen. Calum led the two horses into the stables to unsaddle, rub down, and feed.

A while later, Ian slipped in. "Sweet Mary, that Augusta is bossy. 'Tis a wonder to me that Hugh can stand it!"

Calum laughed as he finished his tasks, closing the last stable box door behind him. "Have ye ever seen her orderin' Hugh about?"

Ian smiled crookedly. "Nay. With him she is as sweet as cream. 'Tis the rest of us she treats like servants."

"Like servants? I've no seen her treatin' anyone like a servant. She works as hard as any of us." Calum eyed his cousin. "Harder than some."

Ian straightened from leaning against the wall. "I work hard," he objected.

Calum grinned. "Aye, ye do. But there's no gettin' by the fact that all this bare livin' is likely harder on the women than it is on us. They're expected to do more with less."

They walked out of the stables together, heading toward the assembled supplies under Augusta's supervision.

"I think ye dinna take kindly to followin' orders from another, Ian."

Ian hefted a small keg on his shoulder, never taking his eyes off Zerrin, who carried away bolts of cloth, her hips swaying. "There's one who doesna give orders," he said.

Calum lifted a keg to his shoulder and, after receiving instructions from a tired-looking Augusta, led the way into the great hall and on to the stairway down to the storerooms. When the two men were alone and had swung the kegs down to stack neatly with the others, Calum turned to his cousin.

"Zerrin gives orders, and no mistake. She just

gives them in her own way." Calum studied the younger man. "Dinna dally with her, Ian. I'll no have ye mistakin' Zerrin for one of yer light o' loves. She's a lady in her own right and deserves better. No to put too fine a point on it, she deserves a husband."

A bright flush moved up Ian's neck, into his face. "I've done naught but look!"

"Aye, well. I wanted to make my position clear on the matter. She's a Christian, Gillian tells me, though she was forced to observe another rite for many years. A fair dowry has been set aside for her. The man who weds her will be fortunate indeed."

"I'm no in the market for a wife, thank ye," Ian said stiffly.

Calum gave a short nod of acknowledgment as they mounted the stairs out of the storerooms. "There are more supplies to be moved. We'll no have our supper until everything's put away, or I don't know my wife and her auntie."

As soon as they safely could, Gillian and Odgers met secretly in an empty room.

"How much did they fetch?" she asked.

"Two thousand five hundred pounds English," he said, passing over a leather bag tied with a thong at the neck. "This is what's left after all I bought." He told her what the sale of the timber had brought, which was less than she had hoped.

" 'Tis better than I feared. We could not expect the best price for a pearl necklace in Inverness."

"Did m'lord notice its absence?" he asked.

"No, though I will tell you I worried greatly at first."

Odgers rubbed his nose. "I obtained almost everything on your list, m'lady, and all on m'lord's. Some goods were just not to be had."

"Did you put out the word about Iolar Glen?," Gillian asked eagerly.

"That we did." Odgers chuckled. "There was quite a row when some fellow made an unflattering remark about his lordship in Gay-lik within our hearing. I didn't understand what he said but Ian did, right enough, and was ready to make the fool eat his words. I and some others had to pull our boy away, and he was not best pleased, I can tell you that."

Gillian sighed unhappily. "I imagine not. But perhaps now some of the MacFuarans will hear how much Iolar has changed for the good and decide to return."

"Likely so, m'lady."

She plucked at the leather thong. "Was Ian suspicious about how much money the timber brought?"

"Astonished, more like."

"I was afraid it would be too much for two wagonloads of wood, but I simply did not know what else to do. As things stood, the crofters and their families wouldn't have made it through the winter. I couldn't let them freeze or starve or both!"

"No, no, of course not. But I do feel you may have trouble on your hands when your husband learns you sold your necklace."

"I know, I know." Gillian had fretted and worried about her decision ever since Calum had last refused her offer to sell her precious pearls. "I know Calum didn't want me to part with my father's gift."

"He's a good man is Calum MacFuaran. Was a time when I never thought I'd be saying that, but we were wrong."

Gillian nodded absently, her thoughts having returned to conditions in the valley and her guilt over sale of the necklace. "Fiona MacFuaran lost her baby today. Beathag believes it was because she didn't get enough to eat. Odgers, most of the women aren't even conceiving. I could not stand by and do *nothing*."

"I'd hardly say you've been doing nothing. And your husband is doing all he can too. Have you taken a close look at him lately? S'truth, child, the man is doing the work of three men. Out in that valley from dawn to dusk, heaving stone and timbers, climbing up on rickety roofs. 'Tis a wonder he's walking, much less working."

Gillian's fingers tightened around the neck of the leather pouch. "I know."

"And you." Odgers continued, his voice gradually rising. "You tend their ungrateful sick, weave their bloody blankets, chop wood, wash, clean, and cook."

"We all help. But many of them are weak, some ailing."

"Yes, and you shall be also if you keep this up!"

"Please. Lower your voice."

"You're working yourself into an early grave," he continued more softly, "and you've just sold the only gift you ever received from your father. I don't know *what* more you can do."

Gillian didn't reply immediately. "Treymoor is his, Odgers."

Odgers went still.

She *was* tired. There seemed to be no end to the misery that surrounded her each day. At night, when her own dreams weren't swirling with emaciated Highlanders and burned-out cottages, Calum's nightmares kept her up. They were coming more frequently now, these terrible amorphous visitations. They left him sweating and shaken, yet all he could remember of them was the suffocating fear.

But it was the lies, her lies, that ate away at her. She hated her deception with a gnawing self-loathing that threatened to consume her. The night of their wedding, she had promised Calum that there would be only truth between them—and even the promise had been a lie. Now she had widened her breech of faith by another betrayal. She felt trapped, stripped of all honor by her own hand.

Odgers waited for her to speak. She knew his opinion on the matter—that she should let well enough alone. The letter would allow the transfer of title to take place without endangering her marriage, without threat of the King's justice. But then, Odgers did not love Calum MacFuaran as she did. And Odgers had not broken a promise to him.

"Let the letter take care of Treymoor, Gillyflower," Odgers said gently. "You've already arranged to have it sent sooner. In time the problem will be behind you."

Wearily, she nodded. She smiled to ease his concern for her. "Thank you so much for your help, Odgers. Because of you, there will be food and shelter for everyone through this winter, and maybe even a bit of a new start in the spring."

After she left Odgers, Gillian went to the well and hauled water to the kitchen to warm for her bath. Zerrin and Barbara welcomed her help with dinner while she waited for the water to heat. Now that supplies had arrived, an invitation to dinner had gone out to the Highlanders. This would be the first such gathering. Tired as she was, Gillian found herself laughing and teasing with the other two women.

"Barbara has an admirer," Zerrin told Gillian, and the two women watched in delight as quiet, sleepy Barbara's round cheeks turned bright pink.

"Pray do not keep me in suspense," Gillian exclaimed. "Who is this discerning fellow?"

Barbara's blush deepened, and she kept her eyes riveted on the stew she stirred in a kettle hanging over the fire.

"He is a Highlander," Zerrin confided as she chopped onions on a long wooden worktable. "Tall." She waved her knife through the air above her own head. Twinkling sloe eyes turned toward the matronly woman tending the stew. "Strong. Most handsome. His hair, it is the color of a nutmeg. He has a small scar above his eye, like so." She drew a short vertical line on her forehead with her finger.

"Donald MacGowan?" The glen dwellers came to Dunncrannog more and more. Some came by invitation to share in the spare evening meal, some to consult with Calum, and others to work on repairs to the castle, which were being overseen by Hugh. Only the worst portions of the castle were being addressed. Calum concentrated his efforts and those of his kinsmen on cottages that must take the weight and moisture of snow and the buffeting of brutal winds.

"Yes," Zerrin confirmed. "Donald MacGowan. A generous man to forgive our Barbara for being English."

Gillian widened her eyes in mock astonishment. "A decided honor! What has he said to you, Barbara?"

Barbara mumbled something into the fireplace.

"Pray, say again."

"He has said," Barbara repeated more loudly, "'A fine day, is it no, Mistress Newey?'"

"And?" Gillian prompted, fascinated with this unlikely courtship.

"That's all"

"All?"

Zerrin's slim black eyebrows lifted. "Ah, but his glances!"

It was a start, Gillian thought. Ties between the castle and the glen would encourage good relations.

When her water was heated, the women hauled it to the tin bathtub in the small room behind the kitchen. How she longed for the luxury of the tiled Turkish bath at Treymoor, so far away.

A tide of homesickness washed through her, leaving a lump in her throat. Gillian missed Pym, and Mrs. Withecombe, and Jenkins, and Sammy. And she certainly missed Lucy Kendrew and the wonderful food she made. She missed the well-meant fussing of John and Alice Varley. In truth, the only person she did not miss was the contemptible Scarth. But he was no longer a worry. A letter from William had recounted how Scarth had run off. He'd left shortly after his encounter with Calum, but Mary had been so ashamed, she'd hidden her husband's desertion as long as she could. Poor Mary.

Then there was the matter of Maynard. Gillian had left him a farewell letter, secretly relieved to have escaped marriage to him and his unhappy mother and the children he would have fathered.

She had no such doubts about Calum's children. They would be beautiful, quick-witted, and utterly adorable. A warm glow filled her. It was well that supplies had arrived, she thought, laying her hand over her still-flat abdomen. If her suspicions proved correct, she would need better nourishment now.

When she finished bathing and returned to the kitchen, she found that Augusta had joined Zerrin and Barbara. Gillian added her helping hands and together they served the largest meal they had prepared since arriving at Dunncrannog.

In the great hall seating was cramped, but she saw no jostling and heard no complaints. In fact, she heard nothing at all.

Highlanders crammed together at the tables, silently rubbing elbows. Among them sat a single Englishman, Odgers, who appeared calm and pleasant, as if being pressed between two towering, glowering Scots was an everyday occurrence.

Gillian, Augusta, Barbara, and Zerrin bore steaming platters of oatcakes and bannocks and tureens of beef and vegetable stew into the stony silence that filled the hall. A woman in her mid-twenties arose from a long bench packed with her clansmen. She walked directly to Gillian, who recognized her as Elspeth MacFuaran. Gillian had helped to nurse Elspeth's little girl through a congestion of the lungs a month past.

The woman held out her hands in an unspoken

offer to carry the burden for Gillian. Without hesitation, Gillian passed the platter of oatcakes to Elspeth, who smiled shyly and carried it to the head of the table, where Calum sat.

Another woman, this one in her middle years, offered to take Barbara's heavy tureen. Two more Highland women rose from the tables and offered their help to Augusta and Zerrin.

After that, the stiffness among the diners eased. Pride swelled within Gillian as she watched her husband's clansmen conferring with him, jesting with him. It seemed that three months' bone-grinding work and deprivation had helped to convince the inhabitants of Iolar Glen that Calum might not be the villian that he had been painted. The steward had lived very well here in Dunncrannog Castle—unlike the laird and his lady did now.

By the time supper had been consumed and conversation dwindled to tired lapses, the hour had crept into the early morning. The guests took their leave with almost solemn ceremony, and after the great hall was put to rights and the kitchen cleaned, Gillian felt she could sleep for a month.

She preceded Calum up the narrow stairway to their chilly room.

Like much of the castle, the once-barren chamber was now equipped with furnishings from Calum's Edinburgh home. On the stone mantel that stood as high as her husband, she'd set figurines of Imperial jade and a glass-cased clock. A draped tester bed occupied the far corner of the room, a richly carved trunk from India at its foot. Two wing chairs and a small round side table sat before the fireplace.

Jewel-hued carpets from France and Italy hung over the cold walls, and one large plush carpet covered the floor.

Calum laid a fire as she struggled to undo the back hooks of her bodice that Zerrin would normally have seen to. Without a word, he came to stand behind her. With deft fingers, he unfastened the bodice.

Gillian gave him a look. "You do that rather too well, my husband. One might think you've had practice."

A corner of Calum's mouth curled up. "I've unhooked a few gowns in my day."

Dangling her bodice in her fingers, Gillian turned to face him, studying his beautiful, beloved face. "You wicked man."

His smiled languidly. "Och, but if I had no learned to take off a wench's gown, I might also no have learned what comes after." He nimbly untied the drawstrings at the neck of her chemise. With his palms, he smoothed the top off her shoulders, low over her breasts. His lips pressed warm kisses over her bare skin.

"I think you are inventive enough with no one's help," she murmured, leaning into him. Since their wedding, he had taught her nightly how much pleasure a man could give a woman—something she considered one of God's more splendid miracles.

"Do ye now?" He peeled off the rest of her clothing. Her fingers dispatched the buttons and ties on his, tugging off each garment and tossing it on the trunk.

"Yes. Mmm." She closed her eyes, thrilling to the

sensations his clever hands evoked. "Superbly inventive." As tired as she was, Gillian eagerly anticipated what he offered.

Calum swept her up into his arms and she twined her arms around his neck, savoring the power of his magnificent body. She followed his gaze down to her ankle.

He lifted an eyebrow. "Ye're wearin' yer ankle bracelet."

She winked at him. "Aye."

"Good." He tumbled her onto the bed, then followed her. "I like it."

"I know."

Starting at the fine gold chain at her ankle, Calum slowly worked his way up her body. His lips, his tongue, his teeth rivaled his hands in sensual ingenuity. By the time he moved above her breasts, Gillian's blood sang through her veins.

He lifted his head. "Where is your necklace?" he asked.

She froze, passion forgotten. "Necklace?" She hadn't worn it for the fortnight that Odgers had been gone, yet Calum had never seemed to notice.

He rolled to one side, never taking his gaze from her. "Yer pearls. Where are they?"

Gillian found she couldn't look him in the eye. Though she'd never enjoyed telling lies, they once had rolled off her tongue with practiced ease.

Until she'd fallen in love with Calum.

His need for truth had instilled in her a desire for the same. Which made lying to him difficult.

"I-I must have misplaced them."

His eyes narrowed as he studied her. "'Tis where

most of the silver came from to buy the supplies, is it not?"

"I . . . well . . . that is to say—"

He sat up, his mouth forming a grim line.

Feeling suddenly chilled, Gillian gathered the covers around her. She sat there in the middle of the bed, miserable with guilt.

"Damn ye, I told ye not to sell them! They were all ye have of yer father. Or was that a lie too?"

"No."

He swung his legs off the bed to stand facing her. "Ye've defied me. And lied about it! Did ye have such little faith in my ability to see my clan through the winter that ye must sell your treasure?"

"No!" She sat up straight, her knees bent beneath her. "No one could have more faith in you than I do. I've seen you work near a miracle in the glen. I've watched you almost kill yourself trying to make Iolar ready for the hard snows." Under his darkened furious eyes, she felt her courage dwindle. She clutched the coverlet to her as she chose her words. "Calum, even a good man, a determined man, cannot hope to defy nature. There was no food for your clansmen. Many of their cottages still are not safe. You could not be expected to work with nothing." Her voice softened. "I'm your wife. Your kinsmen have become my kinsmen. When a woman loses a baby, I grieve. When a man is taken by fever, I sorrow. Both happen too often." Her fingers moved to the empty place at the base of her throat. "If the people of Iolar did not have food and shelter, by spring there might have been no one left in the glen. What is a necklace compared to the lives of our people?"

A muscle tightened in his jaw as he stared into the fire for a moment. Then he turned back toward her. "Ye lied to me. Ye gave me yer promise, and still ye lied."

"Yes. Yes, I did. For that I am humbly sorry."

He raked his hand through his hair. "I dinna want ye to have to sell yer precious pearls."

"I know."

"Damn Farnum's black soul," Calum said, cursing the steward. "Damn him! I always feel that if I could work just a wee bit harder, a bit harder still, a few hours longer, then we'd finish before the heavy snows. I've told myself that for three months now."

"No other man could have accomplished what you have."

" 'Tis not as if I'm the only one workin'. They work. They work alongside me, day after day."

She slipped off the bed and padded over to him, wrapping her arms around him. Immediately, his arms enfolded her, holding her close.

"You need tools, Calum. All of us need food. You've spent every farthing you have on repairing the damage."

He held her at arm's length. "I know ye came to me first, and I refused for reasons that were no good enough. I know ye made a rare sacrifice. But I canna abide deception, Gillian. Please. Never lie to me again."

19

Gillian frantically scrabbled under the bed for the chamber pot. No sooner had she pulled it out than the remnants of her morning meal launched from her stomach. As she hunched miserably over the receptacle, she heard the door to the bedchamber open. An instant later she felt soothing hands gathering her hair back from her face, stroking her forehead.

"So, lady sister, it seems your wish has been granted," Zerrin said, a note of humor in her voice.

"I assure you, I have never wished to be sick." She got to her feet, aided by Zerrin's steadying hands. At the washstand she rinsed her mouth with icy water.

"Does this happen each day?" Zerrin asked.

"This is the second time."

"Have you had your moon flow?"

Gillian sat wearily on the bed. "'Tis late."

Zerrin's dark eyes smiled above her veil. "I believe you are with child."

A tired smile curved Gillian's mouth. "I believe so too."

Zerrin came to sit on the edge of the bed, her slender bracelets tinkling. "What has my lord to say of the matter?"

Gillian levered herself up on her bent elbows. "Before I raise Calum's hopes, I want to be certain I am with child and not merely suffering from a bit of bad porridge."

"A wise decision," Zerrin said. Then her eyes sparkled with excitement. "But I cannot see how you restrain yourself from running to my lord this minute."

Gillian laughed. "With great difficulty, Zerrin. Truly, I wish to run all the way to the library and interrupt him, regardless of his business with Mr. Mawbry. That gentleman has had sufficient time to give Calum whatever correspondence he brought with him from Edinburgh and to relate every detail from Balfour. But I shall wait. Better to be certain than to rejoice and be disappointed. A few weeks will settle the matter, don't you think?"

Zerrin nodded. "If it is sickness, it will make itself known in that time." She reached out and took Gillian's hand. "We shall hope it is a baby."

Gillian's heart soared at the very word. Baby. Her baby. Calum's baby.

She and Zerrin parted to go to their separate tasks, and as Gillian crossed the snowy inner ward she gave a quiet prayer of thanks that Calum and his kinsmen had managed to complete the repairs to the cottages. The work had gone three times as fast after the arrival of the tools, materials, and food.

She smiled as she lifted a stool from its wall peg in the byre and set it at the side of the first cow.

"Good morning, Florence," she said, stroking the animal's neck. "Thank you for sharing with us." Gillian sat down and went to work. She thought about the progress that had been made in mending the relationship between Calum and his kinsmen. It did not hurt that Beathag and Fergus had crusaded for him.

Beathag had stayed on at Dunncrannog. She'd proved to be an able healer and midwife. Despite her age, she had learned from Ian to ride ably, which allowed her to tend those in the glen as well as the slowly increasing number of castle residents.

Calum had persuaded Fergus to become steward, arguing that he'd been neglecting his mercantile business too long and he'd need the money from that to continue his program of improvements to the valley.

In rote rhythm, Gillian's fingers moved up and down on the cow's warm udders. Streams of milk shot into the pail, sending up steam in the cold morning air.

The cottages had been mended, and there was— God willing—sufficient food to see them all through even a difficult winter. In the spring there would be calves and lambs to increase the new flocks and herds in Iolar.

Donald had asked Calum's permission to court Barbara. Augusta and Hugh were . . . well, still

Augusta and Hugh. Hugh would not budge on the issue of his being able to provide Augusta the kind of life he felt she needed and deserved—despite her protestations to the contrary. And though Gillian was still afraid to count on it, it seemed she might be carrying Calum's child. The world was gradually turning into a perfect place.

Perfect but for one dark, festering sin.

Her lie to Calum spread over her heart like a cancer, tainting her every word, choking off her laughter, poisoning her happiness.

He trusted her. She saw it there in his eyes when he kissed her awake each morning, when she held him after one of his nightmares. His faith in her would have been the crowning jewel of her life—but she did not deserve it. While he had lived by the difficult strictures of his honor, she had lived by the corroding dictates of deception. And now it appeared she must pay.

Each day she prayed the letter would arrive. She told herself that fold of paper would deliver to Calum his due, which she felt certain he would treat with fairness. She held desperately to the belief that the letter and the subsequent deliverance of Treymoor to its rightful owner would remove the blight on her conscience. If only she could escape that haunting doubt.

When one pail was filled, Gillian retrieved another. She moved from cow to cow, pausing to stroke each neck, calling each animal by name.

A small boy came running into the byre. His brown hair was escaping his queue. Large blue eyes regarded her earnestly from an angelic freckled face. Angus MacFuaran reminded Gillian painfully of

Sammy. How she missed sweet little Sammy Blenkin. How she missed all of them!

"Excuse me, Lady Iolar, but the laird asks if ye'll see him in the library at yer earliest convenience."

"Please tell him that I will see him in the library as soon as I finish milking."

"Aye, milady." With dignified precision, Angus turned and strode away, his kilt swinging jauntily around his coltish legs. Then he burst into a run, dashing out of the byre to carry her message to the laird.

Gillian returned to her work, certain that Fergus must be proud of his youngest grandson. Would her son have such freckles? Would her daughter? She spent the rest of her task imagining what the child would look like. Like Calum, she hoped. Beautiful and strong like Calum.

Gillian swept smiling into the tower chamber that served as a library, housing the impressive collection of books that had arrived with the contents of the Edinburgh house. Despite the fire crackling in the fireplace, the room, like so many in the castle, was cold.

Calum stood looking out the window, his back to the door.

"You will be pleased to hear that all our cows are in excellent health," she announced blithely as she crossed the floor to him.

He turned, and immediately she knew something was wrong. Despite his composed expression, his eyes betrayed deep concern.

"What?" she demanded. "What has happened?"

Her fingers curled into the wool of his coat. "Has it to do with Treymoor? Is someone ill? Or is it your ships? What has befallen your ships?"

Calum took firm but gentle hold of her upper arms, commanding her gaze to meet his. "Hush, sweetheart. Dinna fash yerself over Treymoor. All is well there as far as I know, and I've heard naught of my ships. Listen to me, Gillian." His green eyes were shadowed with sympathy. " 'Tis yer father."

"My father?" She found she could not swallow.

"Aye, lass. Before we left Treymoor, I wrote to yer father, explainin' the situation, makin' a clean breast of it. I asked his forgiveness for what I'd done to ye and promised I'd make ye a good husband, that I would protect ye with my life. And of course I sent him copies of the marriage agreement." He lifted one of his hands and touched her cheek. "He never arrived in Turkey."

Gillian stared at him. "What?"

"Yer father never arrived in Istanbul. His hired people decamped months ago when he dinna show up."

"You . . . you wrote?"

Calum looked down at the worn oak planks of the floor for a moment, then back at her. "I couldna do less. Though I dinna approve of the way he treated ye, he was yer father. He deserved to know what kind of husband ye were gettin'." His deep voice grew harsh. "A dishonorable one."

Guilt and shame and anxiety boiled up inside Gillian, bleeding across her heart like hot pitch at the sight of his distress over this breach in his code of honor. He had wasted precious time at Treymoor because of her deceit. Had she been a fraction as honest as he had always been with her, he would not have tied his fortune up in a risky business venture. He would have had more time in which to prepare the valley. And he would not have had to withdraw from a portion of Dunncrannog Castle deemed unsafe because sufficient monies could not be spared for repairs. Calum would never have stayed at Treymoor and become . . . entrapped.

Suddenly she could no longer bear the lie. Her lie. This man had given her his name, his honor, and his love. And now, please God, his child. There could be no more deceit.

"You are the most honorable man I know," she said.

"Listen to me, Gillian. Yer father . . . I think we must accept the possibility that he may be dead."

Gillian breathed in deeply, trying to steady her resolve. She met Calum's solemn gaze.

"My father is dead."

"We canna be certain, sweetheart, but there is a verra strong likelihood."

"Calum—" her voice rasped into silence. She swallowed dryly and tried again. "I know my father is dead."

His eyebrows drew down in a puzzled frown. "How can ye know such a thing? No one has seen him in months."

She held his gaze, silently pleading for him to understand, to forgive. Her heart beat wildly. "I saw him die," she whispered.

Calum's eyes widened. "Ye saw him die?" He gave her a small shake. "Ye're talkin' wild. 'Twas a dream, perhaps, no more."

"He slipped in the fountain and struck his head."

"There, see? A nasty dream. Surely yer father would no get into a fountain—"

"He was foxed," she interrupted dully, as the awful memories poured back. She struggled to hold them at bay, to keep them at a distance where they couldn't touch her again, couldn't strip her of her security, couldn't haunt her with the image of moonlight reflected in her father's dead eyes. "He danced in the fountain and sang. He was wearing a hat—" Her throat closed. That silly-looking hat.

Calum had gone quiet.

"I put him in the icehouse." There could be no turning back now, she thought, fighting down a flair of panic. "The estate is entailed, you see, so I knew I could not inherit, but I wasn't certain who would. There seemed to be two candidates. Both their reputations were alarming."

Calum's face betrayed no hint of what he might be thinking.

"There was Nicholas Vallance," she said. "A gambler, a man of violent repute who I heard had fled to France. The other man was . . . well, your father, another adventurer who would always need money. He had even less attachment to Treymoor than my father. What was there to keep him from stripping it bare? I'd seen it happen before." She straightened as she recalled the fate of Frampton Park. "I decided I would not allow that to occur at my home. And then you arrived."

He remained silent, but what she read in his eyes caused Gillian to look away, guilt and anguish roiling inside her. Dear God, had her need for absolution destroyed all she'd built with Calum? The thought made her sick with grief. Swallowing hard, she forced herself to go on.

"It was then I learned your father had died. That put you as heir to Treymoor. Only"—she paced distractedly—"only your reputation was worse than either of the previous possible heirs: a repudiated son who had stripped bare his father's only estate. And I knew Treymoor would hold no sway over such an unscrupulous man's heart." She faced him. "Don't you see? I couldn't risk my people, my home, with a-a stranger. A dangerous stranger. So I formed a plan."

Calum looked at her, his expression impossible to read. "A plan?"

"Yes. I thought"—she breathed in deeply—"I thought if I could marry and have a baby—a son—my child would inherit before . . . you." Her last word dwindled to a wretched whisper.

"Verra enterprisin'. 'Twould explain yer desperate search for a husband." He might have been conducting a pleasant conversation with a stranger, for all the emotion he revealed.

She nodded.

"Where is yer father now?"

"In the family crypt."

"Ye managed this all by yerself, did ye?"

Gillian refused to implicate her friends in her crime, but she would not lie. "I planned it."

She thought Calum appeared remarkably composed until she noticed his hands balled into fists at his sides. Bright pearls of blood marked his palms.

"I didn't know you then," she pleaded hoarsely. She took a step toward him. "I didn't know—"

"No," he spat. "Ye dinna know me at all. And, it seems, I dinna know ye either." He turned on his heel and stalked from the library.

Soundless sobs shook her body as Gillian watched him leave.

Calum did not so much as glance in her direction during dinner that evening. He never came to their bedchamber.

A fortnight passed of his looking through her or avoiding her altogether. Once she was able to corner him in the stables as he saddled his horse to go into the glen. Once he would have asked her to go with him.

"I could have remained silent," she'd said, standing just inside the door. "I'd already arranged to have a letter delivered that would have made it look as if my father had died on his way to Turkey. Treymoor would have gone to you and you never would have been the wiser."

He tightened the cinch, gathered his horse's reins, and led him past Gillian, out of the stables. "A letter, is it? I can no imagine ye turnin' yer precious Treymoor over to an unscrupulous bastard like me with anything as final as a letter. Seems it got lost."

Anger displaced her misery. She stepped in front of him, blocking his path. "You've gone on and on about being a bastard. Well, your parentage, or alleged lack of it, never bothered me. The world is full of the illegitimate. I thought you were a bastard for destroying Iolar Glen. When I believed it."

For the first time in two weeks, Calum looked

directly at her. He met her eyes. "Please step aside," he said evenly. "Ye're blocking my way."

She held his gaze for a moment, then moved out of his path. "It seems we were both wrong," she said, as he led his horse farther into the courtyard and mounted. With the touch of his bootheel he urged his horse into a canter. He never looked back.

Gillian whirled around and hugged herself against the raw grief that tore through her. She blinked rapidly in the winter cold, trying to force back the hopeless tears.

Her stomach heaved. She barely made it into the privy before her breakfast went the way of many other breakfasts she'd eaten in the past weeks.

She felt certain she must be with child. Her child. Calum wanted no part of her. He would want no part of any babe she bore.

Suddenly, she wanted to be away, far away from this isolated island in Scotland. She yearned for the familiar comfort of Treymoor, of the people who lived there, who cared about her. She'd begun to think of Dunncrannog Castle and Iolar Glen as home, but now she saw how mistaken she'd been.

She went in search of Augusta. When she explained her intentions, her aunt stared at her in astonishment.

"You jest, of course," Augusta said.

"No. I'm quite serious. I'm going home."

"Dear, *this* is your home now."

"I am going back to Treymoor, Aunt Augusta," Gillian insisted stubbornly.

Augusta studied her for a moment. "This disagreement we've all been watching between you and Calum—it's not just a lovers' spat, is it?"

394 TERRI LYNN WILHELM

Gillian swallowed convulsively. "No." The word was a choked sob.

Augusta's eyes widened in alarm. "Dear God, you didn't tell Calum about your father? About the ownership of Treymoor? Please assure me that you were not so foolish."

"It was a lie!" Gillian cried. "A black festering lie, and I wanted to be honest with him. He's not like anyone else. He *needs* the truth. And now I find . . . God help me, *I* need the truth!"

Augusta gathered Gillian into her arms, crooning and stroking. "Oh, my poor innocent. The truth is quite dangerous. One cannot simply bandy it about."

"I did not bandy it," Gillian protested against her aunt's shawl-covered shoulder.

Augusta sighed heavily. "Very well. You did not bandy the truth. But can one assume that you did, indeed, inform Calum of your father's demise?"

Gillian lifted her head. "I told him I did it all."

"Yes, and I'm certain he will believe *that*."

"I would not have told him if I thought he might blame anyone else."

"My dear, he loves you. Of course he will blame someone else."

"No." Gillian's throat closed. She drew away from Augusta's embrace to angrily dash infuriating tears from her eyes with the backs of her hands. "He does not love me. Not anymore. And I will not stay here and endure his treatment of me. I am going back to Treymoor. *Now*." She stalked off toward her bedchamber.

Augusta hurried to catch up with her. "But this is folly! We must plan, pack, arrange—why, we don't even know our way to Edinburgh! And Calum will never allow it. He will refuse to let you go. He loves you, you stubborn girl! You must give the fellow a chance to digest what you have told him. I'm certain 'twas a great shock to him. He was hurt. Don't you see? *This is a mistake!*"

Gillian set her jaw and continued on her way.

Augusta gathered her skirts and dashed off in another direction. Feeling betrayed, yet determined to go, Gillian swept through the great hall and up the stairs. She threw open the door of the bedchamber where she'd slept alone since she'd told Calum about her father's death. She knew she could never heft any of her trunks, so she chose her warmest, most serviceable clothing and laid it out in the center of the coverlet. To that pile she added quilts and a few other necessities.

She paused a long time over her silver incense burner. With the tip of one finger, she followed its graceful outline. Zerrin had brought this as a gift, all the way from Turkey, and Gillian had used it faithfully. She remembered how exotic the incense burner had seemed when Zerrin had first showed her what to do. Reluctantly, she set it aside.

Gillian chewed her bottom lip as she finished packing. She had waited so long for her prince. And she'd had so little time with him. Unconsciously, her hand went to her trim abdomen, and through her tears she smiled. She would have something of him to cherish.

As she drew up the four corners of the coverlet and tied them, Zerrin swept into the room, followed closely by Augusta.

Zerrin took one look at Gillian's pack and set her hands primly on her hips. "This is not wise."

Gillian straightened and lifted her chin. "He doesn't want me. I am going."

"And you thought to go without telling me?" Zerrin muttered darkly in Turkish. "A great stupidness, this journey. There is snow. There are bandits. There are—"

"I am going," Gillian repeated, shouldering her pack.

Augusta stepped forward. "Zerrin tells me you are with child, niece. How can you even think of enduring that awful journey we made here in such a delicate condition?"

"I have no intention of returning that way. I plan to go to Inverness and take passage on a ship going down the coast. I will go ashore in Yorkshire and proceed home from there. 'Twill not be as direct a route, but I will not get lost or run as great a risk of encountering highwaymen." Gillian made toward the door, hunched under the weight of her burden. "And now, ladies, if you will excuse me, I wish to get some food from the kitchen before I leave."

"We could stop you," Augusta announced.

Gillian met her aunt's eyes. "But you won't."

Augusta held the gaze for a moment, then issued a long-suffering sigh. "No."

She and Zerrin followed Gillian downstairs, through the great hall into the kitchens, and finally into the courtyard.

There Gillian found Odgers and Beathag standing with five saddled horses and two packhorses already bearing several bundles similar to hers.

"What?" Gillian turned to Augusta and Zerrin in question. For the first time she noticed that they were dressed for travel.

Zerrin walked back into the hall and returned with greatcoats and shawls for them all.

"We had to try to talk you out of this madness," Augusta explained. "But we shall not let you attempt this alone."

"I forbid you to come with me. There are too many risks. I'll not have you endangered because of my problem."

A familiar stubborn light entered Augusta's eyes. "Forbid all you like. We shall simply follow along behind you."

"But it is not safe!"

Zerrin's shoulder moved in a graceful shrug. "What is? Coming here was not safe, but we came. Now we will go."

Reluctantly, Gillian gave in. She hugged her two dear friends, then went to Odgers and embraced him. He held her tightly.

"If my little Gillyflower wants to go back to Treymoor, then, by God, I'll do my best to see she gets there," he said, his voice curiously husky.

She kissed him on the cheek. Then she turned to Beathag. "I own I am surprised to see you here. I cannot imagine that you yearn to see England."

"Nay, lass, I've lived my whole life verra nicely without ever leavin' this glen, but I've got an interest in what ye're carryin'."

Gillian cast a resigned glance at Zerrin. "Does everyone know?"

"I have told only the Lady Augusta, Mr. Odgers,

and Beathag," Zerrin replied, unperturbed. "You need Beathag. The rest of us know nothing of babies. She is wise in such matters and will advise you."

"I've no doubt."

Beathag laughed. "Aye, I'll advise ye, and I'll expect ye to heed what I say."

"Yes, Beathag," Gillian said with feigned meekness. Then she grew serious. "This journey may prove arduous. Are you certain you're up to it? I will be careful, if that is what you're concerned over. There will be a midwife at Treymoor."

"Ha! As if I'd have anyone else deliverin' my laddie's wean. I canna say what happened between ye and Calum, but I dinna think either of ye would want anything but what's best for the wean."

"Of course!"

"Then I'm comin' with ye."

Gillian embraced the wise old woman. "I'm glad."

"Och, lass, I'm no best pleased that ye're leavin', but judgin' from what I've seen, were I in your place I'd likely do the same."

Gillian looked up at the high walls and towers of Dunncrannog, now wearing a trim of shimmering snow. They had become familiar and dear to her. The castle, the valley, the people—she would miss them all. But she had been wrong to think Calum loved her enough to forgive. Her error had cost her the place she'd made for herself here, but more importantly it had cost her Calum.

She tightened her grasp on the pommel, fit her foot into the stirrup, and swung up onto the sidesaddle. Her lesson here had been hard but valuable. Love between a man and a woman was a fragile thing. Never again would she trust in its strength.

Everyone mounted, and she nudged Atlanta with the heel of her boot. "Come," she told the others. "We have many miles to cover."

Single file, the party rode out of the courtyard, following Gillian back to Treymoor.

"Ye have much to be proud of, lad," Fergus said, as Calum and he rode through the glen, taking stock of how the buildings were bearing up under the weight of winter snows, of how supplies among the people were holding out. "I'd no be surprised come spring to find families moving back to Iolar."

Hearing his name shouted, Calum turned to see a rider bearing down on them. As the horse sped closer, he recognized Hugh.

The big Scot reined his mount in, sending snow and clumps of frozen sod flying. "Calum, she's gone!" Hugh waved a piece of paper. "She's gone!"

Hugh's unusual display of urgency alarmed Calum. "Make yerself clear, man," he snapped.

"Yer wife, she's gone. And she's taken Augusta with her. And Beathag and Zerrin and Thomas Odgers. Barbara dinna wish to leave because of Donald. Just packed up and rode off as bold as ye please. I was out huntin' with Ian and came back to this note Augusta left me."

Calum snatched the note from his cousin's hand, anxiously scanning each line of Augusta's flowing script. The words confirmed what Hugh had told him. The message was brief, little more than bald facts. No destination was given, but Calum could guess. Dear God, he could guess too well.

Fear for Gillian squeezed tight in Calum's chest. "The bloody little fool! When did she leave?"

"Barbara says they left this morning, shortly after ye. They're travelin' light, barely takin' anything with them. Just some clothes and food. Took two packhorses." Hugh's face grew more solemn. "And Calum, there's something else."

The fear squeezed tighter. "What?"

"Gillian is with child."

Stunned, Calum stared at his cousin. "She said nothing."

" 'Twould appear she's been unsure and delayed tellin' ye until she was certain."

Calum shoved the piece of paper back at Hugh. "Fergus, ye're my steward," he shot out. "Do as ye must." With that, he dug his heels into his horse and charged toward the castle.

Another horse thundered up beside him, and from the corner of his eye he glimpsed Hugh, leaning low in the saddle.

Ian met them at the shore side of the bridge, the reins of a single packhorse in his hand as he sat astride his own mount. A glance told Calum that the younger man had brought supplies and blankets for three. Without a word, they guided their horses to the mountain pass that would take them out of this land of Clan MacFuaran.

His wife had left him, Calum thought, fury and dread burning in his gut. She had left him and taken their unborn child. Dangers lurked everywhere. She did not know her way. She had no family to which she could turn.

Loathing swelled within him. He was little better than his father. He'd made his wife so miserable she preferred flight and all the risks and hazards that came of having no family to protect her.

Well, whether or not she chose to acknowledge the fact, Gillian had family now—a husband. And this husband keenly felt his responsibility. She might lie to him and try to steal from him, but he was still her husband. He had a duty to keep her safe.

Calum cursed the snow and the ice that slowed their pace, forcing them to allow their horses to pick their way down the descending trail. He hated the distance that separated him from Gillian.

A duty, he reminded himself. Only a duty.

Gillian gave one last yearning look out the window in her room at the Inverness inn. She'd hoped he'd come after her.

Futile not to let it die, this flickering hope inside her. If she needed evidence that he did not care, here it was. She'd sat in this tiny room for two days, waiting for a ship that could take them down the coast to Yorkshire. Two days and no sign of Calum.

Augusta lightly rapped on the door, then opened it. "If we are to take passage, we must leave now. The captain told Odgers he will not delay."

Gillian swallowed hard and nodded. She drew on her greatcoat and shawl.

He was not coming.

Without another backward look, she left.

20

Calum caught sight of the stately Palladian villa and turned his horse to canter back to the wagon Hugh drove. "We've finally arrived!" he called with forced cheer, concealing his deep weariness. "Ian, did ye hear? Soon ye'll be lyin' on a great soft bed."

"Och, anything that doesna move." Ian, flat on his back on tattered quilts, his left lower leg bound in splints, managed a wan smile.

"Ye'll no be movin' till spring," Hugh assured him.

Calum rode beside the wagon as it rumbled up the long drive. He'd never expected to see this place again. Now the estate was his. The snow-covered fields, the impressive house—all his. Once that would have brought him great satisfaction.

The front door opened and Augusta came out, flanked by Pym, Jenkins, and Odgers. They stood on the portico steps as Hugh reined the team of horses to a halt. As Calum dismounted, he knew the picture he and his kinsmen must present. None of them had shaved for weeks. They'd slept in their clothes. Food and bathwater had been rare.

Augusta's longing gaze moved over Hugh. Then she looked at Calum. "She does not wish to see you."

Calum ignored her. "Odgers, help Hugh and me with Ian."

Without a word, Odgers descended the stairs to lean over the side panel of the wagon. Compassion moved in his face when he saw Ian. Together the three men eased the young Scot from the bed of the wagon and carried him into the house.

"She doesn't want to see you," Augusta repeated halfheartedly as she followed them through the entry hall.

Calum carefully maneuvered Ian's shoulders past a column. "I dinna give a damn what she wants."

Augusta worriedly studied Ian. "This way." She directed them to an empty suite of rooms on the ground level, hastening ahead of them to sweep the holland cloths from the bed. "Oh, Ian, you poor boy." She brushed a lock of hair away from his eyes and looked up at Hugh. "He really should have fresh linens. And, dear heavens, he needs a bath."

"*I* shall tend him," came a voice from the bed-chamber doorway. Everyone turned to see Zerrin. On silent slippered feet, she went directly to Ian's side. Ian painfully lifted his hand to her, and she clasped it gently between both of hers. "Please leave now," Zerrin directed the others.

Outside in the corridor, Calum asked Augusta, "Where is she?"

Augusta sighed. "In the library."

As Calum turned to go, she stopped him with a touch on his arm. "Please, Calum. She has suffered."

He met her gaze directly. "So have we all, madam."

When he entered the library, he found Gillian standing at a window, looking out onto the snow-covered garden. She turned at the sound of the door closing, her eyes widening in her pale face.

His heart twisted at the sight of her. She'd grown too thin. The half circles beneath her eyes looked like bruises.

She took a step toward him, then stopped. "I'm surprised to see you."

His mouth twisted in a bitter smile as he tossed his three-cornered hat onto a chair. "As well ye may be. Many times I dinna believe I would see ye again."

Fire crackled in the fireplace.

"Why are you here, Calum?"

He stared at her. "Is that all ye have to say for yer-self? 'Why are ye here?'" His voice was hoarse from fatigue and he could barely stand.

She lifted her chin. "You don't want me. You made that more than clear."

Anger set his jaw. It burned around his heart.

"For two days we waited in Inverness for a ship to take us down the coast." Gillian dropped her gaze to the crumpled handkerchief she worried between her fingers. "I had hoped you might have a change of heart. That you might come to bring me back." She looked back up. "You never did."

"I did come after ye. But we were trapped for

days by a snowstorm. Ian broke his leg. By the time we reached Inverness, we'd no eaten for two days, and we feared Ian's leg beyond repair. Only by the grace of God was there a good bone-setter in port for a few days. When I thought to settle Ian in town with Hugh, then follow ye myself, Ian nearly did himself in shoutin'. Hugh dinna wish to stay either, but would have for Ian's sake."

"Where is Ian now? How is he?"

"The journey went hard on him. Zerrin's tendin' him."

"You never truly answered my question, Calum. *Why* did you come?"

In her soft gray eyes, in her trembling mouth he read the answer she wanted from him. And more than anything he wanted to give it. But she'd lost his trust. Never had he given anyone the power over his heart and soul that he had given this woman. And she'd lied to him. Again and again, she'd lied.

"Ye are my wife. Ye carry my child."

"I see. I had hoped it was more."

"Once it would have been." He tried to harden himself against her shimmering tears.

"Oh, Calum, I want back what we had."

"Ye tell me that ye concealed yer father's death, that ye willingly committed a criminal act to make certain I did not get my greedy hands on Treymoor, and then ye expect things to be the same between us? Have ye so little regard for me, then?"

Gillian looked away.

"Ye promised me there'd be no more lies between us. Ye *promised*. Yet even yer promise was a damnable lie! I dare ye to deny it."

Her throat worked for a moment. "I cannot."

Her words stabbed into him like a poisoned dirk. Somehow, despite all the evidence, he'd wanted to believe in her innocence. Red fury surged in him, swirling with his desire to deny her betrayal. Blindly, he swept his arm across the table.

Papers exploded in a blizzard of white. The inkpot flew to the floor, its black contents bleeding onto the priceless carpet. The quill drifted down to soak in the stain.

As he regarded the wreckage, his rage ebbed, leaving behind the ashes of his dreams, dreams that had all included Gillian.

"I can't live with lies." His voice was raw with grief. "Not anymore."

She lowered her head for a moment. Then she looked up, meeting his gaze. "I was afraid to tell you."

"Afraid? Afraid of what? Of *me*?" Disbelief and indignation flashed through him.

A wavering smile curved her lips. Her eyes glistened. "I was so happy with you, Calum. It frightened me. I was afraid that if I told you"—her voice caught on a sob—"we would lose that happiness."

Yet she had told him.

Calum's head ached. He needed time to think.

Absently he rubbed his forehead. "'Tis been a long journey and I'm sore tired. I'll seek my bed now." He picked up his hat from the chair and gave her a slight bow. "Your servant, madam."

He walked through the long corridors that led to the room he'd occupied on his previous visit.

He didn't want to stay there. He wanted a room

in a less isolated wing. He wanted a longer damned bed. Most of all, he wanted Gillian.

He missed discussing the events of the day with her and hearing her warm, throaty laughter at his stupid jests. He missed all the little wifely things she did to ensure his comfort, and her sweet sighs as he stroked her when they made love. But especially he missed their shared hope for a brighter future.

Could he ever trust her again?

"Wake up, lad. Wake up."

Calum bolted from gut-clenching fear, escaping up toward the familiar voice.

Hugh leaned over him, gently shaking him. "Wake up, Calum." A single candle lit the shadowed room. The older man was clad only in breeches, and his hair stuck out in all directions.

Calum gripped Hugh's shoulders, trying to still the shudders that ran through his sweating body. He fought to free himself from the awful, suffocating miasma of fear.

This time the dream had been different.

"I remember, Hugh!" he gasped. "I remember."

Hugh frowned. He sat on the edge of the bed. "Can ye speak of it?"

Calum leaned back against the headboard. Gradually his breathing eased and his heart slowed its thundering. "Someone was smotherin' me with a pillow. I struggled, but he was much bigger, much stronger than I. I-I couldn't get any air. The pillow slipped, and I grabbed hold of his dressin' gown. I glimpsed a strange scar on his shoulder, a kind of

X." Calum drew a long breath. "Then ye woke me. I thank ye for it, Hugh." As shaky as he felt inside, Calum smiled. "That was enough for me."

"Perhaps this rememberin' is a good sign," Hugh suggested. "It could mean an end to this nightmare."

Calum found comfort in that thought. " 'Twould be a godsend and no mistake."

A clock somewhere in the house struck twelve, casting off the sonorous chimes in funeral cadence.

Calum shoved his hair off his forehead. "I dinna mean to sleep so long. How fares Ian?"

Hugh grinned. "Flourishin' under the tender ministrations of the fair Zerrin."

"And yerself, Hugh?" Calum asked quietly.

Hugh released a long sigh. "I dinna like bein' parted from Augusta, Calum."

"Then marry her."

Hugh lowered his brown eyes, plucking absently at the coverlet. "Ye know my feelin's on the matter."

" 'Tis strange reasonin', Hugh. Families are joined all the time for the purpose of increasin' wealth. If yer pride canna bear the thought of comin' to yer bride with less than she offers, think of it as offerin' her a family. Hers are all dead, save Gillian. And ye can give her more family yet."

Hugh's mouth formed a stubborn line.

"Do ye no want her?"

"Aye! I fair burn for that woman."

Calum nodded. "That's as it should be. Now tell me, what will ye do if something happens to the ships?"

Hugh's face reflected his torment. "I dinna ken."

Calum's gaze drifted to the place on the wall

where there had once been a peephole. Across the house, his wife lay sleeping, her sweet womanly body cradling his child. Their child.

She had told him of her lie. At great cost, she had given him the truth.

A fierce yearning twisted inside him. "Dinna count on what ye dinna have."

Hugh looked at him for a moment, then rose from the bed with a companionable slap to Calum's shoulder. "We're a fine pair, are we no?"

After the door closed behind Hugh, Calum shoved his fingers into his hair, resting his forehead on the heels of his palm.

Dinna count on what ye dinna have.

The following morning Gillian was listlessly eating her bland breakfast of tea and toast and Augusta was enjoying a more robust meal when Pym quietly entered the morning room. Despite his usual composure, Gillian instantly sensed his tension.

"There is a gentleman here to see you, m'lady," he said. "He claims to be the Marquess of Iolar."

"The Marquess of Iolar?" Augusta echoed. "Quite ridiculous. Give the fellow the boot, Pym."

Pym lifted an eyebrow at Gillian. "I believe you may wish to see him. He is an *older* gentleman."

She rose, tossing down her napkin. "Very well."

Augusta stayed protectively at her side as Gillian followed Pym to the small drawing room. Everyone had been treating her like a helpless chick lately.

The visitor rose from the settee as she and Augusta entered, giving Gillian a chance to study him.

She guessed him to be in his late fifties and as darkly tanned as her father had been. He was tall, only an inch or two shorter than Calum. Curiously, he had that same breadth of shoulders her husband possessed, the same stubborn jaw. And there was a faint similarity about the eyes, though his were a dark murky green where Calum's were light and clear as crystal. The visitor was well dressed. The jewels on his shoe buckles winked in the sunlight from the windows. Not a hair of his auburn bag wig was out of place.

He smiled at her, and a cold chill passed up her back.

Gillian did not invite him to sit. How dare this person try to usurp Calum's birthright! "I understand you represent yourself as the Marquess of Iolar," she said. "I own I am confused. My husband, you see, is the Marquess of Iolar."

He inclined his head, acknowledging her claim. "Of course it was to be expected that my resurrection would cause awkwardness. But the report of my death was mistaken. 'Twas my poor brother Alan who died when we were set upon by bandits in India. I survived, nursed by hospitable natives. It took months for me to recover sufficiently to travel, and months more to make my way back to Calcutta. When I arrived, I learned not only that I had been reported dead but that my dear friend Benjamin Ellicott had appointed me guardian of his daughter."

Blood drained from Gillian's face. She swayed. How had the news reached India?

Augusta quickly lent an arm to steady her. Pym, who'd been hovering in the doorway, immediately swept Gillian up in his arms and carried her to a wing chair.

"I pray you will have a care," Augusta stiffly said to the stranger. "My niece is unwell."

He turned to Gillian. "Please accept my most humble apologies."

Augusta straightened, continuing to clasp Gillian's hand. "As we have only just received the news of her father's intentions, I should be interested to hear how you came to learn of it months ago in Calcutta."

"I was informed by a friend."

"I suggest, sir, that your friend must be a carrier pigeon to have gotten the news to you so promptly."

"Or a passenger on a swift ship."

Gillian lightly tapped her fan against the arm of the chair. "A ruby signet belongs to the marquess. I do not see it on your hand, sir. It is, in fact, worn by my husband."

"I left the ring with my solicitor," the visitor said. "Of course I would not take so valuable an item as the signet into the wilds of India. My man had instructions to turn it over to the new Marquess of Iolar in the event of my death. But as you can see, I'm quite alive."

A terrible cold spread over Gillian. If this man were who he claimed to be, everything was lost: Treymoor as well as Iolar Glen. All she'd worked for. All Calum had aspired to. Gone. They would be left without so much as a roof over their heads. And if Calum's trading venture proved unsuccessful, their child's only inheritance would be poverty.

"What is this about the new Marquess of Iolar?" a familiar voice asked from the door.

Everyone turned to find Calum standing there. He went still when he caught sight of the visitor.

The older man walked slowly across the room as if he were caught in a dream. He stopped in front of Calum, who looked every bit as stunned. Seeing the two men together, Gillian could not deny the marked resemblance.

"'Tis been a long time, Calum," the older man said softly.

"Father?"

The serpent's smile reappeared. Murky green eyes glinted. "Aye. None other."

21

Three days had passed, but to Gillian it seemed like months. It sickened her to think that Treymoor and Iolar Glen now belonged to the new—rather, the old—Marquess of Iolar. Not for a second did she believe her people were safe with the man. And she was powerless to save them.

As she sat at her needlework frame in the morning room, stabbing her needle into the linen, her throat constricted. Now she had neither Treymoor nor a husband. Calum showed her every courtesy, but she could tell he was avoiding her.

She reached unsteadily for her teacup and swallowed a gulp of the tepid stuff. Calum's father had already assumed the role of lord of the manor. To his annoyance, the servants and tenants still answered to Gillian. She savored her small victory, even though she knew she must soon convince everyone, for their sakes, that Robert MacFuaran was the new Earl of Molyneux. All that remained was to notify her father's solicitor so the change could be made official.

Gillian heard the door open and turned in her chair to find Calum looking at her.

"I trust I am no disturbin' ye," he said politely.

Hungrily, she filled her eyes with the sight of him. "No, of course not."

He walked to the tea service and poured some for himself. He held up the silver pot in a silent offer to refill her cup, which she extended to him. She thanked him and turned back to her needlework, as if she could even thread the needle at this moment, when all she could think of was Calum. Yearning filled her with a terrible hollow ache.

"Are ye well?" he asked, his eyes searching her face, then moving down over her. "Zerrin told me ye were still sick of a mornin'."

Zerrin talked entirely too much, Gillian thought peevishly. "I'm quite well, thank you. Beathag has assured me 'tis a normal thing to have a delicate stomach at such a time."

Calum nodded. As he sipped his tea, his gaze moved around the room. Moved everywhere but to her.

Gillian cleared her throat. "And you? Have you been well?"

"Verra well, thank ye."

Gillian wanted to scream. This meaningless chit-chat was useless. It did not begin to approach what she really wanted to say, what she wanted to hear. But these awkward, shallow questions and answers were as close to a conversation as they'd come in so long that she found herself hoping they would continue.

She inserted her needle into the taut linen, barely aware of placing the stitch of blue silk. "I imagine it was something of a surprise to see your father after so long."

His mouth tightened. "Aye."

She ducked her head, pretending to focus on her needlework. Of all the foolish questions she could have asked, that took the prize. Oh, she was turning into such a hopeless cake! Quickly she tried to come up with another pointless question or comment, unwilling to risk a silence that might drive Calum from the room.

"Ian appears to be regaining his strength," she said, congratulating herself on the neutrality of the subject.

Calum set his cup and saucer on a small table. "I think 'tis safe to credit Zerrin with his improvement. Such glances as I've seen pass between them might prompt me to post Jenkins—or, better yet, Hugh—in the room."

"Yes," she said, trying to untangle the knotted silk floss. "We certainly would not want—" Abruptly she bit off her words as she realized where they led.

Calum regarded her for a moment. "We would no want what?" His deep voice rolled through her, bearing with it a mélange of piercingly sweet memories that threatened to tear her heart to pieces.

Her fingers shook, and she abandoned her attempt to free the strands of silk. She could not look at Calum. A spurt of anger shot through her. Why had he come when he could not forgive her?

"Gillian?" he prompted softly. "What would we no want?"

Could hearts truly bleed? she wondered. She thought they must when they hurt as badly as hers.

She met Calum's waiting gaze. "I was going to say, we would not want them to have to wed, would we?"

He was silent a moment. "Has it truly been so bad?"

"Only weeks ago I would have counseled them to wed immediately, that they might find the happiness I knew with you." She turned her gaze to the window. All the flowers in the garden had died, blasted by the freezing breath of winter.

Calum stepped toward her.

The door banged open.

"Och, there ye are!" The marquess caught sight of Gillian. "Well, well. How pleasant to have ye both together. And how rare. One would almost think ye had no likin' for each other." Satisfaction oozed through his words.

Calum stiffened. The look he cast his father was dark with dislike.

The older man smirked. "I suppose now is as good a time as any. I have a wee matter I wish to discuss with ye."

He went to the tea service but found no cup. Sighing heavily, he reached for the bell cord. "'Tis a dull place, this. The servants are surly and unresponsive."

Gillian regarded him coldly. "No, sir, they are not. 'Tis your manner that brings you slow service."

He laughed. "A fearless little she-cat, are ye no?" He strolled over to her and lifted one of her curls. She snatched her head away from his touch and glared up at him. He chuckled. "I do enjoy a woman with spirit."

Calum was at her side in two steps. "Keep yer hands off her," he warned in a low, feral tone.

The marquess's smile faded. "If ye dinna want her, lad, 'tis damnable ungenerous of ye not to let anyone else have her."

Calum towered next to her speaking with savage intensity. "She is my wife, sirrah, and ye'll treat her like the lady she is."

"Perhaps I misread the matter." The marquess moved to the writing table. "But enough of pleasantries. I wished to speak to you of another concern." He leaned back against the edge of the table as he faced them.

Gillian noticed the absence of the ruby signet on his finger. A quick glance to Calum's hand revealed that he still wore the carved gemstone. Why?

"This estate is rich and comfortable." His mouth curved into the snake's smile that Gillian hated. "Unlike Iolar Glen, which is a wasteland."

"So Beathag was right," Calum said. "Farnum's instructions *did* come from ye."

The older man's smile grew, revealing his teeth. "Aye, the orders came from me. I thought I'd made my fortune at the time and no longer needed Iolar Glen. I wanted ye to have the valley ye loved so well, only I dinna wish ye to enjoy it. Ye were ever a thorn in my side."

Calum stared at his father. "I knew ye had no use for me, but I never thought ye'd bring such terrible sufferin' to yer own clansmen to spite me. Though 'tis sayin' little, ye're no the man I thought ye were, Robert MacFuaran. At least I though ye cared for yer home, for most of yer kin. Instead I find ye're . . . evil."

The marquess laughed. "Evil, am I? Ye canna begin to know the way of it. Iolar, or what's left of it, is yers. I give it to ye. Much happiness ye'll have from it, with the hatred of yer own kin surroundin' ye. Ah, but ye've already had a taste of it, have ye no? I'm astonished they let ye out alive. MacFuarans are no known for their mercy."

Gillian's hands clenched around the edges of the needlework frame. What could a seven-year-old boy have done to engender such hatred? Calum was right. This man was evil.

"And now we come to the matter of Benjamin Ellicott," the marquess continued. "He is dead. Which makes Treymoor mine."

Gillian's heart froze. The moment had come. Calum must acknowledge her father's death.

"What makes ye think the earl is dead?" Calum asked.

Gillian blinked down at the nest of colored silk in her lap, confused by Calum's response.

The marquess's ugly smile turned smug. "I have a source of information."

"Aye? Pray what did this source tell ye?"

Robert MacFuaran examined the lace that engulfed his wrist. "He told me poor Benjamin had died here several months ago. Curious, is it no? His death was never reported." Murky green eyes centered on Gillian.

Paralyzing terror gripped Gillian. Despite the chill in the room, she sweated.

" 'Twould appear that yer so-called source of information is no verra good. To our knowledge, the earl is alive and well and in Turkey. At least, that's what his letter said."

Gillian tried not to stare at Calum. He was lying!

The marquess's eyes narrowed. "Letter?"

"It arrived at Dunncrannog just before we left."

The older Scot's mouth turned grim. "I verra much doubt that."

"Are ye callin' me a liar, sir?" Calum asked with deceptive softness.

The marquess regarded him a moment. "I would no put it quite like that."

"Then how would ye put it?"

"My source was reliable," Calum's father insisted.

"Was?"

"He met with an unfortunate end. Crocodiles."

"Pity. But then, liars deserve to meet a foul end."

The marquess thumped the edge of the table with his fist. "The earl is dead!"

Gillian swayed, feigning an oncoming swoon. She had little to pretend.

Calum immediately moved to steady her. She drew strength from the feel of his strong hands on her shoulders.

"Have a care, sir," Calum snapped. "You speak of my wife's dear father."

With a desperate surge of relief, Gillian detected the first trace of doubt in the marquess's expression.

"Oh, vile canard," she said, moaning, clinging to Calum like a fragile maiden. "Truly, only a fiend would spread such lies!" She raised wide eyes to Calum. "What do you suppose the varlet hoped to gain by carrying such a terrible story?"

Calum looked down into her eyes. "Who can say?" he asked dryly.

"He hoped to gain gold," the marquess said. "But,

as I mentioned before, the fellow tripped and fell among crocodiles." He clucked his tongue. "A most unfortunate end. But"—he shrugged—"clearly one he deserved."

Gillian thought no one could deserve to die so hideously. But, who would know the true circumstances of her father's death? Suddenly a chill shivered through her. The creature in the cemetery.

"I knew Scarth was a liar, of course. After all, he once claimed to have saved Benjamin's life, when I know verra well the real hero was killed in the confusion of battle." The marquess shook his head. "The little weasel had the audacity to claim he'd been drunk in the graveyard one night when along came a secret funeral procession, right into the earl's crypt. Scarth made it sound quite convincin', laughin' over how he'd frightened everyone by pretendin' to be an evil spirit." Calum's father sighed. "I'm glad I never actually paid the man."

Scarth! The graveyard phantom had been Scarth. Gillian hoped the crocodiles had not suffered for their meal.

"Seems ye were misdirected," Calum observed. "Now I ask ye to leave."

"Och, I shall. I suppose I must take Iolar Glen back from ye. I dinna want to, ye understand. But a man must live somewhere, and Dunncrannog Castle will do." The slithery smile returned. "I'm certain ye made it more comfortable." The marquess gave them a sweeping bow and then turned and left.

Gillian surveyed the closed door. "Do you truly believe he will go?"

"Aye. For the moment."

She didn't trust the marquess to do anything as simple as leave. Everyone must be warned.

Were it not for Calum, the only warning she would now be giving her people would be to escape before the soldiers arrived.

Years of uncompromising honor—sacrificed.

Calum had lied.

Gillian knew he would never lie for himself. Which meant that he had done it for her.

She set aside her needlework frame and rose from the chair. Without a word she went to him.

His arms came around her in a desperate embrace, crushing her to him as if he never planned to let her go. She held him tightly, glorying in the warm strength she'd feared never to feel around her again, breathing in the familiar scent that was his alone. He lifted her head, framing her face with his hands.

Reaching up, she traced his cheekbones with fingers that trembled slightly. "I thought I had lost you."

Calum shook his head. "Nay. Never that." His gaze met hers and held with such intensity Gillian stopped breathing. "I shall love ye till the day I die and beyond. 'Tis only . . . I love ye so well, Gillian, it is difficult to remember we've no always been one. The demands of yer life were verra different from mine. To learn that ye hated me so much ye were willin' to commit a crime to keep me from yer life—"

"I never hated you! I only feared what you might do."

"—that even after ye did want me, ye made me a promise ye no intended to keep. I would rather have had a knife in my heart than that."

Gillian's throat swelled with tears she'd thought

never to have again, she'd wept so much and so often these past weeks. "I feared to lose you, my love. I'd never known such happiness before, you see, and I was desperate to hang on to it. But my lie ate at me. It gave me no peace. Then, when you were so gentle in telling me the news of my father, when I saw how guilty you felt over what you perceived as your betrayal of his trust, I could not let you suffer. I knew *you* were not the one at fault. I was. For everything."

He tucked her head against his chest and rested his cheek upon her crown. They stood there awhile, quiet in each other's arms.

"Ye were locked in the circumstances of the yer life, I can see that now," Calum said softly. "After yer own manner, ye have been more than honorable. Ye took on an enormous responsibility for a lass of fifteen years. Ye've seen to it that yer people were fed and sheltered in spite of yer father's heedless spending. Ye held Treymoor for your children."

A silent song of jubilation filled Gillian. She had not lost Calum. He loved her still.

Gradually, worry nudged back in. "What shall we do about your father?" she asked.

"Dinna fash yerself over him. Let him be my concern."

"How can I not fash myself?" she insisted. "I'm the one who concealed my father's death. You are innocent."

Calum chuckled, the sound rumbling in his chest. "No innocent man could be a decent husband to ye. Perhaps 'tis my boyish face that confuses ye."

She stood on tiptoe and brushed her lips over

his. "There's nothing boyish about you, Calum MacFuaran."

In answer he claimed her in a hungry open-mouthed kiss that seared through her and left her dizzy.

He stepped to the door and turned the key in the lock with a resounding *click*. She watched him with wide eyes, reading his intention in his sensual smile.

"Calum, this is the drawing room!"

"Aye, so it is." He advanced on her. "Have ye never considered the romantic potential of a writin' table?"

"N-no," she admitted as he took her by the waist and sat her on the edge of the table.

He edged her knees apart and stepped between them. His lips moved persuasively along the side of her throat. She curved her arms around his neck.

He caught her earlobe tantalizingly between his teeth. "A woman of yer talents should find this a verra excitin'"—he slid his hand under her petticoat to stroke her bare thigh, and she shivered against him—"challenge."

Gillian slept peacefully beside him. Quietly, Calum left their bed and dressed in the dark, then slipped out of the room.

The marquess had vacated Treymoor by noon, but Calum didn't believe the man would give up so easily. No, he'd be back to try to claim Treymoor and Iolar Glen and, in doing so, establish Gillian's guilt.

Calum refused to stand by while his father worked to prove her concealment of the earl's death. Instead, he would ensure her fraud could not be proved.

Like a shadow, he made his way through the silent house. He went to the stables, where he'd earlier hidden a crowbar and a length of rope. Then, the rope coiled around one shoulder, iron bar in hand, he set off to undertake his grisly task.

Gliding through the deep shade cast by trees and hedges, he made his way toward the cemetery.

In the moonlight, moldering headstones and statuary vied for room with crypts and ancient spreading trees in the crowded graveyard.

It was not easy picking the lock of the crypt's old iron gate in the dark, but finally, with a shrill creak, the metal door swung open. In the anteroom, Calum lit a candle. The door into the vault unlocked more easily.

He looked around the silent room, his breath frosting the air. Stately columns rose to a high ceiling. Among the pale limestone statues, a single dark one stoodout, a towering black marble knight bearing shield and sword, watching sightlessly over the stone sarcophagi.

Calum easily found the one in which the earl had been laid to rest. The lid had been set fully in place, yet the stone bore no name.

He set his rope and candle on the floor. For a moment he stared at the unmarked limestone coffin, his fingers flexing on the crowbar. Only his love for Gillian could ever prompt him to even think about what he now proposed to do.

Reminding himself that he had only a few hours before sunrise, he sent up a short prayer asking forgiveness, took a deep breath, and rammed the sharp edge of the crowbar under the lid of the stone coffin.

After what seemed like an eternity of labor, Calum had inched the massive lid open almost wide enough to remove the earl's remains. Over and over again, he reminded himself of what was sure to happen if he did not complete his awful task.

"So the dear departed Earl of Molyneux does indeed rest here," said a familiar despised voice.

Calum whirled to find his father lounging in the vault's doorway. "I should have expected ye'd be slinkin' around like some slimy worm." He *should* have expected it, but he had not. A part of him had tried to believe his father was not truly the vicious mercenary he seemed. Now there would be a price to pay.

The older man clucked his tongue in mock disapproval. "Is that any way for a son to speak to his father? 'How sharper than a serpent's tooth it is to have a thankless child!'"

Rage, dark and thick, surged in Calum. His fingers clenched around the crowbar. "For what have I to thank ye?" he demanded. "For namin' my mother a whore and me the get of another man? For drivin' her from her home and to her death? For strippin' Iolar Glen to the bare bone and leavin' yer clansmen to starve? Nay, I owe ye no loyalty and certainly no thanks."

The marquess strolled slowly toward Calum. "What do you care for a tribe of ignorant peasants?"

Calum's eyes narrowed. "Odd, but I dinna consider them either ignorant or peasants. And I dinna remember ye thinkin' of them so."

The other man moved closer. "It's been twenty years, lad. People do change. Ye can no guess what hardships I've suffered."

Calum regarded the marquess. "I dinna care for yer sufferings. Ye've already destroyed one good woman in my life. I'll no let ye destroy another."

"Och, but that's where ye're wrong." The marquess struck as quickly as an adder, lashing out at the crowbar.

Years of street fighting in unfriendly ports served Calum well. He jumped back and swung the heavy iron tool at his opponent's head. The sharp edge clipped the marquess's temple before he could dodge out of the way.

The marquess's booted foot cut a blurred arc through the air, striking the crowbar and sending it flying from Calum's hands. It clanged to the floor across the room.

The older man drew away to dab delicately at his wound. His fingers came away bloody. "Bastard!" he hissed. "Ye damned bastard."

Calum bared his teeth in a fierce grin. "If I'm a bastard, what does that make *ye*?"

The marquess drew a dagger from within his coat. It had two parallel bars connected by a cross-piece forming a horizontal grip. Calum had once seen such a weapon used in a fight. It was a *katar*, a deadly thrusting dagger from India.

Calum eyed the crowbar on the other side of the vault. If only he could get to it! He stepped back as the other man moved in to strike.

The marquess pounced, and as he did, Calum dived under his opponent's arm and rolled to his feet, sweeping the heavy coil of rope up with him.

They circled slowly, warily, like enemy wolves, each searching for a weakness in the other's defense.

Again the marquess lunged, his face a set mask of fury.

Calum swung the coil of rope, striking the other man's wrist. The *katar* flew out of the marquess's fingers and rang against the marble knight.

Both men dived toward the fallen blade. They grappled with each other. Calum grasped his opponent by his coat collar, hooking his fingers into the cloth of his shirt, and struggled to pull him farther from the knife.

There was a sound of tearing fabric. The coat and shirt tore away from the marquess's shoulder, revealing a white scar, livid against tanned flesh.

A scar in the shape of an X.

At the sight of the mark, memories long hidden flooded back to Calum. His opponent used the second's distraction to grab the weapon. Calum recovered in time to roll away, but the deadly blade sliced through his sleeve and into the flesh of his upper arm. Blood drenched once-white cambric.

Calum staggered to his feet, backing quickly out of the other man's thrusting range and toward the crowbar.

"Ye're no my father," he said, panting, struggling to keep his attention on his uncle's movements despite the torrent of nightmare memories. "Where is he?"

"Dead," his uncle said, his breath coming heavily as he circled. "We *were* set upon by bandits, but it was yer father who was murdered, not yer dear uncle. 'Twas most convenient for me to assume his name and possessions. He'd insisted on stayin' away from people as much as possible after yer mother died, so no one knew us well enough to tell us apart. Not even you," Alan MacFuaran said.

"Why did ye try to smother me? I was naught but seven. Ye were my uncle, for God's sake."

"I would much rather have been your father's heir. And until yer mother bore ye, that's what I was."

"But ye stood up for my mother publicly when my father accused her of adultery," Calum objected, not wanting to believe that even his uncle had turned on him.

"Of course I did. I knew she was innocent," the imposter said. " But I convinced yer father in private that she had betrayed him. If he doubted ye were his, ye could no verra well be his heir, now, could ye? And Iolar Glen would come to me. Och, it was a plum then, the glen, and I had such plans for it. But after my interrupted attempt to smother ye, yer mother grew suspicious of me, so I had to take steps. Then she left and took ye with her. Yer father was never the same after that."

Alan jabbed at Calum. Calum crabbed back, frustrated that his movement did not take him closer to the crowbar.

"So why dinna my father leave ye the title and estate?" he asked.

"The stupid sod came to distrust me." Alan's teeth flashed in an unpleasant grin. "It hurt me deeply. So I forged yer father's handwritin', fired the old steward, and hired a new one loyal to me. The money from his activities went into my accounts. I got rich and you took the blame. Fittin', I think. Now ye're goin' to die, and I'll not only get Iolar Glen and Dunncrannog but Treymoor as well. Yer little wife will go to prison." He brandished the *katar*. "Perhaps I'll convince the authorities that she murdered her father. Hmm. Mayhap she'll even have killed ye."

Calum quaked with rage. This evil man had destroyed Calum's family and had tried to destroy him. With no regret, Alan MacFuaran had savaged the home of his own clansmen. This spawn of the devil was capable of anything.

Struggling to regain control, to draw on exhausted reserves, Calum studied his opponent's every shift in weight, every movement.

"Ye'll no harm my wife." Calum spoke with the knowledge of absolute determination. He had something he was willing to die for, something that was worth dying for. His uncle would never know that feeling.

Alan ran his tongue over his lips. "Ye'll have no say in what I do to yer wife."

Calum edged closer to the crowbar. Gradually maneuvered his uncle until that man's back was almost against a statue. "Ye'll no harm my wife," Calum repeated. A little farther, and the crowbar would be within reach.

Suddenly, Alan MacFuaran flew at Calum, thrusting the *katar* toward his heart. Calum feinted his uncle's attack with a forearm, then threw his weight against him, driving Alan back against the statue with an audible thud.

Sinews straining against his enemy's considerable power, Calum slowly deflected the point of the blade away from his own chest. Every fiber of Calum's body focused on his life-or-death labor. Distantly, he heard of voices, but locked in his struggle, he paid no heed. Above him, there came a gravelly sound.

A clear voice cut through his awareness. "Calum! The shield! Look out!"

He flung himself away. The massive stone shield crashed down from its high place at the knight's arm, striking Calum's shoulder a bruising blow, sending him hard against a sarcophagus. A man's scream tore the cold air.

Stunned, Calum lay where he'd fallen. Then Gillian was beside him, her warm breath clouding white, her hands moving over him.

"Calum! Where does it hurt? Can you speak?" Her fingers tested his scalp.

He winced from the stab of pain.

"Oh, dear, I'm sorry! You're covered with cuts and scrapes!"

He eased his arm from her anxious hands. "I'll live." A groan escaped him as he tried to get up. Instantly, there were several pairs of hands helping him. He blinked to focus his vision. Gillian's wide, worried eyes searched his face. Surrounding her were Mrs. Appleyard and at least half the household of Treymoor, all dressed in their night clothes.

"He's dead," Hugh said, and Calum painfully turned his throbbing head to see his cousin and Mr. Appleyard, Odgers, and Pym gathered at the foot of the statue. Alan MacFuaran lay still beneath the stone shield.

Calum walked over to the fallen form of his uncle. He thought he should feel regret, but he did not. He felt only relief. Relief that he had not been forced to take his uncle's life. Relief that a man who had planned to harm Gillian and kill him was gone forever.

The fallen shield had driven the *katar* into Alan MacFuaran's heart.

Calum draped his good arm over Gillian's shoulder. "What are ye doin' here?" he asked, brushing his lips over the silken crown of her head.

"I woke to find you gone and you were nowhere in the house." She looked at the partially opened sarcophogus. "I knew you would try to protect me from your father, and this was the only way it might be done."

"Destroying the evidence."

"It could not have been easy for you to consider such a course."

"Nay." He shuddered. "I'd make a poor grave robber."

Gillian stroked his back soothingly. "We arrived just as the shield broke from the statue."

Calum regarded the still form on the floor. "He was no my father."

Gillian's hand stilled. "He wasn't?"

"Nay. He was my uncle, Alan MacFuaran. He turned adventurer with my father, after my mother left Iolar Glen. He said my father was never the same after she left."

Gillian held Calum more tightly. "Perhaps he loved her after all."

"I would like to think so. My uncle, ye see, wanted Iolar Glen for his own, but first he had to get rid of me. That's what my nightmares have been about—the pillow he forced over my face when he tried to murder me. But I could no remember. Perhaps he became careless, for my mother grew suspicious of him."

"And that's why he convinced your father she had been unfaithful." Gillian studied Alan MacFuaran's silent body, all of the upper half but one outflung arm concealed by the stone. "He was evil, Calum," she said. "Evil, and dangerous to the good in this world."

Calum hugged her close to him, silently sending up a prayer of thanks. Here in his arms was a good his uncle had not destroyed. And the people of Treymoor and Iolar Glen had been spared his devastating hand.

"Mr. Appleyard, will ye record Benjamin Ellicott's death in yer register today?" he asked.

The rector smiled. "Gladly, Lord Iolar."

Hugh and Pym and Odgers moved the lid of the late Earl of Molyneux's sarcophogus back into place. Tomorrow Calum would see that a name was carved into the smooth limestone.

As they walked back to the house with Calum's arm wrapped firmly around Gillian, the horizon lit with the pale gray and pink of sunrise.

"We *will* live in clean, sweet-smelling places, Calum," Gillian said, "and so shall our children."

Calum looked into her eyes and smiled. "Full of sunshine."

She laced her fingers through his. "Full of hope."

"Aye."

Golden sunlight poured gradually over the land. Calum held Gillian close to his heart as they watched the miracle together. Something within him made him believe that this would be the first of many miracles they would share.

"Full of hope," he whispered.

Epilogue

Gillian leaned back on the stool, luxuriating in the hot, soothing water Calum poured over her body. Her unbound hair clung to her neck and back. A sigh of pleasure escaped her lips.

Clad only in his breeches, Calum chuckled as he set aside the brass bucket. The low sound echoed in the colorfully tiled room of the Turkish bath. He'd had it built here at Dunncrannog two years ago when the ships had returned from Java, making the cousins wealthy men. Hugh and Augusta now had one on their estate in Kent, where their glasshouses produced rare flowers for the quality of London, and, of course, Ian and Zerrin had a Turkish bath on their lands just outside Inverness, where Ian had established a distillery that produced excellent whisky.

"Dinna go to sleep on me, sweetheart," Calum said. "I have a surprise for ye."

Gillian straightened, delighted. "I thought you had forgotten."

Calum smiled down at her. He brushed his fingertips across her cheek. "Nay, wife. I couldna ever forget the anniversary of our wedding day. Four years." He shook his head. "Much has happened."

She cupped his hand in hers and pressed a kiss into his palm. "You've saved Iolar Glen—"

"*We* saved Iolar Glen. My kinsmen have returned—"

"Dunncrannog has been restored—"

"Ye've given me a fine strong son and a bonny wee daughter. My business prospers, as does Treymoor." Calum frowned. "Are ye content to live only a few months of each year at Treymoor?"

She smiled. "Yes, my love. As dear as Treymoor is to me, my true home will always be with you, wherever that may be."

He leaned over her and claimed her lips with his in a tender, lingering kiss. "Now close yer eyes," he whispered.

Naked and wet, Gillian did as he asked. A familiar weight settled at the base of her throat.

Instantly, her fingers sought to confirm what she dared not hope. She looked down to see the bottom tip of a ruby pendant. "My pearl necklace," she whispered brokenly. "Oh, Calum!" In one motion, she rose and launched herself into her husband's arms.

He caught her to him and held her firmly in arms that had years ago become her haven. "Hush now, sweetheart. Dinna weep. 'Tis a surprise meant to gladden yer heart."

"It does. Oh, it does! I thought never to see my pearls again." Gillian lifted her face from his warm chest and gave him a watery smile. "You could not have given me a more wonderful surprise."

Calum caught one of her tears on his thumb. He brought it to his lips. "I would have returned them to ye sooner, but it took above two years to find them. They had made their way to Holland."

Joy soared within her. Although she had never mentioned how difficult it had been for her to part with her father's gift, Calum had known. "Yet you got them back for me."

"Aye," he said softly. " I could do no less."

They stood there quietly for a moment, holding each other.

Finally, Calum spoke. "I've been thinkin' of buyin' a sugar plantation in Barbados. Or land in America. We need to be lookin' at the future, and I believe there will be great growth in the New World. It wouldna hurt to establish a hold in such a place, ye know."

Gillian reached up to twine her arms around his neck and drew his head down to hers. "Later," she whispered. "Now *I* have a surprise for *you*."

COMING SOON

Vows Made in Wine by Susan Wiggs

Mistress Lark had no need for passion. All her devotion went to a secret cause she embraced with her whole heart—until she met Oliver de Lacey, a pleasure seeker with no time for love. Has Oliver finally met the woman who will change his reckless ways?

Almost Paradise by Barbara Ankrum

Grace Turner never dreamed she would find herself in a real-life Wild West adventure as exciting and romantic as the dime novels she had read. Trying to rescue her brother from Mexican Imperialists, she enlists the help of rugged ex–Texas Ranger Reese Donovan, and along the way, the two find true love.

Chickadee by Deborah Bedford

Long ago, Sarah left Jim, her high school sweetheart, in search of a new life. Upon returning to Star Valley, she faces the heartwrenching choices she made and must find a way to recapture the love of the man she has never forgotten.

A Window in Time by Carolyn Lampman

A delightful romp through time when Brianna Daniels trades places with her great-grandmother, Anna, who arrived in Wyoming Territory in 1860 to become the mail-order bride that Lucas Daniels never ordered. In the meantime, Anna falls in love with the hot-air balloon pilot she encounters in 1995.

Danny Boy by Leigh Riker

For most of their thirteen-year marriage, Erin Sinclair has lived apart from her husband Danny, a professional rodeo rider. Now he's back, and after years of hardening her heart to the man whose dreams of being a champion made a life together impossible, does she even dare to dream again?

Nothing Else Matters by Susan Sizemore

In the splendor of Medieval Scotland, a gently bred maiden's courtship is interrupted when her bridegroom's quest for revenge nearly tears them apart. Then the young lovers realize that nothing else matters once you have found the love of a lifetime.

Winds of Glory by Susan Wiggs

Wealthy Bethany had loved her family's indentured servant Ashton since childhood, but when his life is threatened for his spying for the Colonial cause, she hatches a wild scheme that results in marriage. Surely such a marriage of convenience would be doomed—unless she can match his defiant bravery, and claim her place in his fiery heart forever.

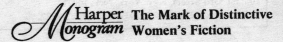

Harper Monogram The Mark of Distinctive Women's Fiction